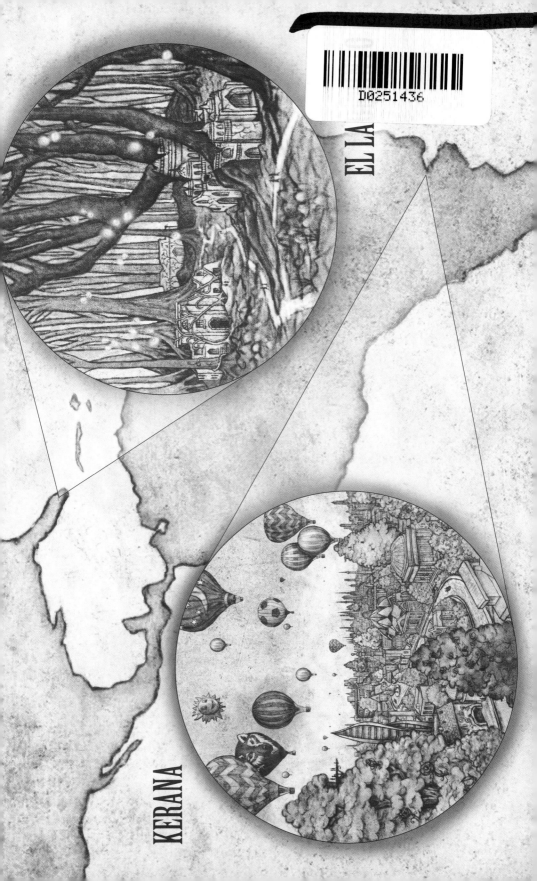

EL LA

KERANA

LOBIZONA

ROMINA GARBER

WEDNESDAY BOOKS
NEW YORK

First published in the United States by Wednesday Books, an imprint of St. Martin's Publishing Group

LOBIZONA. Copyright © 2020 by Romina Garber. All rights reserved. Printed in the United States of America. For information, address St. Martin's Publishing Group, 120 Broadway, New York, NY 10271.

www.wednesdaybooks.com

Endpaper art and interior illustrations by Rhys Davies

Designed by Anna Gorovoy

The Library of Congress Cataloging-in-Publication Data is available upon request.

ISBN 978-1-250-23912-9 (hardcover)
ISBN 978-1-250-23914-3 (ebook)

Our books may be purchased in bulk for promotional, educational, or business use. Please contact your local bookseller or the Macmillan Corporate and Premium Sales Department at 1-800-221-7945, extension 5442, or by email at MacmillanSpecialMarkets@macmillan.com.

First Edition: May 2020

10 9 8 7 6 5 4 3 2 1

For all our children caught in the crosshairs of nationalism.

Y para mamá, mi ídola, por absolutamente todo.

Debajo de tu piel vive la luna.

—PABLO NERUDA

The moon lives in the lining of your skin.

—PABLO NERUDA,
AS TRANSLATED BY NATHANIEL TARN

PROLOGUE

The morning takes a deep breath. And holds it.

A shadow stains the sunny horizon. A black SUV with blue lights flashing.

Don't come here, don't come here, don't come here.

The air grows stale as the vehicle stops outside our building. The street is so still, it could be playing dead.

Five men in bulletproof vests jump out. That's when I react.

I storm into the stairwell and race down from the rooftop. Ten stories below, the agents thunder up.

I'm out of breath by the time I burst into the apartment.

"ICE is here!"

Ma leaps to her feet and tosses all the food she just made, stacking the utensils in the sink so it looks like the dishes have been piling up. There's pounding on a door one level beneath us, and a man's voice bellows out, *"We're looking for Guillermo Salazar!"*

We rush to Perla's room, where Ma drops to the floor and rolls under the bed. When it's my turn, I look at Perla and say, *"They can't come in without a warrant—"*

"You don't know what they can't do."

The horrors Perla left behind when she came to this country darken her glassy gaze, and I realize she never got away. No matter how many borders we cross, we can't seem to outrun the fear of not feeling safe in our own homes.

Screaming starts.

Followed by scuffling.

There are other people shouting now, and I recognize the voices of those neighbors whose papers are in order, yelling at the officers in Guillermo's defense. Everyone else is probably hiding like us.

I have to pee and my leg has a cramp, but we stay under Perla's bed for forty-five minutes. Ma and I don't even speak until we hear the SUV drive away.

When the morning exhales, the street looks untouched.

But it's not.

PHASE I

1

I always bleed on the full moon.

Ma blames the lunar cycle for hijacking my menstrual cycle, so she calls my condition *lunaritis*—a made-up diagnosis that depending upon inflection can sound like English or Spanish.

"Comé bien que en una hora empieza lunaritis," Ma reminds me as she shuts the oven door and places the seasoned carne al horno on the table to start carving.

My mouth waters with a whiff of the meat's smoky aroma. "Obvio," I say, agreeing to eat my fill. Even if this weren't one of my favorite meals, I'd still need sustenance for my sixty-hour fast.

I feel a quiver of discomfort in my uterus, and I pry my sticky thighs from the plastic chair to readjust my legs. The apartment's ancient air conditioner has a hard enough time battling the Miami sun, but it can't compete with the heat of Ma's cooking.

"Cuando te despertés seguimos con *Cien Años de Soledad,*" says Perla as I'm squeezing salsa golf over my roasted potato wedges. Ninety-year-old Perla has been homeschooling me since we moved in with her eight years ago, so she's used to lesson-planning around lunaritis.

"Sí," I say as I slice into the tender oven roast and spear my first bite of succulent pink meat. A delicious warmth fills my mouth and body as I chew, and I fleetingly feel sorry for Rebeca from *One Hundred Years of Solitude* who would only eat whitewash and dirt. Sucks that I won't get to finish that book until lunaritis ends.

A tremor shoots up my belly, and my hand clenches around the red-and-white checkered tablecloth—a warning shot that soon I'll be in excruciating agony. I stop chewing and close my eyes to focus on my breaths. When I open them again, three bright blue pills line the outer rim of my dinner plate.

I meet Ma's concerned brown eyes.

The first few nights of my period are so painful that I can only endure them sedated. These chalky tablets plunge me so deep within my mind that it takes me nearly three nights to climb back out—long enough to miss my gut-contorting menstrual cramps.

I cup the pills in my palm, and for the first time I notice a faint Z etched into their center. Strange, since the blue bottle they come in says they're called Septis. Maybe the Z stands for the zzz's they provide.

I pop the meds in my mouth and chew them with the meat and potatoes.

"Maldita luna," says Ma, glaring out the window. *Damn moon.* Perla follows up Ma's declaration with a spitting sound, as if saying *luna* out loud could invite bad luck.

They think the moon cursed me, so they run through this ritual every month. Only, unlike them, I don't dread lunaritis.

I count down to it.

I chase the food and pills with water and gaze out the window at the dusky violet sky. Any moment now, the shift will happen, and I'll be transported to the only place where I don't have to hide. The one world where it's safe to be me.

I come alive on the full moon.

2

I awaken with a jolt.

It takes me a moment to register that I've been out for three days. I can tell by the well-rested feeling in my bones—I don't sleep this well any other time of the month.

The first thing I'm aware of as I sit up is an urgent need to use the bathroom. My muscles are heavy from lack of use, and it takes some concentration to keep my steps light so I won't wake Ma or Perla. I leave the lights off to avoid meeting my gaze in the mirror, and after tossing out my heavy-duty period pad and replacing it with a tampon, I tiptoe back to Ma's and my room.

I'm always disoriented after lunaritis, so I feel separate from my waking life as I survey my teetering stacks of journals and used books, Ma's yoga mat and collection of weights, and the posters on the wall of the planets and constellations I hope to visit one day.

After a moment, my shoulders slump in disappointment. This month has officially peaked.

I yank the bleach-stained blue sheets off the mattress and slide out the pillows from their cases, balling up the bedding to wash later. My body feels like a crumpled piece of paper that needs to be stretched, so I plant my feet together in the tiny area between the bed and the door, and I raise my hands and arch my back, lengthening my spine disc by disc. The pull on my tendons releases stored tension, and I exhale in relief.

Something tugs at my consciousness, an unresolved riddle that must have timed out when I surfaced . . . but the harder I focus, the quicker I forget. Swinging my head forward, I reach down to touch my toes and stretch my spine the other way—

My ears pop so hard, I gasp.

I stumble back to the mattress, and I cradle my head in my hands as a rush of noise invades my mind. The buzzing of a fly in the window blinds, the gunning of a car engine on the street below, the groaning of our building's prehistoric elevator. Each sound is so crisp, it's like a filter was just peeled back from my hearing.

My pulse picks up as I slide my hands away from my temples to trace the outlines of my ears. I think the top parts feel a little . . . *pointier.*

I ignore the tingling in my eardrums as I cut through the living room to the kitchen, and I fill a stained green bowl with cold water. Ma's asleep on the turquoise couch because we don't share our bed this time of the month. She says I thrash around too much in my drugged dreams.

I carefully shut the apartment door behind me as I step out into the building's hallway, and I crack open our neighbor's window to slide the bowl through. A black cat leaps over to lap up the drink.

"Hola, Mimitos," I say, stroking his velvety head. Since we're both confined to this building, I hear him meowing any time his owner, Fanny, forgets to feed him. I think she's going senile.

"I'll take you up with me later, after lunch. And I'll bring you some turkey," I add, shutting the window again quickly. I usually let him come with me, but I prefer to spend the mornings after lunaritis alone. Even if I'm no longer dreaming, I'm not awake either.

My heart is still beating unusually fast as I clamber up six flights of stairs. But I savor the burn of my sedentary muscles, and when at last I reach the highest point, I swing open the door to the rooftop.

It's not quite morning yet, and the sky looks like blue-tinged steel. Surrounding me are balconies festooned with colorful clotheslines, broken-down properties with boarded-up windows, fuzzy-leaved palm trees reaching up from the pitted streets . . . and in the distance, the ground and sky blur where the Atlantic swallows the horizon.

El Retiro is a rundown apartment complex with all elderly residents—mostly Cuban, Colombian, Venezuelan, Nicara-guan, and Argentine immigrants. There's just one slow, loud elevator in the building, and since I'm the youngest person here, I never use it in case someone else needs it.

I came up here hoping for a breath of fresh air, but since it's summertime, there's no caress of a breeze to greet me. Just the suffocating embrace of Miami's humidity.

Smothering me.

I close my eyes and take in deep gulps of musty oxygen, trying to push the dread down to where it can't touch me. The way Perla taught me to do whenever I get anxious.

My metamorphosis started this year. I first felt something

was different four full moons ago, when I no longer needed to squint to study the ground from up here. I simply opened my eyes to perfect vision.

The following month, my hair thickened so much that I had to buy bigger clips to pin it back. Next menstrual cycle came the growth spurt that left my jeans three inches too short, and last lunaritis I awoke with such a heightened sense of smell that I could sniff out what Ma and Perla had for dinner all three nights I was out.

It's bad enough to feel the outside world pressing in on me, but now even my insides are spinning out of my control.

As Perla's breathing exercises relax my thoughts, I begin to feel the stirrings of my dreamworld calling me back. I slide onto the rooftop's ledge and lie back along the warm cement, my body as stagnant as the stale air. A dragon-shaped cloud comes apart like cotton, and I let my gaze drift with Miami's hypnotic sky, trying to call up the dream's details before they fade . . .

What Ma and Perla don't know about the Septis is they don't simply sedate me for sixty hours—*they transport me.*

Every lunaritis, I visit the same nameless land of magic and mist and monsters. There's the golden grass that ticks off time by turning silver as the day ages; the black-leafed trees that can cry up storms, their dewdrop tears rolling down their bark to form rivers; the colorful waterfalls that warn onlookers of oncoming danger; the hope-sucking Sombras that dwell in darkness and attach like parasitic shadows . . .

And the Citadel.

It's a place I instinctively know I'm not allowed to go, yet I'm always trying to get to. Whenever I think I'm going to make it inside, I wake up with a start.

Picturing the black stone wall, I see the thorny ivy that

twines across its surface like a nest of guardian snakes, slithering and bunching up wherever it senses a threat.

The sharper the image, the sleepier I feel, like I'm slowly sliding back into my dream, until I reach my hand out tentatively. If I could just move faster than the ivy, I could finally grip the opal doorknob before the thorns—

Howling breaks my reverie.

I blink, and the dream disappears as I spring to sitting and scour the battered buildings. For a moment, I'm sure I heard a wolf.

My spine locks at the sight of a far more dangerous threat: A cop car is careening in the distance, its lights flashing and siren wailing. Even though the black-and-white is still too far away to see me, I leap down from the ledge and take cover behind it, the old mantra running through my mind.

Don't come here, don't come here, don't come here.

A familiar claustrophobia claws at my skin, an affliction forged of rage and shame and powerlessness that's been my companion as long as I've been in this country. Ma tells me I should let *her* worry about this stuff and only concern myself with studying, so when our papers come through, I can take my GED and one day make it to NASA—but it's impossible not to worry when I'm constantly having to hide.

My muscles don't uncoil until the siren's howling fades and the police are gone, but the morning's spell of stillness has broken. A door slams, and I instinctively turn toward the pink building across the street that's tattooed with territorial graffiti. Where the alternate version of me lives.

I call her *Other Manu.*

The first thing I ever noticed about her was her Argentine fútbol jersey: *#10 Lionel Messi.* Then I saw her face and realized we look a lot alike. I was reading Borges at the time, and it occurred to me that she and I could be the same person in overlapping parallel universes.

But it's an older man and not Other Manu who lopes down the street. She wouldn't be up this early on a Sunday anyway. I arch my back again, and thankfully this time, the only pop I hear is in my joints.

The sun's golden glare is strong enough that I almost wish I had my sunglasses. But this rooftop is sacred to me because it's the only place where Ma doesn't make me wear them, since no one else comes up here.

I'm reaching for the stairwell door when I hear it.

Faint footsteps are growing louder, like someone's racing up. My heart shoots into my throat, and I leap around the corner right as the door swings open.

The person who steps out is too light on their feet to be someone who lives here. No El Retiro resident could make it up the stairs that fast. I flatten myself against the wall.

"Creo que encontré algo, pero por ahora no quiero decir nada."

Whenever Ma is upset with me, I have a habit of translating her words into English without processing them. I asked Perla about it to see if it's a common bilingual thing, and she said it's probably my way of keeping Ma's anger at a distance; if I can deconstruct her words into language—something detached that can be studied and dissected—I can strip them of their charge.

As my anxiety kicks in, my mind goes into automatic translation mode: *I think I found something, but I don't want to say anything yet.*

The woman or girl (it's hard to tell her age) has a deep, throaty voice that's sultry and soulful, yet her singsongy accent is unquestionably Argentine. Or Uruguayan. They sound similar.

My cheek is pressed to the wall as I make myself as flat as possible, in case she crosses my line of vision.

"Si tengo razón, me harán la capitana más joven en la historia de los Cazadores."

If I'm right, they'll make me the youngest captain in the history of the . . . Cazadores? That means *hunters.*

In my eight years living here, I've never seen another person on this rooftop. Curious, I edge closer, but I don't dare peek around the corner. I want to see this stranger's face, but not badly enough to let her see mine.

"¿El encuentro es ahora? Che, Nacho, ¿vos no me podrías cubrir?"

Is the meeting right now? Couldn't you cover for me, Nacho?

The *che* and *vos* sound like Argentinespeak. What if it's Other Manu?

The exciting possibility brings me a half step closer, and now my nose is inches from rounding the corner. Maybe I can sneak a peek without her noticing.

"Okay," I hear her say, and her voice sounds like she's just a few paces away.

I suck in a quick inhale, and before I can overthink it, I pop my head out—

And see the door swinging shut.

I scramble over and tug it open, desperate to spot even a hint of her hair, any clue at all to confirm it was Other Manu—but she's already gone.

All that remains is a wisp of red smoke that vanishes with the swiftness of a morning cloud.

3

The aroma of sizzling bacon and eggs snaps me from the mysterious Argentine's spell, and after picking up Mimitos's bowl, I find Ma and Perla at the kitchen table, huddled over the caramel-colored calabaza gourd.

They stop talking as soon as they see me, and I wish I'd been paying more attention. It's too late to eavesdrop now.

"Welcome back, baby," says Ma as she refills the mate with hot water. She hands the drink to Perla.

"What's up?" I ask, looking from one to the other.

"You, apparently." Ma gets to her feet and plants a kiss on my forehead. Then she walks barefoot to the stove to check on the food.

She wasn't always this casual about sedating me for three nights. At first, Ma would do a full workup when I awoke— pulse, blood pressure, temperature.

My period started on the first full moon after my thirteenth birthday. I don't remember much about that cycle because by nightfall, my body was in such raging agony that I slammed my head into the bedroom wall hard enough to leave a dent, and knocked myself out. The dent is still there, concealed by my poster of Jupiter's moons.

I was still in pain when I came to, and Ma offered me the blue pills. She knew about the sedatives from her days as a nurse in Argentina, and she had Perla request a rush prescription from her doctor. They're so potent that just one tablet can knock a person out for twenty hours—which is why I take three.

"What'd I miss? Has there been any news?"

Ma keeps her focus trained on the eggs. I look to Perla, but she just stares back and sucks on the mate's metal bombilla—a straw with a strainer at one end that filters out the yerba leaves. Her glassy eyes may be a blink away from blindness, but her gaze still feels as invasive as a microscope.

I sidle up next to Ma and set Mimitos's bowl beside the fat blue glass filled with water that Perla changes out every day. She says it's to ward off envy.

Ma seems smaller to me today, and I wonder if I grew taller this lunaritis. The thought leads to the same question I've been asking myself for months—*Does Ma notice the changes in me?*

She *has* to . . . but then why doesn't she say anything? Should I ask her? Will she think I'm losing it?

Am I losing it?

I stare at her root line as she flips the bacon, tracing the graying locks layered in among the darker ones. And on an impulse, I tip my face down and kiss her head.

We usually only kiss each other in greeting, so Ma's eyebrows arc up as she meets my gaze. "What was that for?"

The shock sugaring her voice makes me feel like a neglectful daughter. "Nada," I mumble, cooling my warm face in the fridge as I pull out an almost-empty carton of orange juice and tip my head back to swallow whatever sweetness remains.

"¿Y esa porquería?" demands Perla in her gravelly voice. She's as disgusted by my drink as I am by hers. "¿Por qué no probás un sorbito de mate?"

I make a face at the mate she's offering me, and Ma goes over to refill the hot water again. "And you call yourself my daughter," she says as she brings the metal bombilla to her own lips.

I seal up the bag of yerba on the counter and make my best effort not to cringe at the bitter herbal smell of the drink that's as sacred to Argentines as dulce de leche. Then I join Perla at the table and pick at a bit of dried sauce on the checkered tablecloth. I can still smell the spaghetti Bolognese they must have had on my second night of lunaritis. Last night, they made milanesas, my all-time favorite meal; when I opened the fridge, I saw they left me a couple of breaded filets of meat for lunch.

Ma turns off the burners and tips the bacon onto a plate, along with two sunny-side up eggs. She places the meal in front of me, then pours a dollop of coffee into my chipped Virgo mug and fills the rest with milk—my favorite drink.

Ma says in Argentina it's called a *lágrima* because it's just a *teardrop* of caffeine. Perla says it's not so much coffee as coffee-flavored milk.

The pans hiss at Ma as she gives them a quick rinse, then she joins us at the table and fills the calabaza gourd with more water. She says she likes to make me the kind of big breakfasts she cooks for Doña Rosa's kids, but she never tastes any of it herself. According to her, Argentines prefer light breakfasts.

I take a bite of crispy bacon, and its crunch is louder than usual, like someone chewing ice in my ear. I wince, and to distract myself I flip through the pages of the local Spanish-language newspaper that's open on the table until I get to the sports section.

"Ganó River," says Ma, her voice flat with annoyance.

"Ugh." I drop my head in shame at our loss.

Ma and I share the same passion: fútbol. We're long-suffering fans of an Argentine team called Racing. River is our biggest rival, and we mourn their every victory.

Ma and Perla trade the mate between them, and since they usually fill every atom of air with words, today's silence is deafening. The tension grows so taut that I shovel down food quickly from nerves and keep riffling through the paper's pages until a headline jumps out at me:

El presidente argentino será padrino del séptimo hijo varón de una familia de Corrientes

I scan the text, skipping over any words I don't know. I can't pinpoint exactly when my default language switched, when I started thinking in English and subtitling Spanish.

"Wait a moment," I say through my mouthful of eggs. "*Ley de padrinazgo presidencial*—by *law* the president of Argentina becomes godparent to the seventh consecutive son or daughter in a family? How the hell did that become a thing?"

"*Language,*" warns Ma. She hands me a napkin to wipe the yolk trickling down my chin.

The seventh child . . .

That reminds me of a story Perla used to tell me when I was little to make me feel better about my alien-looking eyes.

She would say I was born in a secret city that's home to

magical creatures, and every time a seventh son or daughter is born in Argentina, they have to make their way to that land to claim their werewolf or witch powers. Whenever I'd point out I'm an only child, she'd say that's what makes me special: I'm the first of my kind—a non-seventh child born with magical powers.

I can't remember the city's name.

"La ley está basada en la leyenda del lobizón," says Perla in her rattly voice.

The law is based on the legend of the werewolf.

I stare into Perla's wrinkled face, her foggy eyes like dusty crystal balls, and I wait for her to crack her sardonic smile. But it never comes. "¿Qué?"

"The lobizón is the South American werewolf," she explains in her academic tone. "It's a mix of European mythology and the legend of the luisón, a different creature rooted in the stories of the Guaraní, people indigenous to South America—"

"Wait," I interrupt. Perla was a middle school teacher before homeschooling me, so I'm used to taking her lessons seriously. Only I can't with this one. "What do werewolves have to do with Argentine *law*?"

Ma brings the bombilla to her lips and nudges my plate, which I abandoned as soon as Perla said *lobizón,* toward me.

"There's a superstition in Argentina that says the seventh consecutive son in a family will become a werewolf," says Perla, her soft g the only sign that English isn't her first language. "I used to tell you about it when you were little. They say that a long time ago, people really believed it, and to stop the abandonment of these children, the government enacted this tradition-turned-law."

Ma makes an impatient noise as she sets the mate down,

and I let my fork fall to the plate, its clang underscoring my disbelief.

I'm no stranger to a good superstition—Perla thinks describing a nightmare before breakfast will make it come true, and Ma is adamant we keep three salters at the table, one for each of us, because it's bad luck to pass the salt hand-to-hand—but I've never heard of a *government-sanctioned* superstition before.

"But why is it still in practice *today,* when we know better?" I demand. "And if the myth is about seventh *sons,* why does the law also apply to daughters?"

Yet even before I finish asking the question, I know the answer. It was in Perla's story.

"Because seventh daughters become—"

"*¡BASTA!*"

Ma's outburst is so abrupt that even the kitchen seems to suck in its breath, leaving little oxygen for the rest of us. She picks up the thermos, and for a few long seconds the only sound in the apartment is the hot water rushing into the calabaza gourd as she refills it.

Perla brings the mate to her lips when Ma hands it to her and doesn't speak again.

"None of that is true," says Ma, her voice rough. "The law started as a tradition brought over by Russian dignitaries who were visiting Argentina. They asked the president to be godfather to their seventh son because it was customary in their country, so we adopted the practice. *That's all.*"

Our discussion has been innocuous enough that Ma's anger must have to do with something else . . . I think back to when I first walked in, how she and Perla seemed to be discussing something, something serious enough to silence them, and fear hardens into a rock in my gut.

I force myself to finish my food, even though my appetite's

gone. When my plate is clean, I bring everything to the sink and pick up Mimitos's bowl to start washing.

"Leave it, Manu."

Ma's voice breaks the tense silence, and when I turn to look at her, she says, "Quiero charlar con vos."

There's a difference between a *charla* and a *conversación*: The first is a chat, the second is a *talk*. Even though Ma said she wants to charlar, by her face and tone, I know she actually wants to have a conversación.

The last time we had one of those was over a year ago when Guillermo from 2B was deported to Colombia. This morning, her forehead is creased with the same worry lines.

My gut is heavy as I follow her out of the kitchen and into our bedroom. When she shuts the door, my throat closes with it.

"I don't want you leaving El Retiro for any reason today."

My chest deflates; I was planning to visit the library to get the newest book in the Victorian fantasy series I'm devouring. "But what if Perla needs me to check something out for our lessons?"

The librarians know Perla from her teaching days, and they think I'm her granddaughter. They love her so much that they don't even give me a hard time for keeping my sunglasses on indoors.

"You'll have to use what's here." Ma scrutinizes my lopsided stacks of books, which she's constantly asking me to tidy up.

"I promise to be quick and discreet—"

"A sixteen-year-old girl out alone in the middle of the day is never discreet," she shoots back.

"A) It's Sunday, and anyway it's summer, so no one's in school. And B) I'll be seventeen in two weeks."

Still, I know the real reason she's worried. I may not have friends, but I spend my days devouring books and television shows, so I'm aware there's a word for someone like me. Someone who looks too different.

(*Freak.*)

"Ma," I say in what I hope is a reassuring tone. "I swear to keep my sunglasses on *at all times,* even in the *bathroom*—"

"Manuela, *suficiente.*"

The sharpness in her voice means this is the kind of conversación where she talks and I listen.

"I heard from Doña Rosa that random immigration sweeps will be happening in our area to meet this administration's deportation quotas. If they ask for your papers, your mirrored lenses won't be enough to shield you. ¿Entendés?"

Ma works as a maid for a wealthy Cuban family that seems to be pretty plugged into the government because they always know when something's coming down. Despite the stifling Miami heat, my fingers feel frozen. For Ma and me, deportation is death.

We came to this country a dozen years ago because we couldn't stay in Argentina. My father was heir to a powerful criminal organization with hooks into the police and government, and his own people killed him for trying to run off with Ma and start a new life. His family blamed Ma for what happened, so she had to run—and when she discovered she was pregnant, she knew she could never go back.

Only we're not safe yet.

Ma says she filed our visa request with her employer's sponsorship, and we're still awaiting an answer. She and I have a deal that she's in charge of our finances and our residency, which means I'm not allowed to stress about either. I don't know the process's particulars, but what I do know is that until our papers come through, we're undocumented. And since Florida banned sanctuary cities, we're always at risk of discovery—so there's a single guiding principle we exist by:

Visibility = Deportation.

And my face is entirely too visible.

Ma is still waiting on a response from me, so I nod my submission. "Good," she says. "Now why don't you go shower, then we'll play a game of chinchón?"

"*Seriously?*" It's been forever since Ma's had time to play cards with me.

"Doña Rosa told me I could come in an hour later today."

I nod eagerly, my mood improved. But as she's leaving, I can't keep from asking, "Any news?"

Without slowing down or twisting to look at me, she says, "Yes, we're citizens now, and I just forgot to tell you."

I perch on the tub's porcelain ledge, waiting for the shower to warm up. I'm still chilly from Ma's warning about ICE sweeps—US Immigration and Customs Enforcement.

The white noise is soothing, and after a while, I let my eyelids droop as the sound of the running faucet fills my head.

My mind drifts back to my dreamscape. Usually after being awake a few hours, that world sinks away. But today, I've felt a pull to get back there all morning, as if I left something behind in my subconscious that I need to retrieve.

I shut my eyes—

Daytime has dimmed to dusk.

I'm racing through a field of wild grass in the same golden dress I always wear in my dreams, flexible but formfitting with a pocket for stashing small weapons. The Citadel looms on the horizon, its black stone as impenetrable as outer space.

The scent of jasmine infects the air, a warning note that night is nearly here. And it's hungry for me.

Shadows stretch across the landscape, veiling the foliage in silver, and I'm sprinting so fast, I stop feeling the ground. The moon-like opal doorknob grows larger, but something flickers in the fringe of my vision, and I stumble.

A puff of red smoke rises from beyond the black wall.

It looks just like the smoke I saw in the stairwell. Did I drag the memory here, or are pieces of my dreamworld now invading my reality?

A flash of green snaps me back to action. The Citadel's spiky veins of ivy uncoil, baring thorns as sharp as shark teeth. They rear up to strike, and I hunch my shoulders to pounce—

But I edge away, feinting left. The armored tentacles mirror my movements, and as soon as the doorknob is unprotected, I leap up, jabbing my hand out—

And my fingers brush against cool, smooth stone.

I gasp, and my eyes fly open.

I'm back in the steamy bathroom, the dream replaced with the realization I just dredged up to my mind's surface.

Last night, I touched the Citadel for the first time.

4

When I step out of the shower, the mirror is completely fogged. I wrap a towel around myself, and I brush my thick hair as gently as I can, so I won't keep losing hairbrush bristles.

A mosquito buzzes onto the glass, and I squash it dead with my palm. The reflex is so immediate that it only registers when the sting reverberates up my arm. I drop my hand into the sink to rinse off the dead bug, and when I look up, there's a clear spot amid the condensation, leaving everything blurry but my eyes.

Unbidden, the memory unfurls . . .

I'm eleven, and it's my first time at a birthday party. I met Ariana at the local playground, and she doesn't mind that I always wear sunglasses—in fact, she even asks her parents for her own pair because she thinks I look cool.

Ma tells Ariana's mom I have something called photophobia *so I can't take my glasses off. When I get to her house, I've never seen so many kids my age in one place. It's instantly the best day of my life—until it becomes the worst.*

A blond boy Ariana has a crush on thinks it would be funny to toss me into the pool even though I can't swim. I scream as his arms wrap around me, and Ariana's mom runs over to tell him to put me down. The boy shoves me so hard that I fall to the floor, and my sunglasses slide to my chin.

It feels like the whole world stops.

Ariana's mom is the only person close enough to see my eyes, and I watch as her outrage at the boy rearranges into shock at me—which is quickly followed by revulsion, and the inevitable question:

"What. Are. You?"

I shake the memory loose from my thoughts as I change into shorts and a tank top, then I meet Ma in Perla's plant-riddled living room. The mingled aroma of eggs and bacon still permeates the apartment, so I throw open a window, ushering in hot air that's webbed with conversation—songbirds' shrill cries, buses' boisterous bellows, construction's discordant crashes.

I join Ma on the worn turquoise couch, which despite its fraying fabric still manages to be the loudest part of the room. The high velvet seatback is rippled like a seashell, and it's tall enough to cushion our heads. When I was ten, it inspired me to spin a fairy tale about Perla—the first story I ever wrote. She keeps it framed on her nightstand.

"Perla has one of her migraines, so I put her back to bed," says Ma as she doles out seven cards for each of us—plus an extra one for me, since I'm up first—and sets the rest face-down on the cushion separating us. Next to the stack is a notepad with two columns: *M* for Manu (me) and *S* for Soledad (Ma).

The game begins when I discard my spare, so I get rid of

my heaviest card—the king of clubs—and am left with seven. Ma picks up a new card from the facedown stack and drops the jack of hearts. To win a round, we have to fit all seven cards into two groupings that can be a set of at least three cards of the same number and/or a sequential run of at least three cards of the same suit. Any leftover cards in your hand count as points against you.

"She says you should finish reading *Cien Años de Soledad* and be prepared for a quiz when she wakes up," Ma goes on as I pick a card from the stack. It's the seven of diamonds, so I slip it between the pair of sevens I'm already holding—*one grouping down*—and drop the nine of spades. The only seven I'm missing now is clubs.

"¿Te gusta Márquez?" she asks as she picks up a new card, and I nod in assent. I've been trying to read Gabriel García Márquez's masterpiece as slowly as possible so I can relish the writing, but it's so good that I'm already two-thirds of the way through.

Ma discards the eight of spades, and I groan; I should have held on to that nine. But my mood improves when I see my new card—*ace of hearts*. I already have the two and three of hearts, so with the ace, that's my second sequence.

Now I just need the four of hearts or the seven of clubs if I want to end the round with a perfect score.

"Does that mean Márquez has the honor of going on your favorites shelf next to Austen and Wharton and Dickens?" Ma prods as she shuffles her cards around like she's also just completed a grouping. "Or are we talking *top shelf,* next to your sainted Harry Potter? I realize the Buendías are no Weasels—"

"*Weasleys—*"

"But it wouldn't kill you to read more Spanish books."

I roll my eyes, but my gut tightens at her taunting. My love for the Weasleys has nothing to do with nationality or language. I love them because they're the family I long to have, and the Burrow is the home I crave. Only I can't admit this stuff to Ma because she's given up everything for us, and I don't want her to think all she's sacrificed isn't enough for me.

That *she* isn't enough for me.

"Are you going to keep ignoring me?" Ma demands.

"No, but if you're going to make fun of something, you should know what it is. Maybe if you tried reading *Harry*—"

"Name one Latino character, and I'll read it."

I'm too weighted down with other worries to play two games at once, so I pull another card from the stack, hoping it's the four or seven I need . . .

Queen of diamonds.

Damn.

"¿Qué te pasa?" Ma doesn't take her turn until I lift my eyes and meet her excavating gaze.

A rare breeze blows in through the third-story window, wafting her almond scent toward me, and I flash back to my younger days, when curling into her neck could make anything better. Something hard dislodges from my chest.

"Even if we get our residency," I hear myself say, "what's going to change? Between my eyes and lunaritis, I'll *never* fit in."

Ma knits her brow, and she stares at me for a long moment. Undeterred, I stare back.

She used to be beautiful. There are still hints of that beauty in her plump lips and high cheekbones and long lashes. But the past few years have stolen most of her youth away. Her skin has lost its glow, her hair has gotten thin, and her curves have deflated with her shrinking frame.

"Didn't you tell me Harry Potter has a scar on his forehead?" she asks, and the stunned expression on my face must be pretty comical because hers splits into a small smirk. "Your eyes are *your* lightning mark—be proud of them."

"How can I be proud of them when they put a target on us?"

"In that case, we'll just have to get healthcare so we can afford your surgery!" I love when she's in a good mood because she becomes an obstinate optimist. "And take it from me, there are worse chronic conditions to have than lunaritis. When you see a real doctor, they'll give you an actual diagnosis and a *cure*—"

"*You* could be a real doctor, Ma," I can't help pointing out. "When we're legal, you could get certified as a nurse again and go to medical school."

"Sí," she says distantly, but she doesn't sound like she believes it. Then she breaks our gaze to take her turn.

Conversación over.

Her eyes light up when she sees her new card, and I fear what's coming next—

"*¿Cortaste?*" I ask incredulously as she slaps a card face-down, ending the round.

She triumphantly bares her full hand to me. She's holding the four of hearts *and* the seven of clubs, so I was never getting the cards I was waiting on.

"¡Menos diez!" She announces her score and starts shuffling the deck for me to deal the next hand. I pull the notepad toward me and write *–10* in her column and *1* in mine, my gaze lingering on my score.

I am that leftover ace of diamonds.

I don't fit into any of the groupings around me, and the things that make me different always seem to count against me.

For the millionth time, I wonder about the person I might have become if we hadn't left Argentina. If my dad's parents and profession had been normal, and I could have been raised with my family, would my differences still alienate me? Ma sets the deck down, and I ask, "What's Buenos Aires like?"

I was only five when we left, so I don't remember much of my homeland. Just impressions that feel more like paintings I saw once in a museum.

"The old-world architecture is breathtaking," she begins, and I ask her this question often enough that I could mouth her answer along with her. "Assuming you can manage to appreciate it under all the graffiti. The sidewalks change from brick to cement to cobblestone for no particular reason, and they're covered in every variety of dog poop that Argentines wouldn't dream of picking up—"

"Yeah, yeah, yeah," I say, interrupting her. "You always give the same answer."

"You always ask the same question."

I roll my eyes. "What does it *feel* like to be in Buenos Aires?"

"It's the most alive city in the world . . . Days start late and nights are never-ending. You sleep so little that life begins to feel like a waking dream—"

"Okay," I say, cutting her off again. She's said this before too, so just to stump her with something unexpected, I ask, "What's it *smell* like?"

"Coffee and leather," she answers without missing a beat. "I used to like visiting high-end stores just to sniff the jackets and handbags. And . . . paper," she adds, her voice growing distant like she's not seeing Perla's apartment anymore. "Buenos Aires has more bookstores per person than any city in the world."

I sit at attention. It's the first new bit of information she's given me in a while, and I thread the detail into the tapestry in my head. "What are the people like?"

"*Warm.*" Her voice dips a few decibels, and I lean forward in anticipation. "Even if it's your first time there, you're not a stranger because everyone treats you like they've always known you, with smiles and hugs and kisses. The salesperson, the cab driver, the hair stylist—with one conversation, they're instant friends."

She must be burnt out because I haven't heard her this unguarded in a long time. So I chance a question that usually shuts her down, in hopes that today she'll give something up.

"What was Dad like?"

The light dims in Ma's brown eyes as the glaze of nostalgia melts into that dark, faraway look she gets whenever I mention him. All I've managed to work out is that he was probably white, since my skin is a lighter shade of brown than Ma's.

I'm not even sure she's told me his real name because when I looked up *Martín Fierro* on a computer at the library, a fictional gaucho from classic Argentine literature came up. She's so terrified of me finding out anything about him that sometimes it feels like he's still around.

"He was . . . passionate," she says, her voice uncharacteristically tender. "Unpredictable. Charming," she adds with the ghost of a smile. "*Hopeful.* He was determined to leave his mark on the world. Sometimes when we went out together, he would carve an *F* somewhere—a table, a door, a tree. He said he wanted to make sure the place was changed by our presence."

She meets my gaze and her face softens, but I know I'm not the person she's seeing.

Ma says I have my father's eyes.

It's the only thing about him I know for sure.

She claims they're the reason she fell in love with him, yet she's always making me hide mine. I know it's just a precaution we need to take, but it makes me feel like they're shameful or repulsive or *wrong*.

It's only natural to be drawn to the unnatural, Ma always tells me—but attention breeds scrutiny, which is dangerous for us because:

Visibility = Deportation.

This equation—plus Ma's fear of my father's family discovering I exist—is why she makes me wear my sunglasses everywhere. Why she won't take me to see a doctor for my lunaritis. Why I'm no longer allowed to have friends . . .

Because you can't be invisible when your irises are yellow suns and your pupils are silver stars.

5

When I was little, Ma used to call me Solcito. *Little sun.*

Since her name is Soledad, I assumed the moniker was meant to make me sound like a diminutive version of her. But once I pieced together that she was always hiding me, I began to believe I was a real drop of sunlight that fell from the sky.

So when she told me I have my dad's eyes, I imagined him as the actual sun, and I made up a story about how the brightest star in the sky fell so in love with Ma that he literally fell to Earth to be with her. And now he watches over us, waiting for me to become an astronaut so I can launch into the stars and find him.

I rarely miss a sunrise.

The truth, of course, is far less glamorous: Ma says I must have inherited a genetic mutation in my father's bloodline.

One time, she brought home dark brown contacts for me to try, and I was convinced my life was finally about to begin. But when I popped them in, the five points of my star-shaped silver pupils were still there, and the yellow glow of my eyes shone through the filter of dark brown like radioactive material.

It's all sunglasses all the time for me now . . . Until I can afford the surgery that will change everything.

Ma brought us to Miami because of the Bascom Palmer Eye Institute. It's the top-ranked eye hospital in the country and my only hope for normalcy. Once our papers come through, Ma says we can get photo IDs, and then we can sign up for healthcare to help cover the costs.

If the eye institute can fix me, I won't have to worry about being linked to my father and his shady past.

I'll be free.

While Ma's at work, I clean the apartment, wash our bedding, and tidy up my books so Ma will quit hassling me about them. The largest stack is my outer space collection, which I've been studying since I learned how to read. I think I was born wanting to see the stars.

I reheat the milanesas for lunch and eat them while watching Perla's favorite telenovela, but it's not the same without her running commentary. After washing the dishes, I warm up some soup and knock softly before opening the door to her room.

The shades are drawn, and the air is dark as night, but my eyes cut through the dim lighting. Her favorite fragrance hangs in the air, a Spanish perfume with a zesty lemon accent. She told me it's been her scent her whole life.

"Perla," I murmur. "¿Tenés hambre?"

She rolls onto her back and shuffles up on her pillow. I place the tray on her thighs and perch next to her.

"Gracias, Ojazos." That's her nickname for me. It means a pair of eyes that are large or striking.

Perla has something called macular degeneration, and by

now she's lost about 90 percent of her vision—but according to her, she can still see my eyes. I sit with her as she blows on the soup and brings the spoon to her mouth.

My framed fairy tale still sits on her nightstand. Stuck into the corners of the mirror on her dresser are black-and-white photographs of her family, dating back to before World War II.

There are no photos of Ma or me anywhere in the apartment. Ma says it's for our own protection—and I can't be sure if she means from ICE or my father's people. I wish I had a picture of him, but Ma says their relationship was so secretive, they couldn't risk any evidence.

Sometimes I hate him for pursuing Ma when he knew his love would place a lifelong target on her back. Then again, if he hadn't, I wouldn't be here. Most of the time, though, I just wish I could have known him.

From the few things Ma's told me, he sounds more like a fictional character than a real person. I wish I'd had the chance to make my own judgment.

I once asked her why she dated Dad if being with him was so dangerous—was he really worth risking it all? I must have been twelve or thirteen at the time, but the pitying look she gave me made me feel about a decade younger. Then she said, "You might as well ask Juliet why she gave up everything for Romeo."

"¿Cómo va la lectura?"

Perla's rattly voice pops my thought bubble. "Great," I say as she brings another spoonful to her mouth. "I'll be done with the book today."

"Cuando lo termines quiero que escribas un ensayo." We often have conversations like these, where she asks in Spanish and I answer in English. "Una exploración del uso de realismo mágico para transmitir la subjetividad de la realidad."

An essay exploring the use of magical realism to convey the subjectivity of reality . . . I translate the words in my head but still don't have a clue. "I have no idea what that means."

"Then I'll be sure to get you a Spanish-to-English dictionary for your birthday." Whenever she feels provoked, Perla switches to English. "Or you can try cracking the one in your brain."

"The subjectivity of reality . . ." I frown. "Does that mean how each character sees the world differently?"

"Go on."

I stretch out at the foot of her bed and hinge my elbow to prop my head in my hand. But I'm less interested in her assignment than I am in the conversation we started this morning. "How come magical realism is such a big part of our literature?"

"Not just literature." I stare at her quizzically as she takes another sip of soup. "We use magical realism in our daily lives too. Consider our superstitions. We are always willing magic into reality—that's our way."

"But *why?*"

She swallows another spoonful before answering. "There are horrors in this world that defy explanation. Márquez's own hometown experienced a massacre much like the one in Macondo . . . Sometimes reality strays so far from what's rational that we can only explain it through fantasy."

She falls silent and focuses on finishing her soup, and I don't ask more questions. Perla doesn't like to talk about her past because it's too painful, but this apartment is too small for secrets. Once I overheard her telling Ma what happened.

Perla lived at home with her parents in Argentina until her late thirties, when she finally met her match. She married Federico Sanchez a few years before the Guerra Sucia broke out, a violent military dictatorship that disappeared people overnight, ripped children from their parents, and killed any-one who spoke out against the regime . . . including Federico.

Perla had an aunt living in Miami who helped her get a visa, and as soon as she was able, she left Argentina forever. She's never even returned to visit.

"That law we were talking about at breakfast," I venture. "It's connected to that story you used to tell me about seventh children?"

She sets the spoon down in the now-empty bowl. "I used an existing superstition to make up a story so you'd feel better."

"But there was a rhyme, wasn't there?" I frown, searching my memory for the words. Something about thunder and the full moon. I used to repeat it to myself to fall asleep, only it's been so long . . .

"Los lobizones le cantan a la luna llena,
las brujas bailan cuando el cielo truena.
Si te cruzas con uno, no dejes que te inquiete:
El secreto está en sus ojos y el número siete."

Perla recites it softly, with none of her usual dramatic flair. Her hushed tone makes it sound more like a religious pas-sage than a silly rhyme. *The werewolves sing at the full moon, the witches dance when the sky thunders. If you come across one, let it not upset you: The secret is in their eyes and the number seven.*

Boy wolves and girl witches. "Is the werewolf versus witch thing based on sex or gender identification?" I blurt. "Because you told me that in 2012 Argentina passed a Gender Identity Law that says a person can choose their own gender—"

"Oh, Ojazos, you're too enlightened for me," she says with a groan, pushing the tray away. "You'll have to write the presi-dent and find out. Ahora dejame dormir un poquito."

"Bueno, descansá," I say, agreeing to let her rest. I lift the tray off her, and she nestles into her pillow.

On my way out, I pass the only color photograph in her room. It's from her wedding, and it hurts to look at because I've never seen Perla smile that big in person.

For some reason I think of *Don Quijote de la Mancha*. When we read it together last year, we were both delighted to find that neither of us believed Don Quijote to be delusional. I think that's the secret that's always bonded Perla and me:

Deep down, we would rather be dreaming than awake.

I keep my word to Mimitos and take him up to the rooftop with me. I hate days like these when I'm confined to this building. I feel like a video game avatar that can only move up or down.

This rooftop is the only place I can see the world without it seeing me. Evenings are my favorite, when the sun casts a fleeting rosy glow over our street, before igniting and setting us all ablaze. I'll lie along the building's ledge and watch the fiery red clouds cool to a purple ash, until night's first bold stars start to wink at me, wooing me to unknown worlds.

Right now, though, is the worst time to be up here. A little after midday, the sky is white and overexposed, making the city look washed out and hot to the touch. My skin is slick with sweat from just standing in place.

I would much rather be in the heavily air-conditioned library, legs cradled in a chilly plastic chair, arms pressed to the cool tabletop, face buried in the woodsy-scented pages of the Victorian fantasy series I'm hooked on. I wouldn't even mind how my sunglasses' tint makes the font hard to read in the fluorescent lighting because the cold would be worth it.

I cast my gaze for cops canvassing the neighborhood, but there are none. Nor do I spot any threatening black SUVs with flashing blue lights in the distance. I'm going to be finished with *Cien Años de Soledad* soon, and since Perla's migraines last all day, I'll have nothing to do until Ma gets home tonight.

I could probably make it to the library and back in thirty minutes if I hurried. Ma would never have to know.

Except we don't break our promises. *Our trust in each other is the only thing they can't take from us*, she's always reminding me—and I'm not about to risk everything over air conditioning.

Mimitos brushes his soft fur across my leg, and I drop down to pet him. "This isn't forever," I tell him as much as myself, scratching under his eye in the spot he likes. "We'll make it out of here." He offers me his other cheek, and I pet him in the same spot, for symmetry. "Did you finish your turkey?"

A girlish giggle floats into the air, and every sector of the city orchestra—cars, construction, conversation—fades into the background. My new and improved hearing singles out the sound, and I snap upright.

Other Manu is in front of the pink building, wearing her Argentine blue-and-white striped fútbol jersey with Messi's name and the number *10* sprawled on the back. She has the same razor-sharp cheekbones I inherited from Ma, my tall and curvy figure, and my heavy brown hair. The only difference between us is her eyes are an acceptable color.

And she has *him*.

A brawny guy draws Other Manu to his chest, smiling at something she says, his white teeth stark against his black skin. He's been her boyfriend for about a year.

I've watched their entire courtship—when he picked her up for their first date in a coat and collared shirt, when she slammed his car door after their first fight, when he pulled her into his chest for their first kiss. Now she tugs on the neckline of his shirt, and as he leans down, I drink in every slow motion second of their mouths meeting.

Other Manu closes her eyes, and a comma forms between her eyebrows, like the kiss is a puzzle it's taking all her concentration to solve. I wonder if I'll look like that too, if I ever get kissed.

Something flickers in my periphery, and I realize I'm not the only one spying on the couple. Leaning against the side of the pink building is a guy wearing a leather jacket in ninety-degree weather.

While he stares at their make-out session, I study him. He's taller than anyone I've ever seen, with dark hair and thick eyebrows, and he's wearing a belt with a flashy buckle that reflects sunlight like a blade. I've never seen anyone like him around here.

I think back to the woman I overheard on the rooftop this morning. It could be coincidental, just a couple of out-of-the-norm occurrences—or this guy could be the person she was on the phone with. *Nacho*.

Are they here to spy on Other Manu? What's she gotten herself into?

The Miami weather being typically temperamental, a light drizzle starts to fall from the white-gray sky. Other Manu squeals, and her boyfriend holds her against his broad chest as they dart to his beat-up Ford. When I look back at Leather Jacket, he's gone.

Mimitos has already dashed to the part of the wall that's sheltered, and I stuff my book up my shirt and follow him. Small drops splash against the hot cement, and a sticky musk clings to my skin as I sit on the floor, my back against the wall. I open my book, and I have to go over the same paragraph a few times to finally focus on the story and not Other Manu's life.

Mimitos curls up next to me, his tail twirling along my leg, and I'm up to the scene where the almost-invisible Santa Sofía de la Piedad takes off on her own when I hear the scream.

It's so faint, it barely registers, but it's coming from inside El Retiro.

I spring to my feet and pull on the stairwell door. Mimitos senses my urgency because he hurries over, and then we're leaping down the stairs, all six stories a blur. *Please let the scream have come from anywhere but our apartment.*

Adrenaline steadies me the whole way to our door, until I swing it open—

"Perla!"

She's in a clump on the living room carpet.

I drop down and grab her wrist, but my own pulse crashes so loudly in my ears that I can't focus on hers. I bring my hand to her nose to check if she's breathing, and that's when I see the blood pooling behind her head.

"No no no no," I moan, my eyes burning and heart racing. "Perla, por favor—"

Her eyes suddenly flicker open, and I gasp. Mimitos jumps on the turquoise couch, his back arched in terror. Perla's hand moves toward me, and I close my fingers around hers. "¿Perla? ¿Me escuchás?"

Her mouth opens and closes like she's trying to talk but no sound comes out. Yanking the phone from its cradle, I dial the number I never thought I'd call.

"911, what's your emergency?"

"We need an ambulance at El Retiro unit 3E! It's for Perla Sanchez—I think she's fallen and hit her head—and she's bleeding! She's unconscious and ninety years old, so hurry!"

I hang up before the operator can ask me anything and lean over Perla, pressing a gentle kiss to her forehead. "Vas a estar bien," I reassure her while we wait for the ambulance. "Estoy con vos."

She suddenly starts to shake her head, like she's having some kind of spasm, and her rattly voice comes out in a breathy whisper. "Corré . . ."

Run?

"Corré . . ." she says again, and I grip her hand tighter.

"I'm staying with you," I say firmly.

"No." Now she tries to move, and more blood trickles out from her wound.

"Perla, por favor, no te muevas," I say, my voice growing shrill.

"Tenés que . . . irte," she says, and her face turns toward me. "Buscá a tu madre. Ahora." *You have to go. Find your mother. Now.*

"I can't leave you," I say, tears streaming down my cheeks.

"Go. *Now.* For me." She seems to have expended the last of her energy because her eyes close again, and a terrified part of me can't help wondering if they'll ever reopen.

I can't leave her here. But I also can't disobey what might be her last wish.

I hear the wail of an ambulance in the distance growing closer. I don't have much time left. If they find me, they could ask questions I can't answer. Ma and I could be discovered. Then I would be the reason we're deported.

Perla must not want that on her conscience either.

"Perdoname," I whisper, apologizing to her for doing as she asked, and I drop her hand as I dash to my room to trade my low-cut tank for a round-necked white tee that won't draw attention. On my way out, I kneel to kiss Perla again, her eyes still closed, and I thank her for everything she's done for us. "Te quiero, Perla. Gracias por salvarnos y por darnos un hogar y una familia. Ahora tenés que *luchar—*"

The words die on my tongue when I see it.

The red smoke I was convinced I'd imagined in the stair-well earlier . . . It curls past me, and I run my fingers through it. The vapor vanishes.

But is it real? Or are hallucinations a bonus this lunaritis?

I shove on my sunglasses, grab my bus pass, and race out of the apartment, leaving Perla and Mimitos behind. A couple of elderly neighbors are in the hallway, searching for the source of the scream, but I don't slow down to explain. I leave the door open so the paramedics can get to Perla without delay, then I duck into the stairwell and soar down to ground level.

The bus stop is at the end of the block, so I don't have to go far. Ma gave me Doña Rosa's address when she started work-ing for her. She told me Doña Rosa warned her against bring-ing her child to work, so I buried the directions in the back of my mind and promised to only go in case of a life-or-death emergency. This will be my first time.

The street seems quieter than usual as I twist the bus pass around and around in my hand. I'm drenched in sweat from the brew of heat and nerves, and I try to keep calm by review-ing Ma's instructions. Instead of the #29 I take to the library, I'm getting on the #21, toward the nicer neighborhoods. I've never gone in that direction before.

When Ma and I first got to the States, we lived in a motel. Ma cleaned rooms for cash, and we stuck it out as long as we could—until the owner's sexual advances became too aggres-sive for Ma to ignore.

We spent a year shuffling between shelters, then Ma met Perla. The latter was crossing the street when a guy on a mo-torcycle zoomed past and yanked on her purse, and Perla fell facedown on the concrete. Ma helped her up, escorted her home to El Retiro, and tended to her injuries.

Maybe it's because we're from the same country, or maybe she just realized she needed help and couldn't afford it, but basically Perla invited us to live with her. We could share a room in her apartment, free of charge, in exchange for looking after her. She also recommended Ma's cleaning services to people she knew so we could earn money. And when she realized I was eight years old and couldn't speak or read English, Perla made my education part of the bargain.

Please let her be okay.

She has *to be okay.*

PLEASE.

I rush onto the bus the instant its doors open, and I take a seat at the very back, where there are fewer people. The passengers stare at my face as I pass, but Ma says it's not me they're looking at—since my sunglasses are mirrored, people only see themselves.

I'm invisible.

The bus pulls away just as an ambulance wails onto the street, its siren singing too loudly in my tender ears, and I hope it makes it to Perla in time.

I'm jostled as we rumble down the pothole-strewn streets, and it makes me think of all the times I've ridden the bus with Perla. She often spent the whole ride railing about the shape of these roads, complaining that our area is too poor to be prioritized by politicians; and if people glared at her to shut up, she only raised her voice louder.

I can't believe I left her there, lying on the floor.

Ma's going to be furious at me for breaking our promise, but she has to forgive me when I tell her what happened. I press my nose to the glass, by now expecting to start seeing the smooth streets and manicured gardens of a comfortable community. Instead, the bus is rolling through a bustling district of discount businesses, and when we get to the stop Ma told me would be Doña Rosa's, we pull up in front of a convenience store.

This can't be right.

Still, I step off the bus, and the sweltering heat swallows me whole. I touch my sunglasses to make sure they're still on. I no longer know if the reflex is cautionary, obsessive-compulsive, or superstitious. Everything else is a carefully calculated choreography: I keep my movements small and inconspicuous, my face mostly averted.

Sandwiched between street vendors and squat storefronts, I walk half a block before I stop in my tracks to survey the grimy and congested sidewalk around me. Panic pricks my belly, its poke shockingly sharp, as I suck in a would-be calming breath that's deep-fried in the cooking oils of churros and empanadas and tostones.

The greasy air does nothing to quell the queasiness in my gut.

There's no way Doña Rosa's nice home can be on the next few blocks. I must have memorized the wrong address years ago. Or maybe the memory just got misshapen over time. *Where do I go now?*

I don't register the woman hurtling toward me until the wheels of her stroller are inches from my foot, and I duck out of the way before we collide—stepping right in front of a deliveryman. After dodging him, I realize I'm drawing too much attention just standing in place, so I join the flow of people walking.

I pull myself together enough to resume my carefully crafted movements, gliding like a ghost down the squat city blocks as I weave around the afternoon foot traffic. I check out the addresses of the storefronts around me and head uptown to hunt down number 21280. Might as well see what it is now that I'm here; it's not like I have any other leads.

Panic pumps harder with every step, like it's hitched a ride with my blood. I stride past a shoe repair place, a pawnshop, a hair salon, a dentist's office, a counter service Mexican joint . . .

"Oye, come here!"

"¡Mira qué chévere!"

"Por favor, niña, no tenemos tiempo para eso."

Different dialects of Spanish and Spanglish fill the air, and I stick to the inside of the sidewalk, taking up as little space as possible, trying to avoid getting roped into conversation.

Outside a carnicería, a man in an apron and bandana blows secondhand smoke in my face, then a pair of women in dangly earrings and stilettos sashays past, dispersing the smoke with their floral perfumes. A pack of teen boys skates down the sidewalk, inconveniencing all of us, but most of all an elderly lady pushing her cart full of groceries. One of the boys tosses an empty plastic bottle into her things, and she mutters something that sounds a lot like *boludo*—a distinctly Argentine dig that means *idiot*. Under different circumstances, I might laugh.

A couple of pierced twenty-somethings walk hand in hand, and the girl studies me so hard that on reflex I touch my sunglasses to make sure they're still there. When she also reaches up and fixes her side-swept bangs, I realize she was using my lenses as mirrors, and my shoulders drop in relief.

"Nice shades!" says a teen guy hanging by a doorstop with two of his buddies. "Can I try them on?"

I ignore him and keep walking, but in my periphery I see him and his friends start to follow me.

Fuck.

I never get hassled—have never even been noticed. Invisibility is pretty much my only talent. But my body's been changing so much lately, I've noticed the side stares.

It's these damn breasts. Especially during my cycle, when they puff up like balloons.

"Why are they mirrored?" He's louder now. Not like he's yelling, but like he's catching up to me. "You a cop?"

I walk faster, and his hand closes around my arm.

I shove back with my elbow and jab it into his chest. He gasps like I knocked his breath away, and I sprint down the block without glancing back until I'm at the intersection.

I exhale in relief to see they're not following.

And that's when I notice the name of the beauty parlor behind me.

Doña Rosa.

6

I approach the glass slowly, in a trance. There are two grave-faced women inside waiting to be serviced, but no one is working the front desk or any of the four stations.

I pull open the door, and a too-loud bell jangles through the space, prompting the women to look up.

One of them is clutching a bundle of fabric to her chest, and when a small foot kicks out, I realize it's a baby. The sound must've roused it, and as the baby starts fussing, its mom and the elderly lady beside her make soothing sounds to calm it down.

A middle-aged woman with a pink streak in her hair darts out from a back door and strides up to me, examining me through kindly brown eyes.

"Hola, señorita. ¿Tiene cita para hoy?" Her articulated Spanish is fluid, and her neutral dialect gives every syllable space, so she's definitely not Argentine . . . Maybe Peruvian?

I answer, "No, I don't have an appointment."

"¿Qué estilo de servicio busca?"

As I consider her question—which service am I interested in?—it hits me that the women waiting look too anxious to be here for personal grooming.

The knot in my stomach may have formed before I walked in, but it's the tension inside this place that's tightened it. Something's not right.

A scream rings out from the back of the parlor, and this time I recognize the voice intimately.

"¡MA!"

I push past Pink Streak and shove through the door she came in from, my pulse in my throat—

Two women whirl away in surprise from a small television where a fútbol match is being broadcast. The older woman is in a white lab coat and the younger one is . . . Ma.

"Manu?" She rushes over, wearing blue scrubs I've never seen before. "¿Qué pasó?" she asks, her concern so consuming that she doesn't consider the scene from my perspective.

Pink Streak bursts through the door behind me as the words spill out: "Perla fell! I think. I heard her scream, and she was bleeding from the head when I found her, and I called an ambulance, but she wouldn't let me stay—"

A sob chokes me, and I swallow it down, blinking quickly behind my sunglasses to stave off tears.

Ma's hand covers her mouth, her own eyes glassy and round and unblinking. "Dios mío," she whispers. The woman in the white coat squeezes her arm, and Pink Streak takes Ma's other hand.

"Dime el hospital más cercano a tu hogar y yo te averiguo lo que está pasando," she says. *Tell me the hospital closest to you, and I'll track down an update.* The three of them speak in hushed tones as they form a plan of action, and I look around, surveying my surroundings . . .

I'm not in a beauty salon anymore.

This back area is twice as large as the front, and judging by the privacy curtains to my left and the medicine-lined walls to my right—not to mention the general antiseptic smell—I know it's some kind of medical office. The privacy curtains are bunched up, revealing a couple of empty patient beds, and all around me is strange equipment I only recognize from television dramas—IV drips, needles, glass tubes, and a chest-high machine that rolls on wheels. There's a hallway in the back corner, but from here I can't make out where it leads.

The only thing that looks familiar is the small television.

It's Perla's old set.

Shock burns off quickly, exposing a heavier emotion simmering just beneath my surface. Ma isn't a maid. She's a nurse again.

At an underground clinic.

Pink Streak suddenly kisses my cheek. "Hola, Manu, soy Julieta. Tu mamá se la pasa hablando de lo inteligente que eres." *Hi, Manu, I'm Julieta. Your mom is always going on about how smart you are.*

The fact that Ma has been praising my intellect even as she's been manipulating me for years only accelerates the fire scalding my chest, bringing the flames closer to my throat and dangerously near my mouth.

"No te enfades con ella," says Julieta, reading my face and coming to Ma's defense. *Don't be mad at her.*

"None of our families know." Julieta sounds less confident as she switches into an accented English, like a person venturing across an untested bridge. "It's a promise we make . . . so if we're caught, the people we love can't get blamed."

I want to understand, but I can't. These other families might operate on secrets, but the only thing Ma and I have is our trust in each other.

Had.

I guess Ma's constant refrain is right: *Our trust in each other is the only thing they can't take from us.* They didn't take it—Ma did.

My mouth fills with all the hurtful words I want to hurl her way, but when our gazes lock, I swallow them.

I've never seen Ma cry. Not even when we lived in a shelter.

"I'm sorry, Manu," she says as tears roll down, and Julieta backs away to give us space. "This was the only way I could . . . take care of you."

It's the pause in her words that tips me off. Like she was going to say something more specific but caught herself.

I scrutinize the room again for a clue, and somehow I know where to look. Scanning the wall of medicines, I spot the telltale blue bottle.

This is how Ma *really* gets me the Septis pills. It's not through Perla's insurance. Ma's working here, risking everything again, for *me.*

Julieta cups my shoulder with her hand, and the woman in the lab coat offers Ma a tissue. She blows her nose.

"How about you get some rest on the couch in the office?" Julieta asks me. "We just finished lunch, and there are only two patients waiting. Let your mom work, and I'll find out about Perla. Okay?"

I nod because it's as much as I can manage.

"Are you hungry?"

"No, thanks."

"Is it really so sunny in here?" She adopts a lighter tone, trying to crack the tension. "Would you like some sunscreen too?"

Before I can even consider the possibility of taking off my sunglasses, Ma's fingers coil around my wrist, and she pulls me away from Julieta. "I'll take her," she says, dragging me down the back hallway, deeper into the space.

I've barely glimpsed a small kitchen/lounge to my right when Ma pulls me through a door to my left and locks it behind us. I slide my sunglasses onto my head.

"I know you're upset with me, and you have every right to be," she says, and since I can't stand to look at her yet, I scan the office. Black synthetic leather couch, L-shaped wooden desk, ominous six-foot safe in the corner.

"I will answer your questions, *I promise*."

I glower at her. She looks like a stranger in those scrubs, and I can't tell if her skin is paling, or if the blue is washing her out.

"But right now, I need you to stay here and wait for me." She strides up to the huge safe and punches a code to unlock it.

I blink.

"What the fuck is going on?"

The words explode out of me, and I brace myself for Ma's reaction.

"We can't go back to Perla's," she says as she reaches into the safe and pulls out a duffel bag. "We'll tell the others we're spending the night on the couch."

When she doesn't yell at me for my language, fear frays the hard edges of my rage.

She sets the bag on the desk and rifles through its contents. "Then once they head home, we'll go." Ma zips the duffel shut again and pins me with one of her no-nonsense stares. "Everything we have left is in that bag. Stay in this room and guard it with your life. *Do not leave this clinic for any reason.* I'll be back as soon as I can."

My breathing shallows as I try to process the speed at which everything in my life is changing. I feel like this morning I woke from a dream into a nightmare.

Ma reaches for the door, and I make to follow her out. "But we don't even know how Perla is—"

She whirls to face me, blocking the exit with her body. "Let me finish with my patients, and I'll figure out a plan. Don't let anyone see you without your glasses."

"Ma!"

I grab her arm, and I'm chilled by the terror glazing her eyes. Trying to infuse my voice with as much hope as I can muster, I say, "Maybe—maybe Perla's fine by now—"

"Perla was attacked, Manu!" she shout-whispers.

I inhale sharply. "What do you—"

"Your father's family found me." Her voice is faint and fragile and foreign from the Ma I know. "Now we need to run, before they find out about you."

The door slams in my face, narrowly missing my nose.

Ma left the office five hundred and thirty-three seconds ago. I know because there's a loud clock over the couch, and I've been counting off its every tick.

Tick.

Ma thinks Perla was attacked.

Tick.

Ma works at an underground clinic.

Tick.

Ma thinks my dad's people found us.

Tick.

We can never go home again.

Tick.

What happens if they catch us?

A tendril of red smoke floats across my field of vision, but I blink and it's gone. This hallucination is really starting to get on my nerves. I leap off the couch and start pacing up and down the office.

To tune out the deafening ticking of time, I try to make sense of a senseless situation. *It's just like playing chinchón,* I tell myself as I deepen my breathing. I've been dealt a hand of unrelated cards, and now I have to discern a pattern and sort them into groups.

I think of Leather Jacket and the woman on the rooftop. Maybe they were there looking for Ma. The woman sounded Argentine—she could be a scout sent by my dad's family.

What if his people really did hurt Perla?

What if they followed me here?

My heart vaults into my throat, and I reach for the door—but I stop myself before opening it. Ma might not be thinking clearly right now, which means it's important that I be the rational one. I have to consider the facts objectively, for both of us.

Perla is a ninety-year-old woman whose health is starting to fail, and it's perfectly logical that she could have fallen on her own. Ma has been running from my father's family my whole life, so it's natural for her to be paranoid.

I sigh and bury my face in my hands. I can't even trust what I know to be true anymore. Until ten minutes ago, I was beyond certain there were no secrets between Ma and me, and now it turns out all we've ever had are secrets.

If Doña Rosa isn't real, Ma's anecdotes about her multi-story house and snotty little kids have all been fabrications. My entire life is made up of dreams and superstitions and lies—even the *real* parts aren't real.

Tick.

So what if Ma's lying about the only thing that matters?

The question surges up my throat like bile. Ma wouldn't betray me like this. She knows our only chance of survival is with legal residency. She knows we desperately need a real home. She knows the hope of our papers coming through is all that's keeping me going.

My eyes latch onto the duffel bag she left on the desk. I've searched Perla's whole apartment for copies of the paperwork Ma filed, just to touch proof of that hope, to know it's real, but I've yet to find it. I always assumed Ma must have a really good hiding place because I never found anything else either, like our savings or my birth certificate.

I dive for the bag.

Sitting at the desk, I rummage through wads of cash, new clothing, unopened toothbrushes and toiletries, a flashlight, power bars, water bottles . . . and at the very bottom, a pile of paperwork.

I pull out the stack and push the duffel away, resting the documents on the desktop to flip through them. The first thing I come across are sketches and photographs of a symbol that looks like a fancy Z and reminds me of an old television series Perla loves called *El Zorro*.

I recognize it as the same symbol etched onto the blue pills.

Next, there are maps of different sectors of Argentina. The city names have all been crossed out, like Ma's searching for something. Or someone.

Behind the diagrams is a manila folder, and on the cover is a name, written in Ma's slanted handwriting: *Manuela Azul.*

Me.

I open it up to find a series of magnified photographs of my eyeballs.

I can't help cringing. Having never seen a photograph of myself, it's jarring to be confronted with close-ups of my most-hated feature. I don't remember posing for these, so they must have been taken when I was very young. The five-point stars of my pupils look like graphite, and my irises aren't at all what I expected.

Woven into the yellow are flecks of copper and amber and burnt gold, and the longer I stare, the more shades I see. Flipping from one photo to the next, I notice the particles of color keep shifting shape and location, like my eyes are golden galaxies orbiting silver stars.

There's text bleeding through the back of the last picture, and I turn it over to read what Ma wrote. One word, in Spanish.

Anormal.

Abnormal. Aberrant. Wrong.

I ignore the stab in my chest, and I shove the file aside to finish reading later. I keep digging through Ma's papers, but all I find are newspaper clippings and pages filled with unintelligible scribbles that could be notes on anything from Ma's patients to the blue pills she's investigating to the location she's trying to track down. By the time I reach the last page, there's nothing at all about our visa application.

Tick.

Because Ma never filed for it.

The answer is so suddenly and strikingly obvious that I feel foolish for even daring to hope. Ma works at an *underground* clinic. She obviously has no employer sponsoring her. If anything, she's just doubled down on our outlaw status.

A numbness seeps into my skin that makes it hard to access my thoughts or outrage or anything else. It's like a vacuum of air building in my head, making the office blur out of focus and filling my mind with a white noise that's intensifying into a full-body buzzing, until I can't stay here anymore.

If I do, I'll have to process that after all these years of waiting, I'm never going to belong here.

I'm never going to go to school.

I'm never going to be rid of these stupid fucking sunglasses.

The realization snaps shackles I've placed on my body my whole life. *Hide, be invisible, take up as little space as possible—share a small bed, in a small room, in a small apartment, in a small corner of the world, limited to a small routine and a small life.*

I've always felt cramped because I've been crammed into an existence too small for me. That's why the only friends I have are fictional. Why the only world I know is within El Retiro's walls. Why the only time I feel free is in my dreams.

But today, my body has outgrown its constraints.

And whatever the consequences, I'm not going back.

I shove my sunglasses back on—not for Ma, but for *me*, to avoid stares—and storm out of the office, knocking someone over.

The teen girl gasps as she tumbles to the floor, her auburn hair fanning around her stunned face. For some reason, her frightened reaction infuriates me, so I glare back and do something I've never done before—I *growl*.

At first, I think I'm going to belch. But instead, this deep, sonorous sound comes out of my mouth that doesn't sound human.

I'm mortified. My cheeks burn like they're pressed to a hot stove, and for a moment the girl and I just stare at each other. Then, without apologizing or helping her up, I *run*.

I'm going so fast, everything is a blur. Julieta dives out of my way as I reach the door that leads into the beauty salon, and even though I hear my name being shouted, I keep going until I've burst onto the street.

This time, pedestrians have to dodge me. My feet are locked into a powerful rhythm, and I don't know how to slow down. The run is a catharsis, and as tears stream down my face, I realize it's the first time since racing home from Ariana's pool party that I've let my body *go*.

Running awake is different from running in my dreams: weightier, harder, more thrilling. My body has changed from what it was just months ago, my muscles somehow stronger despite my lack of exercise. It's like I've been transforming moon by moon, becoming something new, someone new . . . But what? And whom?

I'm crying hard enough that I can barely see, until I lose track of the blocks, and I don't know where I am. I have no idea where my life goes from here.

I don't know if things with Ma can ever get back to normal. Can I stay in hiding with her if it's forever? And where will we go now?

I only stop moving when I run out of land. As my sneakers hit sand, the impact on my body is instant: My knees wobble from the exertion, my muscles sting, and my breaths come in tidal waves. I must have covered four or five miles. I hinge my hands on my thighs and bend my spine, as I wait for my heart to slow down.

The beach is packed. Parents with children splash in the ocean's shallows, and all along the shore people are lying out or playing volleyball or eating food, everyone basking and baking in the sun's rays.

But the warmth won't penetrate my skin.

My damp shirt clings to me, and the roots of my hair are itchy with sweat. The world grew deafening overnight; as a symphony of brassy conversations and stringy seagulls and crashing waves blares in my ears, I stare off into the sparkly blue Atlantic, yearning for a home that's as elusive as the horizon. And I'm tempted to slip into the sea's womblike embrace and drown out all the noise.

I suck in a deep inhale of briny air to snap out of it.

For a moment, I consider what it would mean if my father's family really found us. Ma's right that we couldn't stick around, waiting to be captured. Especially not if they hurt Perla just for being in their way.

But if I'm going to agree to run, then Ma needs to agree to file an asylum claim with the US government. I don't want to hear her excuses that the accusation might tip off my dad's people to my existence and our whereabouts—because if they're already onto us, we have nothing to lose.

I should have researched this residency stuff for myself instead of trusting her to handle it. She's obviously been keeping me in the dark for a reason.

The only thing I'm sure of anymore is I *can't* go back to how things were. I've already spent too many years fast-forwarding through a series of identical days, self-medicating every full moon, living a lonely and friendless existence. But at least then I had hope. I can't do this without it.

Stepping back onto the hard concrete of reality, I retrace my steps to Doña Rosa, only this time I'm not running. As I cut through the city blocks in a clipped and determined gait, something starts to unsettle me.

At first, I think it's the calm hollowness emanating from my decision. Then I register how much the sidewalks have emptied. Earlier, they were swarming with foot traffic, and now, I could be one of the last people left in the city.

Like the street is playing dead.

My heart stalls, and I'm back with Ma under Perla's bed. Waiting for agents to storm in and take us away.

I don't know when I make the decision to run. All I know is I'm rocketing through the empty streets, moving faster than I've ever moved, each desperate second echoing in my head.

Tick.

I see the blue lights first.

Tick.

Flashing atop a black SUV.

Tick.

ICE is at Doña Rosa.

7

Agents in bulletproof vests are congregated in front of the salon, jamming the sidewalk. My heart rams my chest like something inside is trying to punch its way out.

I duck into a laundromat on the adjacent block. Flying by rows of identical machines, I spot a back door at the end of the space and push past it into a narrow alley lined with city dumpsters.

The stench of garbage baking in the heat makes my breathing shallow, and I feel tears of sweat trickling down my back. I tread toward Doña Rosa slowly, swallowing gulps of fresh air when I reach the end of the block. Then I sprint across the street, sticking to the alley, and scan the back exits for the one that belongs to the salon.

A door swings open, and I dive behind a grimy green dumpster, holding my breath.

After a few interminable seconds, I hear a man call out, "Clear!"

Closing my eyes in relief, I concentrate on my improved hearing, hoping to catch what's going on inside. "Everyone's rounded up, then," I hear someone else say, his voice coming from deep within the salon.

Shit.

They have Ma.

My chest seizes, and I start to stand—

"The investigators are on their way to ask questions," says a woman's voice. "Then we'll book them."

My chest reinflates, the putrid air filling my lungs. I wait a while to make sure no one else is coming, then I rise to my full height.

Now is my only shot.

Either I break Ma out, or I get deported with her.

I creep out from my hiding spot and edge along the wall. Pressing my ear to the salon's door, I hear heavy footfalls, furniture being moved, things being tossed, the static of radio transmissions, the woman agent shouting questions, the tiny baby wailing . . .

I have to do something. The investigators could show up any minute.

My hand trembles as I try the doorknob, hoping it doesn't lock automatically. I could almost smile when I feel it turn.

As gently as I can, I open the door just far enough to squeeze myself through, then I shut it soundlessly behind me. I spin around to find a place to hide, and I stifle my gasp.

An officer is just a few feet away, his back to me as he rummages through the drawers of a cabinet.

Nerves churn into nausea in my stomach, and the milanesas I had for lunch threaten to make a spectacular exit.

Not even daring to breathe, I case my surroundings. Ahead is the hall I walked down before, with the kitchen on one side and the office on the other. My knees tremble as I tiptoe past the agent into the kitchen, and I duck inside. Then I go to cram myself in the crevice behind the door, only someone has beaten me to it.

The teen girl I knocked down earlier is staring at me through wide russet eyes.

How did she manage to stay hidden?

Her hoodie is zipped up to her chin, and her stomach looks bigger than before, like she's harboring something. For a stupid moment I hope it's the baby. Then I realize it's most likely drugs.

Since I'm visible from the hallway, I stuff myself behind the refrigerator, even though it's a less secure spot, and wait.

"Williams, over here," I hear a man say, and the officer by the cabinet walks past to the medical area.

The girl and I lock gazes. Strangely, she seems less scared now than she did when I shoved her.

"Vamos," she mouths, gesturing for me to follow.

I slip out behind her, and we spy the two agents up ahead, in the medical area, inspecting a clipboard. The girl pads to the back door, the one I came in through, but I stay pressed against the hallway wall.

I need a chance to slip past ICE and find Ma. She's probably being held in the salon up front.

The girl looks at me quizzically, and I shake my head. Narrowing her gaze like I'm mad, she carefully opens the door while I keep watch on the officers for a reaction. When I glance at her again, she's holding it open, giving me one last chance to escape despite how I treated her.

I shake my head again but give her a small smile that I hope conveys both my apology and gratitude. She nods, and my whole body cringes in anticipation of the lock's quiet click as she slips out—

The door slams so hard, the walls rattle.

"Go!" shouts one of the officers, and my pulse leaps up my throat as I dive into the kitchen again.

Cold sweat coats my face as footsteps race past, and a moment later the door to the salon opens as the woman agent chases after her partners. When she's followed them into the alley, I run out too, but in the opposite direction.

Weaving through the chaos of items strewn across the floor, I fling myself into the beauty salon.

Ma, Julieta, the woman in the white lab coat, and the two patients from earlier are handcuffed to a row of chairs bolted to the floor. The baby is in a bassinet at its mother's feet, where she can't comfort it.

"Manu!"

Ma looks more terrified than relieved to see me as I run over and throw my arms around her. "¿Qué hacés acá?" she asks in my ear. "¡Corré!"

"I'm not leaving without you," I say, refusing her order to run. I may have obeyed Perla when she told me to go, but I could never abandon Ma. I study her handcuffs, wondering how I can free her and the others.

"There are more agents outside!" Ma says in a strained whisper.

I turn, and through the glass I see them. One is on the phone, and another two are interrogating a street vendor. I drop down by Ma's knees, next to the bassinet.

"Por favor, fíjate cómo está mi bebé," says the baby's mother, her voice choked with tears. I look at her baby like she asks. The little girl is asleep, dried tearstains caked on her cheeks like she tuckered herself out from crying.

The government often separates undocumented parents from their children—and since this girl was probably born in this country, who knows what will happen to her. In this moment, all I want to do is spare this baby everything that's coming. But just like everyone else here, I'm powerless to protect her.

The whole world has failed her.

My heart squirms like it's been caught in someone's fist, the numbing effect of the shock and adrenaline wearing off. The fear, fury, injustice of it all brews in my belly like a boiling cauldron that's been left over flames for too long—and now the feelings are frothing up my chest, into my throat.

None of this is fucking right.

Man-made borders shouldn't matter more than people.

"Está durmiendo," I finally whisper, letting the woman know her baby is sleeping. The words come out squeezed, like they're being pushed past a boulder lodged in the back of my mouth.

I lean over and press a kiss to the girl's head, and her sweet scent rushes up my nostrils. It's like nothing I've ever smelled before, and I let my lips linger on her skin a moment longer.

A car screeches up, and we all snap our gazes to the street.

A couple of men climb out of the vehicle, and all three ICE agents approach them. They must be the investigators who've come to question Ma and the others.

"Manu, you have to go," says Ma, her tone urgent.

"No. I'll stay and get deported with you. We'll go home together—"

"You can't!" she cries out, and I flinch, worried they heard her outside. But all five men are huddled together, trading notes. Any moment now, they'll walk in here, or the three agents in the alley will return—

"I'll be fine," says Ma, her brown eyes sparkling as they

stare into mine. "I'll be with my family." Her expression lightens, and she almost looks like some part of her longed for this—but that's ridiculous.

"*I'm* your family." It comes out fiercer than I intended.

"Listen to me. Perla is at Hospital de los Santos. Find her and do whatever she tells you. I'll contact her as soon as I can to check in. We'll figure this out—"

I yank off my sunglasses in defiance. If she won't listen, then I'll have to show her I'm not following her orders anymore.

I'm not going anywhere without her.

The four women gasp out loud at the sight of my eyes, and the one in the white coat asks, "¿Qué tiene?" *What's wrong with her?*

Like I'm diseased.

Ignoring her, Ma says, "Your eyes will always give you away, Solcito." Tears flow freely down her face, and my own eyes burn at the sound of the old nickname.

"If you come back to Argentina, they'll know you're his daughter," she goes on. "Right now, you're safe because they don't know you exist—they're only after me, probably because of the Septis."

"What do you mean?" I ask, frowning. My dad's family is connected to the blue sedatives?

"Perla's friends will take you in until she's out of the hospital." A vein in Ma's forehead pulses as she begs me to go. "Por favor, haceme caso. Do this for me."

I cup her face in my hands and wipe the water away with my thumbs, but more drops keep coming. I think of the black-leafed trees from my dreams that can cry up storms. The pain wringing my insides certainly feels like it could set off a tempest.

"If they catch you, forget me," she whispers, her tone urgent. "Rewrite your story."

Nausea works its way up my throat again, and my fingers tremble on Ma's skin. "Mami, por favor—"

Her red-rimmed eyes suddenly open so wide that someone must be behind me. My hands fall from her face, but before I can spin around, she says, "My bag! The files, my papers—you have to get them!"

"Paper—why are you thinking about that now?" I ask, anger invading my voice.

"Do as I tell you, Manuela." For a moment, she's the Ma from this morning, still strong and in control of our destiny. "Go now!"

"Ma, I *can't*—"

She snaps her gaze from me to Julieta, and the latter seems to understand something I don't. Then Julieta starts shouting at the top of her lungs.

"¡Déjenos ir! ¡BRUTOS! ¡SON UNOS ANIMALES! ¡Déjenos ir ahora mismo!" She goes on insulting the ICE agents and demanding they let them go.

My body reacts before my brain, and my legs move so fast that it seems like one second I'm in the salon, and the next I'm in the clinic. I don't have enough time to think; my limbs simply act on Ma's commands, like they've always done.

I shove my sunglasses back down and dart into the office, spotting Ma's duffel with its contents spilled across the floor. As I rummage through the mess, the bell on the front door jangles. I hear someone enter the salon, and I slow my movements to keep quiet.

"What's going on here?" a man's voice lashes out, and my spine curls in fear for Ma and everyone else.

"You can't do this! We're part of this country and have been for years! No piece of paper can tell us who we are!" Julieta shoots back. "This is our home!"

The baby starts crying again, and I reflexively stand—ready to do I-don't-know-what—when I hear the back door being flung open. I dive under the desk, hoping the agents don't enter this room.

Don't come here, don't come here, don't come here.

I watch with relief as all three sets of shoes run past the doorway, to the front of the salon. "Someone escaped," I hear the woman say, her voice breathless.

"We searched, but they're gone," adds one of the men.

"Who else was here?" demands the man who shouted at Julieta. "Give us names *now!*"

I need to get out of here . . . But I can't ignore Ma's request. *Where the fuck is that paperwork?*

I find the clothing Ma packed for us, the power bars, the water bottles . . . I start stuffing everything I might need back into the duffel, but I don't see the files anywhere. Did ICE already find them?

Panic amplifies my desperation as I realize I should have read through everything before running off. For all I know, there could have been something in there about my dad.

The man is still shouting questions, and I use the cover of his booming voice to pad into the medical area, tossing things around in hopes of spotting the documents. The familiar blue bottles are lying on the floor amid a sea of other medications, and I grab as many as I can, stashing them in my bag—

Heavy footsteps approach.

I'm out of time.

Slinging the duffel's strap across my chest, I head for the alley. Looking back, I glimpse the door to the salon starting to open, and I dart out, shutting the back door as carefully as possible. Then I run, as hard and fast as I can.

I don't know if I've been spotted, so I sprint down the alley at full tilt. At the end of the block, I cut onto the sidewalk, slowing my pace and forcing myself to move casually even though my heart feels close to exploding. When at last I can't take the suspense anymore, I finally look behind me.

They're bringing everyone out of Doña Rosa, and I see Ma's slim frame and dark hair as she's led into the back of the black SUV. Julieta with her pink streak is right behind her, followed by the doctor and two patients. The woman agent carries the baby, and I feel a punch of hatred in my gut.

My hands curl into fists at my sides. Right now I'm capable of anything.

My gaze jumps to Ma again, hoping to catch her eye, but she's already inside. Every inch of me longs to give myself up and join her. Whatever happens next, we should face it together.

I don't care if I'm deported, or if my dad's family finds me, or if the whole world discovers I'm a freak. I just want my ma.

I take a step forward, but before my next foot falls, I meet Julieta's stare. And I know she sees what I'm doing.

She turns suddenly to the ICE agent flanking her and spits on his chest, the highest part of him she can reach.

I freeze, as does everyone else, and for a moment it's like the world is on pause.

Then the man raises his hand and bashes his fist into her face.

I gasp as he pulls back and strikes her again and again and again, until Julieta is limp on the ground, her brown face completely covered in blood. My fingers are gripping my cheeks so hard it hurts but I can't pull them away. Two agents lift Julieta's unconscious body into the SUV, and the other women follow obediently, the mother staring only at her baby in the woman agent's arms.

I'm still paralyzed in place when the blue lights flash past.

I don't know how long I stand there, horrified.

It's not until I spy a flicker of red in the fringe of my vision that I finally drop my hands from my face. I look down for the source of the movement, but all I see is the unzipped duffel. And as I'm sealing it shut, a wisp of red smoke curls free . . .

In the shape of the letter Z.

8

I've been to Hospital de los Santos before.

The morning Perla's sight really started to fail, I brought her here to see an eye doctor because Ma was at work. Perla was far more concerned about me than herself, so she made me wait for her outdoors, in the blindingly sunny day where my sunglasses wouldn't be conspicuous.

Today, I walk inside and go straight to the help desk, where a woman in green scrubs is staring at a computer screen.

"I'm looking for Perla Sanchez." My voice is so steady that it takes me aback, causing me to stumble through the rest of my words. "Sh-she came in a few hours ago. After hitting her head."

I wait for a reaction for so long that I start to wonder whether I actually spoke out loud. Then, without looking up, she asks, "Are you family?"

"I-I'm her granddaughter. I live with her. I don't have anyone else—" My voice breaks, and I close my mouth, not trusting myself to say more.

The woman finally looks up, and she frowns, probably at my sunglasses. I'm sure I look like a too-cool teen to her, keeping my shades on indoors. "She's in recovery on the fourth floor. You'll have to go up to that waiting room and ask one of the nurses if she's stable enough for visitors."

I nod and shuffle away, keeping my head ducked while I search for the elevators. It's not until I see an old man with tinted sunglasses that I realize I might not look as conspicuous as I fear; for all anyone knows, I could have just had an eye operation.

As I join the queue for the elevators, my mind keeps trying to piece together the few facts I know, same as I've been doing the entire bus ride here. It's an unending loop, but it's the only distraction I have from what Ma must be—

I can't go there. I can't afford to let my mind wander.

I have to stick with the cards in my hand: The Argentine woman on El Retiro's rooftop, the man in the leather jacket who could be Nacho, Perla either falling or being attacked, the blue pills that are somehow tied to my dad's people, the red smoke that's here and in my dreams, the letter Z . . . and whatever Ma's been searching for in Argentina.

When I step onto the fourth floor, there's a doctor leading a family of seven through the double doors toward the patient rooms. I trail closely behind them, blending in like I belong. Once I'm through, I veer off, striding slowly past every room until I inhale notes of zesty lemon.

I knock as a warning that I'm coming in, then I step inside.

The room is outfitted for two patients, but the first bed is empty. There's a curtain partitioning the space, and when I peek around it, my breath catches in my throat.

Perla has tubes sticking out from her arms, her head is bandaged in white gauze, and an IV drip like the ones from Ma's clinic is stationed at her side. But she's awake.

"Perla!" Relief floods through me as I take her hand, her paper-thin skin so delicate, I'm afraid of hurting her with my touch.

"Ojazos," she moans, her voice so insubstantial that I feel tears forming in the corners of my eyes. Her fingers curl around mine.

"They took her."

The words tumble out of me. I don't know if I'm speaking English or Spanish, or even what I'm going to say next, because my voice is no longer under my control. I'm just spilling it all out.

"ICE raided the clinic." I assume Perla is in on Ma's lie—after all, she acted like the Septis were her own prescription. "They have Ma. We're alone."

Water wells up in Perla's irises, and her frosted glass gaze seems to be seeing the future instead of me. Then she turns to me with surprising determination.

"Oíme." Her voice is raspy yet somehow infused with strength as she orders me to listen. "De acá te vas a la casa de mi amiga Luisita." She inhales, the air rattling through her. "Ahí me esperás. Ahora mismo la llamo para avisarle."

I know Perla's friend Luisita because they meet for mate every couple of weeks, but she's never seen me without my sunglasses. If I stay at her house like Perla's ordering me to do, she'll eventually see my eyes. Will she still protect me if she's repulsed by me? "Si me ve los ojos se va a asustar y no me va a querer ayudar," I say, voicing my concerns out loud. "Me va a tener asco."

"¿Asco?" repeats Perla, like she's never heard the word before.

"She'll be disgusted," I translate.

"So now *you're* going to teach *me* Spanish?" she demands, both breathless and annoyed. "I know what the damn word means. What I don't know is how it applies to you."

Perla may be too blind to see my eyes well now, but she has to remember what they look like from when her vision was better. "When people see my eyes, they're grossed out—"

"No es así." She frowns in disagreement and stares at me so intently that I feel like she's seeing through me. "For your own good, you need to listen to me, Manuela."

She's only called me by my full name a handful of times, and I remember them all.

"Your mom doesn't hide you because you're shocking or ugly or wrong in any way—like it or not, humans simply aren't drawn to what's unpleasant. You're powerful because you're one of a kind. That's what makes you so beautiful." She takes another rattly breath, and I pick up the plastic cup of water from the table and bring the straw toward her, but she waves me away.

"Like I told your mother millions of times, beauty can be a weapon too. A girl like you can't hide forever."

She's definitely too blind to see me if she thinks I'm beautiful, but since I don't want to burden Perla with more of my problems, I just nod. "I'll go to Luisita's. But first—what happened? Did you fall, or . . . ?" I dangle the question without finishing it because the other possibility still feels too far-fetched to voice.

She shakes her head. "I just remember falling. Now listen to me." After giving me very detailed directions, she adds, "Don't even think of returning to the apartment, ¿me oíste? They could be waiting for you."

My pulse skips. Who does she think will be waiting for me there? ICE or my father's people? I start to ask, "Who—?"

"You need to hurry," she says, cutting me off. I follow her gaze out the window. "Go to Luisita's now, while it's still light out."

She's right—sunset is only an hour away, so I need to get going. Ma never lets me out after dark. A small slip of my sunglasses would put everything at risk, since darkness reveals more than light. The gold and silver of my eyes glow even brighter at night.

"Te quiero, Perla," I say, the first bit of warmth spiking my blood, relief that I haven't lost her.

Her hand squirms in mine, and when I realize what she wants, I let my fingers go limp so she can bring them to her lips. Planting a soft kiss on my skin, she whispers, "I love you too, Ojazos."

Outside, the egg-yolk sky is ripening to blood orange. Once it blazes fiery red, I'll only have moments before the day combusts into the pinks and purples of dusk.

In the dying light, patients, paramedics, and other personnel walk around me, in and out of the hospital. But I'm paused on the sidewalk, waiting for someone to hit play on my life again.

I know I should be moving. The bus stop is only a few strides away. I watch buses roll in and out, passengers get on and off, yet I can't bring myself to bridge the gap.

I've always done everything Ma and Perla have told me to do. I never even questioned their guidance because I knew their decisions were in my best interest. That was as true to me as the Earth being round and spinning on its axis and orbiting the sun.

I don't know who I am outside their rules. I'm not sure I've ever made a decision that's purely my own.

If I could have chosen, I would have stayed with Perla when I found her on the floor of the apartment.

If I could have chosen, I would have stayed with Ma when ICE raided the clinic.

And if I could choose now?

. . . I know what I would do.

I get off the bus a stop early, five blocks from El Retiro. The sky is as crimson as a raw wound.

My heart thudding in my ears, I hurry down the darkening sidewalk without slackening my pace until I see the familiar pink building with its graffiti tattoos. If someone is really scouting El Retiro, I'm going to scout them first.

I inhale strong citrusy notes, and I look up to see an elderly woman with a bulbous forehead sitting on the pink building's stoop while chewing on mandarina rinds. She's a regular fixture out here, always snooping on the neighbors and gossiping with anyone within earshot.

"¿Asere que bola?"

I stare back at her, unsure how to respond. Though I know she spoke Spanish, I have no clue what she said.

Growing up in El Retiro, I've learned that dialects and vocabularies vary enough from country to country that Spanish is a living, breathing language. It's a different melody everywhere it's spoken.

"¿Hablas Español?" The way she drops the s makes me think she's probably Cuban. "Una desgracia como los jóvenes de hoy no conocen el idioma de sus abuelos," she goes on, bemoaning the fact that so many Latinx kids can't communicate with their Spanish-speaking grandparents.

"Yo soy Manu y vengo a darle una sorpresa a mi prima." *I'm Manu, and I've come to surprise my cousin.* She's bound to know Other Manu, and I'm banking on her noticing the similarities in our features.

Her brow arcs when she hears me speak Spanish. "¿Usted es argentina?" she asks, the telltale singsongy accent giving me away. Funny how people rarely ask if I'm Uruguayan.

"Sí," I say, hoping she doesn't harbor a grudge against Argentines. Perla told me all Latin American countries have a stereotype, and Argentines are considered by our neighbors to be *arrogant.*

The purpling evening is rapidly running out of light.

The woman stands from the stoop, her colorful skirt unfolding and freeing a mandarina peel that tumbles to the ground. She climbs down and stops two rungs above me so we're face to face. Frowning, she scrutinizes my features like she's trying to see my eyes. My gut churns as I ready myself for her to ask me to take off my sunglasses—

"¡Micaela de 5B! ¡Pues lucen igualitas!" *Micaela from 5B! You look identical!*

Micaela. Her name even sounds like mine.

"Oye, ¿qué tú sabes de ese noviecito que tiene? ¿Va al colegio? ¿Tiene trabajo?" She's asking for the lowdown on Micaela's boyfriend—*Does he go to school? Does he have a job?*

"Es el heredero de una gran fortuna," I blurt. *He's the heir to a great fortune.* I'm not sure why I feel defensive of him and Micaela. Maybe I'm just trying to protect my fantasy.

The woman's eyes grow round, and without another word, she opens the door for me.

I step into a tacky lobby with pink-and-green carpeted floors and flamingo wallpaper that's peeling away from the walls. I climb up the stairwell, and when I reach the fifth floor, I'm tempted to knock on Micaela's door and finally meet her after all these years.

But for the first time, I have my own life to live.

I keep going until I get to the door labeled ROOFTOP ACCESS. Outside, the horizon is settling into a cool blue, and I pad across the pebbled ground toward the ledge that looks in the direction of El Retiro.

I've never seen my building from this perspective, and it strikes me how much it resembles a concrete jail. *Or a castle tower.*

The comparison reminds me of my last argument with Perla, back when the new presidential administration came into power. Ma was so paranoid about the party's anti-immigrant politics that she didn't let me leave the apartment for a whole month. One day I waited for her to go to work, and the instant I was alone with Perla, I snapped.

"My fucking life is ruled by more protocols than a Jane Austen character!"

It might have been the nerdiest meltdown in history.

I knew better than to curse in front of Ma; Perla, on the other hand, is too old to be rattled by words. "One of these days you should read a book written after the nineteenth century," was all she said to me. "Cuando eras chiquitita, te gustaban los cuentos de hadas."

When you were little, you liked fairy tales.

Ever since I wrote her that story, she'd gotten it into her head that I was an idealistic dreamer at heart but my fears of the world had made me so afraid to dream that I turned to the repressive evils of the Victorian genre. It's an absolutely ridiculous theory—but then, Perla thinks yawning too much is a sign you've been hexed by mal de ojo. *The evil eye.*

"You want the fairy tale version instead?" I shouted at her. "Fine! I'm a cursed princess, this stupid building is the castle tower imprisoning me, and Ma is the fire-breathing dragon keeping me locked up. Oh, and the charming prince I'm waiting on? He's an inanimate green card!"

"Muy bien," she said approvingly, like we were having an exemplar lesson, "pero te olvidaste la mejor parte del cuento de hadas." I stared at her blankly, wondering what was the best part of a fairy tale that I'd apparently left out.

"The ending, Manuela. Princesses who don't give up get to live happily ever after."

After that, I stopped looking at the bars of my cage and started looking between them. If my life sucks, that just means it hasn't peaked yet. I'm in the middle of my story. And every tomorrow could be my happily ever after.

It takes me a moment to realize I've been staring at Leather Jacket for a long minute. He's not standing by the pink building anymore—he's outside mine.

I keep my eyes on him for what feels like an hour. Two. My stomach grumbles with gnawing hunger, but I stay on watch.

The guy doesn't budge, and his stillness is almost unnatural. *I need to know why he's here.*

I race back down the stairwell, and when I leave the building, the elderly woman is still keeping watch from her same spot. "¿Le dijo a su prima que fui yo la que le abrió?" *Did you tell your cousin I was the one who let you in?*

I cross the street, my sight fixed on the back of Leather Jacket's head, careful to keep out of view. From down here, I realize he's not just atypically tall, but he's also broader than anyone I've ever seen and could probably crush me without much effort.

My heart beats harder as I step onto my block, only instead of walking toward El Retiro, I take cover behind the corner building. Pressed against the wall, I cast my gaze for anyone who might be with him, but after a while I have to admit he seems to be alone.

I exhale in exhaustion. I'm weak from thirst and hunger and everything I lost today, and I really need to change my tampon—but I can't leave this spot. There's got to be a clue to what this guy's about . . .

My gaze travels down his leather jacket to his dark jeans, and I again glimpse his flashy silver belt buckle. Only it looks like there's a logo emblazoned on it.

I squint until the design grows clearer.

It's a Z.

"They're only after me, probably because of the Septis."

My father's family must produce the Septis. Somehow, Ma managed to get ahold of them—*for me*—and that must have tipped them off to her whereabouts. Maybe Ma was trying to track down the city in Argentina where they're headquartered—

Leather Jacket finally moves.

I snap into action, trailing him down the block. By now the night is inky black, and my sunglasses look bizarrely out of place, but the only other person out here is a homeless woman sleeping a few feet away.

Leather Jacket unlocks a gray pickup truck and climbs into the driver's seat. *Now what?*

I hover by the back tire as the engine roars awake, blasting my eardrums.

I should turn around and head to Luisita's. Perla's definitely called her by now, and they're probably out of their minds with worry that I haven't shown up. If I don't go, I'll lose my only connection to Ma, and she'll have no way of contacting me.

Once I talk to Ma, I can help her piece all the clues together. She was right—my father's people found us. They must have attacked Perla. And maybe they're the ones who called ICE.

The truck's tires start to roll forward, and I'm out of time.

Adrenaline courses through me, muffling my thoughts, and before I can consider what I'm doing, I grab hold of the vehicle. My other hand clamps around the duffel by my waist, and I pull myself into the open truck bed.

I don't know if I'm more shocked by my daring or how lightly I land. I guess when your only friend is a cat, you learn a few tricks.

I drop down and cover myself with my duffel, holding my breath while I try to decide if the driver noticed me by determining if he's slowing down. But we just rumble on down the street without interruption, and after a few tense minutes of expecting the worst, I ease my grip on my bag.

Staring up at the dark and starless sky, it feels fitting that the world is void of light tonight. With nowhere to go, and my pulse still blaring in my ears, my mind beelines to the thoughts I've been blocking off for hours . . . Only now I don't have the strength to resist.

Mami.

I curl into myself as the tears cascade down, a sharp pain piercing my chest as I sob. Until I'm choking on my cries, until my skin screams for Ma, until I have nothing left inside. Is she in jail or at a detention center? Is she alone, or is Julieta with her? How soon before she lands in Argentina and my father's family catches up with her?

What if they do to her what they did to him?

My body starts trembling so much that it's beyond my control. The shaking extends from my teeth to my toes, until I'm freezing in the ninety-degree air. If I don't stop thinking of Ma, I'll die.

The truck winds through unknown Miami streets, and I stare up at the blanket of blackness above, awaiting my fate. As usual, it's in someone else's hands.

I'm a passenger not just in this vehicle, but in my body, in this country, in my life. Defined by decisions I didn't make.

My undocumented status.

My father's family.

My eyes.

It's a long time before my body stills. And in that stillness, a new kind of terror grips my mind as I process the monumentally dangerous decision I made jumping in here. If this man hurt Perla, how exactly am I going to survive when he catches me?

My pounding pulse pumps fear through my organs, and as it spreads, the only small source of strength comes from knowing that whatever happens next, jumping into this pickup was *my* choice.

Wherever it leads, for the first time, I'm in charge of my own destiny . . . Even if this is the first and last decision I ever make.

We've been driving for so long that I'm surprised we haven't fallen into the ocean yet. I stopped seeing buildings and traffic lights a while ago, and now there's only treetops.

I slide the duffel off my torso and lift myself up on my elbows, craning my neck to survey my surroundings. We're driving down a narrow paved road, cutting past so much foliage that we've left civilization far behind.

The greenery grows thicker and more encompassing the farther we go, and I've no idea where we could possibly be.

YOU ARE LEAVING THE EVERGLADES. I blink at the sign on the opposite side of the road. If the other direction is away from the Everglades, that means . . .

Why is he driving into the Everglades?

The truck takes a sharp right, and I almost fall as we pull off the asphalt onto an uneven dirt path that slices through the tangle of mangroves. I have to grip the side of the pickup to keep from being tossed around, and my gut is as knotted up as the lattice of limbs enclosing us.

The canopy of leaves overhead filters out any inkling of light, and at last I pull off my sunglasses and stuff them in my bag. The glow of my irises illuminates the view a little, enough to let me make out a few details.

We're sailing past trees so intricately interwoven that it seems impossible we're not crashing into them. As I gawk at the mangroves, searching for some semblance of a destination, I register a symbol carved into some of the trunks. It looks like someone's initials. Or grave markers.

I squint to try making out the letters—or *letter.*

Understanding zaps through me like lightning.

Either El Zorro has been fighting crime in the Everglades, or my dad's people are hiding out here.

A far more terrifying thought crosses my mind: Does the truck driver know I'm in here? He seemed determined enough to wait all night outside El Retiro, but he gave up his post prematurely. Could it be because he spotted me? What if he was counting on me jumping into his truck all along?

Heart hammering my chest, I keep my body low as I twist toward the truck's cab to see if Leather Jacket is watching me in the rearview. But the back window is tinted, and I can't see anything.

Cold sweat trickles down my back. I've seen enough mafia movies to know there's only one reason to bring someone to the middle of nowhere. *I can't be inside this pickup when it stops.*

I'm on all fours in the truck's bed as we weave down a path that seems specially measured for this vehicle. All I see around me is the letter Z, flashing past like a persistent warning of my doom.

Something tingles through my body, like I've just walked through water. My skin pebbles, and my hair stands on end, as if we've crossed some type of invisible barrier.

Even though we're going deeper into the Everglades, the ride begins to smooth out, the ground growing firmer. I start to sense the truck slowing down, and my muscles tense—*I have to get off now.*

I sling the duffel's strap across my chest again, and I crouch down lower, knees bent, arms at my sides. When I see the next low-hanging tree limb, I jump.

The skin of my fingers rips as I cinch my hands around the tree and pull my body up with all my might, curling my legs around the branch. Leaves scratch my face as I bury it into the mangrove's arm, my bag dangling under me.

I can't hold on for very long, so when I don't immediately hear the pickup's brakes screech, I uncross my legs and drop to the ground. Until today, I didn't think I had a jot of athleticism in me—but apparently all I needed was enough space to stretch.

My heavy breathing is all I hear, the exertion exhausting all my muscles at once. I'm so drained, I can't even move.

As the engine's rumble fades into the distance, other sounds begin to replace it. The sharp, high-pitched buzzing of insects, the hooting of owls, the scurrying of small creatures, the low drone of frogs, the chirping of crickets, the whistling of birds . . . The longer I stand and listen, the louder the swamp's soundtrack becomes, until it's almost overwhelming.

We drove for so long that I don't know how I'm going to get back home. And where is home anyway? El Retiro? The hospital? Luisita's? I can't go back to just waiting around for Ma and Perla's next instruction. And I've already come this far . . .

I tread along the dirt path in the direction the truck was headed, careful to stick to the tree's shadows in case another car drives up. The air here isn't hot and muggy like I expected, but cool and misty. I thought this place would be *marshier*. Swampy. Squelchy.

My arms itch from the suggestion of mosquitos, yet I don't actually feel any bites. At home, Ma and Perla are constantly on me for opening windows since they always awaken to itchy red bumps, but I never get bit. Here, though, I hear their buzzing everywhere, so my luck is bound to run out.

I don't see any more Z symbols etched onto the mangrove trunks, and as the soundtrack of the Everglades grows louder, so do my doubts in this plan. What do I say when I come face-to-face with my father's murderers? And how exactly am I going to hold my own against Leather Jacket—?

"That's it for the tour!"

A loud voice zings through the air, and I dive into the trees' tentacles, nearly falling headfirst into the brush.

"You must be beat from today, so let's get you some dinner before bed." A few people clap in agreement.

"Es hora de comer," translates another voice, and this time cheers break out from what sounds like a dozen people. "Recuerden que es la última vez que les vamos a hablar en español," she goes on, her accent Argentine. "Mientras estén en el Laberinto, tienen que hablar inglés."

Remember this is the last time we'll speak to you in Spanish— while you're in the Labyrinth, you must speak English.

I wonder if El Laberinto is what the Everglades is called in Spanish.

The voices sound like they're coming from up ahead, so I tread through the trees as quietly as I can, picking my way through the raised roots and bristly branches. When at last I glimpse shadows on the dirt path, I slow down.

It seems brighter where these people are, like the area is being illuminated by something.

Looking up, I see golden stars winking through the treetops, and I'm so distracted by their light that I don't immediately realize I've reached the edge of the woods. I look down just in time to see the mangroves fall away, revealing a clearing filled with shooting stars.

No, not stars—

Insects.

They look like dancing bubbles of light. Their frenzied flying draws golden designs in the black air, uncloaking the landscape ahead.

I must have left reality and stepped into a dream. The world beyond looks like an ancient city that got swallowed up by this swamp.

Giant stone structures rise from the soil, as deeply rooted to the land as the foliage ensnaring them, making it impossible to know where nature ends and man begins. I stick to the treeline as the group I overheard disappears around the corner of a building with the largest tree I've ever seen grow-ing inside. Its giant branches burst through the sky-high roof, reaching into the stars.

Across the way sits a smaller off-white palace, with a crum-bling corner that leaves its top story partially exposed. A swarm of green vines reaches inside, twining through the place like an invading army. Farther down, I glimpse a mansion half-buried in a mound of dirt, with flowers of every color growing along its walls.

The way these structures seem as married to the marsh as the timeless trees makes me think of the Citadel from my lunaritis dreams.

There's an ancient world buried deep within the Everglades. How is this possible? Where am I?

I hear a rustling in the foliage, and I duck down as a man steps forth from the woods into the clearing. From this van-tage point, all I can see is his profile. He looks middle-aged.

A breeze stirs through the swamp, bumping my back like a friendly nudge forward. The wind carries wisps of a tantaliz-ing scent, and as I breathe it in, it stirs something lodged deep within me, painful like nostalgia but also exciting, a bouquet of possibilities—

The man twists around like he smells it too.

When I see his face, my heart feels like it's being squeezed. Then it cracks open like a walnut, and all the hopes I've been stockpiling spill out.

The answer I've been seeking my whole life just magically appeared before me. Now I know I must be dreaming.

Long after the man turns away, all I can do is stare at his receding figure, unable to process what can't be real.

His eyes . . .

They're just like mine.

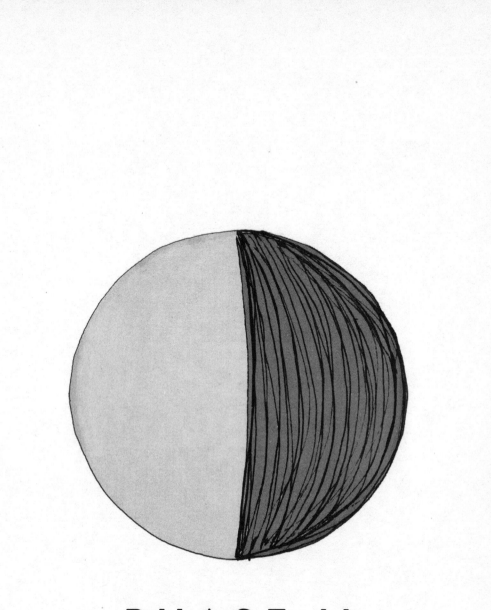

PHASE II

10

Dad?

This is definitely a dream. Or a delusion.

My heart revs like a car engine whose driver just gunned the accelerator, and before I can think it through, I'm chasing after him.

The light bugs fly frantically overhead, charting the frenzied patterns of my heartbeats. I feel exposed the instant I leave the trees' protection, but I can't slow down because the man has already disappeared in the same direction as the tour group.

I can't lose him.

I curve around the structure with the tree trapped inside, and a new aroma rushes up my nose that's mouthwatering and familiar. Ahead sprawls an overgrown garden where a few dozen people are standing around holding plates, eating, and socializing. On instinct, I pull on my sunglasses.

I stick to the garden's outskirts as I approach, taking cover behind the pale petals of a flowering dogwood. Peeking through its ghostly blooms, I spy seven massive stones aligned in a crescent formation. A different cut of meat is being grilled on each surface, and the food's smoky smell is strangely comforting. On the stone closest to me, I see chorizo, beside it are mollejas—my favorite—and I'm pretty sure the others are entraña, vacío, bife de chorizo, tira de asado, morcilla . . . It's an Argentine parrillada.

We have these in El Retiro's outdoor courtyard for celebrations like birthdays and retirements. It's usually Jorge of 4C doing the grilling.

But here, there's no charcoal or open flame. The seven stones themselves are lit up like embers, and the heat seems to be originating within the rock, encasing each one in an orange glow. As the meat sears, it pumps red smoke into the air—

The same red smoke I've been seeing all day.

I'm barely breathing as I scan the crowd for the man who might be my father, and as I study the people here for the first time, I shudder.

My temperature dips, as if I just lost power for a beat or two.

Not Dad.

Not alone.

I draw in oxygen slowly, like Perla taught me, until I've paved a path through the pain and panic.

My whole life, I thought my dad saw the world through the same sunny lens as me. But now I get what Ma meant when she said I have his eyes.

Every person here has star-shaped pupils and glow-in-the-dark irises.

In every color.

A tsunami of relief slams through my veins, shaking my world. *There are others like me.* I can hardly believe it. And yet, I also feel a small twinge of loss.

My father's eyes are the only part of him I've ever been able to picture. The one feature I thought we shared. And now I don't know if they were yellow like mine.

I breathe through my wave of emotions and try to get a grip on what's going on. There are about a dozen teens and a dozen adults here. The guys are all congregated around the men, while the girls surround the women. The scene looks like one of those gender-segregated middle school parties from teen movies—only these people are too old to act this way.

I shut my eyes and cast out with my mind to try eavesdropping on individual conversations. The current of the crowd is pretty strong, and whenever I start listening to someone, another person's voice grows louder and takes over.

I've always wanted to attend this academy—

Of course I read your studies on the evolution of our reproduction! I would love to help with your research—

My mom always says her years here were the best of her life—

Your soil is ideal for growing yappas! I've been exploring their effects—

You guys have the best Septibol team in the junior league—

I open my eyes, feeling a little lightheaded and a lot clueless. This is a *school*?

I flash to the opening chapters of *Harry Potter*, when Mr. Dursley kept the owls from delivering Harry's admission letter to Hogwarts. And for one fleeting instant, I let myself believe there's a world that actually wants me.

But the hope deflates as quickly as it came. For all Ma's secrets, she's nothing like the Dursleys. Everything she's sacrificed has been to protect my potential, not stifle it. If she's never wanted these people to find me, there *has* to be a reason. After all, I doubt Leather Jacket was simply trying to deliver my acceptance letter.

As I picture his heavy clothes and flashy belt buckle, he materializes before me. I blink, and then I realize he's here, talking to someone in a corner of the garden. A woman everyone has been sneaking glances at but few dare approach. All I can make out from here is she's tall with long hair and wearing a formfitting purple dress.

At the sight of the pickup driver, all semblance of rational thought leaves my mind, and I back away as swiftly as I can, retracing my steps to the clearing. I have no idea if he was just after Ma, or if he knows about me too, but I can't take any risks.

I'm going straight to Luisita's and waiting for Ma to call.

Now that I've seen all this, she owes me the rest of our story. *My* story.

Back in the safety of the mangroves, I pick my way through the raised tree roots back toward civilization, keeping an eye on the dirt road to make sure I don't get lost. Even though the tight-packed tree limbs scratch at my arms, and the underbrush prickles my legs, I don't dare step onto the path, where I would be visible.

Thunder rumbles ominously, making the woods quiver, and I quicken my pace, tunneling deeper into the mangroves in case of a downpour.

Now that my fear has mostly burned off, I start to question the logic in my decision to run away so quickly. Setting aside my curiosity, I also have no idea how to get to Luisita's from here. It took hours to get to the Everglades by car, so I'm going to be walking all night. And when I finally hit a real street, I'll have no idea which direction to go.

The scent from earlier tickles my nose, and I inhale deeply. The earthy musk reminds me of a cedarwood and thyme candle Ma brought home once, only this one is spiced with something wild and headrush-y. Like peppermint or eucalyptus or nostalgia.

When I scan the greenery for the rare bloom, I realize I've strayed pretty far from the path. Lightning illuminates the horizon, and I see the mangroves have grown more spaced out. There's a pile of boulders ahead, where the ground tilts uphill, then darkness falls with a thunderous clap before I can locate the road.

"You lost?"

I stop moving.

Most vexing of all is how stealthy the stranger had to be for me not to hear him in this underbrush.

"Get separated from the group?"

His low, velvety voice is so melodic that goose bumps rise up my arms. He sounds like he's made of music.

I keep my back to him while I try to figure out what to do. Smack him with my duffel and make a run for it? It's not heavy enough to slow him down. There's no point in trying to outrun him either because even if I'm faster, he'll just go back and tell the others. I'm hours away from civilization—I'll never make it.

"Paranoid much?"

I can almost hear the smirk sewn into the folds of his voice. "Didn't trust us to deliver your things to your room?"

He must assume I'm part of that tour group I overheard. I should just lie and get this over with. The sooner I get rid of this person, the sooner I can go.

I spin around to face him, but when my mouth opens, no words come out.

The guy laughs, an unexpected bark of a sound. "Definitely paranoid. Why are you wearing sunglasses at *night*?"

When I still don't speak, he frowns and says, "Let's get you back to the group, okay?" His tone has softened. "I can carry that for you if you'd like."

He reaches out with his hand, and I take a step back.

"Or not . . . It's okay. I won't bite." He flashes that breathtaking smirk, like we're in on the same joke, only my mouth is still hanging open.

The ocean is in his eyes.

It's my first cohesive thought.

His eyes have the same genetic mutation as mine, only his are remarkable. They're dazzling sapphires.

"It's really not safe to be out here alone at night so soon after the full moon. Let me take you indoors—"

"No!"

My shout startles us both, and his dark eyebrows knit together questioningly.

I swallow, my mouth dry after hanging open for so long, and I pull in my lower lip to wet it. His gaze drops to my mouth, and heat inexplicably surges through me. "I was just . . . lost," I say, staring down at my beat-up sneakers. "Like you said."

I don't dare look up until I feel the flush fade from my cheeks.

"Well, I'm happy to be of service." Relief floods my veins when I hear the friendliness in his voice. "I'm Tiago. Short for Santiago."

I lift my chin. "I'm . . . Manu." I meant to lie and say Micaela, but the truth falls out when I look at him. "Short for Manuela."

"Nice to meet you, Manu. What's with the shades?"

"Um, something irritated my eye." I go with the first excuse that comes to mind. "A mosquito, I think."

"A mosquito?" he repeats, and I just barely detect a note of suspicion altering the melody of his voice. I thought the excuse sounded plausible enough under the circumstances, but now I wish I'd come up with a better lie. My brain rummages for something else to say, but I can't make out any individual thought.

"You should probably lose those now."

Tiago's tone takes me aback. It almost sounds like a command. "You can't come any farther unless you show your eyes."

Since it doesn't seem like I have much of a choice, I slide off my mirrored shades. Then I inhale deeply before lifting my gaze.

I don't miss the way Tiago's orbs widen with surprise, and immediately I wonder if I've made a huge mistake. My hand twitches, and I'm about to shove the glasses back on—

"You're not alone."

My breathing stalls as a warm intimacy invades his voice, and I feel like he sees me—*really* sees me. "W-what do you mean?" I ask, my heart beating faster.

"It's hard on all of us, leaving home." I pick up on a slight accent in his low-pitched voice that wasn't there before. It's so subtle that it only shows up now, when he sounds less guarded.

My eyes must still be rimmed red from crying the whole ride here, and Tiago thinks I was wearing my glasses to hide my tears.

A gust of cold air blows on my back, and it strikes me how disconnected the Everglades feels from the rest of South Florida. Here, the climate feels cooler and windier and . . . *louder.*

A whirring sound that makes me think of a helicopter flying

too close to the ground comes into focus. Tiago hears it too, because he tilts his head, and we both squint searchingly into the trees. Until now, it was a distant background buzz, but it's growing louder at an alarmingly exponential rate—

"Run!"

Tiago's shout barely registers over my scream.

A funnel of twisting air is tearing toward us through the mangroves, ringed in a cloud of debris, ripping off branches like they're blades of grass.

My body leaps into action before my mind can process— just like when I jumped into the pickup truck—and I run. The spinning air tugs at my muscles, like a whirlpool trying to suck me into its jaws, and I push my legs to work harder.

As we race through the marsh, Tiago keeps stealing glances at me, seeming almost surprised that I'm keeping up. Like he expected the storm to get me by now.

The harder I run, the less afraid and more exhilarated I feel. It's like I'm shedding layers as I go, leaving my old skins behind.

The whipping wind blasts in my ears, gaining more and more ground on us. Until it's so close, I can hear past the snapping of tree limbs to the howling heart of the storm.

Rocks and twigs spray my legs and arms, and I stub my toe against an upraised root. My duffel breaks my fall. The wind is like a giant vacuum, and my clothes cling to me, my hair flapping like a flag. I try getting to my feet, but the gales are solid walls, keeping me from standing upright.

There's a crack somewhere above me. A branch breaks off and spirals at my head, and I shut my eyes right as it's going to impale me—

But then I'm lifted off the ground, pulled into the storm's orbit. I'm soaring at superhuman speed through the air, the wind pressing into my face like a hard wall—

Too hard.

And pulsing, like a drumbeat.

I open my eyes. Tiago's arms are cinched around me, my duffel pressed between us, my head nestled into his shirt.

The winds die down as suddenly as they began, and eventually the only gusts in the air are our heavy breaths. I know the Miami weather is eccentric, but this is beyond anything I've ever experienced.

I'm hit with a headrush of cedarwood and thyme, and I lift my head off Tiago's chest to scan the foliage around me, searching for the source of that mysterious scent.

"Always wondered if I could outrun one of those."

When I look up at him, I'm dazed to survey his sculpted features from this close. Then I scowl because I can't believe what I'm seeing.

He's grinning from ear to ear.

"Exciting first day, huh?" he asks, raising his eyebrows.

"Are you serious?" I push against him to free myself, and he obligingly sets me down. My knees wobble like they're still too unsteady to hold my weight, and his arms linger at my sides.

"I'm sorry," he says, his smile wilting. "I wouldn't have picked you up without asking, but there wasn't time. And I figured since girls can't run as fast as guys—"

"What the hell does my gender have to do with anything?" I shout.

He looks startled by my anger, and he holds up both hands as if in surrender. I never imagined myself as a confrontational person, and I don't know where this reaction is coming from. I guess there's some Elizabeth Bennett in me after all.

"Let me walk you back to the group," he says in a conciliatory tone, and I nod because I don't trust myself to speak again. I wish I'd had a chance to roll on deodorant today. Pretty sure I smell like one of those green city dumpsters.

Tiago gestures to my duffel and flashes me a small smile that does nothing to slow my pulse. "Last chance to let me carry that for you?"

"Since apparently guys don't listen as well as girls, I'll say it again—*no, thanks.*"

His eyes grow comically round, and I feel a strange satisfaction at causing the expression.

"You know, I think I'm going to stroll for a bit longer," I go on, seizing my advantage. "I'll see you around—"

"And take on the next storm by yourself?" He shakes his head. "Let's go, Shades. It's nearly curfew anyway."

Even if I try to run, he's already proven he has no trouble keeping up.

I'm out of options.

So I fall in step beside him and walk into the jaws of the monster that destroyed my family.

When we get to the clearing, I don't hear voices or smell meat grilling. Everyone seems to have disbanded.

My heart is still thumping too loud, and I watch the golden bugs buzz in their zigzag patterns. "They're called doraditos," says Tiago, catching me staring. "But I'm sure they already covered that in the orientation tour."

"I, um, wasn't paying much attention."

"It's a lot to take in," he says, running a hand through his tousled dark hair. I watch the bulge in his arm grow bigger as his elbow bends, and it dawns on me how recklessly brave he was, coming back to rescue me. He could have run off and saved himself.

"When I moved here five years ago, it took me a whole moon to get the hang of this place," he says.

A whole moon? Who talks like that?

Tiago leads us to the colossal structure with the tree growing inside. The stone walls are bruised and cratered, and in the moonlight they look more otherworldly than ancient. He pulls open the heavy door, and I hesitate.

Am I really going to enter this place that could be connected to my dad's murder and the attack on Perla? What would Ma say if she knew I was here? After all she's sacrificed to protect me from these people, am I ready to willingly walk into their custody?

Something cold and wet brushes my ankle, and I jump back.

"Just a snake," says Tiago with a shrug. "If you're determined to sleep out here, I'd watch out for the gators."

I dart through the open doorway, and I hear a soft chuckle that I choose to ignore.

We cross into a round marble chamber that's so vast and towering, I can't hold back my gasp. A thick staircase outlines the space, married to the cracked walls, spiraling all the way up. The balconies of at least a dozen stories ring the chamber, all rimmed with crumbling columns. And in the center of the hall, breaking through the marble, is an enormous tree that's about the size of El Retiro.

Its branches reach across the various levels of the place, needling through the gaps between banisters. The tree's crown is so high, it pierces the night sky.

Glowing white blossoms bloom from the bark, giving off a soft light that's the only illumination in the place. There are petals strewn across the floor, and every few seconds another one floats down, like a feather. On impulse, I pick one up.

Its silky texture feels watery and light, and when I bring it to my nose, I inhale a whole forest. The scent is so overwhelming that I pull away quickly, feeling a little lightheaded. It's like there's a whole world inside that one petal.

"They're called blancanieves," says Tiago, his voice a whisper, like we're inside a sacred place. *Snow whites.*

When I look up at him, I almost gasp. Outside, the doraditos gave off more light than I realized; in this dimmer setting, the blue of Tiago's irises glimmers like crystallized water. Panes of sapphire flicker and flare in the flowers' white glow, an ocean of frozen starlight, and I'm so absorbed in his eyes that it's only now I register he's staring just as intently into mine.

"I've never seen anyone with your eye color," he murmurs suddenly, and the old knot in my gut is back, whispering, *I'm a freak, I'm a freak, I'm a freak.*

"It's like staring into the sun."

Solcito. Ma's old nickname is a punch to my gut, and to keep my shit together, I change the subject. "What is this place?"

"El jardín." *The garden.* "I like to think it's short for 'El jardín de senderos que se bifurcan.'" *The Garden of Forking Paths.*

"Borges," I say, recognizing the short story. He's one of my favorite authors.

Tiago's face goes slack with shock. It's a strange reaction, considering Jorge Luis Borges is one of the most famous Argentine authors in history. Did he think I was illiterate?

"I thought I was the only one who . . ." His slight accent resurfaces, and he clears his throat. "Friendly advice, I wouldn't publicize that you're familiar with their authors. Maybe your *manada* is more open-minded, but it's still against the law to read their works."

I have no idea what any of that means.

Manada? I think that's the Spanish word for pack. *Their works?* What and who is he talking about? It's like hearing an unfamiliar Spanish dialect, only it's not simply Tiago's words that are lost in translation but his entire world.

"You don't speak English with an accent," he says, like it just occurred to him. "Which manada are you from?"

Before I can scramble for an answer to a question I don't understand, a sharp voice rings out.

"What is the meaning of this?"

Tiago and I jump at the sight of a woman with light hair and glowing amethyst eyes. My heartrate doubles when I recognize her as the person Leather Jacket was talking to in the garden.

Tiago straightens like a soldier before his sergeant. "Señora Jazmín, I was just escorting a transfer who got separated from the group. This is Manu."

The woman walks closer, her gait so fluid, she could be floating. Her features are chiseled and blade-sharp, and there's nothing of the Argentine warmth Ma described to me. Standing eye-to-eye with me, her gaze scrutinizes every detail, like an art collector assessing a new piece.

"Thank you, Tiago. I can take *Manu* from here."

He nods, and without so much as a glance back, he sets off toward the spiral staircase. I feel a stab of panic the instant he's gone.

"Manu *what?*" asks Señora Jazmín.

"M-Márquez." I give the first name that comes to mind, so she won't associate me with my dad and his crimes.

Jazmín frowns, and I know I said the wrong thing. She studies me a little longer, her brow set in a skeptical knot. "I don't recall any student transfers registered by that name."

"It was a last-minute change. I just—I really needed to get away from my *manada*." I hope I used that word right and resist the impulse to cringe.

Her forehead remains furrowed with suspicion, and my fingers fidget nervously with the zipper of my duffel. Hoping Spanish will score me extra points, I say, "Por favor, necesito alejarme de mi familia por un tiempo." *Please, I need to get away from my family for a while.*

She still looks unmoved, and I tug too hard on the zipper, sending blue bottles spilling onto the marble floor. I scramble to pick them up before they roll too far, and I stuff them back into my bag, my stomach in a knot. *Shit shit shit shit*—

"The Cazadores checked your Huella at the border?" she asks.

I nod without thinking, unsure what she's referring to since *huella* means footprint.

She looks me up and down, and I feel self-conscious in my shorts and T-shirt, especially compared to her elegant purple dress. Then again, Tiago was wearing the same outfit as me, and she didn't seem to mind.

"This way."

She practically glides away from me, and I follow her up the stairs. I keep a few steps between us as we spiral up so that we can't settle into conversation.

A prickle of unease snakes up my spine as we keep climbing, until at last we stride down a hall bathed in a soft white glow. The ceiling is draped with strings of blancanieves braided together, like holiday lights. We pass a series of doors until we reach the last room.

Jazmín opens it without knocking.

Inside is a meticulously appointed bedroom that looks like a princess's boudoir. It's roughly the size of Perla's entire apartment, and everything is a shade of white or cream, with accents of gold embroidered into the throw rugs and billowy curtains and canopied bedding.

Two teen girls in shorts and oversized shirts are sitting on the massive four-poster, laughing conspiratorially. Their voices cut out at our intrusion.

"Ma, don't you knock?" says the girl with longer hair who looks like a younger version of Señora Jazmín. They have the same light skin, willowy figures, and golden-brown hair.

"I don't have to knock. I'm the head of this academy."

Her daughter rolls her pink eyes. "Now there's a job perk. Don't let the power go to your head."

"Privileges can be taken away, Catalina."

There's an iciness in Jazmín's tone that silences her daughter. Whatever privileges she enjoys, it's clear she wants to hold on to them.

"There was an extra transfer this moon who wasn't accounted for," Jazmín goes on after a measure of silence. "As there are no other available rooms, she's going to stay with you."

The girl looks as horrified as I feel. "*Me?* It's supposed to be up to four to a room—let her bunk in one of the three-girl rooms!"

"Why would I do that when there's plenty of space in here? You have this entire bedroom to yourself—unless you count Saysa, who always seems to be in here. Buenas noches, Saysa."

The other girl smiles at Jazmín, and adorable twin dimples mark her brown cheeks. She looks familiar to me somehow, but I'm not sure where I've seen her before.

"Good night, Señora Jazmín." When the girl passes me, she only comes up to my chest. "What's your name?"

"Manu."

"Welcome to El Laberinto," she says, her lime-green eyes bright. "I'm Saysa, and that's Cata."

"Catalina," corrects my haughty new roommate.

"She prefers *Cata*," Saysa assures me as she slips out the door.

Cata or Catalina opens her mouth to keep arguing, but Jazmín casts her a dark glare that cowers her daughter into closing it. She only finds her voice once her mom leaves and we're alone.

"You're lucky there's a second bed, or you'd be sleeping on the floor."

I look around, and the closest thing I see is a small cot against the bay window, adorned with a handful of delicately sewn dolls. At the sight of a place to rest, something in me unhooks. After the worst day of my life, the adrenaline-glued seams that had been holding me together are giving out.

I walk gratefully to the mattress, and Catalina's cold voice warns, "Careful with my collection."

I don't have it in me to call up my inner Elizabeth Bennet again. Besides, it's obvious to me—if not to Catalina—that her mother placed me here so her daughter could keep an eye on me. I'll have a better chance at winning her trust with kindness.

I gently move one doll at a time onto the windowsill, freeing up the cot for myself. There are seven in total, and each one has a different word stitched onto its sweater, but my vision is too bleary from exhaustion to bother reading them.

The lights suddenly shut off, even though Catalina hasn't left her bed or spoken any command. She doesn't say another word as she settles into her sheets, and I climb into the cot fully clothed.

I watch the small pink glow of her eyes until it fades to darkness. I'm drained beyond my breaking point, but I couldn't sleep if I tried. Not after the past twelve hours.

Even though this cot is a joke compared to Catalina's regal bed, it's the most comfortable place I've ever rested in. The sheets are foamy soft, and before I can stop myself, I'm wondering if Ma ever touched fabrics like these, or slept in a bed this nice, or spent time in a place this luxurious. Where is she sleeping now? A hard slab of concrete? A flea-infested mattress?

I force myself out of bed to break my thought spiral, and at last I use the bathroom.

It's as pristine as the bedroom and infused with a lavender scent that seems to be coming from a large body-lotion dispenser. I quietly root through the drawers and cabinets until I find period stuff beneath the sink. While I'm washing my hands, I catch my reflection in the mirror and cringe. My hair is greasy and matted, my eyes are glassy and bloodshot, and I'm wearing the revolted expression of one who's just realized the moldy odor she keeps smelling is coming from herself.

The glass-paneled shower is just a few paces away, but I'm afraid of waking up Catalina. Still, I can't go to bed like this, so I strip off my clothes and step inside. I turn the faucet toward *hot* and let the water scorch my skin. I hope the shower masks the sounds of my bawling.

When I'm done, I pull on a towel, and I spot the Z embroidered in gold. I bring it up to my nose and examine the letter closely . . .

It's not necessarily a Z. There's a gap separating the top and bottom halves of the letter. It could just be a fancy design touch, or it could mean something else.

Actually, it could be a pair of numbers.

Two *sevens*.

I dart back out to the bedroom and inspect the dolls.

The first one I pick up says *Septimus*. The second says *Septibol*. No idea what the words mean, but they're clearly derivations of *Septis*, the name of the blue pills.

The third doll says *Cazadores*. I heard that word earlier today, on the rooftop of El Retiro, and just a moment ago when Jazmín asked if the Cazadores checked my Huella. It means hunters.

I reach for the next one.

Lunaris.

I bite back my gasp. Is that a misspelling? Is it supposed to be lunaritis?

Gut clenched, I pick up the next two.

Bruja. Witch.

Lobizón. Werewolf.

I swallow, my throat parched, as I read the seventh and final doll.

Kerana.

My lungs seize up as the memory comes rushing back to me. I know that word: It's the name of the secret city from Perla's story, the land where magical creatures go to claim their powers.

Los lobizones le cantan a la luna llena,
las brujas bailan cuando el cielo truena.
Si te cruzas con uno, no dejes que te inquiete:
El secreto está en sus ojos y el número siete.

Perla's old poem plays in my head, the last line on a loop: *The secret is in their eyes and the number seven.*

I feel a shiver go through me as I stare at the creepy dolls, and I think of the superstition about seventh children. I know it's impossible, and still I wonder—

Could it be real?

12

I reach into my duffel, and I tear open the plastic bags of fresh shirts and underwear, pulling out one of each. I'm too unnerved to stay here another second. Once I'm dressed, I grab my bag and run for the door—but when I twist the handle, it won't budge.

I push with all my might, summoning every last vestige of strength in my muscles, but it's completely stuck. I consider going out the window, but I'm too high off the ground to survive the jump. I'm sealed inside with this—this—*witch*.

As soon as I think the word, I'm overcome with the urge to laugh.

I'm being ridiculous. If Catalina, Jazmín, and Saysa are witches, then Tiago is a *werewolf*.

This time I do laugh.

I'd sooner believe I'm institutionalized in an asylum and

experiencing a very vivid hallucination. Or that I'm still lunaritis-dreaming and haven't woken up yet.

I perch on the edge of the cot, hugging my duffel to my chest, casting glances at Catalina on her larger-than-life four-poster bed. This is too far-fetched, even for my life. Until the red smoke, I'd never seen anything remotely resembling magic, aside from Perla's *curaciones*—when she claims to cure our mal de ojo with a ritual using water and oil.

There has to be another explanation. A *nonfiction* one.

I finally loosen my grip on the duffel and let it fall to the floor. Then I slip off my shorts and bra, draping them over my bag, and get under the covers. With one last look at Catalina—still asleep—I rest my wet hair on the cool pillow.

But by the time dawn's blue light breaks through the gap in the billowy curtains, I'm not sure I slept at all. I hear Catalina stirring, and I burrow deeper into the mattress, already too tense and exhausted to take on whatever lies ahead.

The curtains blast apart, as though on a gust of wind, and I sit bolt upright.

Catalina slips into the bathroom, and I roll my eyes when I hear the click of the door locking. As if I would want to walk in on her.

I breathe easier now that she's not in the room, and I un-pack a new toothbrush and pair of socks from the duffel, then I stuff the bag under my cot and fix the bed exactly as I found it, down to the placement of each doll. I try not to dwell on the words embroidered onto them as I yank the tag off my white cotton shirt and pull my denim shorts on.

When Catalina comes out, wrapped in a towel, the sneer she gives me could cool the sun. "You can't wear that."

"Well, I don't have any wizarding robes," I blurt, then I bite my tongue.

She narrows her pink gaze at me. "What manada are you from?"

"Now you want to be friends?" I snap.

Her nostrils flare, and I stalk deliberately past her to the bathroom, locking the door behind me just as she did.

By now, my period is pretty much over, so I put on a light pad. I watch myself in the mirror as I brush my teeth, examining my face. I can't think of the last time I cared about how I looked. My dark hair is a thick mane, my eyelids are puffy, and red lightning webs the whites of my eyes, but at least I smell better than I did last night.

When I return to the room, Catalina is gone. The space is empty, and the door is ajar.

My heart pumps an extra-hard beat. I'm alone, and no one is watching. This is my chance to run. I pull on my shoes and reach for my duffel—

"Manu?"

The door swings open to reveal a small girl with short hair wearing an ankle-length, lime-green dress. Saysa looks like Tinkerbell.

"We wanted to see if you'd like to go down to breakfast with us," she says, flashing me her dimples. She's obviously using the royal *we* because Catalina is leaning against the wall and staring pointedly away.

"We'll wait here while you change," says Saysa, shutting the door on herself.

Change? I frown and look around, and I notice a dress has been draped on my cot. It looks just like Saysa's, only mine is a burnt gold color that makes me think of one of the shades of my eyes in that magnified photograph Ma had. I pull it on, and the fabric is formfitting at the top and loose-flowing over my legs, clinging closer to my chest and hips than it does on Saysa.

I've never worn anything this fancy before, and I admire the way the gold glows against my brown skin. I run my hands along the skirt, and my fingers slide into a pocket. I instinctively feel around for sticks and rocks and other small weapons, like I've worn this dress many times before.

Air snags in my throat as I dart to the mirror to look at myself. And I flash to seeing my reflection in the cascading waterfalls.

This is the dress from my lunaritis dreams.

How is that even possible?

I take deep breaths until my pulse normalizes. I need to swallow my questions if I'm going to find answers. I can't let on that I'm any different from anyone here, no matter how much strangeness I see today.

Instead of my threadbare sneakers, I pull on two sock-like strips of gold that look like they could fit either foot. Immediately, I sense the particles readjusting, the material molding to me, like memory foam only . . . *sentient.*

They look like ballet flats and fit so comfortably, I can't even feel them.

Saysa's gaze is bright with approval, but Catalina doesn't look at me. "I'm *starving*," she says, peeling away from the wall and padding to the staircase.

Saysa and I trail behind her. "How'd you sleep?" she asks, studying my face like she's reading the answer.

"Fine," I lie.

The tree's branches look lower this morning than they did last night, which must be an illusion of the light. I expect us to climb down to the ground floor, but Catalina heads up. Since Saysa follows her, I do too.

A thick limb pokes through the stone railing, and instead of going around, Catalina scales it. I think she's just showing off, but then she steps over the banister, toward the tree.

I watch in amazement as she crosses the branch like it's a tightrope, moving with her mother's grace, as though they command the air around them. She keeps her balance all the way to the other side, where she steps into an opening in the trunk.

"What is she—?"

A body suddenly flings itself off a higher story and falls toward the branch, right where Catalina had just been. I scream as the guy lands—

On his feet, without stumbling. Then he bounds into the opening so fast that by my next blink, he's vanished.

"Let's go," says Saysa, like this is all perfectly normal. She climbs onto the branch just as Catalina did.

"I'm scared," I blurt, before she abandons me here.

She looks back, her expression almost surprised. Like *my* reaction is the abnormal one. "She's not going to drop you. But if heights throw you, just don't look down."

She?

Saysa crosses just as confidently as her friend, only instead of appearing to glide through the air, Saysa's feet are so grounded that she might as well be another limb growing from the tree. When she gets to the other end, she gestures for me to follow.

I steal a glance down the stairs.

I could make a run for it.

"Come on, Manu!" she calls. "I *promise* you're not going to fall."

Catalina's face pokes through the opening. "Es una cagona," I hear her mutter under her breath. *She's a chickenshit.*

Well, I've come this far.

I climb onto the branch, and I step tentatively over the banister. Adrenaline rushes up my veins, and that sense of aliveness I felt running with Tiago is back.

I take a second step, and I find myself trusting my body more than I expected. Even though I don't work out, these past twenty-four hours, it's felt like I've discovered new muscles.

Since I'm finding it so easy to keep my balance, I move faster, until I'm on the cusp of a sprint. Saysa smiles at me encouragingly, but Catalina frowns with disappointment.

Halfway there, I speed up even more, wondering if I can run the rest of it as fast as that guy did. Only I teeter too far to the side, and suddenly the marble floor tilts up at me from a dozen stories below—

The tree twists beneath me, and my weight shifts.

The branch helped me regain my balance.

It's a miracle I don't collapse from sheer shock. I'm out of breath when I make it to the opening, and Saysa cups my shoulder firmly. "You okay?"

I nod and lock my jaw, the nerves from my close call making my teeth chatter. Then the tension melts when I look around me.

We're in a vast and seemingly unending library lined with wall-to-wall books. The fact that it's inside a tree makes it feel somewhat cannibalistic.

The texts are pristine, printed in colors so brilliant, the ink looks fresh. Every few feet, a spine pushes in between adjacent texts, like a new book has just been birthed.

It's a *living* library.

A gap begins to widen between shelves, like a portal opening, and a passage unfolds, leading deeper into the tree's core.

Even if I could excuse last night's twister as the temperamental Miami weather, and the star-like light bugs as a

species native to the Everglades, and these giant stone structures as archeological remnants of an earlier civilization—I
can't explain this tree.

"What is this place?" I whisper.

"Every time a Septimus publishes a text, it gets reproduced
inside this library," Saysa explains. There's that word again,
sewn onto the first doll. *Septimus*.

We go down the passage, and the smooth brown walls feel
alive, like I've been swallowed by a sentient being.

"Stop me if you already know this stuff, because Cata thinks
I get too excited about this place," says Saysa, her words speeding up. "El Laberinto was the first Lunaris-formed territory
abroad, so this academy is the most ancient training institute
outside of Kerana. And it's the number-one-ranked Septimus
school thanks to her. Since she's such a good teacher."

Laberinto, Lunaris, Kerana, Septimus . . . And there's that *she*
again. "She?"

Saysa nods. "Flora. Her roots reach all the way to Lunaris."

Roots. She's talking about this *tree*.

Based on what she's saying, El Laberinto, Kerana, and Lunaris sound like different locations. But why does that last
word sound so much like lunaritis?

I can't help wondering how many more secrets Ma was
keeping from me. But I push that thought back into the re-
cesses of my mind, because I can't afford to think about Ma
and Perla right now, or I'll fall apart.

Light grows brighter ahead, and the tunnel ends above air,
in the tree's crown. I step into the crook of a thick branch.

There are around a hundred teens spread out in clusters
on what looks like a large green field. The ground is actually a
thatchwork of leaves, their edges like the lines between floor
tiles, only these patterns are too complex to be reproduced.

No two leaves are identical, and the level of detail is almost overwhelming.

Each group is gathered around a picnic basket that looks like a large bird's nest. There are also round pillows that look like huge dandelion balls, which some people are using as backrests.

Catalina is the first of us to leap onto the greenery, followed by Saysa. When neither of them falls through the foliage, I join them.

The leafy floor is startlingly sturdy. I look down and admire how the sun illuminates every intricate vein line and gradient of green. We're nestled beneath arcing branches that create a kind of awning over us, breaking up the Florida daylight and making it bearable instead of blinding.

As we weave through the students, I notice the girls are all wearing dresses like ours, while the guys are in shorts and T-shirts reminiscent of my original outfit from this morning. Catalina catches me eyeing everyone, and when our gazes cross, she quickens her pace.

Tiago springs up from one of the dozen groups, and I can hardly contain the thrill of excitement that tingles down my spine as he makes his way over to us. My greedy gaze takes in his dark windswept hair and sculpted arms and sapphire eyes . . .

Eyes that are trained on Catalina.

Time slows down as I watch her stride up and clasp her arms around his neck. His hands circle her waist, and my stomach plummets to the ground as they hug.

"It's so good to see you after the *awful* night I just had," says Catalina when they pull apart.

"Why? What happened?"

At the sound of his voice, I'm once more taken aback by its melody. Like rediscovering a new favorite song.

"I got a roommate," she says glumly, twisting around to pin me with her glare.

Tiago's gaze jumps to me, and his eyes grow wide with recognition.

"This is Manu," chirps Saysa, reaching up to link her arm with mine. "Manu, that's Tiago. My brother."

I start at the word *brother*. No wonder there was something familiar about her. Seeing them together, I notice their skin is the same warm shade of brown and their smiles are equally beguiling. Only while Tiago is tall and muscular, Saysa is scrawny and tinier than most of her classmates.

Tiago's lips flex into that roguish grin from last night, and before he can say anything about our encounter, I blurt, "Nice to meet you."

His brow furrows, but he doesn't look angry—more confused. After a moment, he says, "You too."

The guilt of making him lie to his sister and Catalina keeps me from meeting his gaze, and he leads us to a group of four guys who have already scarfed down half the baked goods in the picnic basket. "This is Manu," he says, sitting next to a light-skinned guy with a baby face and boulder-like body that makes me think of an overgrown boy.

"Javier," says the big guy in a booming voice, and when I sit beside him, he leans over and plants his lips on my cheek.

I gasp. And then quickly cough, remembering Argentines are affectionate in their greetings.

Still, it's the first time a boy's kissed me. The first time I've hung out with kids my own age without my sunglasses. The first time I get to be *me*—whoever that is.

"This is Pablo, Nico, and Diego," says Tiago, going down the line. The guy sitting to his other side—Pablo—nods at me. He's the only one wearing a shirt that isn't white but black, just like his long hair, leather wrist cuffs, and eyes. He looks as if in a typical school he'd be labeled a goth kid. But there's nothing typical about this place.

"Bienvenida," says the guy next to him, whom I assume to be Nico. His gaze takes a moment of adjustment because his irises are almost the same shade of silver as his pupils, so the two blend together. It makes his eyes seem enormous.

The last guy doesn't look up from the book he's reading, and Catalina jabs him with her elbow. His face pops up, and for some reason, I'm surprised to see he's wearing reading glasses. I guess I just assumed our bizarre eyes gave us all good vision.

"Sorry," he says, sparing me a kind smile that extends to his periwinkle gaze. "I'm Diego. Nice to meet you, Manu."

His attention returns to his book before I can respond.

"Where'd Gus and Bibi go?" asks Tiago. "And Carlos?"

Goth guy points to a couple nestled in a thicket of branches— "Making out"—then to a group of girls making room for a handsome guy to sit among them—"and hoping to make out."

My gaze lingers on the girls. I watch one of them fill a colorful calabaza gourd with hot water. The sight of the familiar custom is an arrow to my gut, and I'm jolted back in time to yesterday morning, when Ma and Perla were drinking mate and sharing secrets.

Has it only been twenty-four hours since I lost my world?

"You probably recognize us as the Septibol champions."

Boulder-boy's booming voice jostles me from my thoughts, his volume carrying across the entire Everglades. I remember *Septibol* was sewn onto the second doll.

"We've got the best team in the junior league!" he bellows, his cherubic face at odds with his Herculean frame.

I smile like I know what he's talking about.

"You play?" he asks, and I shake my head no.

"Cata and I are on the team," says Saysa, who's sitting on my other side. I nod like that means something. "You should come to practice!"

Across from me, the guy in all black—*Pablo*—asks, "How do we know she's not a spy?" His gaze drills into my face. "What manada are you from?"

This question is going to be the end of me.

Just then, Saysa passes me the calabaza gourd. Thankful for an excuse to turn away from Pablo, I twist toward her and say, "I don't like mate, actually."

"You're joking."

Pablo's words hang in the air, and when Saysa doesn't jump to defend me, I scan the rest of their faces. His incredulous reaction seems to be unanimous.

"It's not my taste," I explain. They start looking to one another now, like I'm speaking a language they don't understand. This isn't like Ma and Perla's fake disappointment—here, my refusal feels like an actual affront.

Suddenly, Saysa laughs.

Like she just got the punchline to a joke I never made.

Boulder-boy guffaws next, followed by a chuckling Tiago, then the rest of the group relaxes into smiles . . . except for one. Catalina's calculating expression never breaks.

"We have sweeteners if you want them," offers Saysa, setting the mate in front of me like she doesn't for one second believe I'm not going to drink it. Everyone's still watching me, and I realize the awkwardness is not going to disband until I sip the Argentine Kool-Aid.

So for Perla and Ma—who won't be having their morning mate together today, or maybe any day—I bring the metal bombilla to my lips. The hot herbal liquid sears my throat. I take two quick swigs and hand it back to Saysa.

Conversation resumes as a couple of the guys start rehashing a Septibol semifinal that took place a couple of nights ago, and I try to follow along so I can figure out the sport. Only I'm feeling weirdly lightheaded. I think it's from the mate.

I force myself to focus and try memorizing the guys' names as I hear them. Pablo's I've got down. The giant with the baby face is Javier. Silver Eyes is Nico. I don't remember Glasses' name, and since he's still reading and not joining the conversation, I don't hear it again.

My stomach grumbles so loudly that Javier turns to look at me. Suddenly ravenous, I snag a medialuna dulce from the basket, my fingers sticky from the sweet glaze, and I devour it. When I reach for a second one, Javier slides a jar of dulce de leche toward me.

I stop counting pastries after that.

The wave of hunger ebbs away as quickly as it rolled in, and I lean back slowly, into the dandelion cloud behind me. It's surprisingly solid, though it feels feathery and plush against my back.

With food warming my belly and mate swirling through my thoughts, my body feels longer and deeper and vaster than ever. I close my eyes, and I sense a black hole at the base of my brain, a drain to another dimension. Like a portal.

Maybe that's where the landscape from my dreams lives.

When I open my eyes again, the view is hazy. I blink, and water splashes from my lids, blurring my vision.

Is this what being drunk feels like? Is that why Argentines love mate so much? Or did someone slip in something extra to mess with me?

Everyone is still discussing Septibol, but across from me silver-eyed Nico and black-clad Pablo are having a side argument. "All I'm saying is if you're not going to cut your hair, at least pull it back when you play—"

"Worry about your own hair!" Pablo snaps at Nico. "And stop getting in my space—"

"It's not my fault; we're making room for Carlos!"

The handsome guy who was sitting with the group of girls squeezes in between Tiago and Nico. "What'd I miss?" he asks, a little out of breath. His emerald-green eyes dart around the group and pause on me. "Who—?"

A girl's shriek pierces the air, and his head shrinks into his shoulders, like a retreating turtle.

"Carlos, what did you do?" asks Catalina, her tone heavy with suspicion. He ignores her and reaches for a pastry.

"Nada más dejame decirte esto." Nico is still trying to get Pablo to listen to him. "Last match, I saw it get in your way. You didn't notice when the ground was icing over—"

"Will you shut the fuck up about my hair already?"

"Just do it for the *championship*—"

Pablo snarls at Nico, a sound more animal than human, cutting off his plea. His black eyes begin to fill with light, like swirling ink, and his deep brown skin begins to glow like something's happening beneath the surface. Then he rears onto his feet and tips his head back, releasing a ghostly howl.

My mouth forms a soundless scream as hair sprouts across Pablo's face, and his limbs begin to crack and stretch. The hair on his body grows thicker and furrier, his ears stand up and sharpen into points, his nails curve into claws, and fangs drop from his mouth.

He looks like a man midtransformation into a wolf. Or a wolf who was once a man.

A *lobizón*.

My pulse thunders in my ears, and I'm too afraid to even breathe.

Pablo swipes at Nico with his lethal claws, and the silver-eyed werewolf transforms in time to block the strike. They start tussling away from us, and I realize I'm shivering, my skin moist with cold sweat.

That's when I notice four blue-and-gray-dressed girls have our group surrounded. They're glaring at Carlos, their blue and gray eyes filling with more and more light, the way Pablo's did before he transformed.

My skin grows even chillier, and I look down to see frost forming on the leaves beneath me. *Are those girls causing—?*

"C-Cata!" Carlos begs. "Do some-th-th-thing!"

My mind grows fuzzy from holding my breath for too long, and I turn toward Catalina as I gasp for oxygen. She's encased in some kind of transparent membrane, like a force field, and seems unaffected by the change in temperature. She shakes her head at Carlos in refusal.

Her eyes meet mine next, and she frowns, like she can't understand why I'm turning blue.

Just as frostbite is about to set in, the ground warms up beneath me, and the glacier recedes. Saysa's area is already frost-free, and her green eyes are lit up like radioactive limes.

Soon, all the ice has vanished except for the bit under Carlos.

"C-come on!" he begs, his voice shaking as his skin pales.

Saysa looks up at one of the four witches surrounding us. "What's it going to take?"

The girl crosses her arms. "I get to ride him for a day in Lunaris. He has to take me anywhere I want."

Beside me, Javier spits out his water. "The fuck? We're not *mules—*"

"D-d-done!"

The last of the ice begins to melt, and a sly smile spreads across Carlos's ashen face. I wonder if he got what he wanted, or if he's just determined not to let anyone see him lose.

The girls walk away, and Carlos keeps his eyes on the victorious one, something flashing in his gaze. Then he leaps up and runs after her, moving at inhuman speed. "I'll be your bitch, witch!"

Pablo and Nico shuffle back over, both of them looking like they could use a weeklong nap. Yet their clothes are unaffected by the transformation. The fabric just adapted to their forms.

My heart speeds up at the memory of the monster within them. And I realize *all* the guys here are monsters.

Even Tiago.

"Who won?" booms Javier.

"Un compromiso," says Nico, his hypnotic silver eyes still overbright, making him look like a celestial being. "He agreed to trim his ends."

The mate's lightheaded effect is back, and I'm starting to realize it comes in waves. I close my eyes and try to tune out all the conversations around me. I can't process anything that's happening. It's either my drugged drink, or I'm just in shock.

I shouldn't be here. That's going to become amply clear to everyone beyond just Catalina soon, since I'm not a *witch*.

This time when I think the word, there's nothing funny about it. I have no idea how it's possible, but I now know for a fact that I'm surrounded by witches and werewolves. *Brujas and lobizones.* The myth is real—except I'm not one of them.

I only look the part.

At least Harry had supernatural incidents in his early childhood that started making sense when he learned he was a wizard. I've never done so much as a card trick.

"Just don't pull a Fierro!"

My eyes fly open in time to see Javier shoving Tiago in what seems to be playful for him but would probably crush anyone else. Tiago doesn't budge in the slightest.

"A what?"

It's my first contribution to the conversation, and judging by the silence that falls over the group, that hasn't gone unnoticed.

"A *Fierro*," repeats Javier after a beat.

I turn to my other side and look at Saysa questioningly, my heart beating too loud to speak. They can't mean my father. I'm sure Ma lied to me about his name.

"Oh, come on, your manada can't be this cut off!" complains Pablo. "If you don't know who Fierro is—"

"Back off."

Tiago's voice is soft and musical, but his command is packed with palpable power. He's determined to make a habit of coming to my rescue. "You're right, she doesn't know who Fierro is. *Do you?*"

Baby-faced Javier rolls his Mars-red eyes. "That's not what he meant—"

"Manu's just never heard the expression." The way Tiago says my name with a Spanish accent makes it sound more intimate than it should.

"To pull a Fierro just means to disappear," he says to me, and for the first time since seeing him hug Catalina, I meet his sapphire gaze. "Just like Fierro did."

I have to force the oxygen down my throat to keep my breaths from growing too short. A man named Fierro who vanished. It's possible we're talking about the same person—but not probable.

Still, I have to know. I can practically feel Catalina sizing me up and growing more suspicious, so I work extra-hard to make my voice as casual as possible when I ask, "Isn't Fierro like—*dead*?"

My voice catches on the last word, and I cough to conceal the sudden thickness in my throat.

"Yes!"

I can hardly believe it when Catalina agrees with me on something. "*Finally* I'm not the only sensible one," she says, for once looking at me without disdain. "He's definitely dead, that's why we haven't heard from him in almost . . . what? Eighteen years?"

Eighteen years.

This time the dizziness in my head isn't from the mate but the conversation. They're talking about a Fierro who disappeared eighteen years ago—just like my father.

"No way," says Saysa, and I turn to her, eager for a more optimistic point of view. "I think he's out there, biding his time, waiting to lead our revolution when we're ready."

"What do you mean?" I can't help asking.

"Oh no," moans Javier on my other side. "Don't get her started—"

"Our culture places too much significance on one's sex, which reinforces a patriarchal system." From Saysa's tone, I gather this is a speech she's got down pat. "Our entire way of life forces Septimus into a male-or-female binary, which is a narrow and outdated approach to identity, especially since our biological sex assignment is tied to our gender and supernatural makeup. Fierro understood that, which is why he wanted to change things. He wasn't an anarchist, he was a progressive—"

"Yes, but the question is *where* he is, not who he was," says Pablo impatiently. "So why don't we go back to trading theories on where Fierro's been hiding?"

"Because we weren't doing that," silver-eyed Nico points out.

While I agree with Saysa's perspective, there's only one thing on my mind right now. "Where do you think Fierro is?" I ask, leaning toward Pablo.

He brushes his long black locks behind his ears, seeming to appraise me anew. Then he steeples his hands together, his leather wrist cuffs touching. "Obviously not Earth. To live off the grid for this long, he's got to be in Lunaris."

Lunaris is another planet? Do these creatures have their own way of traveling through space? I can't ask without giving away that I'm not one of them. But there's something more pressing I need to know.

So I say the one thing that might tell me once and for all if Fierro is my father.

"I-I heard he fell in love," I mutter in a trembling tone, "a-and he got in trouble for trying to run away with her."

My heart holds its next beat until Pablo speaks.

"With a *human.*"

My next heartbeat never comes.

It has to be him.

"Can you imagine if one of us moved in among the humans?" Catalina's voice is low, like even the suggestion is treasonous.

"We'd be discovered in no time," says Javier, dialing down his volume too.

My gut hardens, like something is growing in there.

"Did he think he would get a human job and buy a house and get married?" asks Nico just as somberly. "It's not like they could ever have a family."

"But what if Fierro did?" presses Pablo. "Gave birth to some freakish thing with that woman?"

My stomach starts to cramp worse than ever, and I lift my knees and hug them to my chest.

"You okay?" Saysa asks me. I nod without meeting her gaze.

"If the attempt at crossbreeding worked—which is a big *if*," clarifies Catalina, "then by law, the thing would be hunted down and destroyed."

"Manu?"

Even though Saysa is sitting beside me, she sounds far away.

"I just need some air," I murmur. "Think I'll check out the view."

"I forgot to show you!" she says, a little over-the-top enthusiastic. "The best lookout point is by that branch shaped like a hook. You can see the whole swamp. I'll take you—"

I shake my head, but before I can speak, Pablo asks again, "But what would happen to it?"

Glasses shuts his book for the first time, and the quiet gesture resounds through the group because every face turns toward him. His skin seems to darken to an even deeper shade of black as his expression grows grave. "Fraternizing with humans is forbidden, so a hybrid's existence would go against our laws."

"But, Diego," insists Pablo, "if Fierro knocked up a human, the thing would be—"

"What I just said," he says, removing his reading glasses. "Illegal."

13

Thing. Hybrid. Freakish.
  Hunted down and destroyed.
  I am illegal.
  Their labels pelt me all the way to the hook-shaped branch, like a haunting haiku. But it's that last word that utterly eviscerates me.

Everything's changed, and yet I'm the same. Still a spare card that doesn't fit any grouping. Still unwanted.

I gaze out at the wild landscape of mangroves sprawling below. Dark, snaking canals disappear beneath swathes of green foliage, against the deep blue backdrop of the endless Atlantic. And I release a soundless scream into the Everglades.

My eyes burn, and my chest feels too constricted for even oxygen. I used to think my worst fear was coming face-to-face with an ICE agent, but at least the US government would just send me back to Argentina to fend for myself.

According to these creatures' laws, I'm not even fit to breathe.

The tears keep rolling, and I don't care if someone comes over and sees me. I don't even know why I'm still here. Ma is in a detention center, Perla is in a hospital, and I'm *fraternizing*—to use Diego's word—with the beings responsible for destroying my family. I'm cosmically cursed.

Ma must have known I would never be safe, not *anywhere*. Yet she encouraged me to study and dream up any future I wanted. She could have started over on her own, at least saved herself, but she chose to give up her family, career, and safety, just to make sure I could go on breathing. And I abandoned her.

I need to get out of here. I have to reunite with her before—

"Manu, was it?"

The melody of Tiago's voice startles me. I dry my cheeks on my arm, but I don't turn around because I don't want him to see I've been crying again.

"If you're mad I lied about us not knowing each other, just tell her the truth. I really don't care."

I don't know why I'm being so snappish. Something about Tiago just brings it out in me. "Maybe then I'll get a new roommate, and you'll be doing us both a favor."

"You're talking about Cata?"

He sounds amused, like he finds this *funny*.

"Who else would I mean?"

"I assumed my sister, since she's the one who introduced us."

I feel the blood rushing to my face, and now I absolutely detest him. I wait awhile for him to walk away, but I can still smell him.

"What do you want?" I ask, finally turning around.

His smile fades, and he looks a lot younger without the

charm. "I know last night was hard for you, and I just wanted to see how you're feeling."

Of course he had noble intentions coming over. I stumble into a world of witches and werewolves, and somehow I manage to be the biggest monster.

"I'm—okay."

He nods like he can hear what I'm not saying. "I know Cata can be a bit chilly—"

"Like the surface of Pluto—"

"But she warms up eventually." His smirk resurfaces. "Pluto, huh?"

"The temperature can fall as low as –387 degrees."

He looks at me funny, like he just noticed something. "What?" I ask.

"It's nothing." He blinks off the expression. "Just that you used Fahrenheit. Like the humans in this country."

Shit. I shrug like it's no big deal, and I turn away to stare at the view. I really need to start thinking before I speak.

"I didn't mean to bother you," he says. "Cata is nicer than she seems. Just give her time to thaw."

"Do you always make her friends for her?" Now I'm the one who sounds like Catalina, but I can't help myself. The more he defends her, the more defeated I feel. These emotions are madness.

Tiago sighs, and I wonder how many times he's had to justify Catalina's wintry ways over the years. "Cata grew up here, and she's always been treated differently because she's the headmistress's daughter. She acts tough, but really she just wants to be liked for herself, not her mom."

I nod like I understand, even though Catalina is the least of my problems.

"We have a practice game later," he says after a stretch of silence. "You should come."

Our gazes lock. In the daylight, his sapphire orbs look like cloudless skies, and I long to fall into them.

"Yo!"

Our spell is broken by Javier's booming voice. Tiago winks and he's gone.

It's dizzying how quickly the guys move, and I amble back to the group in a daze. By now, only the girls remain. The green space is dappled with dresses of every color, the fabrics matching the shade of the wearer's eyes. Like labels.

I spot Catalina and Saysa having a private conversation in the corner, but before I can make my way over, a purple dress sweeps across my view.

I look up to see Jazmín as she glides over to the only other adult here, a woman in a wine-red dress. I concentrate on their conversation.

"She transferred last minute and wasn't on the official list," Jazmín tells her.

"Why not contact her manada?"

"There might be a problem back home. I'd like you to keep an eye on her so we can determine the appropriate course of action."

"Feeling better?"

My focus breaks as Saysa comes over, with Catalina in tow. "Yeah, thanks," I answer, and when I look to Jazmín again, her figure is receding into Flora's trunk.

"Buen día, hermanas."

The brujas gather around the woman in the dark wine dress. Her Afro is red at the ends and black at the roots, so that in the sunlight her hair flickers like flames. "For the new trans-fers, I'm Señora Lupe. Let's everyone introduce ourselves."

My tendons tighten with tension as we go around the group.

Bibi, Estefania, Lily, Melisa, Daiana, Noemí, Valeria, Catalina, Saysa . . .

"Manu."

"Welcome to El Laberinto," says Señora Lupe once we get through all forty-nine of us. "Now please spread out, pick a spot, and sit down. Relax, and let us begin our day with some emotional alignment."

Saysa gestures for me to follow her, and we sit by Catalina, keeping a wide berth of space around us. Everyone folds their legs and closes their eyes. Their chests rise and fall in a synchronized pattern, and I copy their posture and try to clear my thoughts.

"Septimus sons are born with the soul of a wolf." Señora Lupe's voice sounds like she's moving around us. "They're hunters, protectors, soldiers. But we Septimus daughters are nature's gardeners, nurturers, healers. Our lobizón brothers have been given the strength to secure our borders, while we have been gifted a sixth sense to care for our population."

I listen eagerly, unable to relax even if I wanted to, drinking in every word like a parched desert wanderer who's come upon a pristine lake.

"Our sixth sense is our magic. Each of us is powered by an element that burns all the way to our eyes. That element exists within us just as surely as any internal organ. The Invocadora is a wind witch. She wears the air around her like a coat. The Jardinera is an earth witch, and her feet are as rooted to the soil as any tree. The Congeladora, or water witch, can freeze any surface. And the Encendedora wields the heat of flames."

Encendedora. That's what Señora Lupe must be. My muscles tighten as I think of the woman on El Retiro's rooftop who left behind the red smoke. Was she a fire witch as well?

"Whatever kind of bruja you are, deep down you are connected to all four elements, as we are all part of a larger whole. Now follow your breaths and burrow into your core."

The breathing exercise reminds me of Perla. She used to say most of our ailments could be cured just by breathing—if we can suck the oxygen in deep enough, we can sanitize our darkest places.

My shoulders drop, and the springs of my neck grow lax, letting my head loll . . .

"Our identity is shaped by yesterday. We carry everything we've experienced within us, even those things we can't name or recall. Our history grows in us like sedimentary layers, each memory feeding our foundation, adding a new dimension to our identity."

I'm aware of the mate's buzz again, and I wonder whether it's really coming in waves, or if it's now become a baseline constant. I don't know how anyone can enjoy this dizzy feeling.

"Ride those clouds of breath through your body, become aware of every centimeter of your being, find the doorway that unlocks the next level . . ."

I sense the black hole at the base of my head, and I hover near it, unwilling to get closer. What if I get stuck down there, and I can't find my way back?

I can't risk it.

I have to stay in control at all times.

Yet the combination of mate and deep breathing has me in a mental headlock. Opening my eyes feels impossible, like I'm too far from my surface. This deep in, the black hole's gravity is too strong, and before I can pull away, I'm overrun with a memory.

"Ayudame."

Ma's call for help is as clear as my own internal monologue, but I can't see her. I know it's a trick of the dark, trying to make me think she's trapped within my depths to lure me down—so I resist.

"No puedo, señora, se tiene que ir ya mismo. Cómo se le ocurrió traer a una criatura por acá . . ."

I can't, ma'am. You need to leave right now. How could you even think to bring a child here . . .

Light begins to streak into the blackness of my mind, until I'm with Ma and an older man inside a bookstore. The memory comes in complete sensory detail, and I inhale the earthy perfume of paper.

I know I'm very young because I'm eye level with the book spines on the third shelf up from the ground. Also, Ma is holding my hand. More like gripping it to the point of strangulation.

I have to tilt my head back to see her face. She looks lifetimes younger, and it's only in remembering her this clearly that I realize how much she's aged. Time's effects would probably have been easier to track if we had photographs around the apartment.

Ma leans into the counter, her face inches from the man behind the register. A quick scan tells me we're alone.

In Spanish, she tells the man, "Why do you think I came back? I don't have any other options. You need to tell me what you know, now."

"I told you everything I knew five years ago, when they wheeled me into your hospital in an ambulance," he answers. "You saw what they were capable of doing just to find you. Imagine what they'll do if they patrol past and see you here! What kind of protection are you giving your daughter?"

Ma's fingers release mine, and my hand feels suddenly cold and cramped. Then she squeezes my chin and swings my face up, whipping off my old plastic pair of Minnie Mouse sunglasses.

I feel as frozen in shock now as the younger me did then. I can't believe this ever happened—or that I forgot it.

"How do you want me to protect her?" Ma demands.

The man's eyes bulge, and he looks from me to Ma and shakes his head. Only he doesn't just look stunned—his shock is shadowed with sadness. Like he understands what this means.

Like he knew my dad.

"I don't know if it's true," he says at last, "but last I heard, they were taking him to Miami."

14

I wake up screaming.

I'm sprawled on the ground, my throat sore, with a circle of girls' faces peering down at me. I've no idea how long I've been spasming.

"You okay?" asks Saysa. She's closest to me.

"Y-yeah," I say, sitting up. I'm mortified as I look to Señora Lupe and the other brujas. I'm supposed to be laying low, not breaking down.

Catalina is squinting at me more curiously than ever, and she's not the only one. Some of the girls are inspecting the area around me. They all look . . . *confused.*

"Okay, everyone, give Manu some room," says our instructor. She comes closer to me and smiles. "That's a perfectly natural reaction. And look"—she gestures to our surroundings—"no harm done! That's some great emotional control."

"Thanks," I mumble, too lost to follow.

"I think that's enough deep diving for today," she tells the class. "Let's bring it in."

I fall in with the others as we shuffle back into Flora, and Catalina comes up to me. I brace myself for her challenge.

"That was impressive," she says. "To completely let go of your emotions like that and still keep your magic under control? I underestimated you."

Saysa nods approvingly at her friend, like she's pleased to see her playing well with others.

But Catalina's pink gaze is unwavering, and somehow her newfound respect doesn't feel all that comforting. In a lower register, she adds, "I *can't wait* to see what you can do with your magic."

Trailing behind the others down another smooth brown passage through the tree, all I can think of is the memory I just accessed.

Now I know the real reason Ma moved us to Miami. There's only one thing that's ever been powerful enough to make her risk everything, including her life—*love.* It's how we both ended up in this whole mess to begin with.

But why couldn't she tell me she thought my dad might still be alive, or that there was a chance he was in this city? I feel like since yesterday, I've been caught between reproach and remorse. I want to be furious with Ma, only I can't be, because she's already going through hell, and she's only suffering because of me.

The passage ends abruptly, and I'm yanked out of my misery by the grove of gigantic, purple-leafed trees that surrounds me. The grass isn't green but golden, and a low mist hangs on the horizon. It's a place I've only seen in my dreams. *Literally.*

I can hardly breathe as I step into my dreamworld, the shock wrapping around me like a shawl muffling all my senses.

This place isn't just a fantasy in my head.

It's real.

"Gather round, ladies," says Señora Lupe, and as we come together, I realize I'm taller than even our teacher. "Today we're going to continue our lessons in control. Big spells are showy, but it's the tiny ones that measure a bruja's true ability to wield magic. So I want each of you to take a basket, and as you walk around, you're going to pluck a single petal from a dozen different flowers without touching them. If you harm a plant, or remove more than one petal, you'll try again. We'll be here until each of you has a full basket."

Saysa scoops up a pair of wicker baskets woven with white ribbon and hands me one. A loose end of ribbon flutters in the air even though there's no breeze blowing. I bring it up to my face and inspect the shiny white fabric that's fringed with tiny feathers or a fine fur—

The ribbon suddenly snaps at me, its sharp jaws chomping just inches from my nose.

I drop the basket to the floor and leap back. "It's a snake!" I say stupidly.

Saysa chuckles, but the other witches look annoyed that I broke their concentration. "That's a vivi—short for vivora. Don't you have them at your school?" I shake my head and hope she doesn't press me for details. "She keeps us honest."

Saysa hands my basket back to me, and I carefully close my fingers around the handle, keeping a watchful eye on the vivi. She curves like a tiny cobra, and though I can't spot any eyes, I have a feeling she can see me.

I follow Saysa deeper into the grove of trees, and when I see a wisp of red smoke, I freeze.

A girl with copper-orange eyes that are glowing like coals is staring at a pink flower with pointy petals. A fine stream of red smoke wafts up from the stem, and a couple of petals fall into her basket, singed.

Her vivi unfolds and strikes, devouring both petals in a single swallow.

"Try again, Noemí," says Señora Lupe, approaching the girl. All I can think as I watch her is she could be the spy on El Retiro's rooftop.

"I was *so close*," Noemí complains, holding up two fingers that are nearly touching.

It's not her. The voice I overheard was low and sultry, not high and nasally.

Catalina stands in front of a tiny tree with silver blooms. Her rose-quartz eyes light up, and a delicate wind whispers through the flower, gently knocking a petal loose. It loops through the air and lands lightly in her basket.

Invocadora.

So Catalina is a *Carrie*. Just when I thought she couldn't get more terrifying.

I turn to find Saysa staring at a plant with brown bulbous flowers that look like onions. Her green eyes glow as she casts her spell.

Whatever she's doing, it doesn't seem to be working. Nothing's happening. The flower isn't moving or changing . . .

It's wilting.

A single petal begins to fade and wrinkle and shrink, until it simply detaches and lands in the basket, an aged corpse. The rest of the blossom is unaffected.

Jardinera. An earth witch.

Though any plucked petal is by definition dead, there's something solemn about Saysa's power. Like it comes with a heftier kind of weight.

"No petals yet?"

Startled, I turn to see Señora Lupe scrutinizing my empty basket. The vivi is curled into a question mark, like it's also wondering where my work is.

"I . . . I'm not feeling great," I say lamely, knowing there's no way this is going to excuse me from anything.

"Maybe it's for the best you don't use your magic today," she says, to my infinite shock. "Not until your emotions have settled." I can't believe my freak-out from earlier is working in my favor.

"Keep me company?" asks Saysa, and I'm all too eager to fall into step with her.

"What is this place?" I chance, hoping the question doesn't raise any alarms.

"Well, you know that each of our territories abroad are hybridized, just like Kerana—they exist partly in this world, and partly in Lunaris, right?" I nod like I know. "Flora is the Lunaris anchor for El Laberinto. She's rooted there but grows here."

Lunaris must be the name of my dreamworld. It's also where Pablo thinks Fierro is hiding.

"Where's your favorite place to pick semillas in Lunaris?" asks Saysa. I ignore the question and pretend to be focused on a bruja in a gray dress. Her eyes brighten like diamonds, and a fine dusting of frost covers one of the yellow petals across from her. It breaks off from the flower and drops into the basket.

Congeladora.

"Manu?" Saysa prods. "Where do you like to pick semillas?"

"It's . . . hard to describe," I say vaguely. "Maybe I can show you?"

"Sure. Show me next moon."

Next moon.

Every answer is a gateway to more questions. Does she mean the next *full moon*?

Class doesn't end until the last bruja has plucked her twelfth petal. We even eat lunch in that grove, stacks of sandwiches de miga.

By the time we return to El Jardín, Catalina and Saysa are practically running. "We're late!" Saysa calls to me, ducking into her room once we get to our hall. I follow Catalina to our room, where she grabs a change of clothes and bolts into the bathroom. She darts out an instant later wearing a baby-blue dress with matching ballet shoes. *El Laberinto Juvenil* is stamped across her chest.

I'm tempted to change into my shorts, but right as I'm reaching for the duffel I hid beneath the cot, Catalina calls out, "Let's go!"

She holds the door open for me, which is probably more a gesture of distrust than chivalry, and we meet Saysa at the end of the hall. She's wearing a matching baby-blue dress, and we race down to the ground floor.

Going outside for real is different from being inside Flora. The air here is cooler, and the breezes carry a medley of aromas from different woods. I look up for the doraditos, but they aren't out. I wonder if they're nocturnal.

The afternoon sun fills the clearing as we pass the structure with the crumbling roof. It's smaller than El Jardín, and I only see guys going in and out. The third structure is draped with flowers, and only girls step through its doors. We keep walking, entering an embrace of trees that look much sturdier than the Everglades' mangroves.

The temperature drops a few degrees, and we follow a narrow path just large enough for the three of us. The trunks grow more elaborate the deeper we go, and the foliage becomes wilder—flowers with rainbow petals, leafy vines that scour the ground like snakes, trees with labyrinthine branches that twist into impossible designs.

The sounds here are also different. More musical. Like the creatures are calling out in harmony, synchronizing their noises into a soundtrack.

The path opens up into another clearing—a vast field with goalposts at either end, surrounded by stadium seating. A dozen guys burst out of a structure at one end, and I spot the wolf design on the door. Must be their locker room.

"Do you have a locker room?" I don't know why I ask.

"No," says Catalina. It's the first time she answers one of my questions. "But we don't play on the field."

"You mean, we're not *allowed* on the field," says Saysa, frowning, and now I get why Catalina volunteered to take this query.

The guys warm up by stretching and kicking the ball around.

"Hey!"

Tiago looks at us from the field, a wild grin on his face. I can't help smiling back. Or noticing how the uniform brings out the blueness of his eyes.

"Manu?"

I blink, and I realize someone's been saying my name. A girl with coppery-orange eyes has joined Saysa and Catalina. She's the Encendedora I was watching in class.

"This is Noemí," says Saysa. "She's also on the team."

"Hi," she says in her high voice. "You thinking of trying out?"

I detect a faint note of rivalry.

"Just here to watch."

Her expression relaxes. Another witch bounds across the

field, toward one of the guys, and he pulls her into his arms. "That's Bibi," says Saysa, following my gaze. "Gus's girlfriend."

"New trainee?"

A man who looks to be in his thirties lopes over to us, sizing me up.

"Coach Charco, this is Manu," says Saysa. "She's a new transfer."

He stares at me an extra-long moment, and I consider what's giving him pause. Is he trying to identify my element by my eye color? Or is it something else?

"Saysa, you training your replacement?" he asks her. I wonder if that means he's placed me as a Jardinera.

"Don't see the harm in letting her watch practice," she says.

He frowns. His eyes are ambery brown, probably the closest to mine I've seen so far. "You know with the championship coming up, there are bound to be scouts . . ."

I hear Pablo's paranoia in his words. Apparently, so does Catalina. "Do you seriously think my mother would put our win at risk?"

This seems to satisfy him, because he says to me, "Remember to keep off the field."

"Come with me," says Saysa, and I join her and Catalina on the sideline. The other brujas station themselves across from us, on the other sideline. "They're our substitutes. We'll start with an A team versus B team match, but later we'll mix it up."

When the game begins, I can't look away.

The guys are beasts. I don't need to be told which team is A or B—*it's obvious*. Mostly thanks to Tiago. He makes me think of Messi. He can kick the ball in from anywhere.

From what I can figure, Septibol is pretty much soccer. There are seven wolves on each team, and it seems like two forwards, two midfielders, two defenders, and a goalie. Tiago is a forward, and his game is so above the rest that I wonder if he's going to pursue this professionally.

Assuming there are professions among Septimus.

Watching them weave around each other, chasing the ball, setting up shots, shooting to score—I feel an unfamiliar urge to join them. To play on that field.

"You two ready?"

The coach looks to Saysa and Catalina, both of whom nod. Then he shouts at the other two brujas across the way— "Match starts *now*!"

I'm confused. I thought the game was already in progress.

Saysa and Catalina spread apart, until they're standing on the sideline on different halves of the field. I stick with Saysa.

I watch a B player steal the ball from silver-eyed Nico, when suddenly the ground begins to tremble, and a full-on earthquake rattles this side of the stadium. I turn to Saysa in alarm, and her eyes are glowing like neon signs.

She's doing this.

Back on the field, the B player loses the ball, and Gus takes it. The shaking stops.

Gus manages to weave around two players, but before he can pass the ball to Tiago, the grass ices over into a glacier and the ball skids off in a new direction.

Gus looks at the witch on the other sideline. Bibi blows her boyfriend a kiss, her gray eyes diamond-bright. He laughs and shakes his head of curls.

Now the B team takes possession, and suddenly everyone's flooding the other goalpost. Pablo is trying to steal the ball back, but Noemí sends a cloud of red smoke his way to slow him down.

Catalina diffuses it with a gust of air, and Pablo makes the steal. I'm not sure how he can see anything with his long black locks curtaining his face, but he thwacks the ball, and it goes soaring over the field in an arc. Tiago leaps up and brings it down with his chest, then he swings his leg and the ball bullets into the net.

They play for hours, past sunset, until the doraditos come out. They're buzzing overhead in swarms, so many of them that there's no need for stadium lighting. The sky is lit up with golden constellations of shooting stars.

When the games end, the guys flock to their locker room to shower and change, and Coach Charco gives the brujas notes. I've been so entranced that only now do I notice the Septimus who've gathered in the stands to watch. They all seem to have their own notes for the coach because soon they're crowding him, and I fall back to give them all space.

I stand on the outskirts, in the shade of the surrounding trees. Then I hear light footsteps behind me, and I spin around.

"Good ears," says Carlos, his hair wet and forest-green eyes dancing. "So what'd you think? Have we got a chance at the championship?"

"Not if you piss off those water witches again, and they turn you into an icicle."

He chuckles. "Good point . . . Maybe for my own safety I should quit playing the field and settle down."

His gaze sears into mine, and heat sizzles my skin. Not the kind that warms, but a fire that *warns*.

"Ready to eat?"

I'm relieved when Saysa and Catalina come find me, and we head back through the opening in the trees. Only this time, the path isn't the same.

It's now wide enough to fit two car lanes.

The woods are also different. The trees here are wider and squatter, and they all have openings in their trunks, like Flora.

Every now and then, I notice a pair of eyes flashing in the gaps. Like there are Septimus living in the branches' intricate networks.

"Are we taking a different path back?"

"The path is always shifting here," says Saysa. "That's why it's a labyrinth."

Behind El Jardín, everyone's eating dinner picnic-style in the garden. Catalina and Saysa make their selections from the buffet and sit with the team, but I don't have enough space for all the milanesas and ensaladas and empanadas I want to taste.

"I'll sell you room on my plate."

The musical voice tickles my spine, and I ask Tiago, "How much?"

"Two bites of everything you store."

"One bite." I cock my head like I'm considering the deal. "And you get the *last* bite of everything."

"How do I know you won't eat the best bites first?"

I feel the ghost of a grin on my lips. "How can there be better and worse bites?"

Saysa crosses between us to get some chimichurri. She doesn't say anything to either of us, but her presence punctures my fantasy. I don't know what's between Catalina and Tiago, but since she doesn't seem to violently hate me at the moment, I'd rather not risk alienating her.

"I'm good, actually." I take my plate to where the others are sitting, and I squeeze in next to Saysa. A quick scan of the garden indicates Gus and Bibi are making out behind a shrub. "Do the doors to our rooms lock us in at night?" I ask Saysa, and she nods.

"Witches and wolves sleep on different floors, and there are attendance checks at curfew, so there's no sneaking out."

I guess that explains why Gus and Bibi are inseparable during the day.

Diego is still absorbed in his book, and I'm almost jealous.

Falling hopelessly into the world of a story was always my favorite feeling. I wonder if he's reading something familiar.

I lean in to try glimpsing the text . . . but all I see is white paper. No words.

Diego flips the page, his brow furrowed with concentration, and I rub my eyes.

"So what drew you to El Laberinto?" asks Carlos. "Was it the studs on the Septibol team?"

Before I can answer, black-clad Pablo asks, "What manada are you from?"

I've no way of getting out of this question now, so I just say, "Guess."

He frowns. "How are we supposed to—"

"Okay, you speak perfect English," booms baby-faced Javier, analyzing me like I'm a hand of cards. "So you grew up in the United States."

"Not necessarily," says Diego, and when he sets aside his book, I worry I've made things too interesting. "Most manadas are multilingual, and English is the fastest growing second language."

"At least give us a clue," says Pablo. "Describe your home."

The word *home* conjures up El Retiro, and the life I'll never get back to. Ma, wherever she might be, and Perla, who must be worried sick. Our small, loving family has been shredded, and I don't know if the three of us will ever be together again. Yet here I am, enjoying myself while they're suffering, probably worried out of their minds—

"Are you okay?" asks Saysa.

"Let's back off our interrogation," says Tiago.

"What interrogation?" demands Pablo. "We only asked what manada she's from. It shouldn't be such a difficult question—"

"She doesn't owe you answers." Catalina jumping to my defense is shocking enough to jolt me out of my sad memories.

She turns to Saysa. "Ma asked if we would help her prepare the yerba for tomorrow's mate. We should go now."

"Sure," says Saysa, getting to her feet.

I sit up straight. If I leave now too, I can run up, grab my bag, and make a run for it—

"Tiago, would you walk Manu back?" asks Catalina, leaning down to plant a kiss on his cheek.

"I can walk alone," I say, looking away from them.

"Sure," he says. "Let me know when you're ready to go."

I cross my arms, determined to wait him out. Whenever he gets dessert, or someone distracts him, I'll leave without him noticing.

"So, Manu, what are you thinking about right now?" says Carlos, his intimate tone at odds with the public setting.

I stand before I can stop myself.

"I'm ready."

The doraditos buzz overhead as Tiago and I walk around to El Jardín's entrance. The sooner I get to the room, the quicker I can grab my things and get out of here, before curfew locks me in.

Entering the dimly lit setting, I'm no less awed by the spiraling marble staircase and glowing white flowers and majestic tree than I was last night. Not to mention my sapphire-eyed escort.

"I want to show you something," he says softly.

Even though there's no time to waste, I already know I don't want to leave without seeing whatever it is. So I follow Tiago to the center of the hall, our steps muffled by hundreds of fallen blancanieves, until we're up close to Flora.

Her trunk very subtly expands and contracts, almost like she's breathing. Her cracked bark betrays the countless lifetimes buried in her layers, and there's something almost sacred about being in her presence.

"I had a hard time when I first got here too," murmurs Tiago, his tone a mournful tune. "I missed home."

He rests a hand on the tree, and I spy the bark's texture smoothing out beneath his fingers. When he pulls away, the imprint of his hand remains.

"Geography lies," he says, and I move closer.

Tentatively, I rest my hand on Flora. Her bark feels like sunbaked sand. It melds to my touch, filling every line of my palm until we're completely connected.

My next breath is a whiff of almonds, with hints of zesty lemon.

For a moment, Ma and Perla don't seem that far away. And our small, loving family isn't broken.

Tiago insists on walking me to my door.

Probably in hopes of seeing Catalina, but I don't argue. I tell myself it's because the sooner we get there, the sooner I can run. And not because I'll take whatever time I can get with him.

"Can I ask you something?" he says as we climb the staircase. I spy his shoulders stiffening, like he's already anticipating friendly fire, and my gut hardens with apprehension.

"Catalina said I don't owe anyone answers," I remind him.

"You don't," he says quickly. "I was just curious—why was it weird when Javier kissed you this morning?"

I blink, the question not at all what I was expecting. I'd hoped I recovered quickly enough that no one noticed my reaction.

"Do you *like* him?" he presses.

There's a sudden lightness in my chest, and I burst into laughter, startling us both. What he's asking is just so *ordinary* that for a few breaths, things feel fractionally less harrowing.

I don't bother answering, but I'm still smiling when I open the door to the room—and the grin melts off my face.

Everything I own is strewn across my cot. Plastic packs of new shirts, socks, and underwear. Granola bars. Wads of human cash. A dozen blue bottles. My duffel lies open-mouthed and empty on the floor.

Saysa is perched on my roommate's bed, her body curled into itself like she wants no part in this.

"You have one chance to tell the truth," says Catalina, standing between me and my belongings. "Or I'm calling the Cazadores."

15

I feel Tiago's breath on my neck as he peers over my head to see what's going on.

There's no point trying to run because he's faster. So I step inside, and an instant later I hear the door click closed behind me.

When I draw a fresh breath, the air rots in my lungs.

"What's going on, Cata?" asks Tiago, a warm intimacy in his voice when he says her name.

She ignores him. "What manada are you from?" she asks me. "You have three seconds."

I need to come up with a sympathetic backstory, something that will make them *want* to help me. Harry grew up not knowing about the wizarding world because his parents were killed . . .

"One."

So he was raised by muggles who kept his own past from him and didn't let him learn the truth for himself—

"Two."

And he finally found a home at Hogwarts.

"Three. Time's up—"

"My parents died when I was a baby, and they left me in the care of a human!" I blurt.

"That's impossible." Catalina doesn't sound the slightest bit moved. "When a bruja crosses into human territory, her magic emits a trace that only Septimus can see. You would have been found by the Cazadores."

The red smoke. That's why I saw it.

She strides past me to the door. "Where are you going?" I ask, my voice quivering.

"I told you—I'm getting the Cazadores. *Move,*" she commands Tiago, and he hesitates, looking from her to Saysa for guidance. He avoids me completely.

If Catalina turns me in to the authorities, it's not just me they'll come after. I'll be putting Ma in more danger than ever.

"Maybe we should just talk to Jazmín," Saysa suggests, her voice lacking conviction. Tiago nods his agreement.

"And make my mom *complicit*?" snaps Catalina. "We need to do this ourselves."

My knees start to shake, and I suck in a deep breath. I can't outrun them, nor can I lie my way out of this.

Tiago steps away from the door, and Catalina reaches for the handle.

It's now or never.

"I was born in Argentina and raised in Miami."

Saying the words out loud, I realize it's as much of my identity as I can be certain of—even my species classification is unclear.

"Liar!" Spittle flies out of Catalina's mouth, and she looks a little mad. "I grew up here, and you're not from this manada!"

"I didn't say anything about a manada."

The stunned silence that follows is the longest moment of my life.

Throat parched, I confess the rest. "I'm the *thing* you were discussing at breakfast. A hybrid."

"What are you talking about?" asks Catalina impatiently.

"My mother is human . . . and my father is Fierro."

Saysa gasps. Tiago cuts across the room to sit next to her, like his legs might give out during this conversation. Only Catalina remains stoic.

Since I may not get another opportunity to tell my story, I barrel on. "In Argentina, my mom and Fierro were in love. They planned to run away before he disappeared. She was afraid his family would find out about me, so she brought me to Miami and raised me in secret."

The silence has grown thick enough to muffle the room's walls. It grows more deafening with every word they don't say, until finally, Saysa speaks.

"You know nothing about us? *Yourself?*"

I shake my head.

"Where's this human now?" demands Catalina in an unfeeling tone.

My heart pounds in my chest as I realize *this human* is a loose end to her. "She's being held somewhere," I say vaguely. "We're not in this country legally. I managed to get away, and I sensed this . . . *pull* . . . leading me here."

"More lies!" Catalina throws her arms in the air. "I've never met a worse liar. Looking past the bad performance, the facts are these: You couldn't have grown up outside our world, not even if you were *invisible*, because there's one time a month when you can't stay on Earth. *The full moon.*"

I jut my chin at the blue bottles.

"My mother would feed me three of those, and I'd sleep through it every month."

Now Catalina's face goes blank, and Saysa takes over. "That's what we do for underage Septimus who feel the stirrings of their magic before they turn thirteen," she says, her voice full of awe. "To get them through the physical pain of the full moon. We call the condition *lunaritis.*"

The last word makes it hard for me to breathe, much less speak.

Ma must've known what I am. She knew about the Septimus. More secrets she kept from me.

"What about mate?" presses Saysa.

It takes me a moment to hear her, then I shake my head. "Ours didn't taste like what I tried today. Was it drugged?"

"It's grown from a Lunaris plant," she explains. "As long as we consume it every day, we keep our abilities during the moon's other phases. We pick the seeds in Lunaris every full moon and plant them here."

That's why she kept asking me where I like to pick semillas.

I think back to what Catalina said—how a bruja emits a trace in the human world that only a Septimus can see. I may not have powers, but I definitely saw the red smoke. That has to mean something.

"But . . ." Saysa knits her brow, and she looks from Tiago to Catalina before finishing her thought out loud. "If you've never had mate, and you always sleep through the full moon, then . . . *you've never done magic.*"

I shake my head.

This silence is deeper than the one that came before.

Saysa won't look at me, but at least she doesn't keep me in suspense for long. "You can't access Lunaris without magic."

No.

Disappointment pangs in my chest. I don't know how my heart could have harbored so much hope when I only just learned that place is real a few hours ago. And yet any chance of finding Fierro vanishes with her words.

Lunaris will forever be what it's always been for me—a dream.

It's not like I was planning to stick around anyway, I tell myself. I have to get back to Ma and Perla. I don't belong here.

"That's irrelevant because she was never going to make it there," says Catalina, like she's reading my mind. "If we don't turn her in to the Cazadores immediately, we'll be charged as accomplices."

"Please," I plead, my insides twisting with desperation. "I know you don't owe me anything, but I'm begging you not to do this. I've spent my whole life locked up, without knowing the truth about myself. I just want a chance to figure out where I belong."

Instead of begging them to let me go, I hear myself begging them to let me stay. Shame sears my skin and burns my eyes. I felt exposed from the moment I saw my stuff strewn on the cot, but now I feel like I've handed over something I'll never get back.

"What happens on the full moon when we all go to Lunaris?" asks Catalina. "Or during training tomorrow when you can't do magic? Or the next day? You're going to get caught, and if we don't turn you in now, you'll take us down with you!"

I don't beg her again.

Not because I'm too proud—*I'm not*—but because that's not anger sharpening her voice. It's fear. For her friends who are her family. I can't ask them to risk everything for me. Besides, she's right—I shouldn't be here. I should be with Ma.

If Catalina is determined to turn me in, I'll have to make a run for it. Tiago could easily catch me, but maybe his sister will feel enough sympathy to ask him to buy me some time—

"Let's help her."

I think I fantasized Saysa's voice, but then I watch her lips move again. "We just need to awaken Manu's magic—"

"Do you even understand what kind of trouble we'll be in?" Catalina snaps. "The trouble our families will be in? Tiago, talk to your sister—"

"If we help her catch up, at least she won't be defenseless," insists Saysa, crossing her arms like she's not going to budge.

"Let's say she awakens her magic," says Catalina, and from her calmer tone, it's clear she's testing a new tactic. "Then what? She doesn't exist in our records. My mom specifically asked me to keep an eye on her, which means she's not going to drop this. Not to mention," she adds, rounding on me, "she's a *terrible* liar!"

"We can fill her in on everything she needs to know," Saysa goes on.

"She can't even answer the basic question of what manada she's from—"

"So we'll craft her backstory."

"And when we get to Lunaris, we can use her to find Fierro." Tiago's musical voice disinfects the stuffy air, like rain driving away smoke.

His words have an obvious effect on Catalina. Even Saysa. The three of them exchange glances, communicating a secret. I don't like that he suggested they use me, but if it gets Catalina to let me stay, I'll go along with their plan.

Besides, I want to find Fierro even more than they do.

"Fine," says Catalina at last. "But if we're breaking Septimus law, your education begins *now*."

Tiago and Saysa return to their rooms for the nightly curfew inspection, and the tension tautens as soon as I'm left alone with Catalina. She doesn't so much as look my way as I pack my things back inside my duffel.

Señora Lupe knocks lightly on our door, then opens it. "Good night, ladies," she says, poking her head in. She's wrapped her Afro in a silky red fabric. "Manu, get some rest. Let's see how you feel in the morning."

"Thank you."

We wait a few minutes, then Catalina grips the door handle and opens it. "How'd you do that?" I whisper, remembering when I tried to get out last night. "It was locked—"

"Don't worry about it."

Halfway down the hall, Saysa is already outside her door, waiting for us. I guess they both have a master key. We hurry toward the stairs, but I throw my arm out.

"Wait," I whisper, concentrating on the faint murmur of voices until they grow clearer.

"She didn't participate?" asks Jazmín.

"No," says Señora Lupe. *"You might be right about trouble at home. What do you want to do?"*

My heart pounds my chest.

"Just keep me updated."

"Will do."

When I can't hear any more, I say, "Okay. Let's go."

Catalina looks at me like I just wasted her time, but Saysa seems impressed. We spiral up to the guys' floor, and Catalina opens the door to Tiago's room. He comes out instantly.

"Hey, where are you—"

Pablo's question cuts off as the door shuts. The rooms must be soundproof because I can't hear anything else.

When we get to the balcony, Flora extends a branch to us, like she's complicit in our plans. Then again, Saysa's lime eyes are bright, so maybe the tree was just obeying her magic.

Tiago leaps the length of the bough, and the rest of us scurry across as quickly as we can. Inside, the book spines begin to reshuffle themselves.

I move toward the closest shelf and peek at the titles popping up: *A History of Septimus, Looking at Lunaris, Tribunal Trials & Tribulations*. The tree seems to be both library and librarian—it's producing the texts we need.

There are words etched into the ceiling: *In Lunaris we were born, and to Lunaris we return*. And the question I've been dying to ask spills out of me: "Where's Lunaris?"

"It's another dimension that's only accessible at the full moon," says Saysa.

"Give her the *abridged* history," says Catalina as she examines a shelf of books and pulls down texts. They fall soundlessly to the cushiony ground.

"Right," says Saysa. "Let's sit." We cross our legs on the ground, facing each other. "A long time ago, seven demons ruled over Lunaris. The youngest was Tao, and he was a troublemaker who had a penchant for wanting what he couldn't have—"

"No time for color," Catalina tosses over her shoulder. "Skip to the point."

Tiago is at the other end of the space, his face buried in a black book whose title is obscured. He doesn't seem to want any part in this plan, even though he was the one who made it possible.

"Fine," says Saysa, her words speeding up. "One day, Tao discovered a window into Earth's mortal dimension, and he fell in love with a human named Kerana. So he broke through the barrier between worlds to have her, creating a bridge to this realm every full moon."

"What happened to Kerana?"

"He violated and impregnated her."

I flinch. It sounds like one of those Zeus myths, and it's hard to believe it's actual history. "I thought Kerana was a place in Argentina?"

"It is. That's our capital city and where most of our population lives. It's named after our Mother."

"What happened to Tao?"

"Turns out that by coming here, he became mortal. Kerana's people killed him. They thought the whole episode was over then, but his blood stained the land with a curse. Kerana gave birth to male septuplets, and the seventh son was born a werewolf."

"And from then on, all seventh consecutive sons were born wolves and seventh consecutive daughters witches," I finish for her.

Saysa, Catalina, and even Tiago stare at me, and I mumble, "There's a myth in the human world about that."

"Well, what isn't *myth* is what those human monsters did to the earliest members of our species," says Catalina through gritted teeth.

"They were scared," says Saysa more sympathetically. "Our powers manifest on the first full moon of our thirteenth year—that's when wolves first transform and witches feel their magic. For the first of us, our human parents didn't understand what was happening. Many thought their children had been possessed by demons."

The first full moon of our thirteenth year—that's when I got my first period.

"Eventually, the surviving Septimus banded together to form the first manada. They looked and felt human most of the month, but the full moon awakened their Lunaris side, and they'd lose themselves to their magic. Many died because their mortal bodies couldn't conduct that much power. They continued to seek out other seventh children, until they gathered enough Septimus to harness their energies and lift the curse from the land, ending the transformation of seventh children. But they couldn't cure themselves."

"Wait," I say, frowning. "Does that mean any seventh consecutive sons and daughters born today are human?"

She nods.

"So, how are the Septimus still around?"

"When the first pair reproduced, their child was born cursed. It's a condition we carry in our blood. That's how our species originated."

"What happened next?" I ask eagerly. I've always been a voracious reader, and this is quite the story.

"Our ancestors located the bridge Tao had opened to Lunaris. They realized that as children of two worlds, the only way to strike the balance our powers require is to honor our dual heritages. That's why every full moon we return to Lunaris."

"The full moon is the only time we can go?"

She nods. "It's too dangerous a place to live year-round. Most of us wouldn't survive. Besides, Septimus younger than thirteen can't make the crossing because they haven't come into their magic yet, and we can't just abandon them here."

So, I'm a stunted Septimus. At nearly seventeen, I'm essentially a prepubescent witch.

Saysa is staring at me hard, and just when it starts to get uncomfortable, she says, "No wonder your eyes are such a unique color."

"What do you mean?"

"Well, wolves inherit their mother's eyes, but a bruja's eye color is determined by her element. Red and black shades are Encendedoras, blue and gray are Congeladoras, pink and purple are Invocadoras, and Jardineras have shades of green and brown. Your eyes are just golden enough to pass off as a super light, bright shade of brown—but they're really something else."

I want to ask what kind of magic she thinks I might have, if my eyes don't exactly fit one of the elements. But what comes out instead is, "What do you know about Fierro?"

"I think that's enough for today."

Catalina's tone is final. Her eyes glow bright pink, and all the books rise into the air at once and shelve themselves.

Neither sibling objects, so we cross the branch back into El Jardín. Tiago plants a kiss on Catalina's forehead before peeling away from us. I wish he would look at me or say something, but all I get is his arm brushing my dress on his way past.

Then again, I don't exactly know how I feel about him after he told the others they should use me for their own ends.

My dress feels heavier where he touched it, and when I peek down, I spy something in my pocket. I don't dare look until I'm in bed, and the pink glow of Catalina's eyes has faded to darkness.

Only then do I sit up and slip my hand into the dress pocket, pulling out a black book.

Finding Fierro.

It's my second sleepless night. But after my sixty-hour lunaritis coma, my body should have enough rest stored to tide me over.

I leaf through Tiago's book until daybreak. According to the text, *Fierro* was a moniker used by "a nonconforming Septimus" who wanted to "change the way things work." My dad believed brujas and lobizones to be equals and lobbied for more brujas to join the tribunal, the Septimus' governing body. He also believed Septimus should come out of hiding and live alongside humans.

Apparently, he was the first of the species to start supplying humans with Septis. He believed that if the Septimus knew a way to lessen another species' suffering, the merciful thing was to share it. Sects of his followers have continued the practice in his absence.

"He was famous for carving his symbol wherever he went to stoke hope in his followers."

I read the line over and over and over.

Ma told me Dad used to mark things with an *F* so the place would be changed by his presence. *Fierro really is my father.*

I thought I believed it before, but it was more that I *wanted* to believe. Even though the timing and circumstances lined up, I still didn't know for sure. Until now.

The book illustrates how Fierro's symbol looks like an *F*, but it's not. It's really two characters combined into one, just like the Septimus symbol.

The *F* is a pair of sevens that are facing forward instead of looking back. It was his way of saying things needed to change.

The mystery of where he went is what shot Fierro to legendary status. Tribunal executions are public and rare, and some speculate he was killed in secret to avoid making him a martyr. Others think he ran off with his human lover and the Cazadores are still hunting them. But the author of this book believes, like Pablo, that Fierro learned how to survive year-round in Lunaris. There are still Septimus who go on search parties for him there every full moon.

I shut the book, suddenly feeling determined to awaken my magic so I can travel to Lunaris and find him.

Ma clearly brought us to Miami to search for him, and now it's my turn to finish the job. My gaze drifts to the stars, thinking of where she might be and how she's doing. I hope Julieta's taking care of her.

If I'm really going to stay here—which is a big *if*—I need to find a way to get word to Ma and Perla. I have to know they're okay. And they need to know the same about me.

When I open the book again, a note slips out from between the pages. I unfold the paper to find a message written in tidy blue lettering.

Ma told me she named me after an Argentine lullaby about a turtle named *Manuelita* who leaves home one day and loses sight of herself, but who eventually finds her way back.

Tiago wrote exactly three words, but they're the perfect three:

Welcome home, Manuelita.

16

By the time Catalina wakes up, I'm bathed and dressed. She doesn't direct a word to me, so it's a relief when Saysa shows up and lightens the tension.

"How are you?" she asks, perching on the cot beside me.

"Better," I say, and I know it's true because the knot in my chest from yesterday is less taut. For the first time, I'm able to be myself around someone outside my family—at least, in this room and Flora's library.

"You sure you want to go through with this?" asks Saysa, and Catalina stops brushing her hair to hear my answer.

I debated leaving all night. I counted down the hours until dawn, waiting to hear the click of the door unlocking.

I know the smart thing to do would be to run before I'm discovered—but I also know that even if I make it back to civilization, nothing will have changed.

I can't help Ma.

I can't even help myself.

Whatever the government—American or Septimus—I'm always powerless. I'm always missing something crucial, like papers or the right eye color or *magic*.

As the first finger of sunlight poked through a crack in the curtains, a new idea took hold. If Saysa's right that my magic is blocked, and by spending time here, my powers will awaken, then once I'm a witch, I can keep us safe.

I see their faces now. Not just Ma and Perla, but Julieta, and the patient with the baby, and all the others.

When I get my magic, I'll save them all.

"Absolutely," I say, holding Saysa's gaze.

Catalina looks away in annoyance, but Saysa examines me closely. "You definitely look ready to work. Another long night?"

"There'll be time to sleep once I find my magic," I say, trying to call up some of Ma's obstinate optimism. And at the thought of her, I ask the question that's been nagging at me all night: "If you guys are a secret, then how come humans know about the curse on seventh children, and that guys are werewolves and girls are witches, and even about a secret city named Kerana?"

"That's how our earliest ancestors were able to get the word out to other seventh children that there was a place for them. So they wouldn't lose hope," says Saysa. "If they found Kerana, they would be safe. The stories sounded childish, so humans wouldn't believe them, but they weren't for their ears anyway. They were meant for Septimus children. Only those with supernatural senses could find our home."

So it's not all that strange that Ma or Perla would have heard about Kerana. But did they know I was one of those lost children?

"I'm starving," says Catalina, herding us toward the door. Before I cross the threshold, her pink glare is in my face. "*Not a word* about any of this once we leave this room. We don't discuss anything until tonight in Flora. Understood?"

I nod.

When we get to Flora's crown for breakfast, I'm bummed to see Tiago isn't with the group.

It's only because I was hoping to discuss the Fierro book with him. Not because in one day his smile has already replaced rooftop sunrises as my favorite way to start the day.

When the mate makes its way to me, I take a few sips without complaint. The headrush is the same as yesterday, the mate pulling at me like it's dragging me down a drain in the depths of my brain, and I try to think past the drugged sensation.

I doubt I'll ever get used to this.

Instead of having class inside Flora, today Señora Lupe leads us out of El Jardín altogether. We pass the rectangular building with the crumbling corner, and I scan the guys' faces for Tiago, but I don't see him. We keep marching to the square edifice that's covered in flowers of every color.

As we approach it, I notice the walls are made of a hard spongy material, like porous stone, and the flowers are blooming out through the crevices. Their stems seem to be planted inside the structure.

"For the new transfers, this is the bruja training house. We call it La Catedral."

I become aware of a persistent thrumming sound, and when the doors open, I see the source: Rain is pouring down inside.

The walls are obscured by a thatchwork of overlapping foliage that makes the plants of Lunaris look tame. The floor is overgrown with grass, and there are clouds blanketing the ceiling.

Ahead of me, the witches enter in pairs of like elements. Two by two, the brujas in purple or pink dresses erect force fields that protect them from the droplets. The brujas in shades of blue or gray redirect the rain so it falls around them. Any drops that touch the brujas dressed in red or black fizzle into steam.

Saysa links her arm through mine and pulls me forward with her. "Try to call that yellow flower to you," she murmurs in my ear, and I look at the umbrella-like blossom. I concentrate on the flower, scrunching my forehead and trying to force the plant to obey me—

Come here.

Come here, please.

Would you please come here?

Suddenly, the yellow flower and its blue neighbor pull away from the wall, and Saysa and I step under their protection. When I look at her, Saysa's eyes are alight. She's doing the spellwork for both of us.

I keep my gaze downcast so the teacher can't see that I'm not doing magic, and we cross into the next room, where it's not raining. The flowers Saysa summoned retreat.

I don't think we're indoors anymore.

We're in what looks like a meadow that's bordered by mismatched foliage. On one side is a cool forest of tall, thick trees, and on the other is a humid swamp with wiry trees that have thin trunks and high roots.

"When we're in Lunaris, the wolves help us hunt for ingredients," says Señora Lupe once everyone is gathered. "Often the most powerful herbs grow from the most dangerous soil, and the wolves escorting us can only buy us a short window of time to find what we need. So today's lesson will be timed.

"You won't know how long you have. As soon as I say *begin*, start filling your baskets with the most useful plants you can find. *Begin!*"

The brujas reach for the pile of baskets stacked on the ground, and they scramble away to explore the two landscapes available. I stare at the vivi warily as I pick up a basket, and its ribbon-like body unfurls and tightens, like it's stretching after a long slumber.

I hurry to keep up with Saysa through the forest, pausing to pluck the same things she gets. Red leaves, black flowers, fuzzy silver plant stems—

My vivi opens its wide jaws, and before I can stop it, the white ribbon shreds everything I collected.

"No!" I cry out, too late. All that's left are scraps of red, black, and silver debris.

"No cheating," trills Señora Lupe, looking at me. "I know this place can feel intimidating, but this training is for your own good. Trust yourself."

I feel the heat flushing my cheeks, and I nod sheepishly. I can't bring myself to meet Saysa's gaze, so I leave her side to explore deeper into the woods.

I don't know who else heard Señora Lupe's admonishment, and I don't want to know what they think of me now. Between yesterday's freak-out and today's cheating, I'm not exactly being as inconspicuous as I'd hoped.

I cut in a different direction and wade through a passage of giant, feathery leaves that look like elephant ears, their soft edges brushing my face and blocking my view. When my vision clears, I'm on a small grassy trail that cuts between black-leafed trees.

I've been here before.

These are the weeping woods that can cry up storms. I'm

always wary here in my dreams because their sadness storms can bring out Sombras. One attached itself to me once, and it was the coldest sensation I've ever felt. Not just a physical cold, but the kind of chill that freezes the heart. A life-sucking frostiness I never want to feel again.

I remember thinking I'd never be able to shake it off, until I fell on a field of pointy plants that give off heat. The funny-looking foliage was red at the roots and black at the tips, like it'd been charred, and it had a soothing effect that repelled the Sombra.

I search for that plant by the trees' roots, trying to forget how hollow the Sombra's hopelessness felt. The cold cut so deep that I was scared to take my blue pills the following full moon. But that wasn't my worst experience in the dream-world.

That honor goes to the time my dream didn't end at the Citadel, but in a stone mountain. My only lunaritis *nightmare*.

The trail grows so dark ahead that I turn around. I'm not sure if there are Sombras here, since we're not technically in Lunaris, but I also don't want to risk finding out. So I head back toward the elephant ears, and just as I pass the last black-leafed tree, I spot something by its roots. A small patch of red-and-black.

I duck and pluck out a leaf, tucking it into my basket. The vivi curves down and inspects it, and I brace myself for another attack—but it winds itself back around the handle without devouring the plant.

"Time!"

At the sound of Señora Lupe's voice, I make my way back to the meadow, my basket embarrassingly light. I should have just grabbed any leaves at random to fill it up.

Everyone forms a circle around our teacher, and though

Saysa waves me over, I stay where I am, between a pair of water witches.

"Excellent, Saysa," says Señora Lupe as she inspects her basket. "Yappas are extremely powerful herbs for brewing truth potions. We're lucky they grow well in El Laberinto's soil, since most manadas have to pick them in Lunaris."

Truth potions.

The phrase sends a chill down my spine. For all the damage that could cause me, it might as well be poison.

"Noemí, in all this time you only found four samples?"

"I was trying to be selective—"

"You mean you were too busy trading gossip with Bibi." Señora Lupe stares Noemí down until the latter's gaze drops. "Remember, this training isn't just about you. We're a community, and that's why you get evaluated as a class, not individuals. When you don't do your best, you're letting down your family."

My heart sinks to the floor as Lupe approaches me and peeks into my basket. Then I look up when she lifts the red-and-black leaf for everyone to see.

"How did you find this?"

"It—" I'm so parched the word creaks out, and I cough to clear my throat. "It was by the roots of the black trees."

"Have you used it in a potion or salve before?"

I think of the effect it had on the Sombra that attacked me and chance, "It's good for depression."

"Precisely," she says, to my great shock and relief. "This plant is called a Felifuego, and it is the only cure we have for the postpartum depression every bruja undergoes after giving birth. As you all know," she says, surveying each of us, "a bruja can only give birth two or three times in her lifetime, and after each baby is born, she loses her abilities. It's believed to be part of Tao's curse, a punishment for Kerana's lineage of daughters."

She turns to me again. "The tribunal commands that every fertile bruja have children, for if we stop reproducing, our species will die out. If not for this plant's healing ability, many of us would never regain our magic." She measures me for a long moment, and I feel every other set of eyes burning through my skin's outer layer. "Felifuego is notoriously hard to spot, so often we must depend on the wolves to locate it for us. Only a true Jardinera could sense its presence. *Excellent* work, Manuela."

Only now do I let myself venture a look in Saysa's direction, hoping to find I've made her proud. But she's frowning back at me. Beside her, Catalina looks livid.

I don't get an explanation until much later, when we're back in Flora's library. Tiago hasn't been around all day, but I've been holding out hope he'll show up now.

"Attention is *not* a good thing for you!" Catalina snaps the instant the three of us are alone. "What were you thinking, showing off like that?"

"I wasn't—"

"You have no idea what you just did," she goes on, shaking her head. "You marked yourself as a witch to watch. A Septimus with promise. That is exactly what you *don't* want. As soon as my mother hears about this, she's going to be even *more* interested in you than before. I can't believe while we're risking our necks for you, you're pulling this shit!"

Even though I know she's right, Catalina's insistence that I hold back reminds me of Ma, and how small she's inadvertently made me feel my whole life. "So I'm just supposed to be nothing forever?" I snap.

I don't know whom I'm madder at—Catalina or Ma or the world.

"I'm not exactly new to this whole hiding thing, you know. Believe it or not, my legal status defines me in the human world too. And while not having a life may have kept me safe from your Cazadores and the American government, it hasn't kept me alive in any of the ways that count."

I suck in my breath, embarrassed to have revealed that much, but Catalina just starts yanking texts off the shelves and ignores me. Saysa wends deeper into the stacks, and I know she hears me following her because I'm not quiet about it. Still, she studies the spines for an extra-long moment before addressing me.

"How did you know about the Felifuego?"

Her voice is casual, but I catch a hint of cautiousness that could be anything from distrust to rivalry.

"Every full moon, when I take the blue pills, I dream of Lunaris. Only I didn't know that's what it was."

Saysa stares at me with open curiosity now. "It's the same with us. We dream about that realm until we turn thirteen. That's when we can finally visit it."

I don't want to dwell on the fact that for me Lunaris will always be just a dream, so I keep talking. "I remembered one time when a Sombra attached itself to me, and I was only able to get away after falling into a patch of those plants."

Her dark eyebrows arc up. "How do you know we call them Sombras?"

"I-I don't. That's just how I think of them in my dreams."

"That's good," she says, her tone growing eager and shedding its suspicious notes. "Information travels through the air in Lunaris. This means you have the ability to access that dimension, and you're vulnerable to its magic—we just have to figure out what's blocking you."

It's the first bit of encouragement I've gotten, and I feel a warm lightness that I haven't felt this keenly in too long, not even when I was living with Ma and Perla.

Hope.

"Do you think the Felifuego could help awaken my magic?" I ask.

"It doesn't work that way. If it did, we would use it to awaken every child's abilities before they turn thirteen. But the first time you access your powers, you have to do it on your own."

Damn.

"Tonight I want to consult some exercises to see if we can stretch your magical muscles," says Saysa, turning back to the titles she was investigating: *Keepers of Earth's Secrets, Reconnecting with Your Element, Earthly Delights.*

Now that she's not looking at me, I muster the courage to ask about *him.* "So, where was your brother today?"

"He and Cata graduate this year, and the Cazadores are gunning for them to enlist," she says as she leafs through one of the manuscripts. "They assume if he joins, she'll follow him." Her voice sharpens, and I can't blame her. Catalina deserves more credit than that.

"He was excused from training today to tour their local station, which is a big deal because they only do that for very few recruits."

"What exactly are the Cazadores?"

"In human terms, they're like our law enforcement and army and intelligence agencies combined."

"You study human affairs?" I ask in surprise.

"And math and science and literature and history—pretty much all our academics are completed by thirteen, when our powers come in. After that, we train in our talents until we're eighteen. The more prestigious the academy, the more likely the Cazadores will notice you, especially if you're a lobizón."

She must see the question mark in my expression because she explains, "Guys outnumber girls four to one. But last year a bruja from this academy got recruited. Her name is Yamila. She's the youngest Cazadora in history, and every time she breaks a record, she brings us all closer to change."

"Do you think Tiago is going to join?" I ask, shivering at the thought of Tiago having to hunt me down one day.

"Depends on what Cata does."

My stomach sinks a little. "So the Cazadores got it wrong, and it's he who'll follow her?"

"Truth is, he's generally paralyzed with indecision," admits Saysa. "He's good at leading others, but when it comes to his own life, he's a mess. The Cazadores aren't the only ones after him. Every Septibol team in the pro league is trying to recruit him, and some of the most prominent manadas in Kerana are offering him positions of power to lure him to their communities. But Tiago has never known what he wants. He has this tendency of just stumbling into things and discovering he's a natural. Sports, academics, music, whatever it is, he makes having talent look like a burden—"

She looks up suddenly from the book she's been flipping through, catching herself. "Sorry, forget I said all that. He'll be back tomorrow. Read this section here." She twists the text around so it's facing me.

I stare down at the page, but the words blur as I mull over everything Saysa just said. I used to dream of having a sibling, a lifelong friend and partner in adventures. But I never considered how it might feel if they went with me everywhere and constantly outshined me. Or if I had to compete with them not just for my parents' affection, but also my best friend's.

Catalina slams an open book down on top of the one I'm supposed to be reading.

"This!" she hisses. "This is what happens if you stand out!"

Unlike the other manuscripts here, this book is small and the yellowing paper smells of decay. I narrow my gaze to bring the letters into focus, and Saysa comes closer to read too.

Offspring between a Septimus and a human being are so rare as to be near impossible. There are only two recorded cases in history:

The first was a witch who was impregnated by a man in 1825. Both she and the offspring died during childbirth. The man was never identified.

The second was a wolf who impregnated a woman in 1933. Both the Septimus and the human were sentenced to execution by the tribunal, and the offspring was stillborn.

My stomach turns, and I feel the blood draining from my face as I reach the final sentence on the page:

In their ruling, the tribunal asserted that had it lived, the hybrid would have suffered its parents' fate.

17

My third sleepless night. This is like a reverse lunaritis.

In the morning we have class inside Flora again, and as soon as we get there, I know Catalina was right. I overreached.

Jazmín is already waiting for us, her dress blending in with the grove of gigantic, purple-leafed trees.

"Señora Jazmín will be supervising our training today," says Señora Lupe, and Catalina casts me a superior look.

I'm screwed.

"We're holding class in here because we're expecting lobizón visitors—"

A pair of wolves enter the grove right as she's announcing them. Even though they're dressed like the other guys, there's something cop-like about their gait.

"Here they are!" The officers don't return her smile. "This isn't anything to be alarmed by. The Cazadores are going to check your Huellas to make sure everyone here was properly processed, then we can begin class."

Jazmín's piercing purple gaze is staring right at me. I don't think it's strayed since I arrived.

"Please line up," says Lupe, and the class files into a row. Catalina, Saysa, and I hold up the rear.

The Cazadores call the first bruja forward. She pulls out a thin booklet from her dress pocket, and an officer holds it up to her face like he's comparing her likeness, then he flips through it and skims the pages. When he's finished, he hands it back to her, and she returns to the line.

They then call up the next bruja, and so on. I glimpse down at Saysa's skirt, and I spot the lime green booklet peeking from her pocket.

I can still feel Jazmín's stare scorching my skull, so I slide my hand in my pocket and pretend there's something in there.

The next two girls are called forward, and my skin grows hot and itchy, my vision blurring. I close my eyes to calm down, and I'm back on El Retiro's rooftop as the black SUV pulls up outside our building.

Racing downstairs, I can hear the agents entering the stairwell on the ground floor.

I'm out of breath as I burst in on Ma and Perla in the kitchen.

"ICE is here!"

"It's okay," I hear someone whisper.

I open my eyes, and I realize I'm trembling. The Cazadores have already gotten a third of the way through the line. I don't know if it's my heart or my head doing the pounding.

"Manu," says Saysa, and I realize she's been speaking to me. When I look at her, her voice drops out, and she's more mouthing than whispering.

"Just say you left yours in your room," she mouths.

But I can't speak or move. I can barely breathe. I close my eyes again to try to focus on my inhales—

Ma drops to the floor and rolls under Perla's bed. When it's my turn, I look at Perla and say, "They can't come through our door without a warrant—"

"You don't know what they can't do."

The look of fear in her frosted gaze reflects how I feel. The horror of it all.

I'll never outrun the monsters.

Like Ma and Perla, I'll live in fear forever.

The pain in my hand snaps me back to the present, and when I open my eyes, the Cazadores are two-thirds of the way through. Saysa is squeezing my fingers.

"Are you okay?" she mouths at me.

I can feel the sheen of sweat on my face, and I know she can tell my hands are clammy. Then a third Cazador enters the grove.

It's Leather Jacket.

My knees grow shaky as I watch him greet Señora Lupe. I gape at Saysa in wide-eyed alarm, unable to break through my paralysis, and she looks as petrified as I feel. She whips around to Catalina and whispers, "Do something!"

Catalina is equally ashen-faced and wide-eyed, but to her credit, she swallows her feelings and a mask of calm falls over her features. Then she strides up to her mother and speaks in her haughtiest tone. "I need to talk to you right now."

"It will have to wait."

"You're never here for me when I need you. It's always about your students and never about me. Fine, then—I'll just go to your office and call Dad."

Jazmín's face snaps to her daughter's like she just said the magic word. "Come here," she says in a deadly tone, and she leads Catalina away from our ears, deeper into the purple trees.

Just a handful of witches separate me from the officers. Saysa is going to be called up within moments. And with Jazmín pulled away and Leather Jacket distracted by our teacher, this is my only chance.

I step back from the line, bending my knees so I can lower my height and hide behind the others. I keep my gaze on the Cazadores' faces as I retreat, and when the two of them are looking down at someone's Huella, I slip behind the nearest tree trunk.

I keep moving back, going from one tree to the next, until I'm safely ensconced in the misty woods. I hear two voices whispering, and I cock my head so I can pick up on Catalina and Jazmín's conversation.

"Have you gone through her things yet?"

"This isn't exactly spy school, Ma."

"You want to be a Cazadora, don't you? Think of this as a chance to prove you're just as good as Yamila."

"What is *that* supposed to mean?" There's real hurt in Catalina's tone, more than I thought her capable of feeling. I remember Saysa said Yamila is some hot shot Cazadora who went to school here. It sounds like she can count Jazmín in her fan club.

"I expected you to be smarter than this," says Jazmín, either ignoring or not hearing her daughter's pain. "She wasn't registered as a transfer, and the manada name she gave me was a lie. Not to mention all the Septis bottles she had in her bag. *There's a reason she's here, and you need to find it.*"

I frown. I never mentioned my manada. I only lied to Jazmín about my last name.

"If you want answers so badly, why don't you ask your beloved *Yamila* to investigate her?"

"Because *you're* my daughter, and I believe in you. Now show me I'm right to place so much faith in you."

I hurry back before they spot me, tree by tree, until I'm behind the trunk closest to Saysa. The line of students has disbanded, so it looks like everyone's been accounted for.

I slip out quickly and pop up next to Saysa.

"Excited for practice," she says to me at random, her voice a few notches higher than usual. "It's been great having you come watch. I hope you don't mind us dragging you each time. But who knows, maybe you'll like it and want to join the team . . ."

She keeps rattling off random bits of nonsense, like that's somehow going to help us blend in better.

I let her blabber on while I watch Jazmín regroup with the Cazadores, noting her disappointment when they tell her everyone checked out. She turns to Leather Jacket, and I concentrate on what they're saying.

"But, Nacho—"

"It's fine," he says, kissing her on the cheek in a way that's meant to come off as polite but is obviously patronizing. "If there's anything we need to know, Yamila will tell us."

By dinnertime, I'm too nauseated to eat. I can see now why Catalina was so hesitant to help me—what we're trying to pull off is impossible. Any moment, someone could ask to see my Huella, and then what?

Not to mention that conversation I overheard her having with Jazmín. Catalina didn't say anything to Saysa and me when she regrouped with us, but she was definitely quieter than she's been around me. Like she's mulling over whether it would be worth exposing me to gain her mother's approval.

After all, their plan to use me to find Fierro is looking less probable by the day; I'm no closer to making a flower bend to my will than I am to becoming a US citizen.

Everyone else is already sitting on the grass eating their meals, but I'm just staring at the milanesas on the cooking stones, holding an empty plate. Too distraught to eat, I spin around to head back to the room, when a flash of sapphire stuns me.

"How are you?" asks Tiago, his face a salve for any ailment.

Even I can admit the eager way we're absorbing each other is inappropriate. It's like we've been apart a year, not a day.

"She's *fine*," says Catalina, who's suddenly at our side. She cuts between us and reaches for a cob of corn. "Your sister and I are fine too."

"Sorry," he says, reaching out for her. But she sidesteps his embrace and rejoins the group a few feet away.

Tiago stuffs his hands in his shorts' pockets and flashes me a sheepish grin. "How's life on Pluto?"

"Thawing . . . *marginally.*"

"So, more Neptunish now?"

I didn't expect him to know that's the next coldest planet, and he can tell he surprised me because his smirk widens.

"How was the recruitment?" I'm only trying to make polite conversation, but the good humor fades from Tiago's features.

He doesn't answer me, and we're much quieter by the time we join the group. In fact, the four of us barely say a word through dinner. It's like the air between us has been hardening with all the words we're swallowing.

So the instant we get to Flora, our feelings boil over.

"I don't know how much *she* told you during your little chat tonight," Catalina says to Tiago, "but yesterday she decided to show off by finding a fucking Felifuego!"

"Wow," says Tiago, and I feel myself swelling with pride from the way he looks at me. "How—?"

"And as a result," Catalina goes on, raising her volume, "*my mother called the Cazadores.*" Her pink eyes are nearly bulging out of her head. "I still have no idea how we didn't get caught."

I wait for her to add something about the private conversation she and her mom had, but she doesn't.

"I can't be the only one who gets how serious this is," she says in a heavy tone. "If she's found, the tribunal will have her *executed.* And what do you think will happen to *us* for being accomplices?"

"What exactly are you saying we should do?" asks Saysa.

Catalina opens her mouth then closes it, like she's rethinking her answer. Instead, she turns to me. "Is this *really* where you think you belong?"

The question stabs me in the gut.

I already knew she didn't like me, but seeing how hard she's trying not to outright ask me to leave sucks. I thought since she helped me in class today, she might be starting to warm up—but it seems her support had more to do with not wanting to alienate Saysa.

"She belongs." This time it's not Saysa but Tiago saying it.

"And what if she never manifests magic?" Catalina shoots back. "*Everyone* will know her secret in a few weeks when she can't access Lunaris!" Her voice takes on a tinge of panic, and I almost feel sorry for her.

So I say what needs to be said.

"If I haven't accessed my magic by the full moon, I'll leave."

Silence meets my words. No one argues because they know there's no other way.

"You'll have to run far," says Catalina, and I don't know if that's a threat or a warning. Either way, she's right.

So I look her in the eye and vow, "You'll never see me again."

Ten days pass, and still no magic.

By now all of us have lost hope—except Tiago.

"It'll happen," he says when, for the dozenth time, I can't summon a limb of blancanieves to bend toward me.

"No, it won't," sings Catalina under her breath from the other end of the library.

Saysa doesn't speak, same as last night. Something's shifted in her, and I can't blame her. I honestly don't know how Tiago can still be so optimistic. It's obvious I'm a lost cause.

"Try again," he says, and I sigh, too tired to argue. It's been almost two weeks now that we've been meeting in Flora, with the three of them taking turns testing my magic and drilling me on Septimus facts.

Catalina is worried it's only a matter of time before her mom springs another surprise on us because she's been so quiet since the day she called the Cazadores. She's convinced the longer it takes her mom to strike, the greater the danger.

"Midnight," says Catalina, slamming a book shut. "We said we'd cut things early tonight for tomorrow's practice."

"We can do half an hour more," says Tiago.

"It's just two weeks until the final, *Captain*," she shoots back. He scowls but doesn't disagree.

Catalina sends all the books soaring back to the shelves, and the three of them march to the opening.

Saysa is the first to realize I'm not with them, and she sweeps her green gaze to me. "Manu? What is it?"

"I'm . . . seventeen."

Midnight means it's my birthday. The first one I'm spending without Ma.

The urge to communicate with Ma and Perla flares stronger than ever. This past week, I used every chance I got to scour El Laberinto for signs of phones or computers or mailboxes. I need to know what's going on with them—and they need to hear from me.

I've flirted with asking Saysa for help, but she's been so withdrawn these past few days that I haven't mustered the courage.

"Happy birthday," says Tiago, his smile lighting up the dimness.

"¡Feliz cumpleaños!" Saysa throws her arms around me in an unexpected hug. I'm relieved, since it seemed like she'd pulled away from me.

Catalina doesn't say anything until we're in bed with the lights off. Then I hear her faint whisper, "Que la luz de la luna te bendiga."

May you be blessed by the moonlight.

I wonder if that's what Septimus say on someone's birthday.

It seems like I've only just fallen asleep when I feel a warm pressure on my arm. My eyes fly open, and I look into a pair of glowing green orbs as bright as sunlit grass. Saysa brings her finger to her closed lips and mouths: "Get dressed."

I sit up and reach for the dress draped at the end of my cot, but she shakes her head. "Human clothes."

I knit my eyebrows and raise my shoulders questioningly, but she just gestures with her hand for me to hurry. That's when I realize she's wearing sneakers, shorts, and a T-shirt.

I drag my duffel out from under the bed and change into my denim shorts and a clean white tee. After using the bathroom, I swipe my sunglasses and follow Saysa out the door.

I don't say a word as we pad down the spiral stairs, and when we get to the shut doors of El Jardín, Saysa pulls out a vial of blood. She opens it and dabs some on her finger, then she cradles the doorknob, and it turns.

Outside, the dark air is alive with doraditos. We run down the path I first took to get here, toward the Everglades and away from El Laberinto. When we reach the trees with the Septimus symbol, we slow down.

Saysa is out of breath and clutching her side, but I feel like I could keep going. In fact, I *want* to keep going. It seems like any time I start running, I don't want to stop.

"This way," she says, weaving between the tight-packed mangroves.

"Where are we going?" I ask now that we can speak out loud.

"You'll see," she tosses back, and I lose sight of her as she slips between the trunks. I hurry and see massive roots that have surfaced like monstrous worms, large enough to consume a person. Saysa walks up to one and vanishes.

I rush over and spot a shadowy hole, like the opening in Flora, and I tentatively step through. Inside is a brown tunnel.

"Trees connect the planet," Saysa explains as I catch up. "As earth witches, we can reroute the roots of special trees, whose seeds are from Lunaris, and use them to cross vast distances."

"So where are we going?"

She stops walking so suddenly that I nearly topple into her. "I'm going to tell you something nobody knows. Not even Cata or Tiago."

The three of them are so tight that it's hard to believe they have any secrets from one another. Then again, Ma kept secrets from me.

"But first, you tell me something," she says, and my gut hardens in warning. "How did you get all those bottles of Septis?"

"My mom," I admit. "She worked at an underground clinic for people like us who are undocumented. I don't know how she got them though."

"From me."

The world suddenly flips upside down.

"What?"

She sucks in a deep breath. "Fierro was the first of us to advocate sharing the Septis with humans. Even after he disappeared, his philosophies spread. Most of us do it because we believe, as he did, that if we can help someone in need—no matter the species—we should."

"So does that mean . . ." My voice grows rough, and I clear my throat before continuing. "Did you meet my mom?"

"No," she says quickly. "We don't interact with people—we just drop off the boxes. They never see us."

I'm both relieved and saddened by her answer. "How do they work on most people? Do they make them dream of Lunaris too?"

She starts walking again as she speaks. "They're intuitive painkillers that numb whatever part of the body is in pain. Or if it's a general agony, they put you to sleep. Which often comes with some pretty wild dreams—but not of Lunaris. Only a Septimus can access that realm."

Something in her expression tells me she's not finished, so I hold the rest of my questions.

"But sometimes, humans get addicted to the pills. There are Septimus who like to take advantage of that—they see it as payback for what humans did to the earliest members of our species. That's why those of us who do this for the right reasons prefer providing the Septis to clinics where they'll be dispensed responsibly."

I nod, trying to process it all. "And this is because of Fierro?"

"He stood for equality—for everyone. Not just brujas and lobizones, but humans too. He valued every life. The tribunal thought they could put an end to his revolutionary ways by stopping him, but his words had already infected our bloodstream. Even when he went away, his ideas didn't."

The mention of *bloodstream* makes me think of the vial of blood she's carrying, and I make a mental note to ask her about it.

"Look, Jazmín knows there are Septimus in El Laberinto delivering bottles in the area, and she's been trying to stop us," she says, the words coming out in a rushed exhale. "I actually think the fact you had those bottles with you is why she let you in. She might have a theory you're here as an undercover Cazadora, investigating us. Either that or she thinks you're part of the smuggling ring."

I remember the night of our first meeting, how Jazmín seemed to change her mind only after the bottles spilled out of my bag. "Could be," I say.

"It's not just me though," she goes on. "If any one of us gets caught, the others would be at risk. That's why I can't tell *anyone*. Just in case."

"But you told me," I say, stating the obvious.

"I figure my secret pales in comparison to yours."

When we've walked in silence for a stretch, I ask, "What's with the vial of blood?"

"Oh. That." Her cheeks dimple. "Well, the thing is, only Jazmín can open doors in El Jardín after curfew—her DNA unlocks them. A loophole Cata takes full advantage of. She gave me some of her blood so I could visit after hours."

"She has no idea what you really use her blood for?"

Saysa shakes her head, and there's something in her expression that's finite, like I've hit upon something intractable. A breaking point.

"If she knew," she says softly, "she would want me to stop." Her green gaze holds mine. "And I won't."

I think of Ma.

If she'd told me her secrets, what would I have done? Would I have gone along with her plan if it meant not filing residency papers?

Probably not.

Ma must have known that.

The tunnel ends, and suddenly we're outside. It's still dark out, so it takes me a moment to realize we're aboveground, in a thicket of trees.

The first thing I feel is the change in the atmosphere—we've traded light, cool air for heavy, sweaty humidity. I follow Saysa through the foliage, and we pop out on the side of a main thoroughfare that seems to lead away from the Everglades toward human civilization. There's a bus bench a few feet away, and Saysa takes a seat atop the graffiti-covered metal.

Soiled napkins and straws litter the ground by her sneakers, and a reflective green sign on the roadway indicates that Miami is twenty-six miles away.

It all looks so normal that I could almost think none of the Septimus world is real—except for Saysa. She's proof the past two weeks really happened.

She looks up at me and taps the bench for me to join her.

But I just stare back at her in shock.

Her eyes . . .

They're *human.*

18

Saysa's gaze widens with the same shock, and we stare at each other with mouths agape.

"How did your eyes change?"

Even I can hear the desperation in my voice.

"They only shift at the full moon," she says in an awed voice. "When Lunaris's influence is strongest on this planet."

"But in El Laberinto—"

"It's a Lunaris colony because the land is hybridized with plants from that realm."

I don't believe this.

Yet another way I got fucked by fate.

"Your eyes *always* look like that?" she asks, and in her sad tone, I hear a deepening of understanding. This is the first time someone is seeing the full me, and I'm pleased that she's horrified. It makes my anger justified.

Twin headlights flash in the distance, and I pull on my sunglasses. I'm going to look ridiculous since the sun isn't even up yet, but I'm used to it.

Saysa produces a bus pass and swipes us both on. She looks so ordinary that I'm again struck by the possibility that the past two weeks were a dream. I drop into the seat next to her, and everything is startlingly mundane. Time feels like it's running a half second slower than it was in El Laberinto, and even the particles of oxygen seem to move sluggishly through my lungs.

The bus is littered with food wrappers and newspapers, and the fabric seats smell slightly of pee and vomit. The three people on board are asleep with their necks tilted back. And I'm once again viewing the world through mirrored lenses.

"Where are we going?" I finally ask.

Saysa sits up and faces me. "For two weeks, you've been waking up with red eyes. I know you cry yourself to sleep at night. What I don't know—or *didn't* know—is why you chose to stay with us. But seeing what it's like for you in the human world, I think I understand. Still, it's your birthday, and I thought maybe you'd want to visit your family."

I'm too moved to speak. The one thing I wanted, that I was too afraid to voice out loud, she already predicted. It's not enough that she's risking it all by helping me cheat in class every day—now she's putting herself at even more jeopardy without my having to ask.

"I'm here often enough that I know my way around," she says in a lower register. Her gaze is steadfast, like she's trying to communicate something without saying it. "We can set a time and a meeting place, and if you don't make it back, I'll explain to the others. We won't go looking for you."

She's telling me to save myself.

Saysa genuinely cares.

Enough to let me go.

And she's right—I don't belong among the Septimus. There's no point waiting out these next two weeks until the full moon because nothing's going to change. I've caused Saysa, Catalina, and Tiago enough trouble, and it's time I let them get back to their lives.

"Come with me," I say. Saysa's eyes widen in surprise, but she nods in agreement.

I consult the transit map over the windows to figure out where we need to transfer to get to Luisita's, and by the time we make it to her building, the sky is a steely predawn gray. "We need to get back before sunup," Saysa murmurs.

My heart flutters.

Not *I*, but *we*.

She seems to catch herself because her lips part like she's going to correct herself, but I just give her a small smile so she knows I get her meaning.

Perla gave me the code to enter Luisita's building, so I buzz us in, and we take the elevator to the sixth floor. I find door number 607 and ring the bell a dozen times. On the thirteenth, a tiny terrified voice from inside asks, "¿Quién es?"

"Luisita, soy Manu. Disculpame por favor, pero tengo que hablar con Perla. ¿Sigue con vos?" I rush through my apology and ask if Perla is still with her.

A heavy chain scrapes the door, and three locks successively click. The door cracks open a notch, leaving barely enough space for me to squeeze through. Saysa slips in behind me, then Luisita shuts the door, setting every lock back into place.

She's in her mid-eighties and wears her hair in a white pompadour that always makes me think of Elvis. Her bony arms reach out for me, and she crushes me to her chest. "Ya no sabíamos qué pensar . . ."

We didn't know what to think.

I hug her back tightly, and she pushes me away like I'm being melodramatic. "Tú y tus espejos," she mumbles, like she does every time she sees me. She thinks I wear these sunglasses to be cool. "¿Y tu amiga que no come nada quién es?"

And who's your friend who doesn't eat?

"Un placer conocerte, Luisita. Yo soy Saysa." Saysa flashes a dimpled smile that's every bit as charming as her brother's and pecks Luisita on the cheek. "Muchas gracias por dejarnos pasar y, por favor, disculpanos por la molestia."

Thank you very much for letting us in, and we're sorry to bother you.

Luisita falls silent, an uncommon occurrence.

"Hoy es el cumpleaños de Manu," Saysa goes on, "y lo único que ella quería era ver a Perla." *Today's Manu's birthday, and all she wanted was to see Perla.*

Saysa's English is flawless, yet there's no doubt Spanish is her first language. The ease of her Argentine accent is undeniable, a veritable verbal stamp certifying her place of birth. And it makes sense, given that she and Tiago lived in Argentina for thirteen years.

"¿La puedo ver?" I ask Luisita if I can see Perla.

"Claro que sí," she says, clapping her hands together. "Andá a despertarla. Ahora vamos a tener una celebración, ¿me oíste?" She sends me to wake up Perla so we can celebrate my birthday. I leave Saysa and Luisita in the kitchen, and I step into the darkened hallway.

A whiff of zesty lemon hits me as soon as I swing open the door to the guest bedroom, and Perla calls out, "¿Quién es?"

She's sitting up, her foggy eyes glassy and bright in the slats of dark gray light seeping in through the blinds. Beside the nightstand is a walker.

"Soy yo," I say.

There's a sharp intake of breath, and her clouded eyes turn in my direction. "¿Manu?" she whispers, her voice cracking. A small golden light pops on, the lamp's illumination casting a candle-like glow that leaves most of the room in darkness.

I drop to my knees next to the bed and take her hand in mine. Her skin feels frailer and crinklier than I remember, like she's aged ten years in the past two weeks.

"Ay, Dios mío," she says, her eyes rolling up and tears sprinkling down her cheeks. "Menos mal que estás bien, no lo puedo creer . . ."

"Perdoname," I breathe. "I had no way of contacting you. I'm so sorry. What do you know about Ma?"

"La tienen en un centro de detención, esperando su *hearing*." *She's in a detention center, awaiting her hearing.*

I swallow hard, and my voice comes out rough. "How bad?"

"I wouldn't know because all she talks about is you. You don't know how happy she'll be to know you're okay, Ojazos!"

Guilt gnaws at my belly, and I ask, "When will you talk to her?"

"She's going before the judge this week. Something called a master calendar hearing. The lawyer said she can try to challenge her deportation if she wants to stay."

"What's she going to do?"

Perla shakes her head. "All your mother cares about is reuniting with you. She's going to do whatever will free her fastest. Doesn't matter the continent they drop her in, she's coming right back for you."

I nod vehemently because that's all I want. To get my family back. I regret all the days I took for granted being stuck in that El Retiro apartment with the two people who mean the most to me in the world. Any world.

I should've gotten here sooner. Perla clearly needs round-the-clock care, and Luisita shouldn't have to provide it. Not to mention whenever Ma can call again, she's going to need to hear my voice.

"¿Y vos como estás?" Perla's tone shifts along with her language, and I know from the way she asks how I am that she's already formulated her own observations.

So I respond with another question. "Did Ma ever tell you about my father?"

"I know his family was dangerous enough that she gave up everything to keep them from discovering you." From her lack of surprise, she's already guessed I've been looking into him.

"Were they the ones that hurt you?" I ask her.

"That's what she asked too. Pero la verdad que no sé. Like I told you at the hospital, I just remember falling." She presses my hand. "Are you safe?"

"Yes. And I'm not alone. I have friends." I have to stifle a smile when I say that last word.

For once, Perla doesn't press me for details. The light through the blinds grows less opaque, lifting the room's blanket of black. "Look at you, Ozajos."

I don't know how much Perla can actually see, but I get the feeling she's not commenting on my physical appearance.

"You're in full bloom."

I kiss her hand and hold it to my cheek. "I'm so sorry it took me this long to return to you."

"It's about time. I warned her it wasn't sustainable." She sounds like she's resuming a conversation we never started. "I told your mother, one day you would outgrow that apartment. But you know how she gets when she wants to believe something will work out—no dose of reality can dampen her faith."

"What are you talking about?"

For a moment I worry she's starting to go senile, but then she pins me with one of those telescopic stares that makes me feel like she sees *everything*.

"You know your mother loves you more than anyone in her entire life." She says it like a disclaimer she wants to get out of the way. "But there was a lot she didn't tell you. Not just about your past."

"What else?"

"There was a reason she made you agree to let her handle the visa process. She didn't want you discovering her lies for yourself. Otherwise, you would have known she couldn't apply for a visa after living here illegally for so many years."

My gut clenches in protest, but I refuse to get upset with Ma. Not when I know all she's done for me.

"I already know she never filed papers."

"It's more than that. She was *never* going to let you get a government-issued photo ID. She wouldn't risk committing your eyes to any record. She wouldn't even take a photograph of you to keep for herself! The plan was always to hide you indefinitely."

It's that last word that drives home what Perla is trying to tell me.

There was never any hope for me here.

"The path you're on," whispers Perla, "that's where you need to be at this moment. You need to be free to make your own choices . . . And so does your mom."

There's a knock on the door, and it opens a crack.

"Manu?" says Saysa softly. "It's getting late. Luisita made us breakfast, and I packed it to eat on the go."

"Saysa, meet Perla," I say, and Saysa slowly edges into the room. "Perla, this is my friend, Saysa."

"Es un honor conocerte," says Saysa. *It's an honor to meet you.* She takes Perla's hand, and I glimpse green vines growing from Saysa's wrists and curling up Perla's arm.

I blink, and they vanish.

Like the red smoke.

"I'll wait for you another minute, then I have to get going," says Saysa, and she leaves the room.

When I'm alone with Perla, she cups her wrists like they feel different, and she looks sturdier, like she was hit with an immunity booster.

"What should I tell your mother from you?"

Perla's dismissal assumes a decision I haven't made—just like when she told me to leave her on the floor of the apartment, or when she sent me to wait for her at Luisita's. Only this time, it doesn't feel like she's choosing for me, because the safer option would be to keep me here, with her, in hiding.

This time, she's choosing me.

She's letting me go.

My eyes burn, but I fight against the tears. "Tell her I'm safe. And if she's been in the same place for two weeks and my dad's people haven't come for her, then so is she. I'm going to be out of touch for a while, but tell her to do whatever she chooses—and as soon as I can, I'll find her. No matter where she is."

Perla nods. "Anything else?"

I almost laugh.

Anything else? Ma has been my lifelong sole confidante, and in the past two weeks, I've lived more than my previous seventeen years put together.

I want to tell her that I finally started school, only it's a supernatural academy in the middle of the Everglades. That I've made friends with a couple of witches who've been helping me cheat in magic class. That I have my first crush.

Only problem is he's in love with my roommate.

And he's a werewolf.

I want to tell her I don't understand why she kept so much of my past secret from me, but I also want her to know how much it means that she gave up everything for my sake. I want to tell her that even though I've met witches and werewolves, she's still the strongest being I know.

"Yeah," I say, planting a kiss on Perla's forehead. "Tell her to sniff some of those high-end leather handbags for me."

19

There are more people on our bus route now that the dawning sky is light gray.

"What did you do to Perla when you took her hand?" I ask Saysa in a low voice.

"Jardineras have healing powers. I was boosting her system."

We keep going in silence for a while, until the question finally bursts out of her: "Why didn't you stay?"

When we left Luisita's together, she didn't question me, but I could tell she was waiting for me to volunteer an explanation. Only I still don't have one because even I don't fully understand yet.

"Believe it or not, it's still easier to pin my hopes on becoming a bruja than a US citizen," I say with a grin.

Saysa rolls her eyes, and I take her small hand in mine. Since we've locked elbows a lot, I didn't think it would be a big deal, but when she angles her head away from me like she's uncomfortable, I free her fingers by pretending I need to fix my sunglasses.

We're silent the whole way back, and the closer we get to El Laberinto, the more confident I feel in my decision. Strange how I lived my whole life as a human, and yet already this place feels more like home. I wonder if that's because I was always happier in my lunaritis dreamscape than at El Retiro. Or maybe it's because I finally have friends.

Saysa unlocks the door to my room, and I exhale in relief to see that Catalina's still sleeping. As I change out of my human clothes into my Septimus dress, it hits me that by coming back here, I'm saying I'd rather risk death than return to my old life. More than anything, it shows me how unhappy I've always been. How much of myself I've repressed over time.

So when we get to Flora's crown for breakfast and Pablo passes me the mate, it strikes me I've been doing the same thing with this drink.

Every morning, I've sipped the bare minimum, desperate to avoid looking inside and seeing what's really at my core. Too terrified to unleash my innermost self after all these years of insisting I'm just waiting on papers for my life to begin.

Even though I'm in El Laberinto sitting among the Septimus, on the inside, I'm still caught in the crevice between worlds. And if I don't eventually take a leap, I might never figure out who I am.

So I down the whole drink to find out.

I barely register when the guys have left and only the girls remain. As soon as I polished off the mate, there was no hope of resisting—the current swept me straight down the black hole.

The brain buzz is too loud to think through, so I let it

spread inside me. It's hard to see how the others can still function when its effect is so strong.

Before we leave Flora's crown, Señora Lupe guides us through meditation. The instant I close my eyes, the drink yanks me deeper, until I lose all hope of surfacing.

My hand is on the doorknob to the Citadel. Exactly where I left off in my dream this past lunaritis.

As I'm turning the knob, a vine strikes at my head, and I duck a split second before it skewers me.

I roll across the silver grass until I'm a safe distance away, then I spring to my feet just as another ivy arrow takes aim at my chest—

Only this time, instead of running, I leap up and wrap my hands around the snakelike plant. I cry out in pain as its sharp-toothed thorns slice into my skin, but I don't loosen my grip.

I'm hanging from the vine as it soars up, and I swing my torso back and forth until I gain enough momentum, then I let go. Looping through the air, I land atop the Citadel wall.

Standing between me and what lies ahead is a rattling nest overflowing with hissing green vines, all of them poised to strike. There's no way I can get past them.

Nor can I jump down from here without crushing every bone in my body. This dream is going to end again, and I'm still not going to make it past this wall.

There's a shift in the mossy mass ahead of me, and I spy a lighter, brighter shade of green amid the ivy. As the vines pull apart, I realize what I'm looking at—

Who I'm looking at.

"Saysa!"

I shout her name, but she can't speak. Every part of her is bound by the ivy, and blood is beginning to seep through the bands of coiled vines as they constrict tighter and tighter.

Watching her suffer and being unable to help is maddening.

I can't just stand here.

I need to do something—

Suddenly my being begins to crack. One moment I'm me, and the next I'm becoming something else.

My fingernails curve into claws, fangs grow past my mouth and down my chin, my hair elongates, my body nearly doubles in size, and my dress expands with my new shape until I'm taller and ripped and deadly.

A vine comes at me, and I thwack it away like it's a shoelace. Another one swings at my feet, and I jump and dive into the nest. I use my claws and sharp teeth to rip through the ivy binding Saysa, and when she's free from its hold, I tuck her into my chest, and I leap off the roof, landing inside the Citadel wall—

My eyes fly open.

I expect to find the world at an angle again, with everyone gathered around me. But instead, I'm sitting upright, and the other brujas are just starting to open their eyes.

The hallucination felt so real that I inspect my fingers to make sure I don't have claws. Maybe I should stick to my two sips of mate from now on. I don't think I'm ready for such a high dose.

As we march to La Catedral, my body still feels larger than usual, my muscles firmer, my joints springier. Only now the mate isn't buzzing in my brain, distracting me. It feels like I've absorbed it into my skin, and it's humming through me in a muted, background sort of way.

As soon as Señora Lupe swings open the door to La Catedral, a blast of heat slams into us. Red and orange flames flicker through the smoky haze like a wall of brilliant gemstones.

La Catedral is on fire.

The realization hits me with a jolt, and I stare at our teacher in alarm as she steps into the fire . . . and walks right through it. Even her wine-red dress is unsinged.

"Whoa," I can't help whispering.

"Definitely the coolest perk of being a fire witch," murmurs Saysa, her eyes also wide.

"And the *showiest*," says Catalina, going inside next. An air tunnel blows through the fire, and the flames curve around the force field, creating a channel. Catalina sashays down the walkway like it's a catwalk.

Saysa snorts.

Bibi goes next. She's so quiet in class that sometimes I think her mouth is so exhausted from making out with Gus that it doesn't have the energy for anything else. Frost forms on her hair and skin, and I feel a refreshingly cool breeze kiss my face as she strides forward in her gray dress.

When she steps into the fire, she looks like she's walking through the flames like Señora Lupe did, only there's a soft hissing sound as icy steam comes off her. The fire evaporates where it touches her, so she's literally cutting through the blaze.

Saysa and I are next. My chest is cramped, and I feel sweaty as she takes my hand and squeezes it reassuringly.

"No!" calls Señora Lupe's voice from across the way. She, Catalina, and Bibi are waiting on the other side, watching us through the smoky flames. "One at a time, please. Saysa, you first."

My lungs collapse.

We always go in pairs.

Saysa's expression tells me she's just as taken aback as I am. But she nods at me slowly, like she's got this covered, then she steps up to the fire.

The ground starts to tremble before her.

The land cracks and crumbles as twin fissures form, snuffing out chunks of the blaze and clearing out a charred path. I watch her every step, my heart beating harder and harder with panic.

Señora Lupe is perfectly positioned at the finish line,

watching. When it's my turn, she'll see that my eyes aren't glowing with magic. She'll know I'm cheating. There's no way to fool her this time.

I don't entirely know what my plan is yet, but when Saysa is halfway there, my body springs into action.

I race down the charred path after her.

Within an instant, I've passed her, and I make it to the other end before she does. Catalina's gawking at me in outrage, and so is Bibi. When at last Saysa makes it over, she's also looking at me like I lost my damn mind.

But that's nothing to Señora Lupe's reaction.

"Manuela, I am absolutely *appalled* at you!" It's the first time I've heard her raise her voice, and I start to feel sick.

"Not only did you blatantly disregard my instructions, but you tried to upstage your classmate, and you didn't even do it with your elemental magic. What you did was worse—you used a performance enhancer."

"A *what*?"

"Quiet," she says, glowering at me. "I don't know what you took, but I hope you know the effects wear off in minutes. Those brews are supposed to be a safety measure if we ever find ourselves in a life-or-death situation—not to show off in front of our friends."

I have no idea what performance enhancer she's talking about, but I'm more concerned by how quickly my body acted. Like it wasn't waiting for my thoughts to catch up.

Catalina's scowl tells me I'm in for another lecture in Flora tonight.

Once we're all gathered in the meadow, our teacher says, "Today, you're going to be dueling in pairs to work on your magical reflexes. Please pick a witch with a different element than yours."

Catalina deliberately steps into my path.

"Your task is to knock the other witch off her feet," says our teacher, circling us as we pair up. Saysa faces Bibi. "First one to fall loses the duel. Begin."

Catalina's brow is set in a hard line. I let my hair cover my eyes so our teacher can't see they're not lit up with magic.

A rock comes sailing at my leg, and I fight the instinct to dodge it.

Right before it hits my kneecap, a branch from the tree behind me swings forward and knocks it out of the way.

Lupe monitors our area for a while, and Catalina keeps up her steady act of shooting rocks, and then subtly blowing the branch over while trying to give the impression it's moving because I'm calling to it.

Coordinating the timing of her magic so that she's fighting herself is taxing, and after a while, Catalina's gusts grow weaker. Thankfully, Señora Lupe has moved along to supervise a different group of pairs.

My body is still vibrating from the mate and the adrenaline rush, and again I feel the irrepressible urge to *do something*.

The rock is coming at me, by now aiming for my ankles instead of my knees. I hear the branch rustling to save me, but this time the arc of its swing is smaller, and I know it's not going to make it.

So I kick the rock out of the way.

It goes sailing over the trees and disappears.

Catalina stares daggers at me, and I stare back just as defiantly. I know she's dying to tell me off, and I feel the grin break through my lips before I can stop it.

Suddenly one of the wooden vats for brewing potions comes flying at my head—

I reach up and catch it.

I've barely set it down before a pointy branch spirals at my arm, whizzing through the air like a spear, and I drop to the ground. It lodges into the tree trunk behind me with a thwack.

I grab the vat by my feet and launch it at Catalina's face.

She only reacts at the last instant, veering it away with a strong wind.

I scan the area to make sure Lupe isn't watching. She's at the far end of the meadow, tending to someone who got hurt. Then I wrest the branch free from the tree and aim it at Catalina's chest.

She looks at me like I've gone completely mad, and I relish the expression. It might be the first time she's shown me any respect.

I heave the spear before she can conjure up a gust of wind, and she dodges a second too late, so it grazes her shoulder. She hisses, and before I can apologize, six rocks rise into the air and fire at me like missiles.

I duck, dive, and leap until I've avoided them all.

Another set of stones rises into the air, and I scoop up three of the rocks she threw at me. As the airbound stones rearrange their formation, I aim the first rock at her injured shoulder—

Something waxy wraps around my ankles, and I shriek as I'm lifted off my feet.

The rocks fall to the ground, and my hands grip the hem of my dress, holding it against my legs as my body hangs upside down in midair. "What the—"

"Let go!"

Catalina's voice cuts me off, and she comes into focus. A thick, snakelike vine is wrapped around her ankles and suspending her upside down too, while her hands also grip the skirt of her dress. "Put me down!" she demands.

My head hits the ground, followed by the rest of my body.

I blink up at Saysa, who's standing over both of us. "Grow the fuck up," she whispers under her breath.

By the time class ends, none of us are on speaking terms.

"Given the importance of the upcoming Septibol final, our afternoon training is canceled," announces Señora Lupe. "I know most of you want to watch tonight's practice match."

Everyone else celebrates, but Saysa, Catalina, and I are too tense to enjoy our early release.

Instead of having lunch in class, today we're eating behind El Jardín. Apparently so are the guys. While Saysa beelines straight for the food, Catalina goes up to Tiago, tugs down on the neckline of his T-shirt, and plants a kiss on his lips.

When she walks away, Tiago stares after her, stunned.

I can't shake the feeling the performance was for my benefit.

Her action sets off a murmur of whispers around us, and I hear reactions like *"Finally!"* and *"I knew they were together!"* and *"Go, Tiago!"*

Saysa glowers at Catalina when she joins her at the buffet, and I want to force myself not to care, but suddenly I'm not hungry. I turn away from them, unsure if I want to stay or go back to the room.

"Happy birthday," says Tiago.

I wish I had the strength to walk away. But when I meet his sapphire gaze, he says, "I have a present for you."

It's alarming how quickly my mind can go blank around him. He rakes his fingers through his dark hair, and as the blue skies of his eyes search mine for a response, the most coherent answer I can muster is, "I—you got me—present?"

"That's the general gist." His roguish smile sets me back a few more brain cells, so this time, I keep my mouth shut and simply nod.

"Let's go," he says, and instead of handing over a package, he sets off, toward the clearing.

"We have to go somewhere?" I ask, jogging to keep up. We stride past El Jardín, and I follow him through the line of mangroves into the Everglades. "Where are we going?"

"The night we met, I wasn't here by accident," he says, and I start to recognize the direction we're headed.

The ground tilts up, and I spot the collection of boulders I saw right before meeting him, when I was hunting his scent. Tiago positions himself between two of the rocks, and his muscles bulge against his skin as he shoves the stones to create a small opening.

He gestures for me with his hand, but I don't move.

"I promise we won't have to outrun any more lunarcanes," he says with a wink.

"Lunarcán?"

"The windstorm from your first night here. They only happen around the full moon, while the portal to Lunaris isn't completely closed."

When I still don't move, another realization seems to dawn on his features. "You're probably too sane to follow a strange lobizón into a dark cave. Just wait here. I'll be back."

As he disappears between the boulders, I think to myself, *Sane, my ass.*

The instant I enter the dark, enclosed space, I inhale Tiago's maddening musk. My eyes only illuminate my immediate area, so I follow his scent until I enter a deeper alcove that's strung up with glowing blancanieves.

The cave is infested with books.

Everywhere I look are precariously stacked towers of texts. Only these aren't like Flora's mostly pristine and durable manuscripts—these copies seem flimsier and flashier.

"They're originals," he says, and from the reverence in his voice I know I'm somewhere sacred to him. "*Human* books."

I pick up a frayed copy of *Dracula* that has a USED sticker on the back. "I don't understand."

"Our stories are retellings. We replaced the human heroes with Septimus." He grins at my expression. "The tribunal banned human media a few centuries ago because it made the species seem sympathetic. Septimus were becoming too curious about people, some even advocating for changes to our laws. So our authors took advantage of the obvious loophole in the law and just rewrote their favorite stories. If no one's allowed to read the originals, who's going to accuse the writers of plagiarizing?"

Now I get why Tiago was surprised when I knew Borges's name my first night. "That's . . . clever," I concede.

"*Romeo and Juliet* are a wolf and witch from rival mana-das. *The Metamorphosis* is about a werewolf who wakes up one morning as a human." His words gain speed like he's enjoying himself. "*Alice in Wonderland* is about a witch who runs from her manada and falls down a rabbit hole into a world without magic. It's called *Wanderland*. And that's all Alice does—she wanders through a depressing landscape and gains a deeper appreciation for home."

I'm battling a smile. "That's a joke, right?"

"Depends on your definition of *joke*," he says with a crooked smirk. "Harry Potter is a werewolf."

"No way."

"Hogwarts is a school of witchcraft and werewolfery."

"Stop."

"The muggles are still human, since they come off terribly. Probably why that series is so popular with our government."

It's all so ridiculous that I burst into belly-aching laughter. The release feels so good that once I start, I can't stop. I bend my waist and clutch my sides, and Tiago chuckles at my reaction. But with my guard down, other feelings surface, from this morning's visit to Perla and the life-changing decision I made by coming back here—and the laughter starts to feel hollow, until I get the urge to sob.

Keeping my face averted, I blink away the tears and force the darker feelings down.

Tiago waits a few beats to continue.

"The originals are better, so I collect them any chance I get." His voice fills the cave with music. "I could tell in Flora's library that books are important to you. I thought maybe you'd want to share this place."

I meet his soft stare, surprised he's paid such close attention. "How could you tell?"

"Your eyes."

He takes a step toward me. Given the cave's size, it closes much of the distance between us. An electrically charged silence spreads through the space, zapping my body with static and driving my mind wild with ideas.

I don't know if Tiago's moved again, or if it's me this time, but his face is close enough to admire each shiny shard of sapphire in his jewellike eyes.

I want so much to touch him.

Too much.

"So." I pan my gaze across the book stacks. "You were going to give me one?"

"Give you one?" he repeats, sounding a little dazed.

"A book. My birthday present? That's why we're here?"

"Right," he says, though he seems unsure. "Pick whatever you want."

I move away from him to clear my mind, which is still buzzing from our proximity. Striding up and down the teetering stacks of English and Spanish spines, I'm having a hard time focusing. I see books I love, books I've never heard of, books I've been hoping to read . . . I want them all. Yet there's something else in this cave I want even more.

"Which one were you going to gift me if I hadn't come in?" I ask from the other end of the space.

"I don't know," he says, stuffing his hands in his pockets.

I pin him with a questioning stare. "But you were coming in to grab a book for me."

"You were bold enough to follow me, so you should get to choose for yourself."

I think of what Saysa said about Tiago's indecisiveness when it comes to his personal life. "Well, I choose for you to pick one for me," I say, crossing my arms.

His face goes blank, like he's not used to taking orders.

I'm not sure where my challenge is coming from. It's almost like I want to get him back for making me weak. And besides, I came into this dark cave alone with him and withstood the power of his smoldering gaze, and now he's too good to step outside his comfort zone to do something that was his idea in the first place?

Tiago reaches for a text that's in the very middle of one of the towers, and I suck in my breath as he plucks it out in one swift movement. Then he presses the book into my hands.

"We should get back before all the food's gone," he murmurs, leading the way out of the cave.

I look down at the dog-eared paperback in my hands, struck speechless by how he noticed the way my gaze kept straying to this particular spine.

Then I tuck *Cien Años de Soledad* into my pocket and follow him out into the daylight.

20

When we get to the Septibol field for today's practice, the stands are packed. Not just with students, but with Septimus families I haven't seen before. They must live in those tree homes.

While the guys head to the locker room, I hang on the sideline near Saysa and Catalina. When at last the team steps onto the field, the crowd goes so wild that it's distracting just standing in place. I can't imagine playing through this much noise.

"It's worse in Lunaris," says Saysa like she can read my thoughts. This is the first time we've spoken since class.

"How much worse?"

"The whole population is in the stands. Almost one million of us."

My face goes slack trying to picture such a huge number of people in one place. It's an overwhelming population for an audience—but it's small for a species. That means humans outnumber Septimus by about 7,799,000,000.

No wonder secrecy is so important.

Catalina casts us an ugly glare, so Saysa steps away from me, and we all go back to silence.

I'm tired of Catalina using me as a pawn in all her cold wars—with Saysa, with Tiago, with her mom. No wonder it took her so long to make a friend. She's merciless.

Tiago shakes hands with a guy who looks to be in his mid-twenties, and I remember that this match isn't team A vs team B. This time the juniors are going up against El Laberinto's professional team.

Saysa and Catalina take position, and Bibi waves me over to sit on the bench with her, Noemí, and the rest of the B team.

The game begins to thunderous applause, and then the field is a blur of color and movement. The pro team has possession until Catalina sends a powerful gale that blows all the players back except Javier, whose boulder-like body withstands the wind. He passes the ball to Nico in midfield, who gets it to Tiago.

The guys are moving too quickly for the brujas on the opposing team. Their Congeladora ices the field, but Tiago's feet stay ahead of the growing glacier. He kicks the ball at the goal, and it sails just beyond the keeper's fingertips, hitting the net.

"Yes!" shouts Coach Charco from the sidelines, and everyone in the stands cheers.

The ball is back in play, but the spectators are still celebrating Tiago's spectacular goal. Chants of "Tiago! Tiago! Tiago!" fill the air, his name shouted in rhythm with my heartbeats.

My mind keeps frisbeeing between the match and his secret

cave, to that moment that almost happened between us, and a thrill of excitement tingles down my spine. My fingers reach into my pocket to trace the pages of the book he gifted me. Then I see Catalina cheering him on as he races to the goal again, and guilt makes me snatch my hand back.

If they weren't secretly dating before, I guess that's going to change now that she kissed him. I don't think I'll be able to stand it if the two of them start making out all the time like Gus and Bibi. At least I won't have to endure it for long, since at this rate I'll be back in the human world before the next full moon, and this whole experience will be just another lunaritis dream.

The crowd's good cheer begins to fade as the pro team gains steam. Rather than bursting onto the field with energy, their game has a slower build, and now it's starting to pay off. Their top scorer doesn't have Tiago's talent, but he gets in more shots because our goalie isn't as solid as theirs.

Diego is good at anticipating the ball's trajectory, but his reflexes aren't quick enough to stop it in time. The extra second it takes him to get out of his head is costing him goals. After he lets in a fifth ball, the mood is somber and the atmosphere tense.

Depression settles over the field, and our team starts to lose its edge. Even Tiago misdirects a kick, and the ball bounces off the goalpost.

It rebounds, and a member of the pro team takes possession, and the current of the match changes direction. Catalina hits the player with a wind spell, but she misjudges the timing, and the bump of air ends up helping him pass the ball to a midfielder, who kicks it to their top scorer.

Pablo sees what's going on, and with a burst of speed, he intercepts the ball. The pro team's Jardinera unleashes a tremor, and Saysa's green eyes light up as she counteracts the spell.

Their competing magic keeps the ground at a sustained tremble, and Pablo's long black hair falls over his face, partially blinding him as he hurries to keep pace with the ball. The pro team's forwards are on his tail, so he has to kick it away, in any direction but the goal.

He swings his leg without looking, and there's a deafening boom as the ball blasts into the air with the power and speed of a bullet.

The whole thing happens so fast.

One instant the players are crowding Pablo, and the next there's a sound like a gunshot, and they all look up, the ball flying too swiftly to bring down.

Saysa's still locked into her magic, trying to stabilize the field against the other Jardinera. She doesn't register the ball that's headed right for her neck, with enough power to break it.

The wolves are closer to her, but they don't immediately register what's about to happen.

Catalina is on the other end of the field, and I'm not sure she has enough time to conjure up a gale strong enough to knock this ball off course.

All of these realizations hit me simultaneously, and I'm running before I know what I'm doing.

Saysa looks up just as the ball is about to slam into her throat—

I launch into the air, my arms and fingers outstretched—

And the ball crashes into my hands.

I drop to the ground with a thud, the impact sending a shooting pain down my side. Rolling over, I hug the ball to my chest, the only sound in the world my pulse pounding in my ears.

My breathing is loud, too loud, and it takes me a moment to realize that's because the stadium has gone silent. I hinge my elbow beneath me and start to sit up, and Tiago appears, lifting me to my feet.

The ball dribbles to the ground.

"Thank you," he says, his eyes shiny.

Saysa is beside him, staring at me in shock, her gaze glassy and wild. Without warning, she wraps her arms around me for a long, hard hug.

When we pull away, Catalina is beside us. She takes Saysa into her arms next and holds her tight. Pablo rushes over and hugs Saysa too. "I'm so sorry," I hear him telling her over and over again.

It's still far too quiet, so I survey the stands.

Every single Septimus is staring at me.

I look to the field, and players from both teams are watching me too.

The murmuring starts all at once, like a brook of water that's rushing closer by the second. There are too many voices for me to isolate any particular conversation, and when I look at Tiago, Saysa, and Catalina, they're also scanning everyone warily, like even they aren't sure what might happen next.

As the conversations grow louder, I catch snippets of what the crowd is saying.

"How did she do that?"

"Brujas can't move like that."

"Who is she?"

"Not normal."

"She can't be a—"

Señora Jazmín and Coach Charco approach. Coach's amber eyes are round with awe, but Jazmín's gaze is narrowed with distrust.

"What was that?" she demands, her expression so severe that I wonder if she missed the part where I saved Saysa's life.

"She saved her," says the last voice I thought would advocate for me. Catalina steps up to her mother, but Jazmín keeps looking past her to me.

"Make the earth shake," she commands.

"E-excuse me?"

"Show us your magic. *Now.*" She glares warningly at Saysa. "And don't you dare help her."

I swallow.

This is it then.

I should have stayed with Perla after all.

"She's not a bruja."

I never knew such a beautiful voice could cut so deep. Tiago's confession crushes me, but if I'm already going down, there's no reason he and the others should have to take the fall with me. Might as well save themselves.

"I'm not," I admit, my voice low so I don't have to hear the words.

I'm not one of them.

I don't belong here.

Or anywhere.

Tiago looks at me, and his eyes begin to glow and churn like real oceans. Hair sprouts across his face as fangs drop from his mouth. His uniform expands as his body grows larger and bulkier and hairier, and by the time he's finished transforming, he looks part-beast, part-man.

He turns to his teammates, and as his gaze grazes them, one by one they each begin to shift. Pablo and Javier go first, followed by Carlos and Nico and Gus and Diego. When Tiago looks at me again, I feel a painful tug in my uterus.

I bend over and hug my stomach, as agonizing cramps twist my insides. Like my body is assuming a new design.

I scream as all my joints crack at once, the bones of my

skeleton breaking off. My spine curves as it elongates, and fangs pierce my gums, my skull tingling as my hair grows out. I stare at my hands in horror as my nails curl into claws, my vision flickering on and off, like I'm going to black out from the pain.

I'm ripping out of my skin.

When the torture ends, I'm crouched on the ground, head buried in the skirt of my dress, just trying to breathe.

Can you hear me?

Tiago's voice sounds in my head, like he's speaking directly into my mind. I look up at him in awe and nod.

Yes.

His jaw falls open on seeing my face.

The other wolves gawk at me as I rise to my full height. Their shock spreads to Jazmín, Coach, Catalina, Saysa, and everyone in the stands. They're all gaping at me like . . .

Like they've never seen a lobizona before.

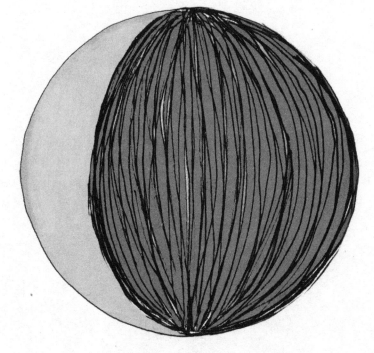

PHASE III

21

Tiago was right. I'm not a bruja.

I'm a werewolf.

Señora Jazmín's penetrating purple eyes are still staring at me, only now we're in her private office inside El Jardín. And I'm back to my usual size.

My transformation barely lasted a minute. So fast it might not have happened at all.

The pain is what makes it real. I can still feel my knees trembling from the impact. Not to mention my jaw is tight, my bones are sore, my head aches, my lungs feel bruised, my chest burns . . . It reminds me of the aftereffects of the period pain I felt at thirteen. Before Ma brought home the blue pills.

All this time, my transformation has been struggling to break free.

I grew taller, my hair thickened, my vision improved, my hearing sharpened . . . because *I'm a lobizona.*

I *belong.*

I blink, and Jazmín's scrutinizing stare comes into focus again. My happy thoughts are extinguished like a candle's flame.

The game ended prematurely.

Jazmín announced that students were to return to their rooms for an early curfew and dinner would be delivered to them. She then ordered Catalina, Saysa, Tiago, Señora Lupe, Coach Charco, and me to follow her.

We're in her office on the top story of El Jardín. The walls are all windows, and we're so high up that the ground looks like a quilt of green beneath a sea of stars. We're sitting around a comfortable curved couch with plushy cushions, probably meant to lull students into lowering their guard.

"So, you're a lobizona," says Jazmín, evidently done waiting for me to speak. She and I are at either end of the C-shaped couch, facing each other. Sitting in a row to our side are Saysa, Catalina, Tiago, Coach, and Señora Lupe.

"Yes."

And just like that, I have an identity.

Not a human, not a bruja, but a lobizona.

The door to the office opens abruptly, and a lanky man with sharp facial features steps inside. Jazmín nods at him, and he walks over to sit beside her. Something about him seems familiar, and I see him wink at Catalina before focusing his coral-colored eyes on me.

"I'm Gael," he says, his voice deep and warm, like an Argentine embrace. "Catalina's uncle."

And Jazmín's brother, I realize, now noticing their similarly chiseled bone structures.

"I'll also be training you, since I'm the instructor for the wolves." He nods at Tiago, who nods back.

"Let's not get ahead of ourselves," says Jazmín, and the

blancanieves illuminating her office seem to dim their glow. "First, we need some answers. Why did you keep your true abilities hidden?"

"I-I was afraid."

I force myself not to look at Catalina, Saysa, or Tiago so that nothing I say sounds rehearsed. Thankfully, Catalina is so thorough that she already came up with a detailed backstory for me in case my lack of magic was ever discovered.

Now I just need to recite what she told me, but replace *lack of magic* with *being a lobizona*.

"Afraid of what?"

"Of being ostracized because I'm different. Like I was back home."

"Which is where? What is your manada?"

We agreed it would be best to claim one of the seedier manadas in Kerana to make it harder for anyone to verify my story. "La Mancha."

"That's not what you told me your first night."

Saysa has explained that Septimus take their manada as their last name, so when I introduced myself as Manu *Márquez*, Jazmín took that for my manada affiliation. So I just say, "You must have misheard me."

She frowns. "What about your schooling?"

"My parents were too ashamed to send me to school, so I studied at home. They didn't want others to know their daughter is different."

"I'm sorry," says Gael, the pity in his voice contrasting sharply with Jazmín's lack of it.

"What I don't understand," says Señora Lupe, who also sounds gentle compared to Jazmín, "is how you've been able to do your assignments in class?"

"I've been cheating," I say quickly, trying to keep the focus on me and not my friends. Since Lupe caught me before, I'm hoping it's not too much of a stretch. "I'm sorry. Saysa and Catalina could tell something was off with me, but I lied to them whenever they asked. I've been deceiving everyone since I got here."

"I don't know why you're so proud of it," says Jazmín, bristling.

"I'm not, I just want to come clean. And confess. Because I'd like a fresh start."

"A fresh start at what? You've misrepresented yourself and snuck into a spot in a competitive training program that you didn't deserve. Your next stop is the Cazadores!"

"I think we should consider the extenuating circumstances," says Gael, frowning at his sister. "This situation seems more innocent than what you're reading into it. Manu is only looking for a chance to fit in. We have an opportunity to make a difference in a young Septimus's life. Isn't that what we're here for?"

"She *lied*," Jazmín reminds him. "She broke the code of conduct for attending our prestigious institution—"

"Jaz, you let her in even though her name wasn't on your list because you must've sensed she needed our help. Now we know why. Let's help her."

"It isn't our place to decide what's best for her. That's up to her parents and the law." She stares stubbornly at me. "Please hand over your Huella, *now*."

"I . . . I didn't bring it."

"Where is it? Your room?"

"It's at home."

Now even Gael looks at me in confusion. "How did you get past the Cazadores patrolling the portal's border? They must have asked you for it when you arrived from Lunaris last moon."

"There was a crowd, and I managed to sneak past," I recite, just as Catalina instructed me.

"How could you leave this realm without your identification?" demands Jazmín. "That's another breach of our laws—"

"It's my parents," I say. "They hold on to it in Lunaris so I can't run away, but this time, I had to escape. I wanted a chance to go to school and make friends." This last part, at least, isn't a lie.

"Well, you'll have to take this up with the Cazadores. This academy can't get between you and your parents. Not to mention the fact that your family concealed the existence of the first known lobizona from our government. They should have reported your condition as soon as it revealed itself."

It didn't work.

I discovered my identity too late to explore it.

And worse, now I've probably put Ma's life at more risk than ever. When I can't give my true manada or my parents' identities to the Cazadores, they could force-feed me a truth potion, and then they'll learn about her—

"The full moon is in two weeks," says Gael, turning to his sister. "We could just let her stay on until then. Who better than us to observe and vet the first lobizona? Once the others learn of her, we might not get the chance."

She scowls at him. "You just want to be the one to train her for the fame and prestige!"

"You said this is a *prestigious* institution. We should be at the forefront of something like this."

"And what of the *law*?"

"We've already had her here two weeks. What's two more? Come on, Jaz."

I can't help seeing Catalina reflected in Jazmín's cornered expression as she's faced with going against her better judgment for the sake of someone she loves. And like her daughter, I have no idea in which direction she'll break.

"You will train with the lobizones under Gael's instruction," she declares to me suddenly, "and if you hold the other students back in any way, *you're out.*"

I nod in agreement, but I don't dare let myself believe it's real.

"When we get to Lunaris, I expect to see your Huella *and* your parents."

I nod again. Those are tomorrow's problems. Right now, I just need to get out of this room—and as far from Jazmín as possible before she changes her mind.

"What about Manu joining the team?"

Everyone turns to Coach Charco at once, and I let out a nervous laugh. His humor may be unconventional, but we could use the comic relief.

"Did you all see that save?" he presses, his amber gaze lit up with what can only be lunacy. "Diego couldn't pull that off on his best day!"

My mouth is suddenly too heavy to close.

"Our team would be *legendary*—"

Jazmín holds up a hand to cut him off, and she looks like it's taking her a moment to summon her voice. She folds her fingers into a fist and uncurls them one at a time.

"First, absolutely not. Second, we don't reward lawbreakers, we punish them. Third, the championship is in two weeks, and we already have a superior team. Lastly, there's that little issue of girls *not being allowed on the Septibol field*—"

"*Brujas* aren't allowed on the field," corrects Coach Charco. "Manu's a lobizona. She has the same abilities as any lobizón here." His chest puffs with pride when he looks at me, and for the first time since entering this office, I don't feel small.

"Coach, I know you're only trying to help, but this isn't the way," says Jazmín decisively. "We have a great team that's gotten us this far. Let's not mess with it."

"We'll train every single day for the next two weeks until she's ready," he argues. "I'll still start Diego, but I want her on the bench just in case. She can be our *secret weapon*."

Secret.

The word hits me in a place that's too profound to pinpoint. Maybe because that's what I've always been, wherever I go—a *secret*. As long as I'm unknown, I'm safe.

The word seems to have an impact on Jazmín too. She leans back against the couch cushion, like she's considering it—which seemed impossible just a few seconds ago. "Have you consulted your captain?"

At last I allow myself to look at Tiago. And I find him staring openly back at me, awe still splayed on his face. I wonder if he's been watching me this whole time.

When our eyes connect, it's like we're back in that moment when we looked at each other as werewolves.

A shiver tingles through me, and I blink.

"Tiago?" asks Coach Charco.

"I think it's entirely up to Manu," he says in a soft, musical murmur. "Would you like to join the team?"

As his sapphire eyes search mine for an answer, I feel seen. And thanks to Coach, I also feel *wanted*.

Gael's help came from a place of personal ambition, but Coach sees talent in me. I swallow, my throat parched.

"Yes."

"How did you know what she was?" Jazmín is scrutinizing Tiago's face like she's looking for more people to punish, and Saysa and Catalina straighten their spines in anticipation of what's coming.

"Small things started to add up," he says, his gaze never straying from mine. "She's taller than any bruja I've ever met. And she runs faster than even most wolves." My face grows warm as I flash back to us outrunning the lunarcán. "And that save she pulled off—no one moves like that."

The way he's watching me, I feel like I might burst out of my skin a second time tonight.

"Okay, then," says Jazmín in a brusque tone. "Tomorrow you train with the lobizones. *Not a word* about her escapes this manada," she adds, panning her purple gaze across every-one. "I'll make sure the others who saw her keep quiet. Until the championship, Manu is our best-kept secret."

Once Catalina and I are alone in our room, I know what's coming. If she was upset about the Felifuego, that's nothing to what I did today. Drawing too much attention to myself would be an understatement.

As soon as the door shuts, she strides up me, and I squeeze my eyes shut, waiting for the blow to land—

Her hands circle my neck, and she breathes in my ear, "Thank you for saving Saysa."

"Oh," I say, too shocked to hug her back, "no problem."

She pulls away and sniffles. "I can't believe I froze like that. I should have blown that ball away. What if you hadn't—"

"Let's not."

She looks really shaken, and I finally start to glimpse what Tiago and Saysa see in her. She may be a pain in the ass, but her friendship is genuine. I think that's what Tiago was trying to tell me that first day.

There's a stack of sandwiches de miga waiting for us on the table, and we each bite into one.

"I can't believe you're a wolf." She shakes her head disbelievingly. "I've never heard of anything like this before. First thing we need to do in Lunaris is get you a fake Huella."

"What exactly is a Huella?" I finally ask. I've been pretending to know what it is since my first night here.

"A small notebook that's got our identification information, and the pages get filled in by every manada we form part of throughout our lives. It's our life story and our identity. The paper comes from a one-of-a-kind Lunaris tree we call El Árbol Dorado. It's what the tribunal uses for all official government ordinances. But there's a black market of Septimus who specialize in fake Huellas—they find imitation barks and forge signatures and match your eye color with the right Lunaris flower to distill its pigment for the cover."

I try to take all that in. "But why would a Septimus need to forge their Huella?"

"If they've been banned from a manada, or there's a restraining order against them, or if they're just unhappy and want a shot at starting a new life in a different manada."

I don't know why I'm surprised to find Septimus are as flawed as humans. After all, they did descend from the human race.

Not to mention there's the fact that they would kill me if they knew my parentage—so clearly they're not perfect.

"At least Coach's plan bought us some time," she says as we're getting into bed. "As long as you're a *secret* weapon, you can't draw attention."

I place the paperback Tiago gifted me inside my duffel, and it hits me that today is still my birthday. The visit to Perla feels like a lifetime ago, and in a way, it was.

I so badly want to share all this with Ma. I can't even imagine how she would react to me telling her I'm a *werewolf.*

I start to picture her in the detention center, cold and hungry and scared, and my heart bangs desperately against my chest. I should be on my way to break her out right now. But I don't even know how to transform or what I can do as a wolf.

I need to train first. Then I can save her.

I can save them all.

"Of course you're not *actually* going to play in the final," says Catalina, summoning a breeze to shut off the lights. "The entire crowd would be all over you after the match. We need more time to work on your new backstory."

I know she's right, and yet I can't help thinking that maybe the reason we haven't heard of any other lobizonas is they're all in hiding. But if no one knows we exist, how can the system ever hope to accommodate us?

I roll over to get comfortable. My body still feels achy from today's transformation. I'm not sure I'll ever believe any of this is real.

"You're going to class with the guys tomorrow."

There's an innocence in the way Catalina's words hang in the darkness, and it makes me almost giddy. I used to fantasize about the day I could go to college and live in a dorm and have a roommate to trade stories with at the end of each day.

Nerves buzzing in my belly, I whisper, "What if I can't keep up?"

What if?

These guys are in superhuman shape, and I've never completed a workout in my life. I've seen Tiago and the others tear up the Septibol field. There's no way I can move like that—

"You're going to leave them in the dust."

Her whisper washes over me like an enchantment, and I feel myself glowing as though I'd swallowed the moon.

This birthday was magic.

22

The next morning, a new outfit for me is delivered to our room. A pair of black shorts and a white T-shirt, all made of the same breathable fabric as my dress.

When I walk into Flora's crown with Cata and Saysa, everything feels different. For starters, the whole school is staring at me. I'm the only girl not wearing a dress.

For someone who's gone invisibly through life, it's unsettling to suddenly be all anyone sees. What makes it bearable is that this is the first time I've been anywhere and known I *belong*.

Conversations die as I approach, and Saysa and Cata close ranks around me. When I see the way my roommate stares down a group of witches ogling me, I feel a swell of gratitude rise up my chest.

The walk to our usual spot feels twice as long, and I'm relieved when we finally join the guys. Tiago and Pablo make space for us, and I sit next to Pablo, who's trimmed his black hair a few inches and keeps running his fingers through it.

We're squeezed in tighter than usual, and I notice Gus and Bibi are actually sitting with us for a change. They're not even making out. They're staring at me.

Like everyone else.

Saysa passes me the mate, and I drink it down. This time there's no drug-like effect; it's just absorbed into my system like water. I wonder if what's changed is that now the energy knows where to go and what it's used for.

"Why didn't you just say something?"

I'm not surprised it's Pablo who says what everyone's thinking. I gaze up at him, and his black eyes probe mine, probably for signs of a deeper conspiracy, so I keep my expression unguarded. "I didn't think you'd accept me."

"That's stupid. You're a wolf, you're part of the pack, period."

"Agreed," says Tiago, and when I look at him, my traitorous heart skips up and down. There must be a way to soundproof its cage.

"I get why you were afraid, but I'm glad you're being truthful with us now," says Nico. I nod but don't quite meet his silver eyes.

"I remember reading about a guy witch once," says Javier in his booming voice. "He lived a long time ago, and even though he got a lot of shit for being different, he eventually became a famous Cazador—"

"That's a *novel*," says Diego. Today he's not wearing glasses or reading his blank book. I asked Saysa about that, and she told me Diego dreams of serving on the tribunal one day, so he checks out a lot of texts that require some measure of security. The words can only be read by the Septimus wearing the glasses.

"But there have been rare cases of boy witches and girl werewolves in the past," argues Javier.

"I've never heard of any outside of fiction," says Diego, his periwinkle eyes studying me, their light blue color contrasting with his black skin. It's unclear if he's going to say more, and it's a testament to how much his friends respect his opinion that no one speaks until he does.

At last he tells me, "I'm not going to lie, you don't have an easy path ahead." He sounds like a doctor delivering a difficult diagnosis. "When someone deviates from an accepted norm, they signal a gap in the system. A hole that hasn't been plugged. The danger with exposing a foundation's failings is it opens the door to the possibility that it's a faulty structure altogether and should be torn down and built anew."

"You're seriously intellectualizing her life right now?" asks Pablo, shaking his head disbelievingly.

"She was scared to come out as a lobizona, so I want her to know why that fear is a waste of time." Diego looks at Pablo patiently, like a teacher waiting for their student to understand the lesson before moving on.

Pablo shrugs and goes back to brushing his fingers through his shorter black locks, and Diego's gaze bounces back to me. "I hope you don't think I'm being patronizing, but I've studied our history and our laws enough that I think I can be helpful." I nod for him to go on. "The truth is, there will be Septimus who can only justify your existence by convincing themselves you're using magic or performance enhancers—because it's easier to dismiss you than to modify the system."

"Yeah, Tao forbid we move beyond a binary system," says Pablo, squaring his shoulders like he's getting worked up. "Humans have more freedom than we do! They're not locked

into a lifestyle at birth, they can define their identity for themselves—"

"They can love who they want," growls Javier, and it's unclear if he meant to say it out loud because he drops his gaze
to the food and stuffs a medialuna in his mouth.

"Well, my work here is done," says Saysa, pretending to
wipe away a tear.

"Whatever happens," says Diego, his face cracking into a
warm smile as he turns to me, "we've got you."

"Fuck the haters!" thunders Javier through a mouthful of
pastry, making the leaves beneath us tremble. There's a pause
in every conversation as heads turn in our direction.

"All I know," says Gus, snaking an arm around Bibi's waist,
"is that for two weeks, you fooled the witches into thinking
you had magical powers. That's *savage.*"

Bibi jabs her elbow into his side, and he clamps his other
arm around her, trapping her in a hold. Her gray eyes glow
with light, and suddenly Gus yelps and his arms spring open.

His skin turned blue where it touched her, and he rubs his
hands on his shirt for heat.

"I still can't believe the way you caught that ball before it
clobbered Saysa," says Pablo, his voice dipping like he's still
swimming in guilt. "I don't know many keepers who could
have made that save."

"I know I couldn't," says Diego, exhaling heavily. "I think
you should start training with us."

One look at Tiago's expression tells me it wasn't supposed
to go down this way.

I'm guessing Tiago planned to address the team at practice.
But this way Diego gets to save face and the others can't get
upset with Tiago for betraying a teammate.

"Is that some sort of joke?"

It's the first time all morning Carlos has opened his mouth. He's sitting on Pablo's other side, so we're not in each other's line of sight. "Girls can't be on the field, remember?"

"That's not the wording of the regulation," says Tiago. "It says only *wolves* can interact with the ball."

"Exactly," says Carlos. "And Diego just explained to us how there's no way we can be sure she's really a wolf."

"Which Diego were you listening to?" asks Pablo.

"We don't know what she is. Only the tribunal can confirm it. Otherwise, any girl could claim to be anything she wants—"

"She transformed right in front of us!" blares Javier, rattling the tree branches arcing over our heads.

"Girls have *magic*," Carlos insists, his emerald eyes flashing. "We can't possibly be sure of everything they can do with it—"

"*Okay*, that's just way too much to unpack." Saysa's voice is deeper than usual, like anger is weighing it down. "*Why* is Manu such a threat to you? Why is it so terrifying that someone with a vagina is joining your field of dicks?"

"Tiago, get your sister in check," says Carlos with a dangerous growl. "This is a *wolf-only* conversation."

"Are you fucking for real?" snaps Cata, her cheeks red and nostrils flaring.

"We're not doing this," says Nico, his tone calm even as the silver of his eyes ripples like liquid mercury. "Carlos, solo queremos entender por qué estás así."

Carlos, we only want to understand why you're so upset.

"Something's wrong with her!" Carlos insists, pointing an accusatory finger at me. "She's not normal. She's a *freak*—"

I wince and look down, so he won't see the hurt in my eyes. Instead, I focus on the black leather cuff around Pablo's wrist, and I notice his hand is balled into a fist.

"According to whom?" demands Saysa.

"To our entire fucking history!"

"Yes, and that's why we call it *his-to-ry*," says Catalina like she's explaining the concept to a two-year-old. "Because we continue to evolve, and those organisms that stay stuck in the past don't make the next cut."

Carlos springs to his feet. "I can't talk with *them* here."

"Them?" Saysa calls after him as he storms off.

Nico is the only one who gets up and follows him.

"We should probably go," says Tiago, and I realize the guys in other groups are disbanding. I forgot that wolves get dismissed first.

Pablo and the others rise, but my knees are shaky as I try to stand. Saysa slides closer and grips my hand. "Forget what that idiot said. I know you're going to crush being a wolf. Tiago will look out for you, but trust your body because your instincts are razor-sharp—I wouldn't be here otherwise."

I squeeze her fingers so she knows I understand, and she flashes me her dimples.

"Now go forth and shatter every convention."

Despite the game of cat's cradle currently twisting up my intestines, I can't help smiling back. What a Saysa thing to say. If she had a car, I could totally see that sticker on her bumper:

Go forth and shatter every convention.

I stick close to Tiago as we leave El Jardín, and we approach the rectangular building with the crumbling ceiling.

"This is La Guarida," says Tiago.

My legs grow heavier the closer I get to the door. "What"—I clear my throat—"happens when we go in?"

"What do you mean?"

"What's the forecast?"

"You want to know the weather *indoors*?" By his confusion, it occurs to me that maybe witches and wolves don't discuss their training spaces.

We step inside, and I brace myself for some kind of environmental test—but nothing happens.

We're in an abandoned estate with naked walls and high ceilings and no doors. From what I can see, its chambers are void of furniture. In the distance beyond, I spy green foliage, like the backside of the building is wide open.

About fifty guys gather in the hollow entrance hall. Some are stretching, some are yanking off their shirts, and some are staring at me. I keep close to Tiago and the rest of the team, most of whom are baring their cut upper bodies.

Tiago is the only one who keeps his shirt on.

"Welcome, Manu," says Gael from the center of the room. Even though I know he's older, there's something so youthful about him that he could be one of the students. It's like he's managed to hold on to a piece of himself that most adults seem to shed.

"I don't think this is funny," calls out one of the wolves watching me.

"She could get killed," someone else adds.

"Is this even allowed?"

"Shouldn't she train with the younger class?"

"Girls can't be werewolves."

Carlos says the last thing. Pablo growls at him, and it reminds me of the way I growled at that girl in the clinic weeks ago.

"Anyone else?" asks Gael, his coral eyes surveying our faces.

Pablo steps closer to me, like he's my bodyguard, and I notice a tattoo near his heart that's just three black lines that look like gashes.

"Manu, this affects you more than anyone else, yet I don't hear you complaining," says our instructor. "Do you want to train with the wolves?"

My throat is parched. I wish I'd drank more water at breakfast.

I nod yes.

"And why is that if some of them are so unwelcoming?"

I don't appreciate the way Gael is putting me on the spot. If he didn't want me to join his class, he shouldn't have spoken up for me last night.

"Because I'm not here for them," I say, thinking of what Diego said. "I'm here for me."

Gael smirks, and I see where Catalina gets her snarkiness. "We're a pack species, so going at it alone is out of the question. To be family means we can disagree, but we are bound by something deeper. *Trust.*"

The guys who objected before now voice their approval—not of me, but of Gael's words. There are murmurs of "that's right" and "exactly" and Carlos says, "I don't trust her."

Gael now turns to my detractors. "The witch tends the garden, the wolf patrols its perimeter. One works the soil, the other protects it. Wolf or witch, it's not an issue of sex—it's a question of worldview."

Not an issue of sex? That's funny, given that everything among the Septimus seems to be tied to one's sex. It feels inescapable.

"Right on!" says Pablo, breaking into solo applause. I think he's being sarcastic, but when I look up, there's no trace of humor on his face.

Gael's gaze lands on me again. "What do you think, cariño?"

I shrug and nod; a mixed message. "I think there's more than one way to be a wolf."

"Show us, then," he says, and I'm not sure if the words are a challenge or an invitation. Then he shouts, "Let's run it out!"

At Gael's command, the guys sprint down the hall toward the greenery on the horizon, and I'm swept up in their momentum.

Beyond the walls is a vast grassy field enclosed by a forest that grows along the back of a mountain. We run laps around the field, moving in sync. The air is cool and slightly breezy, the sun golden and warm, and this run is delightful.

Stretching my limbs, working up a sweat, my lungs burning, my muscles crying . . . I am *awake*.

I don't know how many miles we cover, but by the time we're done, I feel like I can't take another step. "Very impressive," says Nico, patting my shoulder.

Before I can thank him, Pablo says, "Don't be a dick."

"I'm not!" says Nico. "I'm telling her she did well—"

"It's condescending that you set the bar that low for her."

"I'm with Pablo," booms Javier.

"Don't be. Pablo's just pissed I gave him a haircut." Nico rolls his silver eyes. "And I'm not sure why, since the brujas seemed to approve—I know you heard them whispering about how good it looks because you wouldn't stop running your damn fingers through it!"

I try hard not to laugh.

Javier tries less hard.

His guffaws are so loud that Gael looks over and shouts, "Everyone line up for ten transformations!" When the guys start to groan, he says, "Don't give me that. This is important. *A transformation in time saves lives.*"

"What's going on?" I ask as the class spreads out.

"We transform ten times in a row to stretch our bones and keep our bodies nimble," explains Nico.

"But I don't know how to make myself transform."

A few of the guys shoot me strange glances, and I immediately wish I hadn't said anything since every wolf here has preternatural hearing. So I add, "I mean, under this much pressure."

"Adrenaline triggers it," says Diego in his kind, steady voice. "But in a gathering of lobizones, we tend to bring out the wolf in one another."

"Start!" calls Gael.

I furrow my brow and tighten my muscles and picture myself turning into a werewolf, but nothing happens. I hear snarls and howls and the snapping of jaws as all around me the guys grow big and hairy and lethal. And after a moment, I feel the twist in my uterus, and my body starts to transform.

I don't have a mirror, but when it's over, I'm much higher off the ground. I see the claws in my fingers, the bulging muscles of my arms and legs, and a fine fur of body hair that's a lighter hue than the guys'.

I apprehensively raise my hands to my cheeks to feel for bushy facial hair—and I exhale in relief when I feel only smooth skin.

There's a piercing pain in my gut as my body shrinks back to its usual form. By my tenth transformation, my muscles are rubbery and my head is pounding. I'm the last one to finish, and as I adjust to my regular shape, I realize all the wolves are watching me. Even Gael.

I drop to the grass, exhausted. Let them stare all they want.

"She's really a wolf," I hear someone say.

"No shit."

That's Pablo.

"You look just like the rest of us," declares Javier. "Except you don't have a beard."

"Y parece que se comió dos melones," adds someone else, and a few guys snicker.

And it looks like she swallowed two melons.

I scowl and look in Gael's direction, expecting him to tell the guy off—but he's watching me with an expression I can't place.

"I told you she's not one of us!" says Carlos accusingly. "She doesn't have fur or facial hair!"

"Her fur is just lighter than ours," counters Nico in a placating tone. "And think of how lions have manes but most lionesses don't."

"Anyway, you can't judge because we don't have a reference for what lobizonas are supposed to look like," Pablo points out.

"That's because they don't exist!" roars Carlos.

"That's enough," says Gael, shutting down the shouting match. "Everyone pair up!"

Tiago is at my side before I can blink. He offers me a hand and pulls me to my feet.

"Go into the forest and practice your howls," says Gael. "Take turns locating one another."

Without further clarification, the class runs uphill into the woods. Tiago keeps pace with me until we hit the trees, then he leads us in a direction far from the others.

My only botany experience is limited to Perla's plant-riddled living room, but I've always had a fascination with trees. I used to leaf through the glossy pages of heavy tomes in the library to try to identify the species where I lived. Mostly palms, oaks, dogwoods, magnolias.

Yet the trees here defy classification. They each vary so much in color and texture and size and design that I think they must have individual names.

"How much farther?" I promised myself I'd only ask if my body was close to giving out.

"Sorry," he says, finally slowing to a stop. "I just didn't want anyone eavesdropping."

I cling to the nearest tree, my limbs melting into the bark like sap. And I try not to think about the fact that Tiago was purposely distancing us from everyone else.

"So what's . . . the assignment?" I ask, not sure my bones will hold me up for much longer.

"Howling is our own language," he explains. "We can use it to locate each other, or to warn of oncoming danger. The pitch and length lets us know the message. Give it a try."

"What, just howl? Right now?"

He nods, and I do my best impression of a wolf.

"That's a human howl."

"A what?"

"It's just a sound. Ours is a *call*. It doesn't come from the same place as words."

I close my eyes and concentrate on how it felt to transform, pulling on that sense of ripping out of my skin—

"*Owoooooooo!*"

"That's it," he says encouragingly, and I gasp to catch my breath.

"It's more natural to track someone in your wolf state," he explains. "So I'm going to hide and howl, and you transform and find me."

He disappears in an eyeblink, and I look around for a clue as to what direction he went. I close my eyes and concentrate so I can transform, but my body doesn't budge. I don't know how to just call it up.

A single, musical note fills the forest.

Tiago's howl is a song.

Its beauty pierces me, and without making the conscious decision to shift, I feel my body changing shape. Then I'm off in the direction of his voice.

I've never moved as a wolf before, and it's exhilarating. I'm covering ground so quickly that I don't know how I'll slow down. Each time his howl sings through the trees, I feel my pointy ears perk up, and my inner compass readjusts its direction. As long as I'm moving, it's easier to maintain this form, and I start to speed up as I pick up his scent and get closer to his location—

I crash into Tiago, and we tumble to the ground.

I feel myself transforming back to human as we roll, until at last he manages to stop our momentum, pinning me beneath him. His breath brushes my skin, and I inhale that fragrance of cedar and thyme and something wild, something that makes my heart leap, something that makes me want to lose control.

"Manu," he whispers, and I hold my inhale. "There's something I—"

"My turn."

He moves off me, and as soon as I'm upright, I take off into the trees, running until I can't breathe his scent on me. Whatever he was about to say, I can't hear it. Not now that Cata and I are finally friends.

I transform mid-run, and when I can't take another step, I close my eyes and howl.

Once.

I hear the rustling of leaves and cracking of twigs, and I twist to see Tiago loping toward me. It took him *seconds*.

Can you hear me?

He speaks into my thoughts again, the way he did yesterday. I concentrate on the spot in my brain where I heard the words, and I try to trace the line of communication back to his mind. *How are you doing that?*

Alpha wolves can forge telepathic connections with members of their pack.

We transform back, and neither of us says anything.

It's becoming too much work to be around him.

"What's the deal with Cata's uncle?" I ask, needing to make her feel present. To remind him. To remind *us*.

"He's brilliant," says Tiago, brushing his dark locks away from his face. "Too brilliant to be teaching a bunch of teens. But he has no other choice."

"What do you mean?"

"He can't return to Kerana, by order of the tribunal."

"Why? For what?"

Tiago exhales heavily, and for a moment I don't think he's going to tell me.

"For failing to capture Fierro."

23

"Gael was the best Cazador we ever had," Tiago explains as we stroll through the trees. "He could track down *anyone,* and he had a reputation for never failing a mission. So as soon as Fierro started making a name for himself, Gael set his sights on him. Only problem was, no one's ever seen Fierro, so he was literally chasing a ghost."

"But it's not fair to punish Gael for something no one else could do," I interject.

"True, but Gael sort of brought it on himself. He'd discovered Fierro's plans to run away with . . ."

Tiago's oceanic eyes pull me into their current, and I supply, "My mom."

He nods. "Gael wanted to be the one to catch him, so he didn't tell anyone."

Just like he wanted to be the one to train me before Jazmín turned me over to the Cazadores.

"Somehow Jazmín caught wind of his plans, and instead of telling the authorities, she teamed up with him. They both had ambitions—he wanted to be head of the Cazadores and she a judge on the tribunal, so they thought they could help each other move up."

"Then what happened?" I ask, breathless.

"Well, Jazmín had second thoughts at the last minute. Cata wasn't even a year old yet, and her husband is a big-time politician, so she decided to confide in him. But he betrayed her. He told the Cazadores what they were doing. When they finally caught up with Gael, he had failed to capture Fierro—but he claimed to know where he was headed. He was convinced Fierro had run to Miami."

The memory of Ma in the bookstore floods my mind. That's where the man told her Fierro had gone. Was he Gael's source?

"But by then, the Cazadores were furious with Gael and didn't trust him, so as punishment, he and Jazmín were sent here. They're not allowed to set foot in Argentina again until they capture Fierro."

"What about Cata's dad?"

Tiago frowns and doesn't meet my gaze. "You should probably ask her. It's her story as much as yours."

Tiago's revelation about Gael plagues me all through training, and I stare at our teacher so hard that I miss everything he says. After howling, we return to the field behind La Guarida to scarf down choripanes, then we sit for guided meditation.

I lower my lids until my eyes look closed, and through the slits I watch Gael. He's cross-legged on the ground, facing us, eyes shut. I'm trying to clear my mind, but too many questions cloud my thoughts. How much does he know about Ma?

Is he the reason my dad never made his meeting with her? Does he have any leads on where Fierro might be now?

"What's going on?" I ask Tiago as everyone stands.

"Yoga," he murmurs from a few feet away. "Gael *just* said it."

"That's the third time you've had to ask," says our teacher from the other end of the field. "If you listened to me half as hard as you stare, you wouldn't miss a word."

Everyone looks at me.

I glare at the back of Gael's head in disbelief.

What an asshole.

When class is over, Cata and Saysa are already waiting for me in our room, holding my new team uniform. "How'd it go?" blurts Saysa before I've even shut the door.

"Fine."

I wonder if I should ask what she knows about the Gael situation before I approach Cata. I still remember that first day at breakfast, how eager Catalina was to believe that Fierro is dead. Maybe her feelings have to do with what happened to her mom and uncle.

"Manu, *this is serious*," says Cata, narrowing her gaze in a very Jazmín-like look of evaluation. "Do you think anyone was suspicious?"

I blink. "Of what?"

"Of what you are!"

"Oh."

Her phrasing stings, but I guess if approached from a biological standpoint, it's accurate.

Assuming that's how one wanted to look at me.

"What she means to say," says Saysa gently, "is: Could they tell you'd never transformed before this week?"

"No—it went well. I didn't feel like I was pretending to be anyone else." The impact of the statement hits me as I say it.

"I was just . . . me. But Tiago said Gael probably went easy on us for my sake, so who knows."

By the time we make it to the Septibol field, everyone is already there. Not just the team, but every student I've taken classes with is sitting in the stands.

I feel like I just swallowed a jagged rock. It scrapes down my throat and settles in my gut.

"Welcome, Manu," says Coach Charco, his amber eyes glinting in the sun like honey. He walks over with Tiago. "We're honored to offer you a spot on the team, as an alternate at first—"

"So, the rest of us don't get a say?"

The guy who spoke is the B team goalie. He wears a white headband on his forehead, and over his shoulder I glimpse a flash of green eyes. Carlos is literally behind this.

"Absolutely not," says Coach, staring Headband down. "This is my kingdom, and it's my discretion to add or remove players from the team. You have a problem with that, Raúl?"

Headband grits his teeth. "I don't understand why she gets to skip tryouts. The rules should apply equally to everyone. She shouldn't get special treatment just because she's a girl."

"If a boy had made that catch yesterday, you wouldn't be questioning my decision—"

"Raúl's right," I say, not wanting to splinter the team. "I should try out."

Coach frowns and throws his hands in the air. "Sure, let's waste time—it's not like we have a championship in two weeks." He plops down on the substitute bench. "Penalty kicks, best two out of three. And make it snappy."

Raúl strides to the net. I guess he's going first.

Carlos positions the ball at regulation distance, and on Coach's whistle, he kicks it at the goal—but Raúl catches it. Still, Carlos served him such an easy ball that no one applauds.

Javier goes next, and this time the ball sails over Raúl's head, hitting the net, and cheers break out from the stands. Tiago is last, and his kick is so powerful that the ball grazes Raúl's shoulder on its way in. Raúl cries out in pain, but Tiago doesn't bother apologizing.

"You saved one out of three," says Coach, his voice flat and unimpressed. "Diego, your turn."

Carlos sends a powerful ball this time, but Diego kicks it out. Javier's goal looks like it's going to go in, but Diego manages to knock it out with his fingertips. Yet when it's Tiago's turn, Diego doesn't stand a chance. Tiago makes the ball defy physics, and Diego ends up diving the wrong way.

"Two out of three," says Coach approvingly. "Manu, you're up."

My heart echoes in my chest as I set foot on the field. I've watched hundreds of fútbol games in my life, but it's nothing like actually being here. As I cut across to the goal, there's a collective intake of breath in the stands, and when I look out, most of the brujas are on their feet, watching me with wonder.

I meet Saysa's and Cata's stares, and they're wearing the same expression of hope mixed with awe. And something else. *Pride.*

I suck in Perla's steadying breaths, trying to keep the moment's momentousness at a distance so I don't let them down.

Javier intersects Carlos before he can get to the ball and positions himself to go first. Maybe he thinks Carlos will throw me off my game.

Coach blows his whistle, and the sound of Javier's kick echoes through the stadium.

The ball rockets into the air, but I don't take my eyes off it until I can predict the rest of its trajectory—then I jump, and it plows into my chest with enough force to knock me off my feet.

My breasts scream in pain, and it feels like there's a crater in my ribs, but I refuse to let them see any of it. I keep my breaths slow and shallow, so their sensitive hearing won't catch my struggle, and I kick the ball back to him.

The crowd is dead silent, but Javier is smiling, not at all upset that I saved his goal.

Carlos takes his place next, and we glare at each other. On Coach's whistle, Carlos sends the ball spiraling toward the top left corner. I leap up and knock it out so emphatically it punts off the ground.

Carlos stalks off the field, and again there's no reaction from the stands.

Now all the focus is on Tiago and me. Even Coach gets to his feet.

Our gazes meet, and I read the respect in Tiago's expression—he's going to go hard.

The whistle goes off, and the ball comes shooting at me with twice the power of the others'. I don't have enough time to figure out where it's going, so I can't tell which way to dive until the very last instant—and I do the opposite.

I throw my arms into the air as the ball sails past me into the net.

Disappointment hits me like a punch to the gut, and I keep my gaze lowered until my expression clears. Even though missing that goal was my choice, it doesn't make me feel any better.

"Two out of three," announces Coach.

Then, all at once, the stands erupt in earth-shattering applause.

Most of the guys are cheering too, but there's no doubt this is the brujas' moment. The field trembles beneath my feet, and I feel a sprinkling of water, followed by a wave of heat, then my clothes flap in a gusty wind. Their emotions awaken their magic, and it's like the whole planet is celebrating.

I look at my friends, and Cata's pink eyes are shiny. She shares a rare smile with me that's purer than any expression I've seen on her face. I wish she knew how breathtaking she looks with her armor down.

Saysa's mouth is a straight line, like she's disappointed. I frown at her questioningly, but she just looks away.

"Diego and Manu tied," announces Coach. "If this were a real trial," he tells Raúl, "you would be off the team. I hope you got what you needed from this exercise because you're benched for today. Manu, you're in."

Diego comes over and bumps fists with me, and I feel myself beaming.

Unlike the tryout, I go all out at practice. I'm having way too much fun to even think about holding back. At one point in the game, I jump so high to pull off a save that I dangle from the top of the goal post and kick the ball in midair.

Everyone in the stands—witches *and* wolves—gets to their feet.

At one point, I catch Coach staring at me the way Gael did when I transformed in his class. Their reactions make me think of how I felt weeks ago, the first time I saw magic.

When we're headed to dinner, everyone's still talking about my hanging save. Some Septimus even greet me at the buffet line.

"Hi, Manu!" says a bruja named Lily.

"You were so good," her friend Melisa tells me.

"That save though!" adds Bibi, looping an arm around my shoulders.

"We're taking the championship!" booms Javier as soon as

I sit. He punches my arm in celebration, and I go flying into Tiago on my other side.

"Sorry," I murmur as I peel my face off his shirt, his wild scent dizzying.

"Don't be," he whispers, and there's something weighty about how he says it that makes me wonder what he's referring to.

We slide apart as a pair of legs pushes between us, and Cata squeezes in. She still looks more lighthearted than I've seen her. Nudging her arm against mine, she says, "I haven't had that much fun playing in so long."

I grin, but in the distance I spot Carlos walking pointedly past us to sit with Raúl and some other guys.

"No te preocupes por él," says Nico, his silver gaze following mine. *Don't worry about him.*

"Why is he so against me?"

"Because Carlos only knows one narrative for guy-girl dynamics—he's the hunter, we're the prey." Saysa's voice thrums with anger, her expression uncharacteristically dark.

"Forget him," says Bibi, who's sitting so close to Gus, they might as well be one organism. "You looked like you were having the time of your life out there."

"I was," I admit.

"Sure," says Gus, "being goalie is a blast since you don't have the wicked witches on your back." He grins at his girlfriend innocently. Bibi smiles back, and when he looks away, she freezes his glass of water into a block of ice.

"Can we talk about that save though?" Pablo turns to me as he runs his hand through his black hair. "I've never seen anyone kick the ball in midair like that. Whose face did you picture popping?"

"Goalie isn't an offensive position," Diego points out. He's not reading today, and it's nice to see him join the conversation. "We're not fighting the ball, we're protecting the net."

"This is the shit I'm talking about. You overthink *everything*!" Pablo looks to Nico and Tiago to back him up, and I get the sense this has been an ongoing conversation. "It slows your reaction time. Your oversized brain is *literally* weighing you down."

Diego quirks his brow. "I'm not sure how to take that."

"Then you're still thinking too hard," says Pablo with an eye-roll. "You need to trust your instincts more, the way Manu does. Watch how she plays—she moves at the speed of thought."

My eyes are rooted to the steak in front of me, and I force myself to focus on eating. If I could move at the speed of thought, I would be far from this conversation by now.

"I'm not sure that kind of innate talent can be taught," says Diego, and I'm relieved he doesn't sound upset. "If something is instinctual or intuitive, it's the opposite of learned."

"Are you fucking with me?"

"Can we not?" injects Nico.

But Pablo plows on. "Diego, you're like the perfect example of what happens when someone socializes more with fictional characters than real ones. I honestly can't tell if you're conversationally challenged or if this is your idea of humor—"

"Pablo, really," says Diego, his periwinkle gaze bright. "You're overthinking this."

Everyone bursts into laughter, and Gus's laugh transitions into coughing as he chokes on the piece of meat he was chewing. Hacking and gasping, he reaches for his glass of water and tips it back—

But it's frozen solid.

"Oops," says Bibi, offering him her drink. "Sorry!"

He glares at his girlfriend as he gulps it down. "Wick"—
cough—"ed!"

After dinner, Saysa comes back to the room with Cata and me.

The door closes, and Cata says, "Okay, as soon as we get to
Lunaris, we'll need to get you a forged Huella. Saysa and I will
write up everything it should say. You did great today, by the
way. I'm proud of you for holding back at the tryout."

I blink, completely taken aback.

"The wolves need to be hustled," she goes on. "Make them
think they have the upper hand, and they won't see you coming."

"I completely disagree." Saysa is glowering at me, her eyes
flashing with the same outrage she showed toward Carlos.
"Do you know how lucky you are to be on that field? How
many of us you're out there representing? How dare you be
less than you are?"

It takes me a moment to react, mainly as I had no idea either
of them noticed I missed the ball on purpose. I'm not sure how
they could have seen that, given the strength of Tiago's kick.

"I was just trying to find my footing—"

"Oh, save the fragile act for someone who buys it," snaps
Saysa. "Anyone who saw the way you moved when the ball
came sailing at my head knows you could have saved all three
of those goals tonight, and you *chose* not to."

"Exactly. I *chose*."

"I need to shower," says Cata, bowing out of our argument.
I doubt she's qualified for the role of peacemaker anyway.

"Manu, I don't want to put you at risk," says Saysa once
Cata goes into the bathroom. "I just don't want fear to hold
you back from everything you can accomplish."

I nod, half hearing her, half listening for the shower's faucet.

As soon as the water starts running, I say, "You're right—but I need to ask you about something else while Cata's not here. Today in class, your brother told me that Gael and Jazmín are here as punishment for going rogue and failing to capture Fierro. Why didn't you tell me?"

Saysa's brow creases with concern, and she shakes her head. "It's not my secret to tell. But if it helps, I've told her to talk to you about it."

I can't get mad at her for being loyal to her best friend, so I drop it.

When Cata comes back out, hairbrush in hand, I say, "My turn."

The bathroom is coated in the sweet lavender scent of Cata's body lotion. I step into the shower, and the water muffles the world around me until I can barely hear the murmur of Cata and Saysa's conversation on the other side of the wall. I could eavesdrop if I want to, but I don't.

Showers are usually where I cry—for Ma, for Perla, for myself—but today, the tears don't come. As monstrous as it feels to admit, this was the best day of my life.

It hurts that I couldn't share it with Ma, but for the first time in weeks, I have hope that we'll be together again soon. And not just us, but Dad too. Somehow, I'm going to recover what she brought us to Miami to find—our family.

Even if that means we have to run to the ends of the world to escape ICE and the Septimus.

And still. If by some miracle I were to track down Fierro, I don't know what I would say. He may not know I exist, but he obviously knows Ma, and he was aware of the danger he was putting her in by spending time with her. A danger he knew she would be running from for the rest of her life. Can I really forgive him for that?

It's not until Cata and I are in bed with the lights off that I say, "I know about Gael, and why he and your mom are here."

"Saysa told me," Cata whispers.

I wait for her to volunteer more.

"My dad didn't want to leave Argentina, so I only see him once a month, in Lunaris. Our situation is pretty unheard of. Septimus mate for life. We don't have *divorces* like humans. That's why unlike every Septimus I know, I don't have a sibling."

No wonder Cata's not a fan of Fierro. Her uncle's obsession with him cost her her family.

"Manu, my mom always talks about how before she came here, she was going places in Kerana. Both she and Gael were. I know she would love the chance to vindicate herself and our family. If she knew the truth about you, she would see you as her redemption."

Catalina's warning lingers in the dark air, and the temperature seems to drop ten degrees.

"Discovering who you are and turning you in would be huge for her . . . Like, ticket-back-to-her-old-life huge."

24

The next morning, Gael is holding open the door to La Guarida as I approach. "Jazmín wants to see you in her office," he tells me. "Report back when you're finished."

"Why does she want to see Manu?" asks Pablo.

"None of your business."

I look at Tiago in alarm, and he says, "I'll go with you."

"No, you're coming to class," says Gael, opening the door wider.

"I'll show her where the office is."

"We were just there two nights ago."

Tiago opens his mouth again to argue, and Gael asks the rest of us, "Who doesn't get that my answer is going to be *no*?"

Apparently only Tiago. "What if—"

"What if you get into class and save your gallantry for my *niece*? Yes, I heard about your kiss—your classmates haven't shut up about it."

"Oh, shit!"

Javier's booming shout is the only sound for miles.

I start walking to El Jardín, and I don't look back.

I haven't seen Tiago and Cata kiss again since my birthday. I was sure she did it to get under my skin, but maybe I was wrong. Maybe since her mom is headmistress, Cata has always had to play it cool because she can't be a regular student like the rest of us.

Regardless, there's no denying how much Tiago cares for her—that's been obvious since my first day here. And I'm not interested in being a consolation prize, or in getting caught in the middle of their love story. I'm so distracted by Gael's dig that I don't consider what I'm about to walk into until I've climbed to the top of the spiraling staircase, and I'm standing outside Jazmín's windowed office.

The door opens on its own.

"Come in," she says from the room beyond.

My gut hardens as I step into the glass-enclosed space. Soft light fills the room, and outside the horizon is streaked with white treadmarks, as if a cloud car just skidded across the sky.

"Take a seat."

I exhale in relief when I see that she's alone and not with a troop of Cazadores. She's sitting at one end of the C-shaped couch, so I take the other end, like last time.

"You seem worried," she says. Her long hair is rolled up in a sleek bun, sharpening the lines of her face. "You're not in trouble. I just want to check in."

"Thanks," I say, though I can't imagine being in this room and feeling relaxed.

"Here, let's have some mate," she says, standing and approaching a small side table with drinks and glasses. "How was your first day of training with the lobizones yesterday?" she asks as she spoons yerba into a calabaza gourd.

"I had a much easier time than I did with the brujas."

"Of course. You're a lobizona," she says, reaching for the hot water. "I know it couldn't have been easy to suppress your real power and pretend to be what you aren't. If you ever need someone to talk to, I'm here."

"Thanks," I say uncertainly as she hands me the mate. The sooner we finish drinking, the quicker this farce will be over.

I clamp my mouth on the metal bombilla and slurp it down as fast as I can. The liquid burns down my throat, but it doesn't taste like the breakfast mate. This one must be of the ordinary variety.

"Tell me about your parents," she says, retrieving the calabaza gourd from me.

"What about them?" I ask, the drink's heat making my face flush.

"How is your home life? Are you close with your mom?"

"We are, but—" I try clamping my mouth shut as a strange lightness comes over my tongue. "But—"

Again, I try to stop speaking, but my mind has grown soft and yielding, like a substance is working its way through my veins, leaving me open and vulnerable.

"But she has her secrets."

I didn't mean to say that, but I couldn't stop myself.

Jazmín perches down at the edge of the coffee table, her face just a few feet from mine. "What kind of secrets?" she prods.

I want to read from the script Cata drafted for me, like I did when I was in here a couple nights ago. But it's like Jazmín has reached down my throat and seized my vocal cords, and I can't pick out my own words.

"She didn't—she never—told me about you."

Even when I tried to cut myself off, my mouth just tried again, until the secret was ripped from me without consent. Jazmín's amethyst eyes are uncomfortably close, and I look away, my gaze settling on the empty calabaza gourd. She never refilled the mate for herself.

"About *me*?" she asks, as the horrible truth dawns on me.

She slipped me something.

Truth potion.

Catalina's warning from last night resounds in my mind. If Jazmín figures out who I am, my life is over. And so is Ma's.

"I mean this—*school*," I say, my pulse booming as I swap out the word *species* at the last instant. I think it only worked because *school* is also technically true.

Maybe I can try shaping the truth into a different design.

"Why didn't she want you knowing about us?" Jazmín presses.

"Because she was afraid I would be targeted for being different," I hear myself say, and then I clamp my lips and hope my mind doesn't volunteer more.

"Where are you from?"

"Argentina," I say carefully.

"What about your dad?"

"I feel like I don't know anything real about him," I hedge.

"It's normal to have these feelings about your parents at this age," she says, dismissing my admission as teenage angst. "What I want to know is how they kept your condition hidden for four years. The Septimus of your manada at least must be aware you're a lobizona. How has the gossip not spread?"

"I don't get out much at home," I say truthfully.

"Not even to Lunaris . . . ?" Her voice fades on the last word, like she's just figured something out. "The blue pills you're carrying aren't for illegal trafficking. They're for *you*."

I don't react, and she narrows her gaze. "Does your mom make you take those on the full moon?"

"Yes."

She doesn't say anything for a long moment, and I hope she stays deep in thought long enough for the potion's effects to wear off. My tongue already feels heavier, like it's returning to my control.

I'm never drinking anything this witch offers me again.

"So, you've never been able to fully explore your abilities as a lobizona. No wonder you were so desperate to escape your monstrous parents."

Guilt sizzles like acid in my stomach for betraying Ma this way, but I force myself to nod in agreement.

"You have other recourses, Manu." Jazmín's humanity comes through her voice for the first time, and even her cold eyes flicker with emotion. "I can set up a confidential meeting with a trusted Cazadora so you can explore your options."

She probably means Yamila, I realize.

"It's okay," I say quickly. At last I feel my words are my own again. "Thank you though."

"I know it's easier to talk to your friends, but they're not qualified to help you. My daughter always thinks she knows best, but she's just a teen girl. I don't want to see her or her friends ruin their futures for you, and I don't think you want that on your conscience either."

"How would they ruin their futures?"

"If they help you break the law, they're accomplices and can be charged alongside you."

I think of how Cata and Saysa are forging my Huella, and I know she's right. I'm dragging them down with me.

Jazmín abruptly stands. "When we go to Lunaris, you are to travel in your dress so no one identifies you as a lobizona before the championship. Understood?"

I rise to my feet too. "Understood."

Sensing my dismissal, I hurry to the door, and as I'm crossing the threshold she says, "I expect to meet your parents next moon."

I nod quickly and dart out. It's only when I'm back on the spiral staircase that I can finally breathe.

I can't believe Jazmín drugged me. I feel completely violated. It's a miracle Cata didn't grow up to be heartless, considering she was raised by Professor Umbridge.

I hurry down the stairs, trying to forget everything about this encounter, but I can't shake one thing Jazmín said. I can't be responsible for ruining my friends' lives.

Maybe instead of going to Lunaris, I should leave now and head to Luisita's. I know how to transform, so I might be able to help Ma break out.

Except I'll need stores of that magical mate that extends our abilities beyond the full moon. And for all I know, Ma could already be in Argentina—

A new idea suddenly strikes me.

I will go to Lunaris . . .

But I won't come back to El Laberinto.

Saysa told me Lunaris has portals to and from every hybrid settlement on Earth. So when the full moon ends, I'll take the door that leads to Kerana.

If we can't stay in the United States, then I'll meet Ma in Argentina.

———

When I get to the field behind La Guarida, the wolves are just finishing their transformation drills. "Great timing," says Gael. "We're hunting!"

Without further explanation, he leads us into the woods up the side of the mountain. Everyone else marches behind him, but my friends hang back until I catch up. "¿Todo bien?" asks Nico.

"Yeah," I say, trying to shake off the remnants of Jazmín's mental assault. "What did Gael mean by *hunting*?" I try to picture myself stalking something like a doe or a bunny and recoil. "Are we—are we actually going to hunt animals?"

"No," says Pablo, and I blow out a breath of relief. "We're going to hunt one another."

I wait for his expression to crack, but his black gaze holds steadfast. "What do you mean?" I ask.

"We pick one student to be the prey," says Nico, his silver eyes reflective in the sunlight, "and the rest of us hunt him—*or her*."

"It can get pretty brutal," adds Javier.

"That's how the captain got his scar," says Gus, clapping Tiago on the back. He looks incomplete without Bibi's body entwined with his.

I frown. "What scar?"

"Called it," says Pablo under his breath. Gus curses and takes something out of his pocket and hands it over to him. Were they just betting on whether I've seen Tiago shirtless?

"Show her your scar," booms Javier, nudging Tiago with his shoulder.

"Another time."

"But she needs to know how dangerous this is!"

Beads of sweat form along my forehead, but I try to stay calm. I don't want to give the wolves more reasons to doubt me.

"Okay, gather round," calls Gael when we reach a clearing surrounded by woolly trees. "Manu, since you've never hunted before, you'll be the prey."

The air never makes it to my lungs.

"The rest of you will break into hunting packs, and the winning team will be the one that incapacitates her first."

My pulse beats like a gong in my ears. *Incapacitates?* What the fuck?

"And, guys, I'd rather not have to report another death to Jazmín, so let's keep the mauling action nonlethal, okay?"

"WHAT?!" I back away from the group, no longer caring what they think of me. "I'm not playing this game!" I shout shakily, glaring at Gael. "You're *insane*—"

The whole class abruptly breaks into laughter, even our teacher.

I roll my eyes when I realize they're hazing me, and I'm not sure if I want to keep yelling or laugh along with them. Pablo bumps fists with me and Nico pats my shoulder, like I was just put through some absurd social test.

I hate that I have to wonder whether they would have pulled this prank if I were a guy—but I do. Because even if I'm part of their pack, I'll always be separate from it too.

"Okay, everyone pair up," says Gael once the guys have quieted down. Tiago cuts over to where I'm standing. He and Diego were the only ones who didn't participate, but they didn't put a stop to it either.

"Our deadliest task in Lunaris," says our teacher, "is to protect the brujas when they visit dangerous territories to harvest ingredients for brews. Most creatures of that realm are beyond our ability to kill, so we need to know how to lose and distract and hold off our opponents. How to create diversions that will buy the brujas time to get a safe distance away. You're going to take turns playing hunter and prey, and you either want to pin your opponent down, or you want to hold them off for as long as possible. *No actual fighting.*"

I've never been violent with anyone, nor do I have any idea how to hunt. But I'm also not particularly eager to be prey.

The guys around us pair off and transform. Tiago's eyes glow a brilliant blue, and his voice grows deeper and gruffer as he speaks, like a radio knob tuning from man to beast.

"I'll give you a head start."

I race into the woolly trees, running up the side of the mountain, my heart punching my chest. The adrenaline is so intense that I feel the pull on my limbs, and my body screams in pain as my bones shift position, and my fangs and claws slide out.

My vision sharpens and expands as I run, and I spy a flicker of silver through the foliage. I hurtle toward it and find a lake of crystal-clear water. Even though I know Tiago could catch up at any moment, I can't keep from edging closer and peeking down.

My jaw drops when I see my reflection, revealing the full length of my sharp fangs. My arms and legs are muscular and strong, coated with body hair that looks like a fine fur, and my hands are capped with curving claws. The hair on my head is wilder than usual, covering everything but the pointy tips of my ears.

My most familiar feature is my eyes. Funny how I've always avoided them for making me look alien, but now they're the only link to my humanity.

I feel my body trembling like it's trying to transform back, so I take off at a run again.

As I leap through the underbrush, it's a thrill to move in this powerful lobizona body. I vault over spiny bushes and swing from tree branches, having so much fun that it takes me a moment to hear the echo. There's someone else moving out here.

I slow down and take cover behind a wide tree.

I can hear your heart racing.

Tiago's voice whispers through my mind like a favorite song.

I shut my eyes and concentrate on the oxygen rushing in through my nose and feeding the rest of my body. I grow steadier with each breath.

Good girl.

I scowl. *Will the creatures of Lunaris also be this condescending when they hunt me?*

A soft chuckle caresses my thoughts. *Got your attention, didn't I?*

I hear the rustling of leaves, and I keep moving through the forest, using the twisty trunks for cover. The effort of climbing uphill makes my breath labored, and a stitch in my side slows me down. I take refuge behind a rocky outcropping and peek out to scout Tiago, but I don't see any sign of movement in the distance.

Will you show me the scar Javier was talking about?

Right after you tell me the truth about your meeting with Jazmín.

I swallow back the memory of the drug, of being forced to speak against my will, and my heart starts racing too fast again.

Maybe it's best we don't talk.

The forest is swathed in a thick silence, and I use my claws to crest the mountain's peak. When I'm at the top, I survey the land below.

There are woods all around, offering ample hiding places,

except for one side of flat grass—it's like someone took a giant razor and cleared a lane of trees. Peering down, I can see all the way to the bottom. Most wolf pairs have already chased each other out of the mountain and are wrestling on the grassy field outside La Guarida.

There's a snap behind me, and I spin around, my gaze darting in every direction. But I'm alone on the mountaintop.

I saw your eyes when you got back from Jazmín's office.

I stiffen. He's just baiting me to lure me out. *What about them?*

Something made their sunlight wane.

My heart flutters, and before I can respond, I see a blaze of sapphire right as something hard collides with me. Tiago's distraction costs me my footing, and I snap my jaws and howl as we fall down the flat side of the mountain.

Air blasts my face and pebbles bounce off my body as we roll down the grass, spinning faster and faster as we gather momentum. Tiago's arms cage me to his chest, and as soon as we start to slow down, I shove away from him and spring to my feet.

His monstrous werewolf form is already facing me.

I'm a tad dizzy, and I wobble. Tiago spies my weakness and rushes at me without warning. He's a faster runner, but I use my quick reflexes to dodge him.

His arms close around air.

Too slow, I taunt.

That was just my warmup.

We start pacing around each other, and the other wolves lose interest in their own matches when they spy ours. One by one they revert to their human shapes, forming a wide circle around us as Tiago and I size each other up. Even Gael joins the crowd.

"*Bets!*" shouts Pablo. "Get your bets in now!"

"Five semillas on Tiago," booms Javier. "Sorry, Manu!"

"Ten on Tiago," calls Gus.

"I got ten on him too!" says someone else.

"Fifteen!"

As they keep calling out numbers, Tiago and I continue to circle each other. *That's a lot of performance pressure,* I tease him. *You sure you can deliver?*

Always do.

"Out of respect for me, you could have at least attempted to do this discreetly," Gael says to Pablo.

"Where's the fun in that?" says Pablo, and at the look Gael gives him, he adds, "Okay, all bets are in! No surprise, everyone is Team Tiago." Then his black eyes lock onto mine. "But I'm betting on gold."

He can't be serious. Even I wouldn't wager on myself.

That's a lot of faith Pablo's placed in you, says Tiago. *You sure you can live up to it?*

While I'm thinking of a clever response, he charges me.

But when he veers too heavily to my right, I know he's feinting. I lean left so he thinks I'm falling for the trick, and when he lunges, I spin just out of reach.

Again, Tiago's arms close around air.

The guys react with a mix of cheers and groans.

Your plan to wear me down won't always work on Lunaris demons, says Tiago. *If you toy with them too much without engaging, they'll lose interest and chase after easier prey, like the brujas you're supposed to be protecting.*

I shrug. *You're welcome to lose interest any time.*

As if I could.

We both stop pacing.

I think his retort took even him by surprise.

I'm vaguely aware that our classmates are saying things, but it's all just a background murmur as Tiago and I stare at each other, locked in a deafening silence. It's surreal to be having this intimate of a moment in the midst of a public showdown.

This time, I know the attack is coming because we've been staring at each other too long. Tiago doesn't have any choice left but to strike.

I stabilize my stance, and when he launches, I don't move. I keep still until he's close enough that I can see the surprise on his face—and right before his arms reach me, I duck.

The force of his leap propels Tiago forward, and I grab a fistful of his shirt and pull myself onto his beastly back.

The guys cheer as I yank on Tiago's arms and shove my knee into his spine.

Tiago growls and drops to the ground. His body shrinks as he transforms back to human, and as I stand upright, I shift back too.

Most of the guys break into applause.

"The captain got his ass kicked by a girl!" Javier booms, and our team surrounds Tiago, messing with him by not letting him get to his feet.

"Pay up, losers!" says Pablo. "Javi, you owe me five. Gus, you bet ten. Hector . . ."

While Pablo settles his accounts, Gael comes over and offers me his hand. I'm so stunned by what just happened that it takes me a moment to shake it.

His fingers are warm and rough with calluses, but his face is smooth and unlined. He looks about ten years younger than his sister. "Well played, cariño."

My moment of triumph is dampened by the pet name. It's the second time he's called me *darling,* and since I doubt he would do that to one of my boy classmates, I say, "*Manu's* good."

His coral eyes narrow for a fraction of a second, like he just remembered or recognized something.

"Have you heard of any other lobizonas?" I blurt.

He shakes his head. "As far as I know, you're the first."

"So I'll always stand out. Everyone I meet will have a ready formed opinion of me based on what I am, not who I am. I'll be loved and loathed . . . *sort of like Fierro.*"

Gael's expression is unfazed by my name-dropping. "The difference is you had no say in being a werewolf. But Fierro chose to become who he was. He earned his reputation through his own bad choices."

"Same way you earned yours."

His eyes widen, and I know I shouldn't have said it—but those bad choices he's referring to include my very existence. And for the first time, it really hits me that I'm staring at the being responsible for foiling my parents' plans.

Gael scrutinizes my face, and I worry he recognizes Fierro in my features. "I'm so sick of you kids and your romantic notions about someone who was nothing more than an outlaw. He's not coming back to save you—he couldn't even save himself." His expression hardens, and he bites off each word. "Get it through your heads. He's gone."

Then he walks away to put an end to Pablo's good times, and I stay rooted to the ground.

There was something deadly in Gael's coral eyes, something he wasn't saying.

Not just hate, but triumph.

Like maybe he already killed my father.

25

"Try not to leave the goal area, even if you start to feel cooped up in there—which you will, since thanks to Tiago, most of the action happens at the other end of the field." Diego takes a running kick at the ball and sends it sailing at the net I'm protecting.

I watch until I have a sense of which way its arc will bend, then I jump up toward the right goalpost—and the ball sails into my hands.

The sky is all pinks and violets, and soon it will be dark. The rest of the team has dispersed, but Coach Charco assigned us extra one-on-one training. He wants me ready to debut in Lunaris, just in case. It came across as a two-sided threat to Diego: *If your performance sucks at the championship, make sure your understudy is ready to step in.*

"What's the danger in leaving the area when the ball isn't even close?" I ask, kicking it back to him.

"Sometimes you forget there's a witch on the other team who's also missing out on the fun. She can't hex the goal area, but she can mess with the rest of the field. Stray too far, and a glacier could catch you unaware and slow you down."

He kicks the ball, and I slam it away, sending it crashing into the bleachers.

"I got it!" I say.

"It's okay, I can get it."

We both end up running into the stands, and he gets to the ball first. As we climb back down, I say, "Can I ask you something more on the legal end of the sport?"

His periwinkle eyes glint in the sunlight. "Sure," he says as we step back onto the grassy field.

"Do you actually think they'll let me play? You said yourself that I'm a challenge to the system, and I'm bound to face resistance."

"The league could make trouble for us if they wanted to," he concedes. "But it's not likely. Our team is the returning champion, and our school is a top-ranked institution, not to mention Coach is a former pro player who has a reputation for being honorable, so we wouldn't pull any tricks. And once they see you play, they'll have no doubt of your abilities."

"But what happens after? I'm not exactly looking to be investigated or studied—"

"Manu," he says seriously, his deep voice dipping. "The truth is, it's hard to believe you've been able to stay under the radar for this long."

I instantly regret opening this door. Diego is way too smart and will figure me out if I ask too many questions.

"Look, you're under Jazmín's protection because you're a student at her school. But now that your secret is out, eventually it will spread. Word of advice?"

"Just one?"

He smirks, and I notice he has a solitary dimple, on his left cheek. "Anything you do that's traditional wolf territory could be challenged by some zealot, and you could wind up before the tribunal. I've been studying their decisions, and they tend to be led by their pragmatism. Our world is gray, and rapidly gray-*ing*, and the tribunal navigates it by sticking to a determinedly black-and-white approach. They rule by the book and can't be swayed by emotion. If you don't fit the exact letter of the law, they see you as going against it."

"So what do I do?"

"You can't break a law that doesn't apply to you."

"Meaning?"

"If you're undocumented, you're *unwritten*. Embrace that."

"You're saying if no one's told my story before . . . I get to tell it the way I want?"

"Exactly."

I nod in appreciation of his advice, but it doesn't ease my nerves because Diego doesn't know that I am breaking the law. Hybrids are forbidden.

A breeze blows from the trees, and I look up when I inhale hints of cedar and thyme.

"Thought you could use an extra pair of legs," says Tiago, looking from our huddled faces to the forgotten ball by our feet. "Everything okay?"

"Good timing," says Diego. He spikes the ball into the air with his toe, and Tiago catches it. "I've passed on all my advice, but as far as sharpening her skills, I'm sure you'll make for a more exciting challenge."

Tiago turns the ball over in his hands while Diego walks away, and the air between us is more strained than ever. We're like a couple of magnets with like charges: The closer we get, the stronger the resistance. Even now, standing a few feet apart and watching the ball whirl in his hands, I feel a repelling force pushing against me, telling me *this is wrong, this is wrong, this is wrong.*

And yet I can't move away.

A sister force is pressing on me from the outside, trying to defy gravity and bring us together.

Tiago drops the ball to the ground. "Want to play?"

"I'm kind of tired," I say, not sure being alone with him is the best idea.

"I'll walk you back." He kicks the ball into the goal, then we tread down the unpredictable path through El Laberinto, beneath a purpling sky. The towering trees block out much of the light, and golden doraditos begin to emerge from the leaves, little droplets of sunlight that are ready to take on the night.

I hope the path is short and direct tonight. There's never any way of knowing how it will unfurl; it could cut through the woods, or meander around a village, or lead us somewhere new altogether.

Neither of us speaks at first. Every time I try to cast around for a conversation starter, I hear his answer when I told him he was free to lose interest in me.

As if I could.

What did he mean by that? Was he talking about the assignment? Or the fact that he has to look out for me?

The sky darkens to charcoal, and stars are strewn across like glitter. The path curves away from the trees, opening up abruptly to a vast glacier.

"How is there a glacier in Miami?" I ask, mouth agape.

"It's not a glacier. It's crystal."

I lean over and peer down, but it's too dark to make out

much detail. I squint and edge a little closer, and my foot steps on the edge of the glassy ground. The crystal cracks where I touched it, and I gasp as silver lines spread from the break, spiderwebbing across the place.

"I broke it!"

"No, you didn't," says Tiago.

I watch the silver fracture lines continue to expand, and when it's over, the ground looks like it's covered with giant crystallized snowflakes.

Tiago sets foot on the design, and the snowflake he's standing on lights up bright blue. I look down. "Are those—?"

"Clothes," he says, and he walks onto another snowflake that lights up neon green. "This is cooking ware and cutlery." He goes on to another that lights up hot pink. "Down here are toys—"

"What is this place?" I ask, stepping onto an area that lights up vivid violet.

"It's our manada's marketplace. This is where we pick up whatever we need."

"So, it's a shopping center?"

"We don't pay for anything. Our currency is the seeds we bring back from Lunaris every month, and they belong to the whole manada."

"So, it's like *socialism*?" I ask, thinking back to Perla's government lessons.

"There's no human equivalent because our values are different. Humans' life goals are often power or comfort based, but we live for the full moon." He must see in my expression that I don't understand. "Just imagine that your version of paradise is a real place you visit every month—what more would you need? Just your loved ones. Teamwork is how we survive. Wolves hunt the semillas, brujas brew the mate."

He makes their culture sound so . . . *liberating.*

But it's not. Like Saysa and Pablo pointed out, Septimus aren't free to be anyone they want. They're born into categories that cage them for life.

And like in the human world, I'm forced to hide because of who I am.

As we walk, the ground beneath us lights up red, pink, yellow, and suddenly I break into a sprint. Looping around the crystal, I trace every snowflake.

The ground illuminates beneath me in a rainbow of colors, their glow decorating the air as I paint the night. I'm having so much fun that I let out a squeal of wild delight.

Tiago's laugh is a honeyed sound that warms the world. He sprints after me, and I run faster. When he gets close to catching me, I switch direction. The ground glows orange and silver and gold.

I hear him coming up behind me again, and when I think he's going to catch up, I twist again—but this time Tiago anticipates my maneuver, and he reaches out to intercept me.

His hands close around my middle, and we whirl along the crystal. Once we stop spinning, we're bathed in turquoise light, and his arms don't fall away.

"Ojazos," he murmurs.

Perla's nickname is a jab to my chest, and I swallow the wave of emotion in my chest.

"No, son más que ojazos," he says. *No, your eyes are more than striking.*

Hearing him speak Spanish feels intimate, like I'm hearing his real voice for the first time. If possible, it sounds even more musical.

"Son solazos."

They're blazing suns.

I realize he's been leaning in when his features blur. His nose brushes mine, and I inhale his heady scent, goose bumps rippling across my body. Our breaths mingle, and my heart races as we stand still in a futile final effort to resist.

His mouth touches mine, and the air seems to leave me all at once.

His lips are softer than I expected, and when I tilt my chin up, they lock onto mine. Blood blasts through my body as lights explode inside me, in more colors than this crystal could hope to contain.

It's my first kiss.

And it's with *Tiago*.

26

Cata's Tiago.

I yank away from him, and Tiago lets go of my waist. "I'm sorry—"

"We should hurry," I say, and I don't look back as I cut across to the path. When he catches up, I stay a few steps ahead so we can't talk.

Guilt gnaws at my gut, and I'm relieved when the trees open up to the familiar sight of La Catedral, La Guarida, and El Jardín. From the aroma of searing meats, I know dinner is well underway, but I can't face Cata right now.

"Tell the others I went to shower," I say without looking back.

"But you'll miss dinner—"

Thankfully there's a trio of brujas eating by El Jardín's front door, so Tiago can't follow me or try to talk. I don't exhale until Tiago peels away to join the others.

As I approach El Jardín, I recognize Noemí, the fire witch on the Septibol team. I'm not near them yet, but I can hear their conversation.

"Shhh, there's a wolf in the area," says a girl named Sara who's wearing a plum-colored dress. I guess sitting out here is the only way for them to speak in semi-privacy.

"It's fine, she's not going to tell anyone about your crush on Hugo," says Noemí.

"Shut up!" says Sara, sending a blast of air at Noemí's face.

"Why was she coming from the woods with Tiago?" asks the bruja in blue. Her name's Olga.

"Haven't you seen the way he looks at her?" asks Noemí. "She's the flavor of this moon."

"Enjoy it, honey," says Olga. "So worth it."

"As long as she doesn't fall in love," says Noemí darkly, and though I keep my eyes lowered, I can still feel the burn of her coppery orange gaze on my skin. "None of us can measure up to his perfect Catalina. He always goes right back to following her around, waiting for the day she'll give him the time of day. Her ever-faithful wolf."

"But Cata kissed him the other day!" injects Sara. "Maybe they're finally together."

"I think she was just marking her territory," says Noemí, and when at last I look up, all three of them are staring at me like they know I'm drinking in their every word.

Once I get close, I don't acknowledge them. I just storm into El Jardín, and I slam the door behind me.

The next ten days pass in a blur of werewolf training and Septibol practices. I've avoided being alone with Tiago since our kiss, and my aversion to being near him is so strong that I can't even finish reading *Cien Años de Soledad* because I don't want to touch anything that's his.

"Tonight is the full moon, so today the barrier between this world and Lunaris is weaker than usual," says Gael, addressing us in the field behind La Guarida. "That means we might experience anomalous weather."

I refuse to remember the lunarcán from my first night here.

Or the way Tiago came back for me.

"It also means some creatures may have breached our borders."

The soul-sucking Sombras flash in my mind, and I really hope those things didn't cross over. Then I remember what nests in the stone mountain from the time my lunaritis dream became a nightmare—and I shiver.

If those things got through, I'll run and never look back.

"You're going to patrol the woods in pairs," says our teacher. "If you come across anything, *howl.*"

I turn to look for Pablo and find myself facing the three black lines of his chest tattoo. "Ready?" he asks, like he's reporting for duty. I've been partnering with him ever since my falling out with Tiago.

I'm pretty sure the guys are convinced Tiago and I hooked up, and whatever was between us is over. For my part, I'm just relieved Cata and Saysa aren't in class with us.

"What kinds of creatures could we run into here?" I ask. In my periphery, I see Tiago walking in Javier's giant shadow, his gaze angled in my direction.

"None of the really dangerous ones," says Pablo, almost sounding disappointed. "Mostly cocorros, since they're drawn to marshy environments." No idea what those are, but at least Pablo doesn't seem too concerned.

We climb the uphill forest, and with every step, I grow more jittery about tonight. It's hard to process that I'm actually going to set foot in the landscape of my dreams. I still can't believe it's a real place.

Cata, Saysa, and I have resumed our nightly Flora visitations. We're been building my backstory and writing the script for my Huella. Saysa's already in touch with a former classmate who does forgeries, and we're meeting her in Lunaris. The more effort I watch them pour into my fake identity, the worse I feel about dragging them down this road.

I can't get what Jazmín said out of my mind. I'm risking my friends' futures, and I know I'm doing it.

Yet I won't be their problem for much longer. I'm not telling them about my plans to run so that they can't be charged as accomplices by the Cazadores. In three days, when I take the portal back to Kerana instead of here, they'll be free of me.

I just wish I knew more about where Fierro might be— assuming Gael hasn't already murdered him. The whole reason Cata, Saysa, and Tiago opted to help me in the first place was in hopes I would somehow lead them to him. I feel like they must have an idea of how I can find him, but I refuse to involve them any more than I already have. I'd rather ask someone who will see it as purely hypothetical.

"Where in Lunaris do you think Fierro's hiding?" I ask Pablo, the words rushing into each other at the beat of my panicked pulse.

"Glad you asked," he says, as eager as ever to trade conspiracies. "I've thought a lot about this, and to survive year-round, he'd have to be on the move. There have always been stories of Septimus who've tried to stay in Lunaris past the full moon, and none of them have been heard from again. We only know they didn't survive because the Caves of Candor didn't reflect their faces back to us anymore. That's why the tribunal ruled it illegal to stay—can't risk dropping our population numbers."

I'm not sure what the Caves of Candor are, but I get the general gist.

"If anyone could survive that place though," says Pablo, his voice taking on a tone of reverence, "it's Fierro."

"Can you think of any way to locate him?"

"So, it's not enough to be the first lobizona, now you're going to bring Fierro home?" Pablo studies my eyes, and I worry I've given too much away. Then he nods approvingly. "I like it."

I smile, but my heart is racing. "Where do we start?"

"I've always thought the Lagoon of the Lost would be worth a try. If he's in Lunaris, the Lagoon will know—problem is, the Septimus asking needs to have something of his to bring into the water. Something valuable to him."

Something of his. Something valuable to him. But what? I don't have any of his possessions.

Besides, I can't swim.

There's a thrashing sound in the bushes behind us, and Pablo and I spin around as the biggest jaws I've ever seen come snapping at me. The creature has the snout of an alligator and the body of a snake, and I scream as it strikes—

Pablo transforms in midair and lands between the cocorro and me. The thing swerves around us, and Pablo lets out a howl that sends every bird flying from the branches overhead.

Adrenaline courses through my heart, and my body begins to shift before I'm even aware the transformation is happening.

The cocorro launches at us again, right as another pair of lobizones jumps in, one of them twice as big as the rest of us—Javier. He's with Tiago.

Are you okay? Tiago asks in my head.

I'm too shaken to respond, and I watch as he and Pablo

corral the creature into a corner. When it's got nowhere to go, Javier takes a running leap and lands on it. The cocorro lets out an ear-splitting shriek, and Tiago reaches out with his claws and slices off its head.

Once it's decapitated, we all transform back, and Tiago runs over to me. "Manu, are you okay?" His sapphire eyes search mine.

I manage a nod, but the truth is I'm not.

I didn't do anything.

I just froze in the face of danger. This was the first part of being a lobizona that didn't come naturally to me. *Violence.*

"We all reacted the same way the first time we came face-to-face with a beast from Lunaris," says Pablo, guessing my thoughts. "If you're not quick to kill, that's nothing to be ashamed of."

Gael shows up, followed by other students. "You all okay?" He looks down and sees the dead cocorro. "Good work. Let's head back to La Guarida."

Tiago falls into step with me. "How've you been—?"

I pick up my pace before the question is fully out of his mouth.

When we're all gathered on the field, Gael says, "We're ending class early so you can save your energy for tonight." He looks at me and the rest of the Septibol team. "Bring home the championship."

The guys cheer, and while everyone else leaves, I hang behind. Tiago lingers, but I avoid his gaze as I approach Gael. "Can I talk to you a moment?"

He looks at me warily and shrugs. Not exactly a *yes,* but not a *no* either.

Since I can't outright ask about Fierro again, I say, "When I first saw the cocorro . . . I kind of froze." In the fringe of my vision I see Tiago finally disappear inside La Guarida.

"That's natural," says Gael gently, and I know I've succeeded in lowering his guard. "Violence is distasteful to you, particularly as your parents' protectiveness hasn't given you a chance to run with other wolves. Give yourself time."

"I'm worried though. I feel like everything I do is going to be judged on a different scale. If I fail, all future lobizonas fail."

"You can't let others' closed mindedness impact your mindset. That's the quickest path to failure. The only thing you can control is yourself."

"Is that why you chose to take on Fierro alone, without backup?"

The alarm is back in his coral eyes, and now he outright asks, "Why is my past with Fierro so concerning to you?"

"It's not," I lie. "I'm just wondering where he went. Like everyone else."

"Well, I obviously don't know, or I wouldn't be here."

"Why not try the Lagoon of the Lost to find him?" I ask in a small voice.

He shakes his head. "Tell me something, since you're so smart: How am I supposed to do that when we don't know his real identity? We have no way of figuring out his bloodline. Let me know when you have an answer."

He walks away convinced he got the last word.

But I can barely breathe.

He just told me how to find my father.

"Are you listening?"

I blink, and Saysa's face comes into focus. She, Cata, and I are huddled in Flora's library, making final tweaks to the details for my Huella.

"What?"

She rolls her lime-green eyes, and this time it's Cata who comes to my defense. "Manu, I know you're nervous, but this plan is going to work."

Jazmín's stern stare flashes in my mind, and I wrap my arms around myself so they can't see I'm shivering. "What if we get caught?"

"We won't."

"Are you sure—?"

"None of this is free of risk," says Saysa, "but it's worth doing if it keeps you alive."

I nod and drop my gaze to the spread of papers scattered around us. The evidence of all the laws they're breaking on my behalf.

"Why are you helping me?" I blurt.

"What do you mean?"

I hear the hurt in Saysa's voice and hurry to clarify. "It's just that on that first night, when you learned the truth about me, it seemed like the only reason you all agreed not to turn me in was because you thought I could help you find Fierro."

Cata blows out a hard breath. "Don't blame Saysa—she would've wanted to help you even if you were half-Septimus half-slug. Same with Tiago. He only said the Fierro thing to sway me. I think selflessness runs in their family."

Guilt gurgles in my belly, and I desperately hope she never finds out about our kiss.

"*I'm* the one who needed to know how helping you would benefit me," she admits.

"I don't blame you," I say honestly. "You were protecting yourself and your friends. And you didn't owe me anything—"

"I know," she says, "but I'm still sorry."

Now that I know her family story, I understand why Tiago felt that finding Fierro would be the ticket to swaying her. After all, he's the reason her family is broken.

Mine too.

"Just so you know, I don't feel that way anymore," she adds gruffly. "I mean, I'd still like to find him, but it's not about that now." Her harsh tone is at odds with her sweet words, but that's because she's not used to making herself vulnerable.

"Shit, look at the time!" she says, jumping to her feet. "It's almost sunset. I need to check in with my mom. Saysa, I'll meet you at the portal." She looks at me and adds, "And I'll see *you* in Lunaris."

Once she's climbed out of the tree hole, I look at Saysa quizzically. "Why won't I see her at the portal?"

"Wolves and witches have different access points." Seeing my face, she adds, "Don't worry, Tiago will go with you." Then she cocks her head with curiosity. "I've been meaning to ask, is everything okay with you two?"

"Yeah," I say too fast.

"Did he try something—?"

"No, nothing like that," I say even more quickly.

She sighs like she can guess what happened and says, "Listen, there's something you need to know about my brother—"

"It's fine, it's none of my business." I spring to my feet, feeling like I'm going to be nauseous if I hear another word. "We should probably head to the portal. I don't even know where to go."

"I'll walk you."

"Wait." Before we step onto the branch-bridge, where werewolf ears could be listening, I ask, "What about my period? It always comes on the full moon. Will there be tampons in Lunaris?"

Deep dimples dig into Saysa's cheeks, and she reaches out and squeezes my hand. "Don't worry—one of the perks of leaving the realm of reality is we don't have to deal with any bodily functions."

"How—?"

She shrugs. "Magic."

The sky is dark enough that the moon will soon be visible. Even if I were indoors, I would know it's close to nighttime because there's a twist in my uterus, like the cramps are just moments away. I haven't been awake for my period since my first one.

My teammates are waiting for me by the path into the trees—everyone but Carlos. "Why are you wearing a *dress*?" demands Pablo.

"Coach wants Manu to be our *secret* weapon," says Tiago like he's talking to a two-year-old. "That means, we don't call attention to her."

"See you on the other side of the moon," says Saysa, winking as she walks away.

I join the guys on the pathway, careful to keep a few bodies between Tiago and me. Tonight, the path is wide and packed with wolves, and when we reach the end of the treeline, we're facing a vast sea.

We have to swim across?

Fuck. Fuck. Fuck. I'm going to die.

I look at Tiago, forgetting everything else that's passed between us. He frowns like he can tell something's wrong but isn't sure what. And I have no way of telepathically telling him unless we transform.

I stare at the endless expanse of water in dread, as the first trickle of silver touches the surface. A ripple skates across the sea, like a wave of energy running through it, and suddenly everyone around me begins to shift.

I feel another stab of pain, and as the cramps begin, so does my transformation. The period pain is worsened by the cracking and elongating of my bones, and the instant I'm in werewolf form, Tiago's musical voice invades my mind.

What's wrong?

I can't swim.

I'll help you. He positions himself beside me, and this time I don't move away.

As the lobizones wade into the water, Tiago and I fall back so that we're the last ones to enter the sea.

He offers me his arm, and I hold on to his bicep as we wade in. The water is warm, and within a few steps it's too deep for me to walk. I cling closer to Tiago and tip my chin up to suck in air.

Relax. Your body wants to float, so let it.

I let the lullaby of Tiago's voice wash over me, and I take in Perla's calming breaths as at last my feet leave the ground. My legs and torso rise until I'm floating on the sea's surface, and Tiago is pulling us both along.

Good. Now kick with your legs.

I do as he says, but I'm still gripping onto his arm for life.

Try holding on to me with just one hand.

My fingers tighten around him as I let go with my other arm. He moves his free arm in long arcs, kicking with his legs, and we glide forward. I copy what he's doing with my free arm, and soon we're swimming as one unit.

We pick up speed, and my terror morphs into excitement. *I'm swimming.* I begged Ma to teach me, but she was too afraid my glasses would slip and someone would see. I can't believe I lived this long in Miami without trying this.

It feels like I'm flying.

I let go of Tiago altogether, trusting my body to know what to do.

And it does.

You're a natural. He smiles at me through his sharp fangs.

How do the brujas get to Lunaris?

Their portal is in the sky. They have to cross some kind of magical storm.

After a while I have to focus all my energy on swimming because it's draining my muscles. I'm starting to feel like we've been going for hours, but judging by the moon's placement, it hasn't been that long. The other lobizones are so far ahead that I can't see them anymore.

When my legs feel like lead and there's still no land in sight, I ask, *How much longer?*

We're halfway there.

Halfway?!

Are you tired? Do you want me to carry you?

The thought of being in his arms sobers me up. *I'm fine,* I say, and it comes out a little harder than I intended.

But suddenly pain spasms in my right leg, and my head goes under. Everything grows muffled, and I want to kick out but my leg is cramped tight, the muscle taut and stinging. The current pulls me farther from the surface, and bubbles stream from my mouth, the air scorching my lungs—

Something hard closes around me, and I'm yanked up, until my head breaches the surface. My wet hair sticks to my face, and I cough to clear my airways, my breaths raspy and shallow.

Tiago's arm is around my waist, and his other hand combs my hair back, away from my eyes. He's careful to use the pads of his fingers and not his claws.

His touch leaves trails of heat on my skin. *Breathe slowly,* he murmurs musically.

I'm tethered tightly to him as the pain in my leg subsides, our faces so close that there's nowhere to look but each other. My pulse picks up again, only this time it's nothing to do with drowning.

Feeling his skin on mine is driving my body wild, and it's a struggle to keep my animal impulses in check. Being alone with him in the middle of nowhere, our bodies entwined, makes me want to give in to my darkest desires.

To the wolf inside me.

Solazos, he whispers through my mind, his sapphire gaze locked on mine. *I'm sorry for what I did. The last thing I wanted was to push you away—*

Please don't. I shove away from him and start swimming again.

He easily keeps pace with me. *Manu, please—*

I said don't.

We keep swimming in silence, and it's a good thing because I need every single store of strength to keep going. I've never in my life been physically active for this long, and my heart and lungs aren't ready. I wish Tiago had thought to tell me that I'd have to cross an ocean to get to Lunaris so I wouldn't have had to learn how to swim along the way.

I'm just about to ask how much farther when he says, *Dive!*

What?

But instead of answering me, he goes under.

Tiago!

I dive down to find him, and the instant my head dips underwater, I'm not in this world anymore.

I'm dry, standing upright, facing the black walls of a place I've only seen in my dreams.

The Citadel.

27

The shimmering sky is streaked with bright blues and golden yellows, making the black onyx stronghold glisten like wet ink.

Night made tangible.

This time, I'm seeing the Citadel from the inside. There are no cracks in its construction, no flowers or trees jutting through—just an inescapable fortress.

"We thought you drowned!"

I whip around to see Pablo, hands propped on his hips like a frustrated parent. He's flanked by Javier and Nico. I stare at them in awe.

"Leg cramp," says Tiago.

"¿Estás bien?" asks Nico, his silver eyes narrowing.

"You do realize the entire championship pretty much rests on your legs," says Pablo, equally concerned.

I can't get over how the guys look—*how I must look*. We're

giants, just like the world around us. Javier is roughly the size of a tree. My head's never been this far from my feet before.

Even though we're in human form, our fangs and claws are still out. We look more like vampires than werewolves.

You can retract them, says Tiago.

It's not enough that he can invade my mind at will, now he's also reading it. I look up and watch his fangs retreat into his gum line. The other guys do the same, and I draw mine in too, along with my claws.

Lunaris is home, so when we're here, we don't transform the same way, Tiago explains. *It's just our claws and fangs that come out.*

Why?

Because this is where our magic comes from, so our bodies are more powerful here. We can harness our wolf senses without the pain.

And you can speak to me telepathically at any time?

Yes.

"Reunion time," says Pablo, clapping his hands together.

The five of us walk into the curtain of mist straight ahead. It only blinds us for an instant, and when it dissipates, we're in a field of enormous flower buds as large as each of us. They're embedded in the grass like lily pads in a lake.

As we weave around them, I watch a wolf approach a lilac-colored bud and water it. The petals begin to bloom before our eyes, and the flower majestically opens.

He tosses something too tiny to see into the blossom and walks away. The flower fluffs its petals and soaks up some sun before slowly closing back up.

There's one for every manada, says Tiago. *They're connected to a plant—in El Laberinto, it's Flora. When we pick seeds, we deposit them here and they travel home.*

Kind of like a bank, I say, and Tiago's chuckle tickles my thoughts.

Beyond the flowers is an even more surreal scene. Hundreds of thousands of Septimus are congregating on what looks like a snowy field, reuniting with friends and family, greeting one another with hugs and kisses and laughter.

Cotton-candy clouds of every color float over their heads, raining down silver stars that are strewn across the ground like snowflakes.

Saysa told me that some Septimus have been in Lunaris for longer, given the different time zones on Earth. According to her, time doesn't work the same way in this dimension. Our bodies don't require sleep, so the whole trip feels like one long day.

Even though the sky will darken just like nightfall, it's technically the various energies of Lunaris cycling through. We have to keep track of the light to know when to return. The third time the sky goes dark marks the closing of the portals.

I follow the guys through the almost million-strong crowd until we somehow manage to find Cata and Saysa. They must have set a meeting point because I don't see how we could have found them any other way. They're standing with an older couple who look too much like Tiago and Saysa to be anyone but their parents.

"Finally!" says Saysa, sounding more relieved than annoyed. "You took forever!"

"Ahí está mi hijo," says Tiago's mother, who shares his exact sapphire eyes. *There's my son.* Tiago wraps her in his arms, then hugs his dad next, and suddenly I miss Ma more than I can stand.

"¿Y quién es esta dama con los ojos soleados?" asks his dad on seeing me. *And who is this lady with the sunny eyes?* He smiles at me warmly. He has Saysa's dimples.

"Soy Manu," I say, and he leans over and kisses my cheek.

"Muy lindo conocerte, Manu." Tiago's mom greets me with a hug and a kiss, and I'm embarrassed when I hold on a second longer than she does. But instead of pulling away, she leaves an arm around my back while she catches up with her family.

There's a flash of forest green, and I notice Carlos staring at me. He's with his parents and a guy who must be his brother. They're gathered with Pablo and his family. It looks like their parents are friends.

Carlos continues to glare, and I force myself not to look away first. I've barely made eye contact with him the past couple of weeks, and I still don't understand why it bothers him so much that I'm a wolf. It's not like I had a say in it. Besides, it's not affecting *his* life. What right does he have to react this way?

"Ready to go?" asks Cata, and I break the staring contest to turn to her.

"Yeah," says Tiago. "See you guys tonight," he tells his family, and I follow him, Cata, and Saysa back the way we came.

"Where are we going?" I ask.

"Out," says Cata in a tone that makes it sound more like *shut up.*

For your Huella, Tiago explains.

Oh.

When we reach the Citadel wall, the opal doorknob is the same as the one I'm always trying to reach in my dreams. It feels so strange to be this close to it that I can just raise my hand and touch—

"Where are you going?"

I look up at the stern voice, and my breath catches in my throat.

It's Leather Jacket.

The Cazador who brought me to El Laberinto.

I drop my gaze to the grass so he can't get a good look at me. I don't know if he saw me by El Retiro, or if he was even aware I existed, but I'd rather be safe.

Tiago greets him with a handshake, pulling him in for a half hug. "We're just going out for a little, we won't go far." His voice is casual and disinterested, like it's really no big deal.

"You know I'm a fan, but I can't let you go with this group. The rule is one wolf per witch—that hasn't changed."

I look up and down the black wall, and I spot Cazadores posted all over. They're standing so still that I didn't notice them.

"Come on, Nacho. Pablo and Javier are meeting us there," says Tiago, still acting nonchalant as he reaches for the door.

But Nacho steps in front of Tiago and blocks the exit. "When they get here, you can go."

A few Cazadores are now looking, like they're trying to decide if they need to come over and offer Nacho some backup.

"Sorry—we're—late!"

Pablo is out of breath by the time he gets to us, and he leans over, panting for air. Javier thumps him on the back, but his attempt to be comforting knocks Pablo facedown to the ground.

"I think I've figured out why you can't get a girlfriend." Pablo's voice is muffled by the grass.

Javier's boyish cheeks flush, and he lifts Pablo to his feet by the scruff of his neck. While Pablo dusts himself off, Javier averts his gaze, but not before I glimpse his expression.

"Can we go now?" Cata asks haughtily, pushing her way between Nacho and Tiago, slicing through their tension.

The view beyond the Citadel is just as I dreamt it—a vast field of golden grass, and a misty horizon that veils whatever lies beyond. Only as we're walking toward the mist, something dark on the ground draws my eye. My shadow.

It's loping away from me.

And it's shaped like a *wolf*.

My wolf-shadow approaches Tiago's, and they sniff each other out. Pablo, Javier, and Nico's wolf-shadows also approach, and they all look one another over. Then they take off at a run, vanishing through the mist.

I keep my gaze lowered until I can school my expression. *What the hell was that?*

Our shadows only show up outside the Citadel, says Tiago. *You know how our manadas are hybrid Lunaris territories? Well, the Citadel is a hybrid mortal territory—because it holds the portals back to our realm. So the rules work a little differently in there.*

Okay, but why are they wolves? *And how come they're not shadowing* us?

Since we're technically part wolf and part man, Lunaris translates our identity this way. They're not just shadows though. They can—

"Now that you called us away from our families who we barely ever see, can we know where we're going?" asks Pablo.

"We're hitting up the waterfalls," says Tiago.

"Fuck yeah!" booms Javier.

Even I'm excited now. The waterfalls are one of my favorite sights to visit in my dreams because I know as long as I can see my reflection in the water, I'm safe.

"Or maybe we should go to the Purple Plains," counters Cata, and I catch her subtly nudging Saysa with her elbow.

"Yeah, let's do that!" she says, her enthusiasm a tad over the top.

I've dreamt of the plains too. They're beautiful, but they're not as exciting as the waterfalls.

"Lame," says Pablo. "I vote waterfalls."

"Okay then, you guys go to the falls, and we'll go to the plains," says Cata, taking my arm and pulling me toward her and Saysa.

"No, not cool," says Pablo, shaking his head of black hair. "The law is one wolf per witch."

"And since when do you care for rules?" asks Saysa, voicing my exact thoughts.

"Since the final is around the corner, and we can't risk our players having to sit it out. Now, if you'd care to do some rule-breaking post-match, I'm your wolf."

"Let's just go to the falls," says Tiago. He sounds a little anxious about something, and Cata seems to hear it too, because she drops my arm and takes Tiago's hand. Saysa looks sulky about the change of plans, but she locks elbows with me, and we follow them.

When the white mist clears, we're facing a forest of emotional black-leafed trees that sometimes succumb to sobbing sessions.

"Sweet, the Weeping Woods!" says Javier, but his enthusiasm sounds just as put on as Saysa's did earlier.

I thought we were going to the falls, I say to Tiago.

Landscapes manifest through the mist when you approach, he narrates into my mind. *Lunaris knows where we want to go, but just like the path in El Laberinto always changes, the destinations here shift around. Nothing ever stays in place, so it's hard to know how long it will take to get somewhere.*

Our wolf-shadows chase and nip at each other. I never in my life would have guessed I could find my shadow endearing.

As beautiful as these woods are, I can't help wondering what happens if a storm blows through and the soul-sucking

Sombras appear. We should have brought Felifuego with us for protection.

What about the Sombras?

Tiago turns his head and scrutinizes me before speaking into my mind, and I wonder if I just gave something away to him without knowing it.

We'll be okay. I promise.

I don't like the intimate way he says that, so I ask about something that's been bugging me. *What's this forest called in Spanish?*

El Bosque Llorón.

I frown. *Weeping Woods, Caves of Candor, Purple Plains . . . why do the names only alliterate in English?*

You'll have to ask the Septimus who translated everything. In French this place is Les Bois Pleureurs.

I don't speak French, but apparently Tiago does. His accent is so beautiful that a catalogue of phrases fills my mind that I'd love for him to translate. Then I shake my head and let the words disperse in my brain like shreds of paper in the wind.

When we enter the familiar forest, I lose sight of our shadows. Our eyes glow in the darkness, like floating orbs. Lime green, sapphire blue, Mars red, rose quartz pink . . . Pablo's black gaze is the only one that's impossible to distinguish.

The reality of these woods is nothing like my dreams. The heavy humidity, the earthy scent, the loamy ground, the bell-like tinkling of the insects that make their homes here—

"I'm pretty sure Fierro left his mark somewhere in this forest," says Pablo.

My heart stalls. "What?"

"There might be one by the falls too. I never fully checked it out."

What's he talking about? I ask Tiago.

Lunaris sometimes invites certain Septimus to leave a mark on the landscape. It's rare and hasn't happened in a while.

Crossing a passage my dad once traveled makes me feel close to him. I squint at every tree trunk, trying to see if I can spot his *F* symbol.

A gust of wind blows through the black leaves, and as they scatter over us, the tree's branches clack together. "Was that you?" Tiago asks Cata.

"No."

"Storm's starting," says Pablo ominously. I touch the trunk closest to me, and my hand comes away wet.

"Who's doing it?" asks Cata, and her pink gaze goes right to me.

"*I* don't know," I say defensively. Why would she think one of us is causing this weather? And why would it be *me* when I don't have any magical powers?

Everything okay? Tiago asks into my mind. He sounds like he's accusing me too.

Why are you asking me that?

The weather is fueled by our emotions . . . Lunaris can manifest our feelings.

I try to digest that. So this whole time, I've been *creating* my own problems in here? And now I'm at it again and putting my friends in danger—

"Sombra!" booms Javier.

Tiago spins around and pulls Cata behind him.

"Where's a fire witch when you need one?" mutters Pablo.

"I take offense at that," says Cata, stepping out from behind Tiago. Her pink eyes glow bright as she summons a powerful wind that blasts the Sombra back into the darkness.

Saysa's lime-green gaze grows luminescent, and she presses

a hand to the closest trunk. Her face flushes, and she shuts her eyes, though her lids flicker like there's a lot of activity going on. It seems like she's communicating with the trees.

After a moment, they stop crying, and the storm's over just as quickly as it started.

Our wolf-shadows are waiting for us in the sunshine when we reach the end of the trees. We cut through another misty barrier, and on the other side are green hills lined with color-ful hot-air balloons that extend endlessly into the horizon. I've never seen this Lunaris landscape before.

You three are going to meet the forger, says Tiago. *I'll draw the guys away so they can't hear you.*

But why here?

Up in the air is the best place to tell secrets. You know exactly who's listening.

"I thought we were going to the falls," whines Pablo. "Why are we in the secret sharing space?"

"What are you talking about?" asks Cata, feigning inno-cence.

"You know exactly what I mean. Who are you meeting here?"

Pablo is too smart for his own good. He's not going to leave us alone.

"Bet I can make it to the last balloon first!" Tiago speeds off, and I almost laugh at his juvenile approach. There's no way Pablo is going to fall for—

Air blasts in my face as Pablo breaks into a supersonic sprint, and Javier takes a flying leap behind him. I blink a few times as their three silhouettes recede into the sunlit horizon.

Well, that was . . . *embarrassing.*

Cata shrugs at the look on my face. "What can I say? Wolves make great pets."

I growl, and the guttural sound takes us both by surprise. My fangs and claws slide out on their own, and a flicker of fear flashes in her eyes.

"You really are one of the pack," she says, and even though she doesn't mean it as a compliment, the words warm me.

"There!" says Saysa, pointing to a pinstriped balloon. A bruja in a silver cloak is waiting inside the wicker basket, and I retract my weapons as we hurry over to join her. Thankfully my wolf-shadow is far off, playing with the others.

"Hi, Zaybet," says Saysa when she steps inside, hugging the water witch. I've noticed that even though the style and fabric of the brujas' outfits vary by manada, their clothes always match their eye color. This girl's outfit makes me think of an elf from Middle-earth.

After greeting Catalina, Zaybet says, "You must be Manu. Nice to meet you."

"You too."

A gust of wind hits the balloon, and we rise into the air. Cata's pink eyes are alight as she navigates us through the sky.

Saysa hands over the information she and Cata drafted for my Huella. "Now I need to capture your likeness," Zaybet says to me as the green hills grow smaller and smaller.

"Sure," I say, expecting her to take out a camera. Instead, she pulls out a mirror with a polished stone handle and hands it to me.

"Look at yourself in there, please."

I hold it up and stare at my face, wondering what exactly I'm doing.

After living with beings who share my unnatural eyes, I thought I would have grown more accustomed to mine, but the sight of the orbiting golden galaxies still jolts me.

"Thank you," she says, taking the mirror back. She uses her sharp nails to remove something from the glass and peels off the filmy top layer of the mirror. My reflection is still plastered there.

My face flutters in the air as the witch stashes the mirror back inside her silver cloak and pulls out a piece of parchment. She flattens my likeness onto the paper, and the result is a rustic-looking photograph that's a perfectly detailed impression of me.

"All that's left is to match your eye color," she says, moving so close to my face that the slightest bump would bring us together. "Hmmm," she muses, her gaze unblinking. "Very unique. Are you earth?"

"Do you think you'll be able to find a match?" asks Saysa, speaking over Zaybet's question.

I'm glad the Huella doesn't include a check box for bruja or lobizón. Of course, that's only because the government equates it with one's sex. For all their magic and might and moon-activated portals, the Septimus seem to be stuck in an earlier century.

"Yeah, I think I know where to look," says Zaybet. "Meet you before the match?"

The balloon starts dropping so suddenly my stomach flips, and the three of us shoot looks at Cata. Her piloting could use some finesse.

"How many semillas?" Saysa asks Zaybet.

"Fifty. Plus something special for the fast turnaround."

As soon as we get to the ground, Zaybet strides up to the mist and vanishes. No farewell. The guys are already running back, and I figure she didn't want to be seen.

"Is this costing you a lot?" I ask Saysa and Catalina in a low voice before the guys arrive.

"She's definitely cutting us a break," says Saysa. "Fifty mate semillas, and by something extra she means a rarer plant."

"Like a Felifuego?"

She nods. "Cata and I already anticipated as much. We took what we needed from El Laberinto's stores."

"*You stole? For me?*"

"It's okay, no one will know." She must see the panic on my face because she says, "There are new seeds every moon, Manu. But there's only one you."

"Finally!" says Pablo when the mist clears and reveals the waterfall coves.

There are ten of them, each one a different color, and a rainbow arches over the set. As we get closer, our reflections appear in the falling water, looming larger than life. Staring at the six of us side by side, I'm struck most by how much I look like the others. Like I belong.

"We have to make it quick," Tiago warns.

"And whose fault is that?" asks Pablo. "If we would've just come straight here—"

"Meet back when the light dims," Tiago commands. He takes Cata's hand, and they split off from the rest of us, going alone to the green cove.

I try to resist sinking into the hole of despair opening in my chest. Averting my gaze, I see that Saysa's also looking after them, like she's annoyed to be left behind.

"Come on," says Pablo, and the four of us walk to the pink waterfall. We have to line up single file to fit onto the stone walkway that curves around the cove, and behind the falling water is an opening into interconnected caves.

Our wolf-shadows leap ahead of us, dancing along the

granite walls, and Pablo follows them into the passage. Saysa goes next. I've never explored these caves before, and as I step inside, I notice Javier isn't behind me.

I turn and see him looking glumly at the water. As I open my mouth to call him, I identify the problem—the cave's opening is too small for his gargantuan frame.

Without thinking, I shout, "Last one in is a cocorro!" And I dive off the stone walkway into the bay.

I plunge through the pink surface in a panic—I literally just learned how to swim moments ago. But my worries fade when I kick up and breach the surface, my body once again coming to my mind's rescue. I rake my heavy wet hair off my face, and I see bubbles in the water from the impact of Javier's dive.

He lets out a roar of laughter as he surfaces, and his boyish grin is one of the purest things I've ever seen. "Race you to the other end!" he booms, and I'm off before his next breath.

His body is so much longer than mine that he easily over-takes me. By the time I make it to the other side, his elbows are hinged on the stone ledge, chin tilted up like he's sunbath-ing. "Oh, you finally made it."

I splash water on his face, which turns out to be a big mistake.

A tidal wave of pink swallows me and pulls me under. We keep messing with each other until we're exhausted, and then we just lie on our backs and float.

Our arms graze past each other, and when I see his face, I spy traces of the sadness I noticed earlier.

"Is . . . everything okay?" I ask softly. I don't think it was *my* emotions that summoned that Sombra.

"Why do you ask?" He floats past my field of vision until I can't see him anymore.

"I just thought—maybe you wanted to talk." He doesn't say anything, and I stare at the pastel-colored sky as I admit, "I guess I've always been invisible, so I know how it feels."

"Invisible," he repeats, like he's testing out the word. "Sharing your secret with us," he says after a stretch, his voice smaller than usual, "Was it worth it?"

I don't say anything.

I can't.

I'm still in hiding.

"Manu! Come quick!"

I look up at the waterfall, where Pablo's waving me over. "I found a Fierro mark! I don't know how long it'll stay—"

My heart leaps into my throat, and I want to go, but I also don't want to abandon Javier.

"Go check it out!" he booms, his voice returning to its jovial volume.

Torn, I look from him to Pablo, just as Saysa pops her head out. "I can't believe you jumped in without *meeeeee*!"

She sings out the last word because Pablo pushes her off the stone. She splashes into the cove, and when she surfaces, her green eyes are overly bright. Suddenly the path Pablo's standing on begins to tremble, and tiny pebbles plunk into the pink water.

"Easy," he says, raising his arms in surrender. "I was just helping you!"

Javier swims under Saysa, and she squeals when he surfaces with her on his back. Since the moment is over anyway, I run up the walkway to join Pablo and follow him through the cave opening. We go single file between glistening stone walls that are so narrow, we have to keep our arms at our sides.

The passage splits into two, and Pablo takes a right. He

starts speeding up, and so do I, my heart beating hard against my chest.

The tunnel spills into a small circular space with blue flames licking the air. Our wolf-shadows are in here, alternately sniffing and pawing and growling at the walls. I look closer to see what they're reacting to—different etchings that surface for a few moments, then melt back into the stone.

"Here," says Pablo, and I dart to his side. Right there, carved into the wall, is Fierro's *F*—a pair of linked inverse 7s.

I instinctively lift my hand to the symbol and trace a finger along the grooves in the rock. It's my first time touching something of Dad's, and the urge to meet him tugs on my heart. It's unfair that all these Septimus got to grow up knowing so much about him when I know nothing.

The mark melts into the stone.

"Where'd it go?"

"Like everything here, it only surfaces when Lunaris wants it to," says Pablo. "She keeps her secrets."

The blue flames go out.

"Shit. We have to go." He pulls me by the hand into the passage. I run with him through the stone maze, until we emerge through the cave's opening, by the pink waterfall. Saysa and Javier are already waiting for us on the grass with Cata and Tiago.

"Let's go!" Tiago calls out.

There's real worry in his voice, and I look up. The pinks and blues and yellows of the sky have turned into reds and purples and oranges. The next step is silver, and then it will be too late to make it back to the Citadel.

Just like in my dreams.

What happens here at night? I ask Tiago as we run.

The Citadel door locks to keep out any Lunaris creatures—and we won't survive out here on our own.

Cata clings to Tiago's side in a way that isn't like her as we make for the misty wall. Whatever happened between them, she seems to need him now more than ever.

I *have* to let him go.

I turn for a final look at the waterfalls before we cross the misty barrier, and I see our wolf-shadows racing after us—except for the smallest.

Mine.

It's standing still, staring at the waterfalls and cowering on the grass, like it's terrified. Our group's reflection is starting to fade from the water, but I know what scared my shadow.

The image shows only five of us.

Where I should be, there's just a dark silhouette . . . like I've been cropped out of the picture.

28

The omen haunts me as I catch up to the others. Am I going to get caught? Is the Huella not going to work? Am I not going to make it out of Lunaris alive?

On the other side of the mist is the vast grassy field that leads to the Citadel. Yet we're so far away that it looks like nothing more than a black dot on the darkening horizon.

The colors of the sky are beginning to blend into gray, and up ahead the golden grass is growing duller by the moment.

"Hurry!"

Tiago's bellow makes me look back, and I instantly regret it. A swath of silver is swiftly overtaking the landscape, chasing our heels. We're literally racing moonlight.

Tiago sweeps Cata off her feet and carries her, the way he carried me during the lunarcán. I turn to help Saysa, but Javier's already pulled her onto his back like a small child.

We put on a burst of speed as we hurtle toward the unforgiving black fortress. The ivy snaps in anticipation, and when we're within striking distance, I hold my breath expecting the vines to attack us—

But they don't.

Pablo reaches the opal doorknob first, and he swings it open for all of us to get through. A handful of Cazadores guarding the entrance yank us in and shut the door behind us.

"Casi casi," says one of them with a dark laugh. *Cutting it close.*

We're too out of breath to respond. Tiago and Javier set Cata and Saysa down, and the six of us amble onward without a word. We drag our feet across another misty barrier—and when it clears, it's already the dead of night.

A night unlike any I've ever seen.

My eyes dance all over the place, trying to take everything in. The full moon is so low in the sky that it looks close enough to touch, and almost a million Septimus are spread out beneath its silvery light. The scarred white orb shines over a majestic midnight garden, where Septimus are lounging on the grass, draped over tree limbs, drinking the flowers—

Drinking the flowers?

A witch brings a red rose to her lips and sucks on a petal. When the ruby tint fully drains, she turns it clockwise and moves on to the next petal, and so on and so on, until the flower wilts and leaves her mouth stained red. She looks like she gets a rush from the pigment because she takes a few tentative steps and stares at the world like it's new.

I only snap out of my awe when my gaze meets Pablo's.

He's watching me.

From the way he knits his dark brow, I know he's seen more than I intended to show. Especially to a conspiracy theorist.

"Where's your family?" he asks, his suspicious tone reminding me of the morning we met.

"I'm about to meet up with them," I say vaguely.

"I'm going to find my folks too," booms Javier, and I'm relieved when Pablo goes with him.

I peek at Tiago and Cata, who are holding hands. Whatever happened at the waterfalls seems to have brought them closer, and though I know I should be a good friend, my heart feels like that wilted rose.

This time when we reunite with Tiago and Saysa's family, it's not just their parents but *everyone*. I meet two sets of grandparents, two sets of aunts and uncles, four teenage cousins, and just when I think the introductions are over, there are extended family members—great-grandparents, great aunts and uncles, second cousins, and more. By the time I've greeted everyone, I'm spent.

I'm also painfully envious. Tiago and Saysa's huge loving family is everything I've ever wanted. Cata knows them all, and from the way they treat her, it's clear they expect her to officially join the family. I watch her with Tiago and Saysa, talking to their cousins, and she becomes a different being. There's no sign of the snarky smirk she shares with her uncle Gael.

I feel like the old me, watching Other Manu live out her dreams in the sunny light of day, while I fantasize about her life from the safety of darkness. Only it's not enough just to watch anymore.

If I play in the championship match, I'll never be invisible again.

The thought both thrills and terrifies me. If I step forth from the shadows, I'll be just like Fierro—caught between fame and infamy. But finally *seen*.

"Manuela de La Mancha," says a deep voice. It sounds

strange to hear such a long name, but that's the manada I'm pretending to be from.

"Hola, Marilén," I say to Tiago and Saysa's great-grandmother, whom I met moments ago.

"No sos bruja."

You're not a witch.

My tongue feels like sandpaper, and my mouth seals dry. Since our wolf-shadows roam outside the Citadel, and my fangs and claws are retracted, I didn't think there would be any indicator of my identity—

"No te preocupes, no vengo a interrogarte." *Don't worry, I'm not here to interrogate you.*

She moves closer, and the way her steely eyes seem to see more than others reminds me of Perla. "Toda la vida soñé con conocerte," she whispers. *My whole life I've dreamt of meeting you.*

Her long black hair is in a tight, elegant bun that pulls her skin, stretching it so that if there's a single wrinkle, I don't see it. "La primera de nosotras que nació fuera de su jaula."

The first of us to be born outside her cage.

Her words warm me, and I feel newfound confidence creep up my features—but it evaporates when I see who's arrived.

Jazmín walks arm in arm with a wolf in black robes who looks like a judge in a courtroom. Or a *tribunal.*

"¡Papi!" Cata runs up and flings herself at her father. The two of them share an affectionate reunion, then she leads him by the hand to greet Tiago and Saysa's family, approaching me last.

"This is a new transfer student, Manuela de *La Mancha,*" says Jazmín, emphasizing my manada like she sees through the lie.

My skin itches and my pulse races. I haven't seen her since

the day she drugged me, and even now I feel unsafe in her presence.

"Nice to meet you," says Cata's father, who speaks with a heavy accent. "I'm Bernardo." Instead of kissing my cheek like the others, he shakes my hand. His grip is so firm that my fingers ache when he frees them.

"Where are your parents, Manu?" asks Jazmín, and it's a struggle to stay still and not run away. "I would like to meet them."

"As would I," says Bernardo. He's examining me too closely not to be in on the secret. Jazmín must have told him what I am.

"They're around," I say vaguely. "I'm meeting them to get my Huella."

"I'd like to take a look when you have it. We'll meet after the howling." Jazmín looks from me to her daughter. "Make sure it happens."

"Manu, come here!" calls Saysa, flashing me a big fake smile. Grateful for the rescue, I start to walk away.

"Are you going to play in the final?"

Jazmín's question lingers in the air, and as much as I'd like to keep moving and pretend I didn't hear her, there's something in her tone that makes me stop and turn back.

"If Coach puts me in," I say noncommittally.

"I hope he does." She cracks a cold smile. "I'm sure we'll know everything there is to know about you then. After all, *the whole species* will be eager to hear your story."

"Try one!" Saysa shoves a bouquet of colorful blooms in my face the instant I join her and Tiago.

You okay? he asks in my head.

I nod in assent.

Cata comes over and circles an arm around my waist. Her expression looks pained, and I feel sorry for the situation I've put her in, pitting her against her parents. She picks out a blue blossom from Saysa's bouquet, Tiago plucks a golden one, and I go for a purple flower.

They each bring a petal to their lips, and I mirror their movement, clamping my mouth on the velvety texture.

An explosion of flavor bursts on my tongue that somehow tastes like the color purple. A cocktail of grapes and frosting and sour candies. I rotate the flower in my hand until I've sucked the pigment from every petal. My body and mind grow energized, like I just ate a complete meal.

Once I've drained the flower, I look up and bite back my gasp. I'm seeing everything through a purple filter.

A subtle buzz spreads through my nerve endings, relaxing me. We keep drinking our way through the flowers until there are none left, and then we wander through the throng in a pleasant daze, greeting Septimus and tasting other plants and ogling the low-hanging moon.

I'm still not used to crowds, and having been taught to avoid them my whole life, I make my way to the outskirts of the garden, where it's quieter. I spot a collection of long-stemmed silver blossoms as tall as Javier that look like thin-trunked trees with silver crowns.

Walking between the stems, I take comfort in the solitude. And as the filter of green from the last flower I consumed fades, I face my reality.

If there was any small part of me holding on to the hope of going back to El Laberinto with my friends, it's officially gone. I have to take the portal to Argentina and try to get lost among the hundreds of thousands of Septimus who live in Kerana. The quicker I'm out of my friends' lives, the better for them.

Jazmín is not going to stop coming for me. She took a dislike to me from the start, and she's determined to get me away from her school.

I wander into a dead end and turn around. Cata thinks that as long as I show her mom my Huella, she'll stop insisting on meeting my parents. But I'm not so sure. The way her dad was watching me tonight tells me they're not going to let this go. Even if they don't know Fierro's my father, they still see a use for me.

When they turn me in to the Cazadores, they'll be the ones who discovered the first lobizona. Cata said so herself—her mother is looking for redemption. And she's sharp enough to recognize she's found it in me.

My life for hers.

"A real werewolf would have heard my approach."

I look up, startled to see Carlos blocking my way.

"Smart move, going back to dresses," he says, his green gaze slowly trailing the length of my body.

I steel myself, swallowing my nerves. "Why does it bother you so much that I'm like you?" I ask, refusing to let him terrify me.

"Because you're *not* like me," he says with a growl. "And your delusion is just going to rile witches up, make them start asking for shit they can't handle, and that's not good for any of us."

I remember the first time I met him, when that Congeladora froze his ass and demanded to ride him around Lunaris for a day. At the time, I thought she was flirting with him, but now I see the full picture.

A bruja can't leave the Citadel without a wolf escort. Carlos wasn't offended by her terms because it wasn't really an insult to him. It was a reminder of a bruja's place.

He moves closer, and my back bumps against the plant

stems. His eyes sear into mine, unblinking, and I force myself not to look away first.

"I *know* you've been drugging yourself with performance enhancement potions," he says in a cold voice. "Show me your magic."

"I can't do magic," I say through gritted teeth. "I'm a *lobizona*."

"If you say so," he murmurs, his face so close to mine that I have to tilt my neck up. "But if all you've got is your physical strength, I've got news for you—"

I gasp as he seizes my wrists and whispers, "Guys will always be stronger than girls."

I raise my knee to kick him in the balls, but he twists me around and shoves me facedown on the ground before I get the chance. My arms and chest ache with pain as he pins me down with his body, trapping my hands behind my back. I try to scream, but he presses my face into the grass.

My mind is too frantic to find the telepathic channel to Tiago, and I try to calm down enough to reach out—

"Go ahead," whispers Carlos in my ear. "Scream. Call out for Tiago. Let him rescue you and prove me right."

I struggle to lift my face, just enough to free my mouth. "You're stronger than me." My voice is strained, but I won't let him silence me. "*So what?* Javier's stronger than you, Tiago's faster than you, Diego's smarter than you—"

"But they're all *guys*," he says gruffly in my ear.

"So what?" I repeat.

"So you're missing a key piece of the puzzle, sweetheart." His hips dig into mine, and I use all my strength to snap my neck back, knocking my skull into his face.

There's a loud crack as I headbutt him, and he cries out in pain. When his grip loosens, I slide out from under him.

We spring to our feet at the same time, but he's still blocking my way out, his fangs lowered, his fingers capped with curving claws.

Where are you?

Tiago's voice breaks into my mind, and instead of answering, I glare at Carlos as my own fangs and claws come out.

I'm done being bullied.

"Your insecurity's showing," I snarl. "Your obsession with me being a girl says more about you than me."

Carlos doesn't believe girls can be werewolves? His mistake. Because I'm about to show him just how much damage a lobizona can do.

"There you are!"

Gael comes up behind Carlos, and I've no idea how he found us. "Coach is looking for you two."

Carlos and I retract our fangs, and Gael's coral eyes dart between us, like he's trying to work out what's going on. "Everything okay?"

Carlos pushes past him without a word. When Gael looks at me, flames are flashing in his eyes, bringing out the coral's fiery undertones. "Did he hurt you?"

I shake my head. "We were just talking."

Gael examines my expression a moment longer, then he says, "Match starts at sunup. Let's go."

I walk side by side with him, and given our last interaction, I don't know what to say. After all, he is my father's would-be murderer.

We cut through a barrier of mist, and on the other side is a stadium that spirals high enough to seat almost a million. Half the stands are already filled.

"Finally!" says Coach, jogging over to me. He thrusts a bundle of baby-blue clothing in my hands. "You have to change into your uniform. Hurry!"

He points me toward the locker rooms. Unlike El Laberinto, there are two here: One is tiny and says *bruja,* and the second is enormous and says *lobizón.* I take an instinctive step toward the wolves' door, then I hesitate, looking from one to the other.

I feel Carlos's disdain all over me, like it's engraved on my skin. And I wonder how many other guys on the team feel as he does but are going along with everything to appease Tiago and Coach.

Coach rests a hand on my shoulder. "*Secret* weapon, remember?" he says, making the decision for me. "That's why I gave you two uniforms."

I examine the clothes, and I see there are three pieces. Shorts and a shirt, with a dress to pull over it.

I look up, and Coach's amber eyes fill with light, growing almost as golden as mine. And I realize the darkness is lifting from the sky. It's almost sunup.

"Let's make an impression no one will forget," he tells me, and I nod, excitement buzzing in my belly at the thought of playing on that field. I reach for the door labeled *bruja,* and as I slip inside, I catch a glimpse of Gael watching me.

He looks disappointed.

"Finally!"

Saysa and Cata are already in their baby-blue uniforms when I step into the locker room. Bibi and Noemí are with them.

"Sorry," I say. "Had one too many flowers."

Noemí snorts and Cata rolls her eyes. "Get changed. Did Coach tell you the plan?"

I nod and hold up my two outfits. Just then a door opens

at the end of the space, and four brujas step through wearing bright red dresses. Their chests say *La Recoleta*.

"¿Tienen *cinco* brujas en su equipo?" one of them asks. *You have* five *witches on your team?*

"We always overprepare," says Cata, arching a brow.

The four of them size me up, their gaze lingering on my eyes like they're trying to determine my element.

"You going to watch her get dressed?" snaps Cata.

When they leave, she looks to Bibi and Noemí. "Make sure they're really gone and keep an eye out so they don't spy."

They nod, and when it's just the three of us, Saysa pulls out a golden notebook. "It's here!"

The three of us crowd over the Huella, examining it. Cata pulls out hers so we can compare them side by side.

"This is great work," muses Saysa.

The cover is a solid imitation material, and it's dyed a golden yellow that feels like a good match for my eyes. My likeness is inside, along with my manada details. Zaybet forged the signatures of officials at La Mancha.

"You're official now," says Catalina, handing me the Huella.

I hold the government-issued photo ID in my hands and stare at it. I know it's fake, but it feels real.

Rewrite your story. I hear Ma's voice in my head for the first time in a while. I did just as she said. I'm holding my new story in my hand.

"I know you must be scared about this match," says Saysa, "but we've got your back."

"Thanks." I set down the Huella and the uniforms so I can change.

"She's not scared because she's not playing," says Cata to Saysa. "She's only pretending because the team is her excuse to lay low."

"*Of course* she's going to play," argues Saysa, frowning at Cata. "She's about to make history!"

The two friends stare at each other in stunned disapproval, and it's obvious neither of them anticipated the degree of the other's reaction. I yank off my golden dress and start getting into uniform, opting to stay out of this particular matchup.

"Playing in one game isn't going to topple over centuries of sexism," says Cata. "You need to be more patient. She's not Fierro!"

"She's his blood! And we've waited long enough. So has Manu for that matter. She deserves a chance to be herself—"

"You can't be this oblivious!"

"And you can't be this *cowardly!*"

Saysa's word is a grenade, and when she lobs it, she flinches in anticipation of an explosion. One look at Cata's broken expression tells me this just became the kind of fight that will stay with them forever.

And like everything else, it's my fault.

I pull the blue dress over my shirt and shorts. It's a snug fit.

"I'm ready," I say to distract them, "but it's not like I can play with these ballet slippers anyway, so—"

"They'll have cleats for you by the bench," says Saysa, turning to me. It's hard to see her delicate features so weighted down with worry. "I know you're both scared, but the moment you step onto that field will change *everything*. You're not just a lobizona, you're practically our best player—"

"She's right." Cata whips around to me, cutting off Saysa. "You'll be a peculiarity, the only one of your kind. This match will make you the most famous Septimus in the history of our species. *Everyone* will want to know your story. From the moment you set foot on that field, there's going to be one word dominating every conversation in every manada on the globe: *LOBIZONA*. Think about it."

And I do.

I think about being someone others want to listen to and spend time with. Having an identity, a place in the system, a purpose on this planet. I picture young girls approaching me in admiration. I think of all the Mariléns, older generations of brujas who will feel emboldened by my existence.

Then I imagine a more ordinary life among the Septimus. A quieter one, where I'm more than just a unique biological specimen or a political revolution—one where I'm my own being. I have friends, and a home, and maybe one day a family.

Yet the picture doesn't end there, because there's still the human side of my family tree. No matter how low-key I keep my existence, *ordinary* just isn't in my cards.

Cata takes a step closer, her eyes as penetrating as her mom's. "This isn't about me or Saysa—it's *your* life, Manu. So ask yourself, is fame really what you're after? Will it keep your secrets safe? Is this what your mom would want?"

Ma's lifelong adages run through my mind:

Attention breeds scrutiny.

Silence is your salvation.

Discovery = ~~Deportation~~ Death.

"Once that spotlight is on you, how long before someone digs deep enough to strike truth?" Cata's voice is gentle, but her words are merciless. "Your Huella will get you access to our world, but all someone has to do is follow-up with the officials whose signatures we forged, and your identity falls apart. *In a pack species, there are no secrets.*"

My entire body tenses over, and I know Cata's right. My life is a testament to the truth in her words because Ma's precautions are the only reason I've survived this long.

Saysa takes my limp hand in hers, interlocking her small fingers with mine. "I know it's not safe or fair, but this isn't just about *you*." Her voice is as soft as a caress, even as she delivers a powerful blow. "It's about everyone who doesn't fit inside the box they were born into. It's about showing closed-minded guys like Carlos that they never had the right to cage us in the first place."

Her grip tightens, and I feel the truth of *her* words in my pounding pulse. "You're a *lobizona*. That word wasn't even in our vocabulary until we met you. You're rewriting everything we know—so why let language ensnare you now?"

Cata takes my other hand. "I know how great Saysa's predictions sound. Her idealism is lovely but naive. You know that better than any of us."

Not to be defeated, Saysa takes my face in her hands and forces me to look right into her lime-green eyes. "Listen to me. Shit isn't working for any of us, and you have the power to change it. You're the spark we've been waiting for—if you ignite, we will fan your flames. Otherwise you'll be alone in the dark forever."

"Stop it," whispers Cata. "Manu can still lead a meaningful life without martyring herself."

"Sure," says Saysa, yet her stare doesn't stray from mine. "But why settle for being a son of the system, when you can mother a movement?"

29

The match begins to ground-shaking applause, beneath a sky streaked with pinks, golds, and blues. The stands are crammed with almost a million Septimus, and I've never seen so many faces in one place before.

"Breathe," Cata whispers in my ear, and I exhale heavily. Our team is already on the field, and I'm with the brujas on the sideline. "Whatever you decide, I'm with you."

"Thanks."

"Brujas, get in position," says Coach Charco, and Cata strides over to her spot, while I trail Bibi and Noemí to the bench.

The game is outrageous.

Our abilities are enhanced in this landscape, so when Saysa unleashes an earthquake, the tremor even reaches the stands; and when Cata blasts the field with a gale of wind, the whole stadium fills with a ghostly howling.

The guys are brutal, but Tiago is the biggest beast of them all. He kicks in goals from *anywhere* on the field, managing to keep possession of the ball any time he comes into contact with it. If I didn't know better, I'd think he took some kind of performance enhancement drug.

There's a conviction in his game that often fluctuates on and off—and right now, he's on fire. But the Recoleta team isn't going down without a fight.

Even though their forwards aren't as assertive as Tiago, they work better in tandem than Tiago and Carlos. Where the latter two seem to be in a competition for goals, the former pair trade off assisting each other and seem to coordinate their choreography. They move like they're dancing.

The score stays pretty even the first half, with us leading 59 to 57. As the clock winds down to halftime, Coach looks at me and nods.

He's going to put me in for the second half.

My breathing grows shallow, and I can't get Saysa's words out of my head. I already know Cata's perspective because it's the same philosophy I've lived with my whole life—but it's Saysa's point I can't shake.

This isn't just about *me.*

She's right—only not in the way she thinks.

Gender equality and freedom of lifestyle are battles I can't take on yet, because first I need to win a different war: *The right to exist.*

If I play in the match and shatter all their conventions, maybe I'll buy myself some goodwill. And then when the truth of my birth is discovered, if enough Septimus support me, maybe against all odds, the tribunal will cave to their pressure and make an exception—and, unlike all the illegally-born Septimus who came before me, I'll be allowed to live.

But that's just it. I'll be the *exception,* not the rule.

I'll be making the case that being a human hybrid, or a lobizona, or any other "other" identity is valid only for anyone who has a talent or is "special" in some way.

What if I sucked at Septibol? What if I hadn't manifested wolf powers? What if I had no abilities at all?

Would that make me any less deserving of breath?

Saysa can't understand that because she's speaking from a place of unquestioned acceptance. She's a full-blooded Septimus. Before I shifted into a lobizona, it was she who took me back to Perla to give me the chance to run. Even she didn't think this was a fight I could win without powers.

I would love to show Carlos and all the other misogynists what a girl werewolf can do with their sport—but if I participate now, I'll be playing the wrong game.

"Manu."

I blink and see that Coach is in front of me, flanked by Cata and Saysa. The entire team is gathered behind him. Including Carlos.

"It's time. You ready?"

My gaze glides from him to Saysa and Cata, their faces shiny and grim. I lift my eyes to Tiago, whose skin and hair are drenched, like he just dipped his head in a bucket of water. He looks equal parts exhausted and excited, and something else—more than conviction, there's a new hopefulness in his expression that hasn't been there before.

If it's about me playing in this match, then I'm about to sorely disappoint him.

"I'm . . . I'm not ready."

Coach's face falls.

I can't stomach seeing Saysa's or Tiago's expressions either, so I find Cata, who nods somberly, like I'm doing the right thing. The only one who seems downright jubilant about my refusal is Carlos. There's a gleam of triumph in his eyes, like he thinks he succeeded in showing me my proper place.

Funny, I expected his reaction to bother me more, but he feels so insignificant compared to everything Cata, Saysa, and I discussed.

Diego squeezes my arm in understanding, and to my surprise, Pablo doesn't say anything. But Javier's voice booms like thunder.

"What are you doing? You're beyond ready! You have to play!"

"It's too soon," I say, guilt bubbling in my stomach. "I don't think I can perform in front of everyone."

Disappointment softens his boyish features, and I wonder if it's because I'm not playing, or if in my refusal, he hears the answer to his question.

Invisibility wins.

We take the championship. The final score is 108 to 104.

The team is giddy as we hit the locker rooms, and I'm especially relieved we won since no one reproaches me for sitting it out. By the time we cross the misty barrier to leave the stadium, the sun shuts off its light, unveiling the universe.

This nightfall is even more spectacular than the last. The moon is now higher up in the sky, but celestial bodies are everywhere, in magnified detail: planetary systems, galaxy clusters, asteroid belts, constellations—the universe feels near enough that I could reach up and scoop a handful of stars.

There are silver sand dunes on the horizon, and their undulating lines make this look like the surface of an unknown

planet. I feel like I'm far out in the cosmos, an astronaut charting new territory, discovering new worlds.

"You have to taste this; it's a delicacy," says Cata, tugging
me by the elbow toward a line of stones that glow like embers.

Skewers of meat are being seared, and I bring one to my
mouth and tear off a bite. A soothing warmth spreads through
my insides, revitalizing me, and I hold back a moan. "What is
this?"

"Bálaga. It's the best thing on the planet." She gets us each
another skewer. "The trek to go fishing for them is so dangerous that we can't always get enough Septimus to volunteer to
go. So the rule is when you see it, you eat it."

Once we've had our fill, we move deeper into the crowd so
that others can reach the food. "What happens with all the
babies and children that stay behind?" I ask.

Cata looks around us and shakes her head, and I get the
message that we shouldn't talk like this out in the open. Not
around so many werewolf ears.

"We deputize twelve-year-olds."

It's the first time Saysa's spoken since the match, and she
doesn't bother to keep her voice down. "We complete our academic education early so that twelve-year-olds will be responsible enough to be left in charge of our manadas three nights
a month."

I try to picture a huge Argentine city populated only by
children and babies for a few days, with the twelve-year-olds
in charge. It sounds more like the premise for a middle-grade
novel than a real thing.

"*Pack* species." Saysa emphasizes the word. "Just imagine
how much help we could offer humans if we showed them
how to care for their communities—"

"Any other questions?" cuts in Cata, her voice pointedly lower than Saysa's.

"Yeah, actually. Why is it so dangerous to be outside the Citadel at nightfall?"

Cata checks for eavesdroppers again, but Saysa jumps right in. "Remember how there were seven demons who ruled Lunaris, and the seventh was the father of our species, Tao?" She looks a little buzzed, and I spot a wilted flower by her feet. "Even though he's dead, the other six demons are still alive and powerful. Night is when they hunt, and let's just say, we're no match for them. I'm sure you know though. From Tiago."

I have no clue what she's talking about, but I can't let myself think about Tiago right now. I'm about to ask how the portals back to Earth work, when I hear it—a faint tune coming from the sand dunes, growing louder as it moves in . . .

"Can you hear that?" I whisper.

The music eases through the throng, a moody, haunting, sensuous melody that makes my hips want to sway even though I've never danced. Not in public, anyway. The Septimus around us begin to pair off, and up and down the dunes I see the silhouettes of partners performing an otherworldly tango.

The synchronized way their bodies move would make even the best human dancers envious. There's an unnatural fluidity that makes the Septimus look less like flesh and bone and more like shadowy animations.

The dancing entrances me, and I can't look away. The rhythm of the song infects my bones, until my dress feels tight and my limbs grow springy and every molecule of my being screams for—

As though summoned by my desire, he appears.

Tiago's sapphire gaze locks onto mine, and I recognize the hunger roiling in the restless sea of his eyes, my body at war with itself. The repelling-attraction is so strong that my muscles are sore from the strain of standing still.

Tiago turns to Cata. "Would you like to dance?"

Just the sound of his velvety voice sends a shiver down my spine, and his eyes dart back to mine like he senses it. Like he feels all of me.

What the fuck is this song doing to me?

"It's okay," says Cata, only the heavy way she says it sounds like she's answering a weightier question. "I need a word with your sister anyway."

Saysa squares her shoulders, and she looks a little pleased, even proud, to be prioritized over Tiago. That was a power move on Cata's part. "Meet us back by the grilling stones when the howling begins," she says to me. "We'll show my mom your Huella, and then we can put all this behind us." Her gaze skips to Tiago before settling back on me. "Go ahead. Dance with him."

Panic grips my pulse. Is she testing me? Or him? Or both of us?

Tiago moves in and offers me his hand. I look around for Javier or Pablo or Nico or Diego—pretty much *anyone*—but in a crowd of almost a million, it's not easy to find friends.

"Cata said so," he says softly, and when I look into his eyes again, I'm sold.

I don't have the strength to keep fighting myself. Tiago's proximity is a revolution to my body. What his stare can do to my pulse, what his mouth can do to my breathing, what his scent can do to my blood.

And I hate it.

My gut twists with warning as my fingers find his, and the instant our skin touches, I don't belong to myself anymore. I'm a note in the song.

Tiago's leading does all the work, and I feel like we're alone again, gliding on that glacierlike crystal marketplace in El Laberinto where we shared our first kiss. It's more than a dance, it's a ritual; our magic, our power, is courting, uniting, giving in to that part of us over which we have no control. The part that's been pulling us toward each other this whole time.

As the music picks up speed, our power begins to lead us. Until we're no longer in control of our bodies. Until we're not in control at all.

Tiago's lips hover by mine, his hand on the small of my back, keeping me close. His intoxicating scent gives me a headrush that makes it impossible to think or slow down or pull apart. I want him, all of him, with every part of me.

His mouth brushes mine, a test, and I know what will happen if I don't put some space between us now. But my mind lost its war to my body weeks ago, and it's just taken my brain a while to hand over the reins.

Tiago's lips are back, and I know this time he's going to kiss me, and I'm going to let him, and we're going to make out in front of everyone. Then they'll all know I'm his latest conquest, just another heart he's going to break before crawling back to Catalina—

I shove him away.

The music fades from my ears. Even though everyone around me is still dancing, I don't hear the melody anymore. All I hear are my breaths and my heartbeat, as overtaxed as if I'd just outrun a lunarcán.

I can live with these feelings for Tiago if I have to.

But I can't live with hating myself.

"You're in love with Cata," I say, glaring at him. "We all know it. So stop playing games with the rest of us. It's fucked up."

"Manu, wait—"

He reaches for my arm, but I'm already sprinting away. I don't slow down or look back as I race through the crowd, tears bursting from the corners of my eyes. I hate him for making me feel this way. But I hate myself more for still wanting him.

When I'm out in the hilly sand dunes, I finally stop to catch my breath. I've ventured beyond the dancers, to a darker, quieter area, and I notice that sometimes the sand looks silver, and other times it's golden, like it's illuminated from the inside. A pair of Septimus brushes past me, and I watch them slip through a dark slit in the dunes that looks like some kind of cave dwelling. After a moment, the sand lights up, like the spot is taken.

A waft of lavender-scented air brushes past me, and I turn in the direction of Cata's familiar body lotion. I trace the aroma all the way to a small dune that's glowing gold. She and Saysa must be in here hashing things out.

I know I should let them talk, but now that I've told Tiago off, I want to give her a piece of my mind too. She's not exactly innocent in all this. She knows how Tiago feels about her, and she toys with his heart and lets other girls get hurt in the process.

I storm inside, and the cave's golden glow burns even brighter, like a warning. My shoulders are tense, and my mouth is already firing off. "Cata, I want to talk to you—"

Two bodies are entwined on the sand, and in a flash their faces pull apart, clutching their dresses to their chests.

"What the fuck?!" demands Cata, leaping to her feet as she pulls the dress straps over her shoulders.

"It's just Manu," says Saysa, sitting up and hugging her knees to her chest.

I look from one to the other, but words won't come. My

gaze just volleys between them, waiting for my brain to catch up and my voice to resurface, until finally I blurt out, *"What's going on?"*

"Read the room, genius!" snaps Cata. But it's obvious her attitude is just a cover for her fear. Her eyes are round and shiny, and her arms are crossed around herself, not like she's annoyed but more like she's exposed.

Saysa exhales heavily. "Look, we wanted to tell you about us, but—"

"But you're a fucking terrible liar," finishes Cata, her anger starting to burn through her fear.

"I don't understand," I say, shaking my head. "So you're both—*together*?"

Saysa nods. "For a couple of years now."

"But Tiago—"

"Is my best friend," says Cata. "And he would do anything to protect us."

"Protect you?" I ask, frowning.

Cata rolls her pink eyes. *"How blind can you be?* Our entire population is equivalent to about one-hundredth of one percent of humans. Most brujas can only give birth twice in their lifetimes, so it's especially hard to grow our numbers. That's why we can't let humans find out about us. It's also why we started settlements abroad—to protect ourselves."

"What does that have to do with—?"

"There's no actual law litigating who you can love," she barrels on, "and flings are fine as long as both spouses consent. But we can't marry someone of the same sex. *Reproduction is everything.* And anyone who doesn't have children—whether by choice or infertility or whatever—can be arrested."

I don't know what to say. I remember what Señora Lupe said the day I found the Felifuego, about the tribunal expecting every fertile bruja to give birth to grow the population, but I didn't register the full implications. The world of *The Handmaid's Tale* suddenly comes to mind.

"That's so fucked up," I whisper.

"Gender identity, sex, sexuality . . . it's all tied into an impossible knot for Septimus," says Cata with a deep sigh. "Saysa's been wanting us to be out in the open, and before you showed up it was pretty much the only thing we argued about. She's never cared for conventions or labels, and that's one of my favorite things about her. But most Septimus don't think like she does."

Cata looks at Saysa, and for the first time I see the adoration in her gaze for what it is—true love. "She thinks that together, we can change our world," says Cata, her tone softer as she rests her hands on Saysa's shoulders. "But if others knew about us, we could lose our freedom, our families, even our lives."

Her pink eyes crack with a loneliness I know intimately. "I love Saysa, but I don't know what that means. All I know is I'm holding her back from being her full self. In an ideal world, I would be proudly by her side, but we don't live in an ideal world—you know that better than most."

I recognize Cata's search for a label that fits her because I've been trying on and discarding labels for what feels like forever. It's hard to define your identity when you lack the language.

"Anyway," she goes on, her vulnerability receding as quickly as it came, "when my mom became suspicious of our friendship, Tiago offered to help by pretending to be in love with me. As long as everyone's distracted by the whole *are they or aren't they* nature of our dynamic, Saysa and I are able to live our lives safely."

"Do you think your mom still suspects anything?" I ask, concern twisting my gut. I know what it's like to have that witch on your back, and it's not fun.

Cata shakes her head. "I can't even think of how she would react if she found out. She'd never let me see Saysa again. She'd shame me, make me feel *off*, like I'm wrong or defective, like . . ."

"Like a lobizona?" I supply.

She smirks, and I feel myself smirking back.

"I get that I'm not the best liar," I say, my voice shaky with the heaviness of this conversation, "but I would never betray you. I hope you know that."

Cata's expression crumbles, her emotions puncturing her mask of invulnerability. "It's not just that, Manu. What he feels for you . . . it's different."

My heart stalls, but I try to keep my face impassive because I can see how much this admission is costing her.

"I knew the moment you found out the truth, you'd quit resisting him." Her eyes sparkle with moisture. "And we'd lose our cover."

I can hardly process her words, so I just say, "I'm sorry you've had no time together since I moved in. And for barging in on you now. And for generally interfering with your lives," I add, and then I purse my lips so I'll stop talking. I could probably apologize forever.

"Less telling, more showing," says Saysa, her cheeks dimpled as she playfully waves me out of their space.

I smile and say, "Message received."

Then I quickly retreat from the cave and step outside beneath the starry sky—where Tiago is standing with his hands in his pockets, waiting for me.

30

I instantly know he heard every word. There's a rawness in his gaze like he's been unmasked for good.

"So," I say. "You and Cata . . ."

"Are best friends who would do anything for each other," he finishes. "I'm sorry we didn't tell you."

"You think I'm a terrible liar too?"

"Oh, definitely." He grins, and when his teeth flash, it's like the whole cosmos just leaned in to snap a photograph. "But I still wanted to tell you the truth. I was just waiting for Cata to come around."

"And today, back at the falls—"

"She agreed to talk to you about it when we got back to El Laberinto."

I shift my weight, guilty about my own secrets. "What about all the girls you've hooked up with?" I ask, my inner

Elizabeth Bennet refusing to give him the upper hand. "Don't you think this was unfair to them?"

"We were just having fun," he says with a shrug. "There were no feelings involved."

"Maybe on your part, but I'm sure you broke some of their hearts—"

"Aw, come on, Solazos!" Tiago raises his hands in surrender, and the way he says that nickname, in that pleading tone, leaving himself completely open to me—it's irresistible.

"What do you want from me, *celibacy*? I never claimed to be a saint—"

And I attack him.

There's no other word for it.

With the guilt gone, all that's left is an incandescent desire burning me up from the inside. My body springs free of whatever remnants of control my mind was clinging onto, and I chain my arms around his neck, parting his lips with my own.

He takes my waist and kisses me back with a fierceness that seizes my breath away. I slide my fingers down his arms, feeling the ripples of his muscles, and when I reach his elbows, he cuffs my wrists in his hands. Pulling my arms behind my back, he holds me against his hard body as he leads me in a new dance.

Without interrupting our makeout, he walks me backward, and I don't resist or worry, entrusting myself to him. He guides me through the entrance into a sand dune dwelling, and warm light flickers on behind my closed eyelids. Tiago presses me against the wall, his tongue trailing down my jawline, neck, collarbone . . .

My moans become gasps as a new sensation spreads through me. It's like a flower planted deep within me is spreading its petals for the first time.

I feel more present, more sensitive, more awake.

He releases my wrists so his fingers can graze my waistline, tracing my figure all the way up, my skin growing tingly when he caresses the sides of my breasts. My hands fly to the hem of his shirt, and I yank it off. His mouth captures mine again, and I press my palms to his smooth, sculpted chest—

I pull away when I feel the ridges in his skin.

"Your scar," I murmur on seeing the three claw-like gashes that just barely missed his heart. "What happened?"

"It was my first time in Lunaris," he says, his hands skating up and down my sides. "I was supposed to stick with my manada, but I went off on my own . . . And I didn't make it back before dark."

The jewels of his eyes flicker with shadows, and my heart races with dread. "And?"

"I came across one of the six demons of Lunaris. I only got away because I'm fast, but eventually the poison paralyzed me, and I passed out. If it hadn't been so close to sunup, the demon would have chased me and finished the job, but I got lucky. The Cazadores found me in time for a Jardinera to heal me."

"But the scar never went away."

He shakes his head. "No one's ever encountered a demon and survived, so we didn't know what to expect. Turns out when they leave their mark, it's permanent."

My heart hurts picturing him as a thirteen-year-old dying alone in the dark. "Pablo's tattoo," I murmur. "It looks like your scar."

"He got it to make me feel more comfortable in my skin," says Tiago, and my scalp tingles as he runs his fingers through my hair. "He wanted the other guys to do it too, but they passed. There's only one Pablo."

"Not sure the world could handle more," I say, tracing the claw marks lightly with my fingertips. I don't look up from the tightly coiled muscles of his torso because there's more I want to say. But it doesn't matter that I'm not meeting his eyes because I can still feel his smoldering gaze on my body, until my heart is beating a billion beats per minute, too fast for coherency—

"You want to share those thoughts out loud?" he murmurs, his voice a sensuous growl, and I feel my face flushing with heat because I'm sure he's hearing my pulse.

"First, I just want to know," I say, trying to stabilize my breathing, "why you went along with this lie for so long."

"Cata and Saysa needed me—"

"So it was one hundred percent pure altruism?" I challenge.

He blows out a hard breath, and I worry I've upset him. "Sorry, I didn't mean to press you—"

"I don't mind," he says, the blue flame's reflection flickering in his eyes. "I like that you want to know me better . . . because I'm aching to know everything about you."

I swallow down my guilt about my plans to abandon them and go to Kerana. Now's not the time to discuss that.

"The truth is we all got something out of it. Cata and Saysa aren't the only ones who needed to redirect people's attention." His accent resurfaces, and its touch makes his voice all the more musical. "As long as everyone believed I was chasing after Cata, they didn't question me about the things I wasn't chasing—like becoming a Cazador or a pro Septibol player. They just assumed Cata and I were going to do things as a unit. Her ambition covered for my lack of it.

"Making decisions doesn't come as easily to me as it does to her, but everywhere we go, they want me to be in charge. No one even questions if that's what I want because it's what I'm expected to want. Cata would make a better team captain, but league rules say only wolves can have that role."

"The alpha werewolf who couldn't make decisions," I muse, taking his hands in mine. "I'd read that book."

"Uh-huh," he says, pulling me closer to him. "Anything else bothering you?"

"Just one thing."

He stares at me expectantly, his expression so naked that I feel like I could ask him anything. "Is it true?" I whisper. "What Cata said?"

From his gaze, I know I don't have to explain.

"I've never felt this way about anyone, Solazos." His grip on my hands tightens, and he breathes the nickname into my mouth. "For the first time, I know exactly what I want."

Blood rushes to my head, and I can't stop myself from saying, "This could be a good time to start working on your dominance . . ."

I'm mortified the minute I say it, but then a roguish grin overtakes Tiago's face.

He radiates so much light, it's like he's solar-powered. The Spanish word for smile is *sonrisa,* which sounds a lot like *sunrise* . . . I've watched the sun rise over the Atlantic from El Retiro's rooftop almost every morning for the past eight years, and yet I've never seen a sunrise as radiant as Tiago's *sonrisa.*

He yanks my hands behind me again, until there's not even a sliver of space between us, and I melt into his mouth. His fingers pull away from mine, and his hands cup my neck, his thumbs sliding along my jawline. His scent hits me like a drug, and I try to move my hands to touch him, but he leans in even harder, locking my arms behind me.

His fingertips graze down my shoulders, sending a thrilling tingle across my skin, and slide under the straps of my dress. Unwilling to break our kiss, I say into his thoughts, *I think this alpha wolf exercise is going to your head . . .*

It was your *idea.*

He pulls down on my dress straps until they dangle loosely off my arms.

I've been a wolf for two weeks, I'm not exactly an expert.

Tiago plants agonizingly slow kisses along the top curve of my cleavage. *Funny, I'm not hearing the word* stop . . .

He tugs on the dress's neckline until it almost slinks off my breasts. *There's so much I want to do,* he says into my mind, the words alone making me dizzy . . . *But we've got time.*

His lips lock with mine for a long moment, and he slides the straps back onto my shoulders. When we pull apart, his gaze is soft and glassy.

"Everything okay?" he asks. "I don't want to push you too far—"

"Not at all. This was perfect."

His eyes narrow with doubt, so I reach up and circle my arms around his neck, breathing in his heady scent. His words cycle through my mind on a loop. *"But we've got time."* Can I really walk away from him and Saysa and Cata after all this? Will they understand why I did it? Will they forgive me?

"Let's go," he says in my ear. "The howling will start soon."

The howling.

That's when Jazmín is meeting us.

Maybe she'll take a look at my Huella and drop her doubts. It could be she's got a tough exterior like her daughter, but inside she's not all bad.

Tiago leads me by the hand across the sand dunes, beneath the glimmering galaxy. *We shouldn't be holding hands in public,* I say.

"I'm done lying," he answers out loud. "I want to be with you, only you, and I don't care who knows it."

"But they're going to talk—"

"Let them," he says, a wild grin on his face. "Yours is the only voice that matters."

My favorite line from one of my favorite books floats into my mind—the one I used to repeat to myself night after night as I fantasized about falling in love: *She was very near hating him now; yet the sound of his voice, the way the light fell on his thin, dark hair, the way he sat and moved and wore his clothes— she was conscious that even these trivial things were inwoven with her deepest life.*

Is that what this is? Is it *love*? The feeling sounds so much better in stories. I never understood the discomfort, the anger, the disappointment in yourself for being so weak and predictable and hopelessly human. But I do now—because suddenly I'm not sure I can leave him. Not even to save myself.

"Hey," says Cata, and I snap out of my heavy thoughts at the sight of her and Saysa. Cata's staring at our linked hands, and the guilt is back, even though I know their feelings were fake. "Do you really think you should be together in public?"

Tiago frowns. "Why not? We already talked about this at the falls, Cata—"

"I know, but I'm only thinking of Manu's best interests. She needs to keep a low profile, and she can't do that if she's dating you. Trust me," she adds in a lower register.

"Seriously? Can't you let my brother be happy?"

Cata looks at Saysa like she just slapped her.

"Why do I always get made out to be the fucking villain when all I do is look out for us?" snaps Catalina.

"Not now and not here," I say fiercely, dropping Tiago's hand.

The three of them hold their tongues and sulk in silence.

The black sky dims to dark gray, and as the stars lose their shine, musical notes start to fill the air. It's a mournful tune that unmistakably marks the end of something, and as it echoes through the air, more and more wolves join in, until a feeling of connectedness swirls inside me, infusing my heart with hope.

When the wave of howls reaches us, I feel Tiago's hand close around mine again as we tip our heads back and—

"Owooooo!"

When my voice joins the pack's, a new feeling comes over me.

The belonging I've been searching for all my life.

I'm home.

A piece of paper drops on the cooking stone in front of us, as light as a feather, as destructive as a bomb. The photograph falls facedown, and its edges begin to burn away with the heat.

But from the recognizable handwriting on the back, I know what it is.

Anormal.

"Hello, Manu."

The sultry voice is familiar, and I look up from Ma's writing to see a girl standing with Nacho. Behind them are ten Septimus I would bet my life are Cazadores.

She's the teen girl from Ma's clinic. The one I pushed down. She was who I overheard on El Retiro's rooftop.

Except her irises aren't russet—they're bloodred.

Now I know what she stashed inside her jacket when she fled. *My file.*

"Hey, Yamila," says Saysa. "You know Manu?"

"We've met." Her lips curl into a snarl-like smirk, and I take an involuntary step back.

"You know, when I got the tip about your mom's clinic selling Septis, at first I just wanted her to lead me to her supplier."

My heart pounds for Saysa, but I don't dare look at her.

"Good thing I like to do my research on the humans I hunt, and I traced your mom's life back to the hospital where she used to work, incidentally one of the last places Fierro was known to frequent. She also disappeared right around the same time he did.

"I knew the rumors, so I decided to spring a trap. I called ICE in the hopes of luring Fierro out . . . but what I didn't count on was *you*. Your mom kept you real hidden, because my brother and I staked out your building, and we had no idea you existed. I stole your mom's files hoping to find a lead on Fierro—and when I looked through them, I saw I'd let the biggest prize slip through my fingers."

My fangs and claws are struggling to come out, yet I try to resist.

What's going on? asks Tiago, but I can't answer.

"So, you know what I did?" asks Yamila in her throaty purr of a voice. "I staked out the detention center. I waited and waited and waited, thinking you would come visit your poor, abandoned mother. Do you know they barely feed her? Do you know the way the men look at her?"

Everything.

Stands.

Still.

"But you were here all along, making friends and having fun, right under Nacho's nose. I guess I should have shared my discovery with him. Sometimes it doesn't pay to be secretive . . . You know?"

Manu, talk to me, says Tiago. But his voice sounds far.

So far.

Too far.

And I'm no longer here.

"Manuela Azul," says Yamila, her sultry tone laced with a

lethal edge. "You are an illegal hybrid. Abnormal. An aberration." She says the words slowly and deliberately, to remind me of Ma's writing on the destroyed photograph.

"By the laws of our tribunal, you are under arrest and subject to execution."

PHASE IV

31

Run!

Tiago's command yanks me back from oblivion, and I shoot off like a bullet.

There's a scuffle behind me, and orders are shouted, but I don't slacken my pace as I race toward the mist.

A pair of Cazadores fly out from the sides to block my way.

There's nowhere to turn, but I can't slow down. The lobizones are bigger and brawnier than me, and at this rate, I'm going to run right into their open arms—

A gust of wind whooshes up from behind me, tripling my speed and slowing them down. The Cazadores are trying to rush at me, but they're battling the gale's forces, and right as they reach out, my feet soar off the ground.

Cata's air current arcs me over the guards, depositing me at the misty barrier, and I vanish into the white haze.

On the other side, the sky is bright again, and sunlight

paints the grass gold. The Citadel's black wall looms ahead, where more Cazadores are waiting for me. Nacho must have gotten word to them telepathically.

Thorny vines of ivy curl up at their sides like weapons poised to strike. Footsteps shake the ground behind me, and I know the others aren't far. I'm sandwiched between Cazadores.

I'm out of options.

I start to slow down, when suddenly the snaky vines turn on the guards, looping around their ankles and sweeping them into the air.

Saysa.

The ivy won't hold them for long, so I hurtle forward and twist the opal doorknob.

My wolf-shadow is already waiting for me outside the Citadel, like it senses my urgency. Together we race across the golden grass until we're swallowed by more white mist.

My only hope now is that Lunaris will lead the Cazadores to a different destination than me.

But when the air clears, I suck in a sharp breath.

I'd rather take my chances with the Cazadores.

The ominous landmark is the only place in Lunaris I've never wanted to see again. *The stone mountain.*

Last time I came here, I never made it out. Even my shadow cowers, its ears pinned back as it paces in front of me.

I look back at the barrier, but no one else comes through. I step into the white steam to try going back, but nothing happens. I'm still in the same place.

The passages only work in one direction.

I have no choice.

Are you there? I ask Tiago.

There's no answer, nor do I feel any telepathic connection to him. I'm probably too far away.

The mountain is so wide that I can't see its edges. The only way to get across is to go through. "Come on," I say to my shadow, trying to sound braver than I feel. "We can't stay here."

I climb through the fissure in the rockface, my wolf-shadow darkening the wall beside me, and we step into the hollowed-out space.

It's cool and dim inside. The feathery ground muffles my steps, which makes it hard to tell if someone's sneaking up on me, so I keep casting backward glances. Yet the real threat in here comes from above.

The birdlike beasts that nest in this mountain are ferocious. They hunt in flocks, and every part of them is deadly.

I tremble at the memory of their talons sinking into my skin right before they flew me to a nest high above to be fed to their monstrously ravenous fledglings—that's when I woke up.

But this time I'm not sleeping. Whatever happens will happen for real.

I break into a soundless sprint, eager to get through this quickly, my wolf-shadow keeping pace with me. But I can't outrun the words pecking at my brain.

"Your poor, abandoned mother."

"Do you know they barely feed her?"

"Do you know the way the men look at her?"

Yamila's husky voice fills every nook of my mind. Was she telling the truth, or was she taunting me?

Both, probably.

I abandoned Ma. I've spent the past month in a fantasy world—going to magic school, making friends with witches, falling in love with a werewolf—while Ma has been fading away, alone, in a cell. Worrying about me.

Thinking of ways to return to me.

My wolf-shadow crosses my path, like it's trying to get my attention, and I slow down. It slinks off to the side, and I follow its lead, taking cover behind a boulder.

I hold my breath as a flock of three massive birds the size of small planes sweeps through the air, patrolling the exact area we were just in. Their beaks look like long, lethal teeth that end in sharp points, and their talons shine like metal.

When they descend on their prey, it's like a claw crane game—only these birds dive so fast that by the time their target sees what's happening, they're captured.

I wait an extra-long time to move, and then I go at a slightly slower pace so my shadow and I can keep watch on our surroundings.

What am I going to do if I ever make it out of this mountain? At nightfall I have to take a portal back to Earth, and Tiago said the portals are all in the Citadel—

There's a flash of silver overhead, and I look up and scream.

A bird is swooping down, its shiny talons coming for my head. I drop to the ground and squeeze my eyes shut, the claws about to tear into my skin—

A *whoosh* of hot air cuts across me, and I look up to see my wolf-shadow. It leaps up, and when it grazes the birds' talons, the monster jerks back, like it's been shocked.

I didn't know my shadow had any powers.

The birds screech as the entire flock is alerted to our presence, and they rocket at us like bullets. "Run!" I shout, and my shadow and I charge forward.

The wind from the flapping wings musses my hair and tugs at the fabric of my dress, and I know they're closing in. My breaths come in gasps, and my muscles scream in agony as another set of talons descends on my head—

My wolf-shadow springs up again, only this time the birds anticipate its defense.

The attacking bird swerves away, and two others sweep in from the sides, spearing my shadow across the middle with their ivory beaks.

I cry out as a scalding pain shoots through me—and I collapse alongside my shadow on the ground, writhing in agony.

The three birds orbit overhead, scavengers anticipating their feast. I dig my claws into the ground and try to drag myself forward, but my fingers just grasp feathers. In my periphery I see the three taking another dive, and this time I know it's over.

I think of Ma and Perla, and how they'll never know what happened to me, and I hope they know I'm sorry—

A growl blasts through the mountain, shaking the stone.

Then a werewolf leaps into the air, sinking its fangs into the first bird and sending the others crashing.

Tiago tumbles to the ground coiled around the monster, and as they roll, the bird tries flapping its wings, but Tiago's hold never breaks.

The other two birds recover, and I scream as they dive down to strike Tiago—and bounce off him like they hit a force field.

I look back and see Cata, her pink eyes swirling with blinding light.

Saysa drops down and helps me to my feet. Tiago's wolf-shadow darts over to mine and licks its wounds, shouldering it up. There's a loud crack as Tiago breaks the bird's neck and kicks its carcass away.

"We have to go!" shouts Cata, and we all follow her gaze. At least a dozen birds are now hovering over us, readying their attack.

"We're going to need some cover!" says Tiago, and Cata's eyes light up again.

All the feathers in our vicinity rise into the air and whirl around us like a funnel, hiding us from the birds' view.

We break into a run, and the feathers keep up with us. Cata soon falls back, the strain of running and doing magic doubly draining her, and Tiago lifts her into his arms. I reach for Saysa's hand, and I pull her along with me.

The feathers keep our position veiled from the birds, but they also blind us to their location—and what lies ahead.

When the feathers flatten into a wall, we know we've hit the other end of the mountain. They fall to the ground, and I gasp when I look up.

Dozens upon dozens of monstrous birds are now gathered above us.

"I don't see the opening!" says Tiago, scanning the rockface for a glint of light, some kind of fissure to get out, and I do the same.

"The stone is too hard to blow away!" says Cata, right as the first battalion of birds dives down—

"Move!"

Saysa's eyes flare neon green, and a rumbling shakes the mountain. Pebbles spike off the ground, and chunks of rock chip off the wall, cascading down and pelting the birds, sending them off course.

Light beams through the trembling stone, and Tiago squeezes his hand through the narrow opening, dislodging more rocks.

"Saysa, the mountain is going to come down on us if you don't stop!" he shouts.

"I'm not doing it anymore!" she calls back.

"It's unstable!" I say, helping Tiago widen the opening. More and more rocks loosen overhead and roll down, and we keep having to dodge to avoid them.

He reaches down and pulls Cata up through the small opening. I shove Saysa ahead of me, and Tiago sends her through too. He offers me his hand next, but I don't take it.

"What are you waiting for?" he shouts over the thunderous rumbling of rocks still raining down.

"You won't fit!"

"Don't worry about me—"

"I'm not going without you!" I shove against the stones to make the hole wider, and Tiago joins me.

I feel the flapping of air on my skin, and I see the massive bird monster shooting for us, its beak moments away from stabbing Tiago, who's trying to shove a giant boulder out of the way.

I yank him down by his shirt, and the bird crashes into the rockface, its toothlike beak blasting the wall open. Tiago and I scramble across the debris to get to Cata and Saysa, who are waiting with our wolf-shadows.

They cry out in relief when they see us, and we all hurtle toward the barrier of mist on the horizon without looking back.

I don't slow down until a new landscape unfurls. Then I breathe a sigh of relief at the sight of a crystal-clear body of smooth aqua-green water, surrounded by mossy boulders and rocky hills.

"The Lagoon of the Lost," says Cata, out of breath, her hands hinged on her knees.

Shock zaps through me, and I can't believe I made it here.

"You must have *really* wanted to get to this place," says Cata, straightening and studying the view around us.

"Why do you say that?" I ask.

"Because Lunaris tested you. She brought you here at a steep price. That mountain is ranked as one of the deadliest locations in this realm—I've only ever read about it."

"How did you find me?"

Cata and Saysa look to Tiago, and he says, "I followed your scent through the mist. I didn't know where it would lead."

"But then the Cazadores could follow it too—" I start.

"Wolves can only pick up the scent of their own blood in Lunaris," says Saysa. "The only exception is . . ." She stares at Tiago like she expects him to finish the explanation, but it doesn't matter anyway.

This is all wrong.

I was supposed to disappear from their lives before they got hurt, and now the Cazadores know they're accomplices in my escape. I've made everything worse.

Perla is bedridden, Ma is in hell, and now my only friends in the world are about to shame their families and suffer who knows what punishment.

I destroy everyone I love.

"You weren't supposed to come!" I blurt out. "It was my plan to run alone. I'm not going back to El Laberinto."

"What are you talking about?" asks Tiago.

"I'm taking a different portal back. Somewhere I'll have a better chance of getting lost in the crowd."

"Like Kerana," Cata supplies.

I nod. "I was trying to avoid dragging you all down with me. I'm sorry—"

"But why come *here*?" she interrupts, her voice cold again, the way it was when we first met.

"I . . . I was just running from the Cazadores."

"Keep lying to us all you want, but why lie to *yourself*?" she snaps.

"Lunaris exposes you," explains Saysa, her voice only slightly less frosty than Catalina's. "The fact we're at the lagoon after braving the mountain means this is what's really in your heart."

I swallow her words, and then I admit it, even to myself.

More than going to Argentina, more than evading the Cazadores, more than reuniting with Ma—"I want to find Fierro."

As soon as I own the wish, there's a stab of pain in my gut, and I feel like the horrible half human I am.

I shouldn't want to meet my father, not after he's taken everything from Ma and me. Not when Ma is still paying for his sins.

But deep down, I know Lunaris is right. I came here secretly hoping to find a lead on his location. I don't know why, since I doubt a famous fugitive will be able to help me much. I guess I just wanted the chance to see him. To show him I exist.

"This past month has been the peak of my life," I say, the blade in my gut twisting. I'm even more of a traitor to Ma for saying my best times were without her. For enjoying myself while she's suffering. For loving our greatest enemies.

"But everyone who's ever tried to protect me has gotten hurt. And that's why I need to be on my own."

"I said this to you when we first met—"

"Cata, back off," says Saysa, the ice already melted from her tone. "None of us knows what it's like to be completely alone the way Manu is."

Cata raises her hand and counts off with her fingers. "She grew up with just her mother—so did I. She felt trapped in her home—so do I. She didn't have any friends before the two of you—neither did I."

"How can you even compare your lives?" asks Saysa, shaking her head. "You may have moments of loneliness, but you're far from alone. You're privileged—"

"You're *always* taking her side—"

"It's not about sides, it's about what's right!"

"Tiago, do you have an opinion?" asks Cata, rounding on him. "She led you on, made us break every law, and all along, she was planning to abandon us."

His sapphire eyes are unreadable as he stares at me.

"Go into the lagoon," he says softly. "You deserve the truth. Only one Septimus can go in at a time, so we'll wait for you here."

"But what if the Cazadores come—"

"They won't," he says. "They're not searching for you anymore. They don't have to. By nightfall, we'll go to them."

32

The instant my foot touches the shore, the lagoon changes color.

The aqua green turns a shimmering gold, like a sea of sunlight. The tide pulls me in, sucking me down deeper and deeper, like quicksand. When it's up to my neck, I inhale as much oxygen as I can, before—

My head submerges, and the water changes consistency. It's soft and pliant and airy, not like water at all.

Welcome to Lunaris, Manuela.

For a moment I think I can't breathe, then I realize I'm in shock.

Lunaris just spoke to me.

Only it wasn't a voice in my head—it was more a flash of lightning. Saysa told me information travels through the air in this realm, and I wonder if this is what she meant.

You have come here in search of your roots. Your mother's world you know, but you wonder about your father's. Yet the question you should be asking is not where is he, but who.

No! I need to find him, to tell him about Ma and me—

What has been lost to you is not your father, but your past.

I don't care about the past right now. I'm running out of time. I'm about to be arrested!

In moments, you will have to make a choice: Which world's justice will you face? Your father cannot decide for you. Yet you can learn from his experiences, as he once made this choice himself.

Images begin to paint the gold air, like projections on a screen, only it's not my father I see.

It's Ma.

Her face is rounder and unlined, and she looks a couple of lifetimes younger. She's wearing green nurse's scrubs that can't conceal her enviable figure, and on her chest is a pin that reads LILIANA RAYUELA.

That's not her name.

She's Soledad Azul.

Ma is sitting behind an L-shaped reception area at a busy hospital, scribbling on what looks like a patient's file. All the signage around her is in Spanish.

A man comes up to the desk, and I can only see the back of his head. In Spanish he says, "Excuse me, miss?"

"I'm busy, please find another nurse," she says without looking up.

"And if I'd rather speak with you?"

Now she looks up. When her eyes land on his face, they take a long moment to focus. "What can I assist you with?" Her tone is less brisk but still guarded.

"Actually I'm here to help you." He stuffs his hand into the messenger bag swung across his chest, and he digs out a blue bottle, setting it on the counter. There are no ingredients or instructions. The only designation is the Z symbol.

"What is this?"

"Intuitive painkillers. When taken, they locate the area of discomfort and numb it entirely. In cases of full-body agony, the pill will put the patient in a painless sleep that lasts twenty hours."

It sounds like a miracle drug, and Ma understandably frowns with distrust. "I don't see the name of the pharmaceutical, nor the ingredients. We can't accept these samples—"

"I'll be back when you need more," he interrupts. Then he takes off, leaving the bottle behind.

The screen cuts to gold before I can see his face.

No! Wait—

The hospital desk reappears.

Ma is still behind it, only this time she keeps looking up from her files, scanning patients' faces like she's searching for someone. I spy the blue bottle peeking out from the pocket of her scrubs.

"What did you think?"

Ma's head snaps up at the sound of his voice, her face filling with light.

"It's a miracle drug! We have a patient, Marco, with terminal pancreatic cancer who was in complete agony until he tried one of your pills. Just one made his pain go away for an entire day! We even discharged him so he can spend his last days with his family, but I need more—"

Ma sounds so excited that it takes me a moment to actually listen to her words. There's a glorious glow illuminating her features, and it's the first time I can see how much healing people means to her. As I watch her eager face, sadness pools in my chest. I never once asked Ma if she missed being a nurse or why she chose that career. I never questioned the real cost of everything she gave up for me.

"Happy to hear it," says Fierro, and even though I can't see his face, I can tell he's affected by Ma's glow because his tone is more tender. "I've brought you more."

Ma leans over the counter and looks down at the five large boxes Fierro wheeled in, and her brow arches in surprise.

"Please wait here so I can call an administrator to draw the paperwork!"

"No need," he says, turning away—and I just barely glimpse the leg of sunglasses buried in his hair before he's out of view.

Once again the projection doesn't follow him.

Thankfully, Ma does.

"Put away these boxes," she instructs another nurse. Then she tails Fierro out of the hospital.

Outdoors, the first thing I notice is the faint outline of the moon pressing into the pink-red atmosphere. It's perfectly round.

No wonder Fierro is wearing sunglasses. His eyes must have started to shift—and soon the rest of his body will follow.

We're on a sidewalk bustling with shoppers, along a wide avenue jammed with traffic. Up and down the street are shops and restaurants and banks and doctor's offices, and I catch a name on a sign—Avenida Cabildo.

Ma weaves between people, nearly running to keep up with Fierro's long strides, until she spots him popping into a bookstore. Through the glass, she watches him approach the register and greet the salesman.

The same man from the memory I dredged up my first day of class.

Dad slips him a bottle, and the store owner pockets it. They trade a few words, then Fierro leaves in a rush. He's cutting it pretty close to nightfall.

Ma follows him down the block, but he vanishes from sight. The only explanation is he must have rounded the corner, so she turns too—

A pair of hands reaches out and grabs her by the shoulders, shoving her into the wall. The back of Fierro's head blocks her face, but I don't need to see her expression to know she's terrified.

"Who sent you?" he demands, his voice a low growl.

"N-no one," she says. "I just wanted to thank you."

He seems to believe her because his hands fall from her arms. And before he can say anything else, Ma reaches up and snatches off his sunglasses.

They stare at each other for a long moment.

On her face is the same awed look she always wears when she looks into my eyes. Then at last the screen pans to reveal Fierro . . .

And I see my father's face, but not for the first time.

My surroundings grow golden again, and a montage of moments flash past. Fragments of time washing up with the tide, like broken seashells.

Ma and Fierro meeting at an abandoned park under a crescent moon. Ma swinging by the bookstore on her way to the hospital and leaving notes for Fierro pressed between the pages of old volumes. Ma stopping by after work to collect Fierro's replies. The two of them together in Fierro's tiny apartment.

"Why don't your eyes look the way they did when we met?" Ma asks him in bed one night.

"How many times do I have to tell you, darling? You were imagining it."

"Then why do you always disappear on the full moon?"

"I suffer from lunaritis," he says, cracking a smile.

She rolls her eyes, and he kisses her. When he pulls away, she asks, "Who are you hiding from?" Only this time she's not speaking Spanish.

"You're practicing your English!" Unlike Ma, Fierro speaks without an accent. Yet the delight in his tone doesn't quite mask the heaviness in his expression.

"You said we will go to Miami together," she says, and I know from her tone that she registers his concern. "Is it the people who make the blue pills? Are the bottles stolen? Is this why you won't tell me about them?"

"Lily," says Fierro, and Ma inhales deeply, accepting the name like it's hers.

And just like that, I know it's her true identity.

My whole life I've called my mother by the wrong name.

"All I can tell you is my family is powerful, connected, and very dangerous," says Fierro in a low rush. "They expect me to take over the business, and *there is no refusing them*." The way he says it leaves little doubt what the alternative to refusing them would be. "The only way for us to be together is on the run. We could never have a home because we won't be safe anywhere in the world. We would be unable to hold down jobs, so we'd have to break laws to get by. We would have to cut ties with our family and friends . . . and we couldn't have any children."

Ma's face is ashen, and she swallows hard. Fierro takes her hands in his. "I selfishly loved you the past few months, knowing I have nothing to offer you. I don't expect you to forgive me for putting you in danger—in fact, you shouldn't. Inserting myself into your life is the cruelest thing I've ever done. All I can say in my defense is that I have never felt for anyone what I feel for you. And if the past six months are all the time I get to feel alive, then I'll die fulfilled, knowing I lived long enough to love you."

Ma's eyes are glassy. Her voice a husky whisper, she leans in and says, "I hope you brought good running shoes."

The images fade to gold, and I try to hold on to the warmth kindled by my parents' love story. Whatever else, their feelings were real. I may have been born into a world that hates me, but I was bred from pure love.

The hospital setting is back.

Ma is at the reception desk as a man is wheeled in surrounded by a flurry of paramedics. She looks up and spies the flash of a familiar face.

The bookstore owner.

She waits anxiously until he's been stabilized and left alone, then she slips into his room and sits beside him. When he opens his eyes, he looks at Ma like she's a ghost.

"Leave," he breathes, the word seeming to eat up all his strength.

"Please," she says, her voice shaky. "What happened?"

He draws a creaky breath. "They killed Juancito. They told me Fierro wouldn't be back. They're looking for *you*."

Ma gasps.

"They'll never stop," he goes on. "You have to run. *Go now.* And don't come back."

The images fade from the water long before they leave my sight. Lunaris seems to sense that I need time to process because she doesn't speak to me again until I've finished screening the entire film a second time in my memory.

Your parents rejected both their worlds. They chose to be anchored only to each other. Yet they did not start running soon enough.

I should have stayed at Luisita's when I had the chance. I was still relatively invisible then, a fake bruja trying to blend in. That was before I knew I was a lobizona. Before Jazmín drugged my drink. Before I fell in love with Tiago.

It is time for you to return to the surface and pick your path.

My thoughts are still muddled, but my body senses some kind of countdown has begun. Instinct leads me up the seafloor, toward oxygen. Toward a world divided into human and Septimus, with no middle ground for someone who doesn't fit either camp.

You seek to discover your true home, yet you no longer have one . . .

Lunaris's whisper lingers on my skin like loneliness.

You have two.

33

When I emerge from the lagoon, my friends aren't alone.

My gut clenches into a knot of dread that eases only slightly when I see that there are no Cazadores here.

"Let me guess, your favorite old student—or should I say, your *dream daughter*—told you I was in trouble with the law. I bet she relished delivering that news."

"Yamila was only doing her job," says Jazmín. "And you need to snap out of this rebellion before it costs you your future."

"And *you*!" Cata shouts at her uncle. "She tricked you! She only told you I was in trouble so you'd use your wolf-nose to track me!"

"You *are* in trouble," says Jazmín, "for aiding a fugitive! I want you to come back to the Citadel with me *right now*."

I set foot on the shore, and everyone notices me. Jazmín glares into my eyes, her purple gaze a starless night.

"Finally," she says softly. "You're coming with me too."

"No, neither of us are," says Cata, cutting over to stand with me. Saysa and Tiago close ranks in solidarity too.

"Manu, don't be a fool," says Jazmín, pleading with me like she knows I'm the weakest link. "Your best chance at leniency is to cooperate. Think of your friends—"

"Can someone tell me what the fuck is going on?" asks Cata's uncle. "You told me Cata was hurt, so I raced to track her down, but she seems fine. And you didn't mention anything about Manu being in trouble."

"I needed a chance to talk to Manu, before it's too late. So she wouldn't ruin her life and the lives of her friends." Jazmín infuses her voice with as much warmth as her wintry heart can generate, but I doubt it's fooling anyone here. "Let me bring you in. I promise I'll work out a good deal for you . . . *and your mom.*"

My heart stalls.

Yamila told her everything.

They know where Ma is.

Suddenly the world turns red, like I just drank the petals of a rose. Only instead of feeling pleasantly buzzed, I'm shaking with fury.

"You mean like the good deal you worked out for your brother?" I growl, and Jazmín's eyes grow round with outrage, and something else.

Fear.

"Does he know?" I press.

"Think about what you're doing," she says carefully. "One more word, and I won't be able to help you."

"I think you will," I say, and my voice comes out so icy that even my friends look at me confused. "Because I know who Fierro is."

At last, I let myself look at him.

"Hi, Gael. I'm your daughter."

Someone gasps, but I don't know who because I don't want to look away. Gael stares at me in utter bewilderment, and I can see the gears of his brain working to catch up. The clueless shock settles into concerned confusion, and at long last, recognition.

The way he's examining my face, it's not me he's seeing anymore.

He's looking for traces of Ma.

"I . . ." His voice comes out stringy, like his body is out of tune. "I didn't think . . . that was possible."

He steps closer to me, his coral eyes shiny.

"I can't believe . . . they told me they knew who she was. If I tried to contact her, they'd kill her. I believed them. I didn't— Manu, I'm so sorry."

Hearing him say my name breaks something within me.

And with perfect fatherly timing, he folds me in his arms, his breathing shallow in my ear. His arms are shaky as they clutch me to him, and my tears freeze on my face at seeing him this moved.

I want so much for this reunion to give me everything I've been missing, heal all my wounds, make me magically whole. But the truth is he's still mostly a stranger to me.

He's not the only family I gained though. As we pull apart, I look to Catalina, my *cousin*, feeling a sudden rush of love for her.

Only she's staring off into the distance, like she's sorting something out.

"How's Lily?" Gael asks me. He keeps a hand on my arm, like he needs the tactile proof this is real. "Where have you two been? How did you find me?"

"She goes by Soledad Azul now, and she's in a deportation

center. We've been in Miami illegally for most of my life. She went on the run the moment she realized she was pregnant, to find you. Only Yamila found us first, so she called ICE. And now she wants to arrest me."

He looks horrified. Seeing the hopelessness reflected in his expression drives home the severity of my situation.

"How long have you known about Manu?" Catalina looks at Jazmín so coolly that a chilly breeze blows past.

"Since *she* told me," says Jazmín, pointing to me.

"What's she talking about?" Cata asks, meeting my gaze.

"I fed her a truth potion," says Jazmín. "What, she didn't trust you enough to tell you?"

I swallow, and my mind goes as numb as it did in her office, when she drugged me with that poison.

"She admitted her mother feeds her the Septis every full moon," Jazmín goes on, sounding every bit as victorious as she feels for fooling me. "That could subdue a twelve-year-old who hasn't fully manifested their powers yet, but not a seventeen-year-old Septimus. Not if she's really one of us. So I did some digging into the clinic Yamila busted and found the identities of the humans taken into custody, and I pieced it all together."

"*You* told Yamila where to find us after the howling," says Catalina to her mom. "You were never going to meet us—you were setting Manu up."

"I *had* to! Yamila approached me at the match already knowing who Manu was. If you would have just reported back your findings like I asked when I put her in your room—or if Yamila had looped me into her investigation instead of wanting to keep the glory for herself—this fiasco could have been averted."

Something's bothering me though.

Yamila may have tipped off ICE, but she said someone

tipped her off first. If it had been another Cazador who dis-covered Ma's clinic, they would have kept the bust for them-selves. Whoever was really behind it would have benefited from ending the illicit trade, while keeping their own hands clean . . . But why wouldn't Jazmín want the credit when she so desperately needs to clear her reputation?

"You told me the Cazadores knew who Lily was," says Gael, staring daggers at his sister. "That I could never reach out to her again. Jaz, what did you do?"

"What needed to be done. *Like always*," she says, her voice growing sharp with anger. "First it was you, getting it into your head to adopt a law-breaking persona and then falling for your own fantasy by falling in love with a *human*! And now *you*"—she points to her daughter—"following his footsteps by break-ing the law and hiding behind a fake romance while you're secretly living a deviant lifestyle!"

The last piece clicks into place.

Jazmín must have known Saysa was the one delivering the Septis. She probably thought she could get rid of Saysa while keeping her hands clean by passing Yamila the tip on the clinic. What she didn't count on was that Yamila's ambi-tion went far beyond arresting some students with misplaced sympathies.

"It's so easy to hate me because I make the hard choices so you can be safe," says Jazmín. "I'm the only one looking out for this family!"

Her words echo Cata's, and Cata seems to sense the simi-larities too because she suddenly declares to her mom, "I'm nothing like you." She takes Saysa's hand in hers. "I love Saysa. And if you can't accept me as I am, we're done."

"Catalina, no me hagas esto," says Jazmín, her purple eyes flashing with parental impatience.

"I'm not doing anything to you. You're the one pulling our strings, manipulating our lives—lying, calling the Cazadores, slipping Manu a truth potion! I don't even know who you are!"

"I'm your mother, and you're coming with me to the Citadel right now. Think about your father, what this would do to him—"

"No, *you* think about him," snaps Cata, "because he's all you have left. I choose Saysa over both of you."

Gael's hand falls off my arm as he steps toward his sister. "Get out," he says in a soft growl that's more terrifying than any shouting. "You're not part of this."

Jazmín's eyes flare with pain, but she extinguishes the emotions as quickly as they came. "Any of you who don't come with me right now will be expelled. Not to mention all the trouble you'll be in with the law when I report this."

"You're not going to say anything unless you want me to confess to being Fierro," says Gael, still speaking in that deadly even tone. "And I'll take you down with me again."

The way they're looking at each other makes the temperature drop about twenty degrees.

Without another word, Jazmín goes through the mist and vanishes.

"Can't she just come back?" I ask. "Or tell them where we are?"

"It's too close to nightfall," says Gael. "By now, their best bet is to run down the clock and wait for us to come to them."

"Yeah, and they're right," says Catalina shakily. "We're five against a million!"

"Is there any other way in?" Saysa asks Gael, pulling Cata closer to her.

"No, I've studied the Citadel extensively, and there's just the one entry point."

This is looking direr by the moment. But I can't shake off Jazmín's words. She's right—just because I'm going down doesn't mean my friends have to too.

The same way Ma didn't let me get taken by ICE with her, and Perla didn't let me wait for the ambulance with her, I have to convince my friends to walk away from me.

Go, I say to Tiago while the others keep discussing. *Please,* I beg him. *If you guys get in trouble, I won't be able to forgive myself.*

"You still don't see," Tiago answers out loud. The others go quiet as he moves toward me. "There isn't a choice," he murmurs musically, and I stare into his sapphire eyes, trying to commit each fleck of brilliant blue to memory. "We're a pack species."

"Which means we're not leaving you," says Saysa. I look from her to Cata and Gael, who seem equally determined.

"Even if it means going before the tribunal," asserts Cata.

"You're part of this pack," says Tiago, his velvet voice laced with alpha werewolf authority.

My chest tightens, and I don't know if I feel better or worse.

"And what are we? Chopped chimichurri?"

We all turn at the sound of Pablo's voice, as he steps forth from the white steam, followed by Javier, Nico, Diego, Gus, and Bibi.

"We heard you decided to dabble in a bit of rule-breaking," says Pablo, "and personally, I'm offended I wasn't invited."

"How'd you know we were here?" asks Saysa.

Pablo's black gaze lands on me. "Just a feeling." He's the one who told me about this lagoon after all. "So tell us, what's going on?"

The law is after us, so it's only a matter of time before the news of what I am reaches the rest of my friends. And I'd rather they hear it from me.

"I'm half human," I spit out. "I didn't grow up among the Septimus like the rest of you. I was raised by my human mom, in Miami."

"Bullshit," says Gus, and everyone else looks just as disbelieving.

"It's true." Gael steps up beside me. "I know because"—his coral eyes meet mine—"I'm her father."

Hearing him say the words sends a blast of warmth through me. *I have a father.* Whatever happens, I pulled off the impossible. I found the missing half of my family.

Now that their teacher is the one saying it, my friends' skeptical masks crack with pure shock. Being the one with the most legal knowledge, Diego is the first to grasp the full implications, because he says, "You *can't* go before the tribunal."

I nod, but I notice my teammates are still hanging back by the mist, like they're not sure whether to stay or go. Cata, Saysa, and Tiago chose to help me knowing the full truth, but it's clear my other friends aren't ready to risk their lives. And I'm relieved to have fewer charges on my conscience.

"I knew there was a revolution in you," says Pablo, and in his voice, I hear real admiration. Even if he doesn't join our band of outlaws, I still have his friendship, and that's all I want.

"I have something to share too," announces Cata. She swallows hard, her chest rising and falling with her heavy breathing. "I'm in love with Saysa."

Saysa's eyes light up like they're filling with a deeper kind of magic, and she springs forward and pulls Cata in for a deep kiss.

Javier bursts into booming laughter, but the other guys stare in stunned silence. Gus and Pablo turn to Tiago like they're awaiting an explanation, but he just stares back like he owes them nothing.

When a beaming Saysa pulls away, she faces the rest of us and says, "I also have a confession. I'm part of a rogue group of Septimus who've been secretly supplying human clinics with Septis."

"What?" snaps Cata, rounding on her. Honeymoon period over.

"How could you do something that dangerous?" demands Tiago, and he and Cata look down on her like disappointed parents.

"Do you even hear the irony in your question?" asks Saysa.

"Not that this isn't all fascinating stuff, but it's getting late," says Pablo, lifting his cuffed wrist to gesture at the sky's dimming daylight. "Are there many more revelations left to go?"

"Just one," says Gael, stepping forward. "I'm Fierro."

34

Cool air bites at my ankles, a sign that night is near.

"*You're* Fierro?"

Pablo has been saying this on a loop for fifteen minutes now. Sometimes he emphasizes the first word, sometimes the second. It's like this final revelation broke him.

"We're out of time, and we need a plan," says Gael. He looks at Pablo, Diego, and the others and says, "You all need to head back now before you're charged as accomplices."

"You're *Fierro*—?"

"What about meeting with the tribunal and negotiating?" asks Nico, his silver eyes heavy with concern.

"No," say both Gael and Diego. Judging by how emphatically they refuse, it's clear the legal route will not end well for me.

"You can take performance enhancers to get past the Cazadores to reach the portals," booms Javier, but Gael is already shaking his head.

"The effects wear off quickly, and we'd be no match against so many. Now, you all need to get going—"

"We use a stand-in."

Everyone turns to Bibi, and Gael asks, "What do you mean?"

"Manu and I have the same skin and hair color. The biggest difference is her height, but we can work around that. We trade dresses, and I'll distract them long enough for her to slip through."

"Absolutely not!" roars Gus, gripping his girlfriend's arm. "You're not getting involved!"

Bibi rests a gentle hand on his jaw. "You've never been excluded from anything because the world is designed for you. So you can't understand how it felt to watch Manu kicking ass on that field. She changed things. And I'm done being on the sidelines."

Gus's face falls in defeat as she presses a kiss to his forehead. Then he turns to Gael, his eyes shiny, and says, "Where she goes, I go."

"Good. Because for this plan to work, we're going to need you."

"But once you're past the wall, then what?" Pablo sounds like he's come down from his Fierro high. "*Where* will Manu be safe?"

Everyone looks at me, and Gael's words to Ma come back to me. "The only way I can survive is on the run."

Gael's coral eyes grow bright with recognition, and he says, "I'm running with you."

"No," I say. "You need to find Ma. Before the Cazadores do."

I know he understands. The only way I can do this is if I know someone is taking care of Ma. Someone who can fend off both human and Septimus foes.

"I'll protect her with my life," he says somberly.

"I know."

"If you run, I run." When Tiago says it, I remember us outrunning the lunarcán, and I feel like we could outrun the world. But even though his tone leaves no room for negotiation, I have to try.

"You have what all of us want. You're about to inherit the world. Before you make this decision, just look at everything you're about to lose."

"That's exactly what I'm looking at," he says, and I can't say anything else because my emotions are too near my throat.

"We're running too," says Saysa.

She's holding hands with Cata, who adds, "We have our own fight with the tribunal."

I turn to Gael, and I think of his expression when Ma learned English. The way his joy battled his dread. And I wonder if that's how I look now.

You're not your mom and me, he says into my mind, confirming my thoughts. *You have what we didn't have*—friends.

Then he looks around at everyone and says out loud, "You have romantic notions of Fierro because you're young and passionate, but he wasn't a leader—he was a rebel. I assumed that disguise because I thought the system was flawed, but I didn't put in the work to change it. I just tried to disrupt it. And when that didn't work, I tried to run. And when I couldn't do that, I gave up.

"But together, you can make a difference. Our civilization was built on the shoulders of exiles. Septimus who believed if you didn't see your path, you paved it. Like our earliest ancestors who banded together after being rejected by mankind and built a new world on top of the old, *you* will do the same now."

He rests a hand on my shoulder, and I feel a powerful rush

of purpose. "Plant your new garden with the seeds of equality, water it with tolerance and empathy, and warm it with the temperate heat of truth."

Pablo claps fervently. "You're Fierro."

The sky is growing redder by the moment. When the guys leave through the mist, I'm left with Tiago, Cata, Saysa, Bibi, Gus, and Gael. Bibi and I have already traded dresses, and she conjured two blocks of ice beneath her feet to give herself more height.

"It's best if the rest of us don't know where you're running, in case we're questioned," says Gael. "So I'll say goodbye here." He hugs Tiago and Saysa, and when he gets to Cata, he holds her for a long moment.

When it's my turn, he whispers in my ear, "Don't worry about your mom. I'll find her, and we'll return to you."

Even though it was my idea, I still wish we didn't have to part so soon. I feel cheated. Yet for some reason what I blurt out is, "You look younger than Ma."

Gael smirks. "We age slower."

"But—why didn't you marry? Or have more children?"

His smile fades. "I loved once, and I lost her. This is the only resistance they left me."

I watch the back of his head until he fades through the mist.

Cata, Saysa, Tiago, and Bibi go next.

Once we're alone, Gus holds out his arm for me, and I nestle into his side the way Bibi does. I know it's important for my cover, but it's weird to be this close to a stranger I've watched hooking up with another girl every single day for a month.

I take a last look at my wolf-shadow, roughhousing with all the others. Like it senses my gaze, it stops to stare at me.

I smile. I hope we see each other again.

When Gus and I clear the white mist, the grassy field appears, with the Citadel just a black shadow on the horizon. We hurry toward the stronghold as hints of jasmine infect the air, and I see a bottleneck of Septimus at the entrance. The Cazadores are checking everyone's Huellas.

We blend into the crowd, keeping an eye on our friends. I glimpse a lobizón making his way toward Bibi, and I recognize Nacho. Tiago steps up, standing between them, negotiating a surrender once they're inside the Citadel, just as we discussed.

Now that they think they have me in custody, the Cazadores call off the identification check—particularly as it's so close to nighttime—and the rest of us easily slip inside.

The Septimus are all running to the misty barrier to catch a portal, and right as I'm going to reach out to Tiago with my mind, we hear the commotion break out.

I spot the flash of gold of my dress and see my friends gathered with the Cazadores, Yamila stomping the ground in frustration. She looks like she's ready to arrest everyone, but Jazmín steps forward and whispers something in her ear.

"Fine," I hear Yamila say to my friends. "Go!"

To all of our shock, they're free.

They make for the white mist, and Gus and I hurry to join them. When we cross to the other side, it's nighttime. And the moon isn't above us—we're standing on it.

The gray ground is rocky and pockmarked and uneven. Around us are craters and caves and canyons. Septimus are scrambling throughout like they're at a busy transportation hub, and while most seem to know where they're going, some look lost and ask questions.

"There they are!" says Gus, and we pull apart as we run to intersect the others. Bibi flings herself at him, and Tiago reaches for me, crushing me to his chest.

"What now?" asks Gus.

"Should we switch back dresses?" asks Bibi.

"No, Manu is still in danger," says Tiago.

"Here." I dig out Bibi's Huella from the pocket of her dress, and she hands me my forged golden one.

"We're too big a group," says Tiago. "We need to split up."

I spot Yamila and Nacho, and I realize they were trailing my friends. Jazmín probably told Yamila to let them go because they'd lead her right to us.

"Run!" I shout, and we scatter just as the Cazadores spring out.

Tiago, Cata, Saysa, and I weave through the crowd, and thankfully it's so packed that it's not hard to lose the Cazadores. We keep going until we've left the throng behind, and the surface begins to tilt downhill. Tiago spies a cave tucked into the gray rockface, and we hurry inside to catch our breath.

"Were—we—followed?" asks Saysa, clutching her side.

"I don't think so," says Tiago. "We need to pick which portal we want to go to." He turns to me.

"Argentina," I say without hesitation.

"Home it is."

Catalina nods grimly. "Since most of our species lives in Kerana, the portals there aren't tied to specific manadas. It should be easier to get past the Cazadores at the border."

"Let's go—"

Tiago's words die on his lips, and I turn to see why. Yamila is standing in the mouth of the cave with Nacho.

"Jazmín was right. You did lead me right to her. I guess a bargain's a bargain."

Her bloodred eyes light up, and Tiago roars as scarlet flames spark to life on his hand. He shakes his arm, but his skin is blackened and boiling.

I cry out like I'm the one being scorched, and Saysa presses her hands to his burn, her eyes glowing green to speed up his healing. Cata glares at Yamila and her pink eyes brighten with a gathering storm, but Nacho shoves her back before she can summon her magic.

I realize too late what he's doing, and suddenly a wall of fire blazes to life, separating me from my friends. Yamila and Nacho were corralling them deeper into the cave, driving a wedge between us.

My friends shout, but it's hard to hear them past the licking of the flames. Nacho stands guard in case they break through, and I turn to Yamila, her red eyes ablaze.

"You don't know our customs," she says to me in her low purr of a voice, "so you probably aren't aware that Encendedoras are the most unstable of all the brujas."

"You don't say."

"*Fire* is willful. She will not be ruled. Most of us will go our whole lives without ever manifesting a single original flame. Yet there are a few of us who have managed to tame her, and when we call, she burns with more power than any ordinary blaze. Your friends aren't getting out of there until you've submitted to my custody."

We stare at each other, and some part of me expected this. Ultimately, no matter how much my friends support me, I'm the one who's out of status.

I'm the one the law wants.

"It's interesting that this whole place isn't swarming with Cazadores and other officials searching for me," I say. "If the whole population knew there was a hybrid hiding out

among them, I'm sure you would have caught me long before now."

"I caught you anyway," she says, shrugging like I'm not getting to her, but I know I'm right.

"This whole time, you wanted to turn me in yourself. That's
why you didn't tell Jazmín what you found at the clinic."

"I knew from the moment I cased the place why she sent me
the tip instead of reporting the operation herself. She didn't
want her daughter blaming her for Saysa's arrest. But I've always
liked Saysa, and it was actually the fact that she was involved
that made me curious about the humans at the clinic—the
people she found worthy of our magic."

"And that's how you found out about my mom."

"Jazmín didn't tell me she had a suspicious student, so I
didn't know why she was so anxious when she didn't hear back
about the results of my investigation. She must have sensed
there was something off about you."

At least Yamila doesn't know about Jazmín's connection to
Fierro.

She doesn't know he's Gael.

"I didn't realize how badly Jazmín would want the credit
for capturing you—but *I found you*. Not her. And when I bring
you in, hybrid, daughter of Fierro, I'm going to be more legendary than he was. The lobizones are going to know they're
not the only ones who can hunt big game. They'll be out-
matched by a *bruja*."

The red glow of her eyes flashes for a second, like a solar
flare, and I know the magic attack is coming. Heat tickles the
skin on my arm, and I slap the spot just as it starts to spark,
cutting off the magic.

Yamila's eyes widen, and I register what just happened. I
anticipated where she was aiming her magic and blocked it.

Yamila's brow furrows in concentration, and I feel warmth searing my wrists, like fiery handcuffs are forming.

I shake my arms before they appear, and the fire goes out.

"How are you doing that?" she bellows.

Her eyes light up like lasers as she sends another magic attack my way, and this time I sense the heat's approach before it even reaches my body. I duck, and the spark hits the ground behind me, scorching a pebble.

It's like my reflexes on the Septibol field have adapted beyond the physical realm so that I'm even starting to feel the invisible threads of magic in the atmosphere.

Yamila's hands ball into fists, and her eyes turn murderous. "What. Are. You?"

It's the same question Ariana's mom asked when she saw my eyes half a decade ago. The same question I've been asking myself the past few weeks.

Only suddenly, it doesn't matter.

If there's no word in any known vocabulary to encapsulate me, that just means language can't define me. A label can't hold me. I'm beyond classification. I'm an original. I'm—

"Undocumented."

Yamila's eyes are alight again, and this time I lunge.

I tackle her to the ground, but her skin burns so much that I scramble away. Yet my strike was enough to disrupt her concentration, and the wall of flames caging my friends snuffs out. Tiago bounds over to me to make sure I'm fine, and I examine his hands, relieved they're unhurt.

Saysa screams, and we turn to see Nacho holding Cata by the throat, his claws digging into the skin of her neck.

"Nobody move, or she's dead."

Blood trickles down his fingers, and panic strangles my heart.

"Tiago, step away from Manu."

I look up at him to tell him it's okay, to do as Nacho says—but his blue gaze is void of emotion. It's like he vacated his body.

And suddenly I know he was holding back when we wrestled in class because I've never seen a more terrifying monster.

Tiago moves so fast, it's like he's flying. I blink, and he's no longer by my side. He's behind Nacho.

"Watch out!"

But Yamila's warning is too late. Tiago yanks back Nacho's head by his hair, and he stabs his claws through his throat, so the Cazador can't scream.

Saysa catches Cata and sets her down gently, running her hand along her skin, healing her. Tiago knocks Nacho into the cave wall and blood gushes down the Cazador's chest.

"Stop!" Yamila's eyes burn, and fire flares on Tiago's shoulder. He drops Nacho on the ground, cursing as he slams into the wall to put himself out.

For a moment I think Nacho's dead, and I can't speak.

Then I see the skin sewing itself back together. Yamila's sprawled on the floor next to her brother, breathless, holding him up.

I rush to Cata, who seems to be regaining her color. Tiago crouches down beside me, and Saysa walks over to Nacho.

Yamila looks at her and says, "Saysa, please."

In her voice, I hear the proof they were friends once. After all, that friendship is what started this whole predicament. Yamila didn't want to arrest Saysa, so she cast out for a bigger fish instead.

Saysa ducks down and rests her hands on Nacho's chest, and at first I think she's curing him.

Then I look at his face.

He looks like a famous painting Perla loves called *The Scream*.

His mouth is twisted in agony, and as the color drains from his skin, his body begins to shrivel. She's sucking his life force.

She's killing him.

"What are you doing?" Yamila shrieks.

"Saysa, stop," I say, but it's like she doesn't hear me. This is the dark side to her magic—the part I've only glimpsed.

"Don't do this, Say." But Tiago's entreaty also goes unheeded.

Yamila's eyes flare, but no spark touches Saysa. The others gather around her, trying to talk her down, but no one touches her. I wonder if that's because anyone who comes into contact with her will also be affected.

"It's okay."

Cata kneels next to Saysa. "You can stop now," she whispers. "It's over. We're all safe."

Saysa blinks, and on registering Nacho's contorted, near-dead face, she pulls her hands off him. She stands, and everyone backs away from her a few paces.

The four of us exit the cave, leaving Yamila sobbing over her barely alive brother. It's far from the hopeful note I would have liked to start this adventure on, and we're all quiet, like we just faced something new in that cave.

Our shadow selves.

"It's right there!"

Tiago, Cata, and Saysa rush toward the crowd of Septimus funneling into a tunnel. According to Tiago, we just have to walk across it to get to Kerana, and then we'll have to show our Huellas. The first test for my forged papers.

Since Yamila and Jazmín haven't told anyone about me yet,

hopefully the border agents won't have any reason to suspect anything is up.

When we reach the entrance to the tunnel, I feel the urge to touch the wall to know what the moon feels like. I press my hand to the rockface, and it softens to clay-like material beneath my fingers.

And I remember what Tiago told me: *"Sometimes Lunaris invites Septimus to leave their mark."*

The others are still walking, and I don't call out to them to stop. I need Lunaris—and myself—to know this isn't the end, but the start of something. So I leave a promise I'll collect on. A symbol of hope. A reason to return.

"What are you doing?" Tiago calls from the shadows.

"Coming!"

I'm not doing what my parents did. I'm not running away. I'm running *toward*.

I'm going to change things. But I can't do that if I'm silenced before I can speak. I can't face a fair trial now, not in any of my worlds. They're not ready for me yet.

But they will be.

I finish carving my symbol—not Fierro's, not the Septimus', but a new one that represents a new day. A new world.

An M for my name, made of two sevens that don't quite touch. Not yet.

I wipe my hand on my dress as I race to catch up to my pack. Tiago's fingers close around mine as we cross through the passage. The air grows black around us, and only our eyes remain visible. After what feels like half an hour, light streaks through the darkness, and fresh air gusts in with an array of new scents.

And as I breathe in the hints of coffee and leather and paper in the air, a smile spreads across my face.

I'm home.

AUTHOR'S NOTE

Dear Reader,

When I was five years old, my mom and dad uprooted my sister and me from our native Buenos Aires, Argentina, and moved our family to Miami, Florida.

My parents met when the *Guerra Sucia* ended, a period of state terrorism that left a permanent mark on the lives of most Argentines. The "Dirty War" was a violent dictatorship during which dissidents disappeared overnight and children were ripped from their families—to this day, the Abuelas de Plaza de Mayo continue to search for their lost grandchildren.

Hoping to raise us in the land of the free, our parents bought into the American dream.

Growing up as immigrants, my little sister and I straddled two worlds: We spoke English at school and Spanish at home. Our classmates' references were lost in translation because we didn't watch the same shows or listen to the same songs. I had such a hard time learning how to read that I struggled with anxiety attacks whenever the teacher called on me. And yet, we were lucky—my dad had a working visa, and after eleven years in the US, we became citizens.

I wrote this book because today's immigrants aren't so lucky. For the crime of coming to this country in search of a safer future, people are being arrested, traumatized, indefinitely detained, separated from their families, deported. *Children are being caged.*

When we use labels like *illegal*, we negate a person's worth and humanity, and the real dangers they're running from—dangers that are not contained by borders because they are born from ideas.

America itself is an idea. Its founding was an act of rebellion. Just as being an immigrant is a rebellion against the arbitrary categories that cage us.

I've spent so much of my life feeling out of place and wondering who I would be if my parents had never left Argentina. The first time I ever felt at home *anywhere* was when I arrived at Hogwarts with Harry. And that's why I write: to build worlds where we can all belong.

Bienvenidos a Lunaris.

Xoxoxo,
Romina

ACKNOWLEDGMENTS

Every lobizona needs her manada, and this book would not exist without mine. Thank you to:

Eileen Rothschild, for believing in Manu and me—it's been a dream working with you and my fellow 305-er Tiffany Shelton! My deepest gratitude to everyone at Wednesday Books and St. Martin's Press—DJ DeSmyter, Lexie Neuville, Meghan Harrington, Sara Goodman, Anne Marie Tallberg, Melanie Sanders, Anna Gorovoy, and the rest of the *Lobizona* team.

Kerri Resnick and Daria Hlazatova, for an *iconic* cover that I will obsess over forever.

Laura Rennert, my champion and my friend, for always having my back. Thank you to Taryn Fagerness, Flora Hackett, and Carolina Beltran for your faith in this story.

Christa Desir, for your fantastic copyedit, and Adriana Martinez, for your excellent sensitivity and authenticity review.

Richie Segal and Sarah Edgecomb, for connecting me with

an awesome team of immigration lawyers—Ben L. Simpson, Rhonda Gelfman, Assma Ali, and Jennifer Healey. I'm so grateful for your invaluable guidance!

My family and friends who relived their own immigration experiences with me—Manu would not exist without you.

Nicole Maggi, my critique partner, twin brain, the Sirius to my James—I miss you more than Harry misses Hogwarts. I can't imagine taking this journey without you as my seatmate. Tomi Adeyemi, when the world made me feel powerless, you reminded me that my words are my weapons. Thank you for your beautiful blurb and your beyond beautiful friendship.

Lilliam Rivera, for inspiring me with your books and supporting me with your blurb—muchas gracias por tu amistad, hermana. Karen Bao, one of my earliest readers, for your invaluable notes. Love to Aditi Khorana, Alexandra Monir, Gretchen McNeil, Maura Milan, Robin Reul, Kerry Kletter, Jeff Garvin, my girl Caden Armstrong, and the rest of the LA YA community. Miss you all so much!

Las Musas and Latinx in Publishing, por todo lo que hacen para amplificar nuestras voces.

Lis, Coco, and Noale—besties since the nineties. Noa's Potatoes forever! Robin, Will, Lizzie, Ashley, Luli, Christine, Gillian, Aurora, and Leslie—love you all to Lunaris and back!

My teachers Mary Kay Sullivan (Sully) and Katherine Vaz, for helping me find my voice and teaching me how to use it.

My grandparents, who were immigrants too. Baba y Bebo, por siempre los llevo en mi corazón.

Superstition was a third language in my childhood home, mostly thanks to the stories handed down by my mom's side. To this day, I still ask tía Fanny to cure my mal de ojo whenever I yawn too much. Te quiero tanto, Fanny.

Mis tíos y primos. Te extrañamos, Gusti.

ACKNOWLEDGMENTS

I named Gus, Bibi, Yamila, and Diego after family members. Diego's character is inspired by my mom's cousin who was a week shy of moving to Perú to work at the Israeli embassy when he was killed in the 2002 terrorist attack at Hebrew University. Nunca te olvidaremos, Dieguito.

Andy, the best brother-in-law ever. Thank you for your friendship and your faith in me—and for my awesome website.

Mels and Mica, you're my everything. Thank you for illuminating my world.

Papi, sos mi inspiración. Gracias por apoyarme en todo lo que hago.

Mami, you're my hero. Thank you for being the best mom in the universe.

Booksellers, librarians, teachers, bookbloggers, and everyone who gets books into teens' hands—you're lifesavers.

Zodai, I write for you. Always.

The seed for *Lobizona* came to me as a teen when I stumbled across a peculiar Argentine law—ley de padrinazgo presidencial 20.843. I wrote my first version of this book a decade ago, but when I tried to get it published, I was told US readers didn't care about Argentine immigrants.

So above all, thank you. For caring.